BREAKING THE RULES

"Could be folks ought not be told what to think," Jack proposed. "Could be someone as intelligent as you might not wait for scoundrels to declare themselves before she recognizes 'em. Could be, *Miss* Garrison, that as long as you insist on holding yourself so all-fired distant from fellows like *me,* you dupe yourself, no assistance required. Maybe instead of marching down here to scold me like I'm one of your pupils, which I am *not,* you ought to be thanking me for not taking worse advantage of that cursed innocence you've been yoked with."

He watched her throat clutch when she swallowed, followed the tip of her tongue when, gazing up at him with wary fascination, she licked her lips. They seemed so close, now.

"You're trying to confuse me," she accused, her voice barely a whisper.

"I'm trying to free you." His voice softened. "Take a gamble, Audra Garrison."

She shuddered, caught her breath, but continued to stare, dazed, up at him.

He leaned nearer, brought his lips close enough to hers that he could taste her breath. "What," he whispered as he closed those last few inches between them, "do you have to lose?"

LEISURE BOOKS  NEW YORK CITY

A LEISURE BOOK®

March 2000

Published by

Dorchester Publishing Co., Inc.
276 Fifth Avenue
New York, NY 10001

ISBN 0-8439-4693-8

Printed in the United States of America.

Dedicated to my sisters,
who remain sisters no matter how near or how far, espe-
cially: Carolyn, Lisa,
Meg, Kristy, and Linda

THE
RANCHER'S
DAUGHTERS:
Behaving Herself

Prologue

1900
Candon, Tarrant County, Texas

Audra's misery did not come upon her suddenly. It had increased over the long train trip from Wyoming to Texas, spoiling what could have been a great adventure. But she had never been a young lady to embrace adventures, even those found in novels. And ever since the scandal, she hardly deserved a happy ending.

No, she had silently suffered for days now. Only when she watched her father sling his saddlebags into the rented buggy, to leave without her, did the ache grow truly unbearable.

She could not do this!

But when he turned back to her, she needed only look at his stoic, weathered face to know that she could do whatever it took. *Poor Papa*. Despite what some people said about cattlemen, he had strong principles. He did not deserve the shame she had brought upon the family. No matter what he said, they would fare better without her these next long months.

And as Aunt Heddy had pointed out—here where nobody knew her past, Audra had a better chance of regaining respectability.

Papa came to her one last time with his awkward walk, the walk of a man who preferred sitting a horse, and stood with his hat in his hand. "Audra," he said solemnly.

The air she breathed seemed too warm for October, and she felt her heart break. "Papa . . ."

"You say the word; I would be pleased to escort you home."

Yes! I want my mother and sisters. Take me home, Papa! But no. He'd spent time and money bringing her here in the first place. And she had accepted a position here, given her word.

"This is a good thing, Papa," she insisted, forcing her words around the ache. "I can start fresh here. They'll let me teach. You know . . . you know I've always wanted to teach."

Papa scowled. "I regret not killin' that Connors boy."

"No!" Audra raised a hand to her father's white-bearded cheek. "He didn't— You did right, Papa. You have *always* done right by me. It's me who . . . who failed. . . ."

He covered her hand with his callused palm. "I will not hear that talk, Audra Sue. You are a good girl. Always have been." He took a deep breath, deliberately looking away from her. "Reckon you'll make me proud in Texas, surely as you done up north."

Audra curled into her father's broad chest for a last embrace, fighting tears. He smelled of soap, horses, leather—and faintly of the tobacco he smoked on the sly that annoyed her mother. The arms he belatedly drew around her felt powerful enough even now to fight Indians or lead cattle drives, as he had done in his youth. But she didn't deserve him. She'd done wrong. She hardly knew how . . . but she'd known the rules of society, and she'd broken one. She deserved this exile.

"You have money for the telegraph," Papa reminded her. "Send word; I'll be here within the week. Weather permittin'."

"Yes, sir," promised Audra.

"Behave yourself."

She nodded. If only she'd managed that back home!

He straightened, his manner stiff once more—even the hug, here in the open, had been surprising for Papa. Then he nodded at her and turned back to the buggy, swung up onto the seat. He would drive it back to Grapevine, catch the train, then continue to Fort Worth, to Denver, to . . . home.

Without her.

"Hedda," he acknowledged as he took up the reins.

Audra's widowed Aunt Heddy stood beside the clapboard home where Audra would stay. "The girl will be safe here," she assured her brother stiffly. "This may be Texas, Jacob, but we're a good farming community. Respectable as they come."

Papa paused with a faintly distasteful expression and suddenly, through her cloying misery, Audra wanted to laugh. As if the society of sodbusters would comfort a rancher! Papa's gray eyes caught hers and warmed. He understood.

"Ladies," he said as a fare-thee-well, clucking the rented horse to work, and drove away. Audra wondered if she could die from homesickness, and if perhaps that would be a blessing.

Aunt Heddy would not let her watch until he vanished. "Best get to work, child," she said. "We've boarder students to prepare for. Idle hands are the devil's playground."

Audra winced at the veiled criticism, but she obeyed. She would do whatever it took to make good here.

This time she would follow the rules.

Chapter One

To keep the school room neat and clean, the teacher must scrub the floor at least once a week with hot, soapy water.

—Rules for Teachers

When the first gales of the blue norther walloped him upside the head, Jack better understood his recent loss at the Dallas racetrack. He had a poor eye for speed and distance. He'd gambled that his bay mare Queen—Queen of Hearts, named after the card that won her—could make the next town toward Fort Worth before the weather turned.

But Jack tended to overestimate chances and underestimate odds, which gave his career at cards the stability of a dancing drunk, though it *did* keep things fun. And Handy Jack Harwood appreciated fun even more than he enjoyed a good game.

Not that he'd had much fun since riding out of Dallas. Especially now that the real storm, not just the buffeting wind, hit with unseasonable, icy rain.

He didn't bother kicking Queen into a lope. He'd ridden her hard enough already today, hoping to find amidst all these truck farms a town with the sense to keep a saloon, or at least a billiard hall. No such luck. Now Jack scanned the scrubby trees and fields on either side of the dirt road through a veil of rain. Despite the cold, he dismissed the first house he saw as too neat. The barn beside and behind it stood in equally good repair, complete with double doors that looked to be—he squinted now—firmly latched. Whatever paragons lived there would either label his innocent visit as trespassing or take him in, feed him, then read from the Bible in the sorry hope of saving his soul.

No, he would rather freeze to death atop this here mare.

The next building Jack approached had a sight more personality—two log cabins separated by a roofed space called a dog run. Shuttered windows gave him hope the occupants might be away. At least that dog run would give him and Queen shelter. At most, he'd find coal in the shed and no locks on the door.

Jack reined Queen toward the cabin, out of the gully-washer and into a pocket of calm. Rain pounded on the roof overhead and blew in on either side, but otherwise was kept at bay.

Jack dismounted with a creak of saddle leather and took off his black hat, pounding it against the side of his thigh a few times to rid it of excess water. Then he saw the bell.

His breath stilled. A church?

Then his senses returned. If there was one thing these hardworking, God-fearing, temperance-minded farmers did right, it was their white-steepled churches. No, this old homestead must be a school. Determined to settle the notion and his unease, both, Jack climbed the puncheon steps to one of the two doors that flanked his shelter. He pulled the latch, glanced in.

Well, now!

He'd found a schoolhouse, all right, and more.

Desks and blackboards caught his notice, true. But only until his gaze skimmed to a lamp in the corner and to a girl—a young lady—standing in its glow, half-turned at his entrance.

She had hair of a sorrel color, pulled back and up, unlike a schoolgirl's. Her fringed, pale eyes widened at him and her lips parted in delicate surprise. The place wasn't empty after all. Not by a long shot. Since he already had his hat in hand, Jack smiled his most charming smile and made a polite bow. "Ma'am."

And the pretty gal said, "You are tracking mud on my floor, sir. I'd thank you to leave."

To Audra's relief, the man in her schoolroom's doorway smiled at her a moment longer, then stepped right back out and even shut the door against the rain. A man. And her alone! Had he not left muddy tracks, she might think she'd created him from her fears of doing something wrong. But he *had* left tracks. When she put down her chalk and ventured to the doorway, she saw that he'd also left drippings of water.

Though she dared not admit it to her aunt, Audra had never scrubbed a floor in all her sixteen years before today. But neither had she dismissed a stranger before he could even say what he wanted, and that made her feel dirtier than the floor. He didn't frighten her. She'd grown up on a ranch among rough cowboys; in comparison, this man had looked rather endearing . . . and very wet. And when she'd told him to leave, he'd gone without protest. Out into the cold.

The wind beat at the walls of the schoolroom and rain drummed, hard, against the roof and shutters. To leave a stranger outside in weather like this seemed wrong. But to let him in, unchaperoned, went against the rules. She ought not risk even the illusion of misconduct.

The misery that had only begun to fade, after several days of acute homesickness, gnawed anew at her insides. What to do? Even Aunt Heddy saw no harm in Audra staying behind to ready her half of the two-room schoolhouse for tomorrow's new term. But neither had anyone foreseen harm in Audra taking a buggy ride alone with a man who was practically her fiancé.

Remembering that, Audra turned dutifully back toward the blackboard to finish preparing for tomorrow.

Then she remembered how mild the Texas weather had been until now. How wet the man had looked. How dangerous storms could become without shelter . . .

Oh, dear.

Resigned, Audra hurried to the door and opened it to call the man back. Wind snatched it out of her grip to bang against the outside wall.

A blanketed bay horse, drop-reined near the end of the dog run, danced back with a snort of fear. The stranger stared up from where he had made a seat of his saddle against the opposite wall—Aunt Heddy's side of the school—with his collar up around his ears, his hat pulled low, and what looked to be playing cards in his hands. Then he stood and caught the door before the wind could slam it the other direction.

Suddenly Audra *did* feel threatened by his nearness, not for her safety or her reputation so much as for . . . what? He was behaving himself, wasn't he? And he was no vagrant. Since the panic of '93, Audra's mother had fed her share of hobos, but not one of them had been as clean-shaven or well dressed as this dark-haired stranger. Under an impeccably cut frock coat, he wore a fine white-ruffled shirt and string tie, both limp with damp. The wet made the texture of his coat, shirt, and even his skin—which threw off its own warmth—somehow more tangible than seemed proper.

Even as they stood there, a bracing burst of wind misted them both. She could hardly blame *him* for the wet!

Perhaps she distrusted his charming smile, or the amusement lacing his dark eyes.

"Ma'am," the stranger greeted, brushing his hat brim with his free hand. If he truly had held cards, they'd vanished. "My apologies for spooking you. I needed shelter through the worst of this here blowup, but I did not intend to . . . intrude."

Her doorway stood at the top of three steps, placing her bodice at an indiscreet level with his head. Despite the rain, Audra flushed at that realization. She took a deep, steadying breath, but his eyes widened at that and her face just got hotter. *Oh, dear.* This was *not* going well.

Thank goodness the man looked away, if belatedly, toward his mare. But even then his eyes sparked like a pine fire and his mouth twitched against less-than-appropriate humor.

Audra swallowed. "I have more chores to complete," she told him in her best ladylike tone. "When I finish, you may come in. Be careful not to track in too much mud, if you will. School starts tomorrow, and I have worked very hard to make my room neat and attractive."

Oh, dear. That did not sound controlled so much as rude. Should she apologize? But she ought not be talking to him at all, should she? They had not been introduced!

"And you've done a fine job, ma'am," assured the stranger, sliding his bright gaze back to her. "Things are most assuredly neat and attractive."

Her already tight throat clenched. He *did* mean the room, didn't he? If not, she should slap his handsome face for such boldness. Torn between suspicion and the injustice of false accusation, Audra chose to ignore his comment and pulled the door shut again, wind or no wind.

Then she sank against it. *There!* Surely that satisfied the requirements for proper behavior . . . didn't it? If she ruined her reputation here—in under a week!—what hope did she have?

Either Jack found the lady colder than this north wind, or about the prettiest piece of calico he'd set eyes upon. Could be both, her being a schoolmarm and all. Except that when she'd stood there, dictating the conditions of her hospitality, he'd not thought her dove gray eyes cold at all. He'd thought them vulnerable, even frightened. That look called to something deep in his gut, something old and painful that he'd rather not pay mind to.

He might not have a say in the matter.

And why wouldn't she be frightened? Though barely old enough to teach, if he called it right, the gal was obviously a lady. Although Jack patronized establishments where ladies' names ought not be spoken; he'd seen enough of the world to know a few of their ways and guessed at more. He couldn't resent her loftiness any more than he'd managed to stop admiring her figure.

A fine, fine figure, indeed. Understated. Elegant.

He fingered the pocketed cards he'd been shuffling to keep his fingers limber out here in the cold, and he wondered why he'd never had truck with a real lady before. Other than the obvious fact of his profession, that was . . .

He gathered his few belongings. "Reckon I might get some shelter after all," he told his mare as he waited, warming his fingers in her breath, listening to the rain.

Queen was still nuzzling his hands, looking for a treat that wouldn't show this evening, when the door from the schoolroom opened again. The horse's head came up, immediately alert—same as Jack's—but this time the schoolmarm held on against the pull of the wind. She wore a blue cape now, and gloves, and a wary expression similar to Queen's.

"Ma'am," greeted Jack, keen to soothe that wariness. "I appreciate your hospitality."

"Just this side," she instructed quickly. She bit her lower lip, then seemed to notice and released it. It was a gem of a lip. "That is . . . I cannot allow you into the other building."

Jack nodded, wondering how he could put her at ease. Before he could figure something up, though, the gal spoke again.

"I should be obliged . . ." She paused, then hurried on. "I should appreciate it if you would avoid mention of meeting me, sir. People might"—she looked down at her gloves and said the last word very softly—"talk."

She might have announced the end of civilization, solemn as she said it. The effect tickled him.

"Now surely a lady of learning like yourself wouldn't suggest I *lie*" teased Jack, smiling—then regretted it.

"Of *course* not!" she exclaimed, taking a step back as if from the force of his accusation. "I *never* lie! I just . . . I mean . . ."

Her eyes grew so large that only his curiosity as to what she *did* mean kept him from an immediate apology.

"Sometimes it *does* seem prudent not to tell the whole truth," she insisted hopefully. "Unless asked, of course. That does not truly count as lying. Does it?"

"No, ma'am," he assured her, not really caring *what* was the truth, simply wanting her eyes to stop aching like that. "Seems to me that's plain good sense. Why burden folks with needless information? That's what I'd say, anyhow."

The wind fluttered loose strands of hair across her face and yanked at the door she held. Hardly noticing, she simply yanked back. "Would you really?" she asked, hopeful.

He nodded up at her, careful to look his most believable.

And then she smiled, and it was a smile of beauty, of salvation. That smile could soothe away pain, warm nights far colder than this one, and tempt a fellow away from sin itself.

All of which made ladies right dangerous, indeed—but at that moment, Jack was lost. He stepped forward to brace the door so that she could stop struggling with it, offered up his free hand. "The name's Harwood, ma'am. John Harwood."

Though when he'd last used the name John, he couldn't remember. He'd been Handy Jack for so long now . . .

For the first time in years, he had no inclination to proudly announce that.

Her gloved fingertips touched his. By the time she'd descended the stairs, her smile had vanished, as if perhaps she weren't certain how to maintain it. Or, just as likely, if she should.

His hand tingled from her touch.

"Thank you, Mr. Harwood," she said. Even without the smile, he no longer found her cold at all, just careful. Whoever she was. She didn't tell him her name.

In fact, she'd asked him to never mention this meeting.

He could see the shackles of propriety behind that request clear enough. And if only to keep that pain out of her dovelike eyes, he meant to honor it, even if he *wasn't* much of a man to follow any rules outside the *Book of Hoyle* . . . and sometimes bent a few of those.

Still, he prodded, "And you would be, ma'am . . . ?"

She pulled a matching hood up around her face. It was a quality garment, he noted; not the sort of cape a farmer's daughter would wear. "I would be leaving now, sir," she parried neatly. "Good day."

Her presence had disoriented him—he only now realized she meant to go out into the storm. He closed the door behind her, so as not to spook Queen. "With it blowing like this?"

"Yes," said the schoolmarm. "I like cold weather."

"Now, ma'am, I'd not be much of a gentleman if I were to allow you to walk out in this storm." Not being much of a gentleman anyway, he put his hand on her arm to stay her.

And *now* he felt the cold. Startled by the ice in her gaze, he immediately removed his hand. He expected she would slap him now, or make some other prim, appropriate response.

Instead she said, "*Allow* me?"

And for a moment, through all that prim frost, he saw unexpected fire. Its heat rushed over him, as surely as her smile had, from its prison deep behind all her rules and moralities.

But like the smile, the icy fire lasted only a moment, then vanished under confusion or embarrassment. The gal escaped into the rain, and he—well, he watched her. Watched her all the way down the road to that clapboard house he'd passed by, where the rain-obscured slip of blue turned in and he knew she'd be safe. He watched for several minutes past that, too.

Fine example of womanhood, that. He doubted he'd be the least bit cold tonight, with her on his mind. Not that he, Handy Jack Harwood, ought to be entertaining himself with thoughts of a lady. Not the kind of thoughts a man dealt himself on a cold night, anyhow. Although he *had* seen fire in her. Short-lived but certain.

Darned good thing Jack would be moving on after tonight. If he were to stay in the area for much longer, he might just overestimate his chances and underestimate his odds again.

Then again . . . things surely would be interesting if he did.

They might even be fun.

Chapter Two

> *Teachers will bring a bucket of water and a scuttle of coal for the day's session, and will start the fire at 7 A.M so the room will be warm by 8 A.M.*
>
> —Rules for Teachers

"Why don't I run ahead?" suggested Audra carefully after one last adjustment to make sure the white tablecloth again hung straight on the kerosene-lit kitchen table.

Aunt Heddy said, "We shall not be *running* anywhere, child."

The implied criticism startled Audra almost as much as being called a child in front of two girls who would be her pupils.

Hardly looking up from examining the drain board, making sure Audra and their two boarders had not merely cleaned the breakfast dishes but the kitchen itself, her aunt added, "Do not bite your lip like that. It is a wholly unattractive habit."

Obediently releasing her lip, Audra felt the most shocking urge to mimic the older woman—and with her mouth pruned up, too. *We shall not be* running *anywhere, child!*

She immediately blamed her nerves. Not only would this morning finally bring her first day as a teacher, a position in which she *must* succeed to regain her self-respect, but she very much feared what would happen if—*Oh, heavens!*

What if Mr. Harwood had not left yet?

She'd kept the enormous secret of him all yesterday afternoon and evening, through her fitful night, through a tasteless breakfast and the numbing solace of morning chores. It provided gentle distraction, and in her defense, the subject of strange men at the schoolhouse had not in fact come up. Aunt Heddy hadn't even asked how Audra's work had gone.

It did not count as an untruth to remain silent. Did it?

Plain good sense, the intriguing Mr. Harwood had assured her, and oh, she hoped he spoke sincerely! And correctly.

But if he remained at the schoolhouse this morning, Aunt Heddy would certainly demand an explanation. Then Audra must either confess to having met and spoken to the man, or else she must flat-out lie. And she must not lie. Not even with her reputation and her future at stake.

Throughout all her missteps last year, she had never actually lied.

But it could not hurt to get to the schoolhouse first . . .

Fourteen-year-old Claudine Reynolds, settling a bonnet atop her dark hair and rechecking it in the window reflection, asked, "Why can't we take the surrey to school?"

Aunt Heddy, not looking up from inspecting the windowsill, did not answer, only corrected, "Why *can* we not."

"The school is so near," Audra reminded Claudine more gently. "We can walk there in the time it would take to harness the horses."

"You know how to do that?" asked Melissa Smith, the older boarding student. Brown-eyed, with remarkably pale hair, Melissa was mere months younger than Audra, but taller.

Audra said, "My parents insisted that my sisters and I learn to drive for ourselves."

"That was Wyoming. Even in Texas, young ladies know not to preen about masculine abilities," scolded Aunt Heddy, turning grim gray eyes back to the three girls. Despite being a fellow teacher, Audra felt like just that to her aunt—no more than another girl.

Except that Audra had a secret. A dangerously scandalous, deliciously personal secret. In this cold, communal household, she had something all her own.

"Who dried the dishes?" demanded Aunt Heddy.

Claudine had, so Audra and Melissa said nothing—but neither did Claudine. Outside the house, a bird began to question the coming dawn with a few loud shrieks.

Aunt Heddy's gray eyes narrowed, as threatening as Papa's could be but with no affection behind their sternness. "I have asked a question, girls!"

Despite her impatience to get to the schoolhouse, Audra kept very still. Only if her aunt asked her straight-out would she tattle. Those were the rules Audra and her five sisters followed.

Perhaps Melissa, raised with brothers, felt differently. Claudine yelped, then frowned at the not-quite-innocent-looking blond girl before admitting, "I did. Every last one of them."

Aunt Heddy said, "Well, you shall *re*wash every last one of them this instant, young lady. Audra, Melissa, go ahead of us and start the fires at the schoolhouse."

Yes! Audra snatched up her blue cloak, her schoolbooks, and her lunch pail, pausing only when Claudine said, "Melissa and I are *paying* to be here. Let Audra do it."

Heddy did not tell Claudine that part of Audra's salary was room and board. Rather than appear petty by saying so herself, Audra fled into the cold, royal-blue morning.

She did not know when she had last felt such relief to escape a place, and not merely for the chance to check on the mysterious and rather handsome Mr. Harwood.

Rather, a chance to make sure he was quite gone.

Audra, perhaps childishly, simply hated living there. Sharing her aunt's room and bed did not bother her—she'd always slept with one or another of her sisters. She did not miss the modern niceties of her mother's telephone, indoor plumbing, or gaslights so much, either—although if her aunt made one more disparaging comment about Wyoming, Audra feared speaking less than respectfully.

No, what Audra hated was the sense that she did not matter, that her existence warmed nobody's day, no more than anyone else's warmed hers. She missed hugs, laughter, the occasional comforting touch or smile. She missed belonging.

Candon, Texas, was so small a town that her family addressed letters here with the extra line, *Tarrant County,* lest the express take them to the two better-known Camdens, in Polk and Gregg counties. But Audra could live with small. She chafed at living with indifferent.

"Are you thinking about school?" asked Melissa Smith. Only then did Audra emerge from her dismals and notice how the black of night had lightened to slate gray in the east, though stars still twinkled in the western sky. Their breath clouded the sharp air with pale puffs.

"Not really," she admitted. In fact, here she was thinking of everything *but* school! Her gaze flew up the hill, toward the shadowed, two-room schoolhouse.

"I could never be so calm as you!" Melissa pulled her own meager cloak more tightly about her, the lard pail for her lunch looped about her wrist. "Here it is, your very first day as a teacher! I would be terrified!"

Audra *was* terrified, especially to teach the big children. But that fear shrank in importance against the sight of dark coal smoke coming out of the school's two stovepipes.

Was he still there?

She looked from the school to Melissa—blowing on her hands, one at a time, as if it were truly cold—and then back to the school, and she thought again of Mr. Harwood. "Perhaps we could walk more quickly," she suggested, speeding her step.

To her dismay, Melissa grinned at her. "Race you!"

And off she ran.

"Wait!" *Oh, no!* Audra had an image to preserve! But . . . what if Melissa reached the school first? What if Mr. Harwood was still there?

Even worse than the fear of discovery: what if the charming stranger were not so harmless as he had seemed?

"Melissa!" Paid no mind, Audra started running.

Melissa had longer legs and, Audra suspected, a better wind. But Audra had desperation. Feet pounding the frosted ground, air tearing in her lungs, somehow she managed to reach the schoolhouse just before her pupil did.

She immediately fell against her own door, blocking Melissa's way in . . . and anybody's way out. What if Melissa had gotten there first? What if something had happened and it were Audra's fault!

Unaware of possible danger, Melissa slumped against the opposite wall, trying to catch her breath between giggles. Her once neat, almost-white hair streamed over her glowing face.

Audra despaired of ever breathing again. But she saw no horse . . .

Melissa caught her breath first. "You shall not . . . be *running . . . !*" She covered her mouth at her own mimicry of Aunt Heddy, her laugh whole and infectious.

But Audra would not be infected. Melissa, though taller, was her pupil, and here, an hour before school even started, she showed no sign of obedience. And why should she? Audra had just undermined her own authority *and* that of another teacher!

"Melissa. . . ." she finally managed, struggling to be stern. "How could you behave so? And on the first day?"

"But Audra, didn't that feel marvelous?"

Marvelous? Audra's face tingled, her lungs burned, and her heart jumped in her chest with each desperate beat. *Marvelous?*

Yes, it had. Along with the fear and the desperation, the race had been . . . fun.

Was there no hope for her?

"How it felt or did not feel is not the issue," Audra insisted breathlessly. "We both must follow certain rules. And . . . and when on the school grounds, please call me Miss Garrison."

The conspiratorial gleam faded from Melissa's eyes and, with it, the first unspoken offer of real friendship in Texas. Perhaps Audra ought not regret that, but perhaps she would never make an adequate teacher, because she did.

And a strange man might yet lurk on the other side of the door she still blocked!

"Please check Aunt Heddy's—that is, Mrs. Cribb's room," Audra managed, sounding somewhat more like a teacher as her panting receded. "I will see to mine."

"Yes, ma'am," said Melissa slowly. "Miss Garrison."

As soon as Melissa vanished into Aunt Heddy's room, Audra darted into her own. She shut the door behind her and waited, at last, for disaster.

Nothing happened.

A fire burned in the stove, warming the room nicely. A full scuttle of coal sat near it. When Audra looked down at her feet, where Mr. Harwood had tracked mud yesterday, the floor looked relatively clean—not as good as when she had finished scrubbing it, but nowhere near as unkempt as she had feared.

But Mr. Harwood himself had left. She and Melissa—and her secret—remained safe.

The void in her chest felt almost like . . . disappointment? Which made no sense. A man's presence would make trouble for her, had he lingered. The way John Harwood's eyes had danced up at her when he'd introduced himself, she little doubted he could make trouble even under better circumstances. What sane young lady would feel disappointment at her escape?

Perhaps she simply missed having him as her secret.

The door behind her opened. Audra stepped out of the way as Melissa hurried in, cheeks still pink. "Audra—rather, Miss Garrison—someone lit the fire! Filled the water bucket, too!"

"The bucket?" Audra crossed to where the pail sat in the corner, a drinking ladle tied to it. True enough, hers also held water, more than she could have carried from the well herself.

"Perhaps one of the men from town came out?" she suggested faintly, wishing it did not sound so much like a lie to her own ears. Even if Mr. Harwood had done all this—and how could it have been anyone else?—he *was* a man. And he *might* be from town.

"Well, it was nice of whoever did," insisted Melissa, pulling pins from her hair to finger-comb it back into some semblance of neatness. Audra shuddered to imagine her own chignon.

"Here," she offered, crossing to the front of the room. Perhaps she could put things to rights between them and still retain her authority. "I put a comb in my desk, so that—"

Then she stopped, blinking. Something was different about the blackboard. Her inspirational rhyme was still there:

Work when you work; play when you play.
One thing each time; that is the way.

And so was her neatly written name: *Miss Garrison.*

But under her name, someone had used the chalk to draw a flower.

Audra felt herself flush at the memory of dripping hair and dancing eyes. *Someone?* Well, she most certainly had not imagined him. He'd most likely spent the night here. In this very room, perhaps stretched out on this part of the floor.

"Miss Garrison?" prompted Melissa. "Is something wrong?"

"No," Audra answered automatically, testing herself for the truth of that answer as she reached her desk. *Was* anything wrong?

She surprised herself with a tiny smile. "No," she repeated steadily, opening her drawer for the comb. "Nothing is wrong at all."

Her smile stilled when she saw a card tucked in the corner of the drawer, bearing a picture of a riverboat and reading, *Steamboat Playing Cards.* She bit her lip, intrigued. A surreptitious flick of the fingers showed her that this card was the jack of hearts. *Oh, my!*

She quickly claimed the comb and shut the drawer with a thump. Perhaps Mr. Harwood had played solitaire on her desk and simply misplaced the card?

He would not ruin an entire deck, simply to leave her a keepsake . . . would he? And even if he had, surely his choice of suits was a coincidence. And on the chance that it was not, she should feel insulted by such impudence, not flattered!

But she felt shockingly, warmly flattered, nonetheless.

Helping Melissa put her hair back to order, then reluctantly accepting the girl's help with her own, Audra wondered at the bold emotions she had felt this morning. They did not bode well, either for her character or her success as a schoolteacher. That sobered her. For the sake of her family, her very honor, she must succeed in this position.

But she also wondered if Mr. John Harwood ever went by the name of Jack.

Chapter Three

Teachers may not smoke cigarettes.

—Rules for Teachers

"I'll see that ten," decided Jack on a contented sigh of smoke, "and raise you five more."

Of the five men around the scarred crate, only the youngest was green enough to widen his eyes at the fellow beside him and then at Jack. "That's—that's all of twenty-three dollars!"

The youth's friend, a quiet fellow near Jack's age with a receding hairline, closed his eyes in silent protest. Then he sloshed some rotgut into an empty jar, threw back a shot, and set the jug on the hay-covered floor. The next fellow, with the tailored look of a banker, swore and inhaled through his own cigarette, a sissified ready-made.

The old-timer who owned this dairy barn started to speak, then crumpled into a long, hacking cough, bracing himself against the crate that served as a table.

The temperance movement had reached Texas. Jack had had to ride as far as Bedford, six miles beyond Candon, to find even a *dairy* with a good game. But discounting the cows, he settled right in. To him the drinking, the coughing, the betting—and the whisper of cards—sang the sweet song of home.

Except for the occasional lowing cow or mew of barn cats.

"Twenty-three dollars!" the boy repeated.

"That's some fine ciphering, son," said Jack. "And a good skill to have in these here wagers. Care to share with the rest of us what you mean to do about the situation?"

The banker snorted.

The boy considered it. "I don't got no twenty-three dollars. I only brought twelve."

And to a two-dollar-minimum game. Where in blazes did a nester boy get even twelve?

Jack hoped it wasn't seed money, or savings to buy his poor granny a wooden leg. "The generally accepted solution to your dilemma, son," he offered gently, "would be to fold."

"But I got five dollars on the table!"

The dairy farmer spit tobacco juice at an empty bean-can spittoon by their crate and only partly missed. "Well dad-gum it, boy, that's why they call it a *gamble!*"

"I . . . I could put up my mule. He's worth twenty-five dollars." On the market, not likely. And if he needed it for plowing next spring, he'd lose far more than market value.

Games of chance surely did show humanity at its most interesting.

"I got two mules already," the dairy farmer protested, wiping tobacco juice off his grizzled chin with the back of his hand. "Don't need a third."

The banker said, "I have no need of a mule."

Even the quiet man said, "I hire out my hauling, Early."

Either they, too, recognized the deep waters this pup paddled toward, or it was just the usual halfheartedness of a midweek game. Early looked at Jack, stubborn and desperate both.

Jack said, "Let the V-spot go. Your cards aren't that good."

It was too easy. "How would you know?"

The old man chuckled. "Well, we do now."

Early scowled, not realizing how lucky he was to have learned so valuable a lesson with so little money on the table.

The quiet fellow sloshed more hooch into his jar, then lifted the jug a tad higher in silent invitation. His companions, Jack included, nudged their assorted glasses—two of which were empty food cans—closer to him. For a man of few words, he seemed right hospitable.

"Me, too, Ham?" asked Early, looking forlorn.

The melancholic Ham stared at him for a long minute. "You gonna fold?"

"Reckon I gotta." And to perhaps everyone's relief, the kid laid down his hand. *Tarnation!* Watching a player that green was like watching a train wreck—morbid and fascinating, both.

Ham placed his own jar in front of Early. "Then have a drink. I call."

The others called as well, including Jack; he rarely risked over thirty on a flush except in truly high-stakes games. The dairy farmer took the hand with four eights, and the win tickled him so much that he laughed, swallowed tobacco juice, and started choking again.

Jack took another draw on his cigarette, then started shuffling the cards—not a new deck, but unmarked; he'd made sure—and then noticed Early watching. The youth's shaggy bowl haircut, his bone structure too strong for his young face, and his eyes somehow dull and enthralled at the same time, all told of a boy with more appetite than sense.

Jack reminded himself that nobody had the right to make the boy's decisions but the boy. No other way to learn. "You in?"

"You just . . . you just lost twenty-three dollars." Early considered the pot he'd lost. "That's over a hunnerd dollars in all. In one hand." So much for his ciphering abilities. He'd forgotten to deduct the twenty-three dollars the winner had put in himself.

Jack said, "It's only money," and, along with the other three, anted up.

"See here," said the banker. "Either you sit in, boy, or you go loiter elsewhere. This isn't school." Then he laughed. "But it is a school night."

Jack grinned. Even that Ham fellow's cheek twitched. The old farmer laughed again. And Early set his jaw with the stubborn look of a bull calf fixing to get into trouble.

Then Ham said, "We're both heading back Candon way. He'd best not leave till I do."

Jack's attention focused sharply. Candon way, was it?

"I can get home without your help," Early protested.

"But can Hamilton get home without yourn?" said the dairy farmer with a cackle.

Jack looked closer at the quiet fellow from Candon—Hamilton. He seemed fair to steady, for someone who might be stewed, but some men just got quiet like that.

"Go roll yourself a smoke, son," Jack suggested, to ease some of the tensions around the crate, and offered the remnants of his makings to Early. "Won't likely be much longer."

The old man said, "Think that way if you're of a mind, stranger."

But at least the boy was persuaded to go sit on a barrel in the corner and occupy himself with none-too-dexterous attempts at building a cigarette. He'd have an easier time of it if one of the barn cats didn't "help" with a swiping paw now and then. That the boy only nudged the animal away with one square-toed boot, instead of venting his frustration on the cat, spoke well of him.

"Rode through Candon just t'other day," Jack admitted sociably—and for a moment, as he set down the deck for a cut, he saw large gray eyes, sorrel-colored hair, and the finest smile this side of heaven. *Miss Garrison,* the gal had written on her blackboard. Jack couldn't recollect the name of the last woman he'd known, in the Biblical sense, back in New Orleans. But the proper little schoolmarm who had barely brushed his fingers with hers and who had called him sir . . . well, he suspected he'd remember her for some time. Miss Garrison.

When he blinked away the memory to deal the cards, he noticed for the first time just how danged smoky the place had gotten. It made him feel a mite empty inside, all of a sudden.

"Small town," he noted to Hamilton, to explain his interest. "Five-card draw, one-eyed jacks are wild." Even if the lady hadn't begged his secrecy, which she most eloquently had, he would not do her the insult of mentioning her in what amounted to a saloon.

But the powerful urge to do so, to learn something about her or at least prove he'd met someone like that, surprised him.

Ham said, "Oh, Candon's not the end of the world, but you can see it from there."

Jack focused fully on his hand, particularly on that saucy queen of hearts that usually brought him so much luck. The old man, ripe with his winnings, opened with a hefty fifteen dollars, and the game got interesting fast, until the farmer called at seventy-five.

Early, now smoking a sorry excuse for a hand-rolled cigarette, risked the banker's wrath by coming closer to watch.

Jack raised ten.

Hamilton saw the ten and raised three. A relatively small bet, compared to the rest, but he hadn't called. Interesting mixture of caution and risk.

The old farmer spat and folded. Fast come, fast go.

The banker started to sweat some as he matched the other raises to stay in.

I would be disinclined to have you as my banker, thought Jack. He matched Ham's raise with a three-dollar coin and slid the last of his paper money out of his vest pocket. "How's twenty more?"

Young Early said, "That's . . . !" But he apparently couldn't manage the arithmetic. A family in these parts could live well for a year off this combined pot, assuming anyone saw his raise.

Hamilton whistled through his teeth, thought a minute, and said, "How about credit?"

Tarnation. Therein lay the danger of closing saloons; in a back room of even as prosperous a burg as Bedford, folks could bet only so high. "Now you seem like a nice enough fellow, friend, but I make it a policy not to extend credit."

"But I *do* make it a policy," Hamilton explained. "I run the mercantile in Candon. Let me see your raise with twenty dollars' credit in my store. Twenty-five, since it's not cash money. I could write the voucher out for you right now."

Jack hesitated. He figured he could take the pot either way; getting Hamilton to fold would just minimize the competition. But he didn't play so much for the money as the gamble. And winning merely by being better staked than a small-town shopkeeper offered no gamble at all.

Not to mention that he liked the looks of this Hamilton fellow. The glazed desperation that had played across young Early's face found no purchase on Hamilton's. While some might see that as cause to minimize the man's losses, Jack saw it as reason to give the man the respect of a free rein—he admired little more than watching a fellow take an open-eyed risk.

Not to mention that doing some marketing in Candon would give him an excuse to double back to the place, maybe catch glimpse of that pretty Miss Garrison one more time.

"I'm of a mind to accept, if our associate here will," he decided, with a nod to the banker.

"Might as well," agreed the banker, a touch flinty. "I go through Tarrant now and then."

"But I do call," added Hamilton, drawing from his pocket a brown cigarette paper and a stubby pencil to write out the promised voucher.

"And I," added the banker, drawing one more note out of his now apparently bare wallet, "raise it *another* twenty."

Hamilton, who'd started writing, grunted and crossed out the number he'd just written.

Jack, not liking the banker's satisfaction, said, "Well, don't you got rocks in your pocket."

The banker said, "If you can't match it, stranger, I expect you'll just have to fold."

Oh. One of those. He'd noticed that Jack's previous bet had emptied his pocket. How downright observant of him.

Rube. If they were playing three-card monte, Jack would own him by now. He slid his gaze back to Hamilton. "Best write fifty, if you mean to match it. I call."

The storekeeper met his gaze, then glanced back at the scrap of paper and began to write again. "I reckon I can give fifty dollars' credit easy as I can twenty-five."

The banker looked nervous all of a sudden. "You gotta match the bet to call, stranger."

Exactly—which was why he hadn't called before. Jack leaned back in his chair and hiked his foot on one knee, to better reach into his boot in full sight. It made for a healthier retrieval, in a tense situation like this, but the banker still said, "You're not going for a gun, are you?"

Well, didn't that perk up everyone's ears? "Now what kind of an idiot would keep a gun in his footwear?" And Jack plunked his emergency fifty-dollar gold piece on the table, then took back thirty dollars of the paper money he had already bet. "Fear I'll have to make change."

Early, staring, started into his refrain of, "That's . . . !"

"It's a fifty-dollar slug, son," informed Jack, patience running low. He could've raised the pot another thirty, but if the banker had much more money stashed on him, too, Jack would end up betting his gold watch. He hesitated to chance his Jürgensen. "It was also a call."

Hamilton finished his voucher for store credit, put it into the pile in the middle of the table, and slid his gaze to the banker. "You raised last."

The banker tried a grin, but what with nobody else folding under his pressure, it didn't come out as cocky as he had likely hoped. He showed his hand—four aces. When the storekeeper discarded his cards facedown, out, the banker's grin started to regain its confidence.

Then Jack turned his hand—a straight flush, all hearts except for that handsome one-eyed jack of spades, filling in for a king high.

"You low-down cardsharp!" The banker rose as if to lunge at Jack. "You chea—"

But he stopped at the single-shot derringer pointed at him. Jack's patience had at last run out. "I said I didn't carry a gun in my boot," he noted. "I said nothing about my sleeve."

"Those aren't legal in this town." But the fellow had lost the worst of his swagger, anyhow. Funny how an up-close view of a muzzle did that to a man.

Jack smiled. "Unlike drinking and gambling."

Hamilton's low, "Go home, Bennet," finished it. High time, too. Folks like that took all the fun out of the game.

As soon as the banker headed out, Jack seated himself and slid the derringer back into his sleeve—that spring-loaded holdout had paid for itself many times over. Then he gathered his winnings, not bothering to count. The only paper his attention lingered on, amid a handful of bills, read: *This voucher entitles the bearer to fifty U.S. dollars' worth of merchandise in the Candon Mercantile, Tarrant County, Texas. Signed: Ferris Hamilton.*

Jack had little use for fifty dollars' worth of merchandise, considering the lack of space in Queen's saddlebags. But he couldn't simply dismiss the voucher. It would be poor business, and an insult to a stand-up fellow like Hamilton besides.

Although Ferris Hamilton seemed to have a touch of difficulty in standing up. That jug beside him looked to be lifting a sight lighter than the last time Jack had noticed. Achieving his feet, Hamilton stared at Jack for a moment, then said, "Thanks for keeping that bastard honest."

Jack smiled one of his first true and honest smiles of the evening. "I look forward to seein' your establishment." *And maybe a few other of the local sights as well.*

The pup, Early, stared at Jack with something akin to worship. "You just won . . . !"

But Hamilton interrupted his latest attempt at ciphering with a hand on the back of his neck. "Come on, Early. Your folks catch you out, they might think I had somethin' to do with it." As the two of them left, Ham swayed. The man was definitely in his cups.

Jack, who'd already gotten leave from the dairy farmer to sleep in his barn that night, didn't like that he hadn't recognized Ferris Hamilton's condition. Playing against drunks lessened his pleasure in winning and downright annoyed him when he lost.

He took a bracing swallow of tonsil varnish from the tin can on the crate and reminded himself that men had the God-given right to ruin their lives in whatever manner they saw fit. Nobody ever kept good sense or a good conscience without challenging it now and again—

Suddenly something walloped the wall, something big enough and heavy enough that Jack spun toward it and almost released his holdout derringer again.

The old farmer said, "Sakes alive!" and started toward the door.

Then young Early appeared. "Ham's horse just throwed him! I think he's hurt bad."

It didn't take much curiosity for Jack to find himself outside in the chill October night. Sure enough, there lay Hamilton. His groans indicated he'd survived, but from the angle of his leg, he'd not survived in full working order.

Well. Tarnation. Tempted to vanish back into the barn and go to sleep, Jack hesitated. The man would need a doctor. Doctors charged a fee. And Jack had all the fellow's cash.

Not that this was Jack's problem.

Except . . . if this Hamilton fellow lost his store, Jack might lose fifty dollars of credit.

He sighed. Nobody waited for him in Fort Worth. Hell's Half-Acre never really closed.

When he went back into the barn for the jug, it was not to avoid the excitement but to bring the liquor out as a painkiller . . . and an indication of his own grudging assistance. Only for the merchandise, he told himself. And maybe one last peek at that schoolmarm.

After that, whether or not this drunken fool killed himself was the sole business of the drunken fool.

Another class day almost over. Audra tried not to will the minutes by more quickly. Candon had given her a job when Sheridan, Wyoming, had revoked their offer. She owed them her best effort. *A full day's work for a full day's pay,* her father always said.

Thus she made herself walk to the back of the classroom again, where the biggest of the big children sat. She took measured steps, kept her back straight and dignified as if she were taller, older . . . a better teacher in general. Until she improved, she could *pretend* competence.

She hoped.

So far, so good. Even those pupils sharing their blue-backed spellers or slates worked quietly. Nobody had hidden a dime novel in his textbook, not since yesterday with *Deadwood Dick's Doom,* now incarcerated in Audra's drawer. And any moment now, it would be time to—

Audra paused, her attention caught by . . . what? She sniffed. For a moment her heart quickened with irrational delight. *Papa?*

Then she realized the full impact of what she had scented. Not her father; he and home remained as far away as ever. No, Audra distinctly smelled tobacco.

One of her pupils had been smoking! Cigarettes?

She glanced at the girls' side of the aisle, but they did not smell of tobacco smoke. Claudine, edging her slate away from the Parker girl, ignored Audra. Melissa, seated with Emily Calloway in back, slid a half-apologetic, half-sympathetic gaze up at her. Apparently Melissa had suspected the breach of conduct as well but, loyal to the other pupils, had remained silent.

Slowly Audra turned to the boys' side. There, in the back desk, sat her culprits. Jerome Newton's shoulders shook slightly, much though he attempted to control them, and Early Rogers' face was flushed plum. And they smelled like a bunkhouse.

Audra had obviously failed in her supervision at recess. Now her stomach sank. Not only must she discipline a boy bigger and older than herself, but she must handle two!

"Jerome, Early," she said, her voice inadequate to her ears. "You will remain after class. Melissa, please tell my aunt that I'll be several more minutes. The rest of you are dismissed."

She turned back to her desk as her pupils fled. Were she teaching younger children, she might linger at the coat hooks to tie cloaks securely under little chins, remind sweet babies not to forget their lunch pails. But Aunt Heddy had the first levels, and thus far Audra had failed to inspire anything approaching her own love of knowledge, even in pupils closer to her age. She could not ride hard on them well enough to prevent such blatant misconduct as smoking!

All too soon, only Jerome and Early remained.

"Come up front," instructed Audra. Once both boys had shuffled closer, they stood almost a foot taller than she and who knew how much wider. They attended school only when their families' farming duties ran light. That meant neither was as far along in his lessons as the girls. In a week, Audra had sensed in them a restlessness she despaired of ever taming.

But it was her job.

The boys shifted their weight uncomfortably, staring at the floor—but from her vantage she could still see their faces. Jerome looked downright amused.

Before she had fully planned it, her question burst out of her. "How *could* you?"

"How could we what?" asked Jerome, his mouth twitching.

Early, still flushed red, said, "You know what, Newton."

Jerome's mouth stopped twitching. "Way to bluff, Rogers!"

"Boys!" This time, heaven help her, Audra actually stomped her foot. At least that got their attention. "You both reek of tobacco. You *must* know that smoking is not allowed at school. It is a coarse, vulgar habit and . . . and it sets a poor example for the younger children!"

She remembered that her first thought, on smelling that particular smoke, had been of her father. That was different. Papa was a cattleman. More important, of course, he was an adult.

"What can you do about it?" challenged Jerome—and meeting his unashamed gaze, Audra felt a stab of fear for something more immediate than her character. There were two of them, and only one of her. And everyone else had gone . . .

She said firmly, desperately, "I shall have to punish you."

"Yes, ma'am," mumbled Early.

Jerome snorted and said, "How?"

The schoolroom door opened. Audra, Jerome, and Early all started at the interruption, and Melissa—slipping apologetically back in—appeared fully aware of her intrusion.

"I'm sorry, Miss Garrison," she said. "Mrs. Cribb told me to wait here and to walk home with you."

For once Audra welcomed her aunt's interference.

"She said . . ." Melissa glanced nervously at the boys, then back at Audra. "She said to tell you not to be too long."

"That is quite all right," Audra said, stronger for the support.

"For your punishment," she decided, "you must each write a composition on the importance of following rules in a well-run society. Tomorrow morning you will each read your composition to the class. Is this understood?"

"Yes, ma'am," said Early.

Jerome said, "Why bother? You're too little to whip us." And he stepped closer, emphasizing his size.

But his nearness also brought the scent of cigarette smoke back to Audra and, with it, the memory of her father. Papa could boss anybody. He never questioned his ability—he just did it. And she was his daughter.

She stood as tall as nature allowed her and stepped boldly forward herself.

Jerome Newton stepped quickly back in surprise.

"I may be small, Jerome, but I can still give my best effort. If you do not fulfill the terms of your punishment, I *will* whip you, and if you sass me again, you may stay home from school tomorrow and explain to your parents why you are no longer welcome in my class, Understood?"

Somehow, Jerome's glare faltered before hers did. "Yes, ma'am," he admitted.

Audra held her breath, so it would not all rush out in a sigh. "Then I must know only one more thing in this matter." And she held out her hand.

"Where did you get the cigarettes?"

"I could *never* have faced down those boys, not in a million years!" exclaimed Melissa, easily matching Audra's determined stride. "It's one thing to bully the younger children into submission, like your aunt does, but Early or Jerome could break you in half. With one hand! Whatever made you think you could make them back down?"

Audra, marching down the dirt road toward Main Street and the mercantile, pondered the question with only the edge of her attention—otherwise, she could never stay this angry. And she must stay angry to maintain her courage.

Someone at the mercantile, not Mr. Hamilton himself but "this feller what helped him out when he busted his leg t'other night," had given tobacco to Early Rogers. *Tobacco!*

"I . . . I had to," she admitted absently, to answer Melissa's question. "My father is not as big as some of his cowhands, but he always makes *them* mind."

But her father *seemed* as big. *He* had never propped himself against a table in the aftermath of a confrontation, fearful of swooning. Her father, she felt sure, had never come close to tears. And he would never hesitate to pursue justice.

How could young men like Early Rogers and Jerome Newton follow the moral path if adults encouraged their disobedience?

The road from the school on Plum Street to Main, then to the mercantile, seemed almost too short. Scrubby elms and black-jack oaks sheltered the girls from even the mild breeze. Almost too soon, they arrived at the store.

Afraid to hesitate, Audra crossed the wooden porch and ventured into the building's neatly cluttered interior.

The crisp smell of new merchandise, apples, and pickles, welcomed her. At first her gaze met a man in a chair, one with a quiet aspect that made her think, Yes, I can do this! Then she saw his splinted leg. Word of the storekeeper's accident had been on everyone's lips yesterday. This must be Mr. Hamilton himself.

"May I help you?" drawled a different voice, sweet as brandy cake. Even as Audra turned to face a second man—most likely her culprit—she felt a sinking premonition of familiarity.

It was the stranger from the schoolhouse.

Mr. John Harwood still had broad shoulders and slender hands, delighted eyes—blue, she realized—and a smiling mouth. Even now his friendly expression brightened, as if the mere sight of her had improved the quality of his day.

It was her Jack of Hearts.

Guilt and indignation had already solidified unpleasantly in Audra's stomach. Now new emotions ruffled her.

Delight to see him again. Apprehension that their unchaperoned meeting could yet be discovered. Confusion—why would a friend of this merchant stay at the schoolhouse? And relief. If he, too, were a storekeeper, perhaps her vague suspicions about him would prove unfounded.

She even felt a moment of immodest flattery that he would appear so glad to see her. As if she were someone special.

And yet mixed with that, disappointment almost suffocated her. Had *he* encouraged Early and Jerome's misbehavior?

Words would not come. But Audra was here for a reason, one she meant to see through. Desperate to know the worst of it, she extended one angry hand and uncurled her fingers to reveal the confiscated muslin pouch with its unseemly *Blackwell's Genuine Durham* label. *There!* Let the man answer the proof of his misdeeds, if not her accusations.

Or better yet, oh, please, let him be innocent.

Mr. Harwood appeared neither confused, as an innocent should, nor pale with guilty admission. Instead he gently retrieved the near-empty bag from her palm and, sapphire eyes sparkling at her, raised it near his clean-shaven face for a discerning sniff.

Audra waited, hopeful and fearful, her heart galloping.

"Why, ma'am," drawled Mr. Harwood, lips widening into a grin of dubious charm. "I do believe we use the same brand."

Chapter Four

Teachers are not to loiter downtown.

—Rules for Teachers

Jack had never known so good a time could be had storekeeping. Since he had more credit than he could use himself, he offered lavish bargains and freely handed out candy to children—even the colored children from nearby Mosier Valley. He even gave credit, special one-time-only Jack Harwood credit, to several customers the serious Ferris Hamilton would never have trusted with the real thing.

"That's coming off your account," Ham repeatedly warned from his post in the corner, one leg up, hazy from pain medication. He marked down each piece of candy, each nickel-off special, each bit of so-called "credit." After the second scruffy, grateful recipient of special Jack Harwood credit walked out, Ham added, "That one's a lousy risk. Can't handle his drink."

Then he took a swig of the pain medicine he'd been hitting all day—a medicine they both knew was more whiskey than not, itself. *He,* the swig said, could handle it.

Jack, plenty of credit to go, just shrugged. He was, after all, a gambler. "Well, if he comes back and pays, you just donate the money to some good cause."

Ham's smile could use some work, but Jack's return grin imparted a sight more humor. He was having too much fun to get testy, so much fun he'd already stayed an extra day.

Best of all, to his way of thinking, was the sheer number of folks who stopped in. Jack generally patronized saloons, pool halls, and barbershops when he wanted company. But in the absence of such sordid establishments, Candon congregated at their mercantile. And unlike saloons, pool halls, and barbershops, the mercantile welcomed womenfolk. Their presence required that Jack check his vocabulary some, but it surely beautified the day.

Especially when Miss Garrison finally swept in.

Jack had just taken a five-dollar bill from some fellow passing through, noted an unusual tear on it, and set it aside. He saw Ham notice—likely waiting for Jack to steal something—but before Jack could explain, in walked the lady of the schoolhouse herself.

Could be the fun of storekeeping wasn't all that held him here, at that.

To his delight, the gal looked every inch as fine as he remembered. Her hair still shone kind of sorrel in its backswept style, showing off the length of her neck, the line of her jaw and cheeks and upturned nose. The silver-gray, puff-sleeved dress she wore today fitted her sleek figure, from high bust to slim waist, before belling from her hips into a flare at her neatly buttoned ankles—hooray for fashion-conscious females. And those sizable eyes of her . . .

Actually, they focused first on Ferris Hamilton. Jack fought back a surge of displeasure. After all, Ham had a busted leg. And while Jack would soon be gone, the lady would likely do business with Ham for some time to come.

That thought didn't ease his irritation one dram.

"May I help you?" Jack asked, and she turned to him. Those dovelike eyes widened in recognition and then—

Jack blinked, startled. Dovelike or not, her gaze nearly froze him where he stood. Shifting her schoolbooks to one hip like some women might hold a baby, the little gal extended her free hand and offered him a near-empty tobacco pouch.

The thrill of seeing the schoolmarm one more time, mixed with his surprise at her icy greeting, must've clouded his thoughts. Surely she wasn't after a replacement! While such an absurdity tickled Jack's sense of humor, he reckoned that he'd best take what she offered.

Definitely tobacco. He sniffed the familiar tang of Bull Durham. Uncertainty began to thaw the lady's eyes. Suddenly Jack wanted nothing more than to have her smile at him again.

"Why, ma'am," he teased. "I do believe we use the same brand."

She did not smile. The friend she'd brought with her, a taller gal with suspiciously pale hair, muffled a laugh. Ham said, "See here, Harwood!" But the schoolmarm's expression stumbled into the same pained confusion that had set Jack's soul to aching back at the schoolhouse. His thoughts scrambled for a fix on how he could reverse the damage when, to his relief, the gal did it herself. Fire, not ice, bloomed back into her cheeks and eyes.

Then she slapped him.

It didn't hurt, of course—just startled him—and at least the gal no longer looked haunted.

"How dare you!" she demanded. She began to turn on her heel, seemed to remember something, then spun back to him. "I would thank you, sir, to stay away from my pupils!"

And then she started to march out—out of the store and out of his life.

Jack vaulted the counter to duck ahead of her. Her pupils? "Ma'am?"

The schoolmarm did not slow.

Jack danced backward, narrowly avoiding a table of lanterns, and stretched his hand out open, purposefully harmless, in her direction. "Miss Garrison, ma'am. Please."

Now the schoolmarm slowed, drawing her schoolbooks in front of her protectively. Jack's stomach lurched in answer. No wonder he rarely had truck with ladies; put him with the real thing and he had all the tact of a goat in a parlor house.

Nobody was to know they'd met.

"You *are* Miss Garrison, aren't you?" he insisted quickly. "I heard tell that was the name of the new schoolteacher, and here you just mentioned your pupils, so I figured . . ."

She finally stood, wariness and hope battling on her face.

Jack risked a step closer. Nothing improper, nothing to frighten her off. Just close enough to catch a whiff of the light, peachy scent she wore, close enough to feel her nearness like sunshine on his face. "Please pardon my presumption, ma'am, if I assume incorrectly. But am I to understand I have somehow wronged one of your charges?"

She hesitated, schoolbooks still shielding her. She didn't trust him. *Smart gal.*

"I would surely appreciate you letting me know how it is I've erred," he insisted. "Make it a mite easier to change my wicked way." That sounded too smooth, even to him. Well, he had another cheek if the lady felt compelled to smite him again.

But to his relief—in fact, to his sheer pleasure—the gal's lips twitched upward before she dropped her gaze and trusted him with an explanation after all.

She nearly ruined her own game in the same moment, too.

Eased by his smile, and determined to err on the side of faith instead of cynicism, Audra attempted to explain. "I caught Early Rogers smoking at school, Mr.—"

"Harwood!" he interrupted, and she jumped. Then she realized how close she had come to exposing them both. As she stared up at him, horrified by her own slip, his eyes danced with their shared secret and her last reservations melted away. He must have a logical explanation. Despite his liberties, he simply did not look like a scoundrel. Though he was in his shirtsleeves, as befitted a man doing actual work, those sleeves had ruffled cuffs of fine white linen, stretched across broad shoulders unweighted by guilt. Noting the brocade of his vest, his gold watch chain, and a barest glimpse of how his striped trousers fit with tailored grace over his trim hips and long legs, she thought that she had never seen so finely dressed a storekeeper. Or scoundrel. And despite the faint flush on one whisker-shadowed cheek, where she had struck him, he appeared more concerned than angry. That hinted at a character to match his well-groomed exterior.

Her hand tingled from rasping across that warm cheek.

"Jack Harwood," he clarified, offering his hand to finish his rescue of her reputation. "And the fellow who's pulled lame over there would be Ferris Hamilton, proprietor of this fine establishment. Pleasure to meet you ladies."

"Ma'am," added the man in the corner, with a nod at her and then Melissa. "Miss."

Even as she nodded back, Audra hardly noticed Mr. Hamilton, or Melissa either. Instead she thought: *Jack. Jack of Hearts.* That she'd guessed right about his name pleased her, and she took his hand instinctively. "Audra Garrison, sir."

Instead of simply touching her fingers, Mr. Harwood raised them to his lips and kissed them. The sensation sang through her hand and her whole being. It was not simply his lips—though who would have thought a man's lips would be so soft?—but the rush of his breath, the smoke in his blue eyes as he smiled up through a boyish fall of dark hair. She should snatch her hand back from such inappropriate gallantry, but for a long moment, all Audra could do was stare back at him and forget to breathe. Peter Connors had never made her tingle like this.

"And this is . . ." he prompted huskily. Holding her gaze, he nodded toward Melissa.

Only as his attention belatedly followed his words, and he opened his hand, did Audra recover both her fingers and some measure of composure.

But her body still sang in a most singular way.

"Melissa," she managed to inform him. "Smith. A boarder pupil." Then she remembered why she had come here. "I *am* the new teacher, Mr. Harwood. I caught Early Rogers smoking at school. And . . . and I am sorry to tell you this, but he said you gave him the tobacco."

Mr. John Harwood—*Jack* Harwood—listened politely. *Oh, heavens*. What if she had been wrong? She had struck him! But before she could castigate herself, he said, "Well, no wonder you're so riled, Miss Garrison. I reckon I would've lit into me, too." This time, when he smiled in that charming way of his, she did not mind half so much. *Trust me,* his smile said. *I can explain everything.* "You mean to say that Early Rogers is young enough to attend school?"

"Why . . . yes," she agreed, and made herself stand straighter. "Both Early Rogers and Jerome Newton are eighth-level pupils. They should be learning their lessons, not dissipation."

"I have not made the acquaintance of any Jerome Newton," Jack—Mr. Harwood—noted pleasantly. "But I met Early Rogers two nights back at a . . . a social gathering, of sorts, and I fear I did indeed overestimate his age. He is a sizable boy."

Audra nodded relieved agreement. It took character to admit one's mistakes.

"I will endeavor to be a sight more clear on the folks to whom I extend my hospitality."

His tobacco was hospitality? For a moment, Audra wondered if perhaps he were a tad *too* sincere, a touch *too* charming. But surely such cynicism belittled her!

Mr. Harwood's gaze drifted downward from her own, as if distracted, and she realized she had bitten her lower lip. Flushing at so childish a habit, she released the lip. Mr. Harwood swallowed, hard enough that his Adam's apple bobbed, but his gaze raised to hers again.

"Such as it is," he added, husky.

What? Oh. The so-called hospitality. The tobacco.

Whatever soap he used smelled wonderful. And he had a tiny nick across his jaw, she imagined from shaving. And his dark blue eyes held hers, almost like a touch . . .

Audra dropped her gaze and clutched her books more securely to her chest. "I would appreciate that," she told him. "For the sake of the children, I mean. Thank you."

She should take Melissa home now. They had chores to finish. Audra took great comfort in her chores; simple, regular work helped ease her homesickness. Yet for the few minutes she had been talking to Jack Harwood, she had not felt homesick in the least.

Still, she must not loiter in a mercantile, especially not with a pupil waiting. So she risked one last glance up at him. He watched her as closely as ever with those clear, blue eyes, as if committing her to memory. The sensation, not unpleasant, rather . . . tickled.

"Thank you for putting my mind at ease, sir. I . . . I am sorry to have slapped you."

"Oh, I reckon I deserved it," he assured her. Again, playful sparks lit his eyes. "One of the better ways to keep rascals like me in line, as a matter of fact. Now if you'd pulled out a six-shooter and plugged me once or twice, that might've proved a shade overzealous."

Even as she blinked at him, taken aback by so wild a suggestion, he unbalanced her further by asking, "May I make poor amends by escorting you two fair ladies home?"

Yes, sang her heart, with the kind of glee it normally reserved for Sunday school picnics or Christmas morning. But that had been before she became a teacher and an example.

"No need," she hedged.

"Two such innocent gals as yourself? I am loath to contradict you, Miss Garrison, but this is Main Street. Quite a few strangers have stopped by this very store today."

Mr. Hamilton, from his chair in the corner, snorted and medicated himself with a brand of cure-all that Audra's parents never allowed in the house.

Melissa, eyes round, asked, "From Mosier Valley?"

Mr. Harwood turned to her, giving Audra a moment to catch her breath. "Now that you mention it, Miss Smith, one or two Mosier Valley folks as well."

That did not sound good, wherever Mosier Valley was.

He'd not asked to escort her home *alone*, Audra reminded herself. That would be almost like courting and, of course, inappropriate for a teacher. Mr. Harwood meant only to behave as a gentleman should. Any cowboy from Papa's ranch would do the same.

She must not let her personal concerns for her reputation endanger Melissa.

"All right," she agreed, oddly dizzy. "You may escort us home, sir. Thank you."

Perhaps she was growing accustomed to his distinctive grin; this time it warmed more than unsettled her. He took but a moment to slip on his coat and hat, say something cryptic about "that five" to Mr. Hamilton, then open the door for her and Melissa to pass through. Then, taking their books, Mr. Harwood offered Audra his free arm as if he were, in fact, walking her home.

She stubbornly took Melissa's hand . . . but wondered what his arm would have felt like.

Mr. Harwood grinned and nodded once, as if he understood perfectly—but if he understood, why would he offer? He dropped his elbow and they continued as a threesome.

Still, Audra felt she should clarify something. "I would never carry a gun, Mr. Harwood."

And he laughed! He had a friendly laugh, joyful and open, but she would have enjoyed it better had she understood. Only then did he say, "And I'd bet you're not likely to smoke cigarettes either, are you?"

"Why no! I . . ." Finally, so come-lately that it embarrassed her, it all made sense. He had been teasing her from the start—about the tobacco, the shooting, and likely the betting, too. Not that they should be joking with one another, of course. Hardly knowing each other as they did, it was terribly familiar of him.

But his grin engaged her, and at that silly image of herself, cigarette in mouth and six-shooter in hand, Audra could not hide her own smile. She peeked at Melissa, who seemed equally amused, and swung their joined hands amiably.

When Audra glanced back at Mr. Harwood, he leaned close enough for her to feel the solid warmth of him and said, low, "How about I handle the dissolution for the both of us, ma'am, since you seem to have full claim on the decency?"

Oh! Looking quickly forward, at the road, Audra hoped that he was joking again. After all, she should not be walking with a dissolute man.

Her own decency had not proven as constant as he seemed to think.

Jack hadn't planned to escort Audra—*Audra!*—Garrison home from the store. The odds of any danger between Ham's place and her clapboard fortress of morality were laughably low. Even the folks from Mosier Valley, the specter of whom had frightened her unnaturally blond friend, seemed as reputable a passel of dirt farmers as he'd ever run into. But he'd conceived the idea, he'd acted on it, and the gamble had paid off.

He might not get the lady on his arm, but he got a considerably larger dose of her fine company, anyhow. Now he just had to think up what to do with it.

No better way to learn a game than to play it. "May I ask how long you've been in Candon, Miss Garrison? Pardon my noticing, but you don't appear to be local-grown."

She seemed determined to study the rutted dirt road, but at his question graced him with a quick, skittish glance. He'd have thought she was wary of him, if it weren't for what he'd wager was curiosity in her shy attention as it swept over him. "Barely a fortnight, sir."

"Audra came all the way from Wyoming!" provided Miss Smith. "On the railroad! She wasn't afraid of robbers, not even up north where those outlaws have been dynamiting trains!"

"My father escorted me," Miss Garrison added. "Of course I was not afraid."

"Wyoming," repeated Jack, making a mental note. To judge by her clothing, Wyoming was doing better for itself than he'd imagined, the notorious Butch Cassidy's train-blasting aside. "Well, that is a far piece. Don't they have need of teachers up thataway? Or were you just anxious to fly the coop, stretch your wings a bit?"

If she wanted to stretch her wings, he could give the lady a discreet lesson or two. But other than flushing pinker and watching her own leather-clad toes as they rhythmically peeked out from beneath her flared skirt, Miss Audra didn't answer his question.

Miss Smith did. "The widow Cribb, she's the schoolteacher who we're boarding with—"

"With whom," corrected the younger schoolteacher softly.

"—with whom we are boarding. She's Audra's aunt. Audra came here to help her."

"Only after the school board hired me," Miss Audra pointed out, finally raising her head to fend off stray compliments. Her composure struck Jack as a mite brittle, her eyes awfully bright, but it was a fair bluff. "*Miss Smith* paints me too kindly."

Ladies must take this last name business seriously in Wyoming.

"Then you aren't escaping an oppressive family?" pursued Jack, a mite disappointed.

"My family is not oppressive, Mr. Harwood," she insisted, meeting his gaze; her eyes warmed and her expression softened. "Far from it."

"Her mother's a suffragette," added Miss Smith, nearly whispering the last word.

If Miss Audra took after her mother, that could bode well for the flying lessons.

"My aunt worries more about Mother than my father ever has," she agreed. "My older sisters are another story. One would think they'd determined the most upsetting ways . . ." For a moment, Jack thought she would laugh at whatever memories entertained her. Her eyes no longer focused on him at all, but she looked so happy, and her happiness was such a pretty thing to see, that he didn't begrudge the attention. In fact, it intrigued him. Imagine, having a family that made a body so happy she perked up just to think of them.

When Miss Audra's attention returned to the present, though, that tinge of loneliness crept back into her pretty face. "Where do you call home, Mr. Harwood? I mean—" Her gaze dropped again, as did her voice, into uncertainty. "That is . . . I gather you are new in town as well?"

"Can't say as there's anyplace I *do* call home, ma'am. My profession moves me around some, as did my father's," Jack admitted. As if his father's calling were any more of a profession than his own! "My mother's folks hailed from Jefferson, back in east Texas. Used to be one hel—"

Miss Audra's head came up even before he got the word out, and Jack turned it into a cough. "Excuse me, ladies. I meant to say, one *humdinger* of a port town, even after the War of Northern Aggression. Nothing much to speak of there since the railroad passed it by."

"Not even your family?" Seeing the schoolmarm's horror at such a concept, Jack faced the reality that she'd not left home to stretch her wings at all. Unless he'd lost his ability to read people, she regretted leaving. It put her selfless assistance to her aging aunt in an even finer light.

"None to speak of," he assured her.

You poor thing, said her eyes, even if she had the grace not to repeat it aloud. Concern radiated off her so thickly that Jack automatically made a bid on it.

"Reckon that puts the both of us a mite far from home," he said solemnly, and felt only a twinge of conscience when she nodded. Now was the moment to mention missing his departed mother's cooking. Odds were he'd get invited to Sunday dinner, his dissolution notwithstanding.

Not that he'd meant to still be in Candon on Sunday.

"My family lives south of here," noted Melissa Smith, roping her friend's polite attention, and there went dinner. Just as well; Jack rarely missed his mother's plain, poor cooking and felt strangely relieved he hadn't told Miss Audra "I Never Lie" Garrison that he did.

A footloose fellow like him had better things to do than dine with ladies, anyhow—especially ladies with morals.

The overly blond girl explained how her home lay a touch too far for her to walk to either Candon or Arlington, and how she, too, meant to become a teacher. . . . Jack only half listened. Unless he'd taken to imagining things, Audra's glance toward the house they approached held no real welcome.

"Have you been a storekeeper for very long, Mr. Harwood?"

"Barely two days," he admitted, scrambling to figure up some answers which wouldn't earn him that second slap after all. "Just helping out my friend Ferris during his time of need."

"He's fortunate to have such a friend," said the lady with a smile. Had it been true, Jack would've taken a great deal of pleasure in her approval. "You have a different line of work, then?"

"Investing." Perhaps he drew a different line in the sand than she when it came to honesty, but Jack's word was generally considered good. No reason to compromise it here.

"Really?" she asked, an easy mark. Not that he meant to mark her. "How exciting."

How did her folks sleep nights, allowing her out in the world where she could fall in with folks like . . . well, like himself? "It has its moments."

By then they'd reached the clapboard teacherage. Audra drew her lower lip between her teeth in that concerned way she had, inspiring in him the sudden and powerful hankering to soothe it and her in a far more enjoyable manner. He'd like to discover just what the lips of a real lady tasted like, just once, before going on his way.

Yup, her folks should be downright ashamed.

"I believe you'll be safe between here and the door," he

assured them with a smile, barely keeping himself from winking. Darned if this gentlemanly behavior didn't take effort.

"Yes," agreed Miss Garrison, after releasing that poor, innocent lip. That old sadness again shadowed her pretty face, her lonely eyes—surely not just for Jack's imminent departure!

Jack forgot what he'd meant to say when, with the sudden slap of a screen door, a true battle-ax stepped out onto the porch. His schoolmarm began to wince and then, so suddenly that it startled him, her face brightened. Jack knew a bluff when he saw it.

"Aunt Heddy," she said, suddenly friendly. "Meet Mr. Harwood. He is helping at the mercantile during Mr. Hamilton's convalescence, and he kindly escorted us home. Mr. Harwood, this is my aunt, Mrs. Cribb."

Jack noted the widow's stern glare and thought: Some fool actually *married* that?

The widow Cribb's grim gaze bore into and through Jack. She looked much as he pictured the famed Carrie Nation, who axed saloons in her crusade against liquor—as though she not only had no truck with fun herself, but resented the barest whiff of it on other folks, too.

"Mr. Harwood." She greeted and dismissed him both.

Jack pasted on his best smile. "Ma'am—"

But she'd already turned to her charges to interrupt him. "Perhaps we had best review your agreement with the school board, Audra."

Miss Garrison raised her chin and met her aunt's gaze evenly. "I am aware of my responsibilities, Aunt." From her aunt's view, it probably looked impressive. But Jack could see the fine tremble in her shoulders, the brightness in her eyes and her otherwise pale cheeks.

Hell, board him with that widow woman and even Jack would feel homesick!

Loath to let her know he saw, Jack slid his gaze to Miss Smith. The younger girl scrunched her mouth and crossed her eyes at him in silent commentary on Mrs. Cribb. Jack decided he liked Miss Smith, whether she bleached her hair or not.

"Ladies," he said easily. "I'll bid you good day. Miss Garrison, thank you for keeping me in line as concerns your pupils. I sincerely doubt they could have lucked into a better teacher."

Especially if the odds were fifty-fifty between her and her aunt.

He took pleasure in watching the lady's eyes warm at him, even sparkle when he overdid things a bit with a gallant bow.

"Thank you, Mr. Harwood. Perhaps I will see you at the store sometime," she said, and his showy pleasure stumbled to a standstill.

"The store," he repeated blankly.

"Audra," warned the battle-ax.

To what Jack thought was her credit, Miss Garrison did not make a face. She fumbled for the schoolbooks Jack still held. He gave them over, a mite embarrassed to have forgotten, and their hands brushed. Such a soft hand she had; by profession, he kept his sensitive enough to appreciate it on so many levels . . .

Head bent over the book exchange, she whispered, "I expect a letter from my parents soon." The mercantile doubled as the post office, he remembered as she scooped her taller charge in front of her with one hand. She *did* hope to see him again.

Too bad he wouldn't be there when she came looking.

Jack returned to the mercantile, still chewing at the thought of disappointing Miss Garrison . . . assuming he merited her disappointment. He didn't much like this turn of events. It made him feel guilty to move on, and him with far less to feel guilty about than usual!

The females off in Fort Worth might not possess smiles nor eyes of her caliber, but he wouldn't have to keep his kisses reined in to mere speculation around them either.

"About time you got back," groused Ham from his chair, as if Jack worked for him. The outer corners of his eyes and mouth looked tight, as if the liquor was wearing off.

"And hello to you, too," greeted Jack, testier than usual himself, and noted the empty store. "I can see you're near to overrun in my absence." Then it occurred to him that Ferris Hamilton was his only source of information just now. "What do you know about ladies?"

"That most of 'em can't be trusted farther than they can be thrown." Ham took another dose of medication. "How did you know about the five?"

"The five?" repeated Jack. How did that relate to ladies?

Ham thunked his medicine bottle back onto the floor beside his chair. "You saved me four dollars. How'd you know?"

Oh! The marked five-dollar bill. Jack helped himself to a stick of horehound candy and noticed that Ham was so addled, he didn't bother to mark it in his writing pad. "Someone gave you a dollar and claimed he gave you a five, did he?"

"A woman. She described that tear in it perfectly. Hell, my leg hurt so bad, I guess I would've believed her, but you'd stuck that five aside, so I knew I wasn't the one what took it."

Huh. Jack took a tangy-sweet bite of the candy and forced his attention momentarily off fine-eyed schoolmarms. It hadn't occurred to him that the swindlers had marked Hamilton specifically. Bad enough to be seriously hurt without having to fend off human vultures, too.

"Runnin' with scoundrels makes for a useful education," he admitted. "So where's the gal what tried to hornswoggle you?"

Ham scowled at a prominently displayed plow.

Jack hitched himself up on the counter. He guessed he knew where she was—halfway to Bedford by now. Or to Irving, or Arlington, or Grapevine, depending on her direction. "See now, that's why she did the pickup instead of the drop-off. I'd wager she cried some when you caught her, too. Said she'd never do it again? Maybe gave you some story about her poor widowed mama, or the eight brothers she's raising, or the banker foreclosing on the farm?"

Hamilton continued to scowl.

"Well, that is refreshing," acknowledged Jack, and took another bite of candy while he wondered what a real lady's lips would taste like. Sweet, or tart? If the lady were Audra Garrison, he knew where he'd lay odds. He just didn't know how a fellow went about determining the answer.

"Refreshing?" Ham demanded.

"That there's still innocence left in this here world," Jack said, impatient to change topics.

"Innocence." Ham snorted. "Ignorance is more like it."

Jack shrugged—no reason he should cheer the fellow up. "Well, for your clarification, I wasn't inquiring about flimflam artists. What do you know about *real* ladies?"

The storekeep lifted his brooding gaze to Jack. "Ladies like that schoolmarm, maybe?"

"Maybe," Jack agreed tartly. "What odds would you give a gal like that stepping out on the arm of a fellow like me?" Assuming a fellow like him stayed in town another week or two.

Ferris snorted. "Money's against you. Schoolteachers can't keep company with men."

Jack stared, the taste of horehound fading against the storekeeper's certainty. "Who says?"

"School board rules about the teachers bein' good examples. Why do you think so many of 'em turn out like her aunt?" The storekeeper's eyes warmed. "You *did* see the aunt, didn't you?"

Jack nodded slowly. The thought of the sweet Miss Audra turning into *that* turned his stomach. "I heard the aunt's a widow. Must've kept company with men at some point."

"Not as a teacher, she didn't," Ferris assured him. "Her and old man Cribb came up from the hill country, but he went and fell off the roof, broke his neck, left her in debt. Some church ladies learned she'd taught school and started one here, so's she wouldn't starve. Since then, she's abided by their rules sure as if Moses made a second trip up the mountain for them."

Jack continued to stare. Miss Audra seemed thoroughly rule-broken herself. But surely . . .

"It's against the rules for lady schoolteachers to have gentlemen callers," Ferris insisted.

"I don't reckon that will be a problem," Jack said. "Not being a gentleman."

Ferris shrugged again, and then looked up as a colored woman entered the store, carrying a basket of clean laundry. She went to the storekeeper as he was likely the one who employed her. Jack didn't bother minding their transactions, just saw that they spoke, and she took the laundry upstairs, and came down without it. Another one of those threatening Mosier Valley types.

It gave him time to ponder the disparity of the school board's mandates. If things were as fair for lady teachers as men, could be he'd have gotten his walk, even his kiss.

He wondered how such limitations sat with a suffragette's daughter. He'd glimpsed the promise of rebellion in her at the schoolhouse, and with her aunt. It'd be a shame to ignore that.

As soon as the laundress left, even while Ham sucked down his longest draw of medicine yet, Jack asked, "Think you might could use a touch more of my assistance, over the next week?"

"Hell, yes," Hamilton replied with a snort. "S'long as you don't implicate the store. Compromise that lady too far, you'll end up married or hanged. Folks here don't tolerate that kind of behavior."

"Not that I plan to," assured Jack with a slow grin. "But just how far *is* too far?"

He had some fairly good guesses, the kind that would, if known, get him slapped for sure. Little wonder Hamilton just rolled his eyes and didn't deign to confirm them.

They were, after all, speaking of a lady.

Chapter Five

Lady teachers may not keep company with men.

—Rules for Teachers

Good girls, went the old saying, left home only in bridal dresses or pine boxes. Perhaps for good reason. Audra would never have spoken so boldly to a man in Wyoming . . . would she?

Still, if she wanted her letters she must face Mr. Harwood. So she went out.

Merchandise crowded every possible inch of the Candon Mercantile. Shelves of ready-made clothing, canned goods, and patent medicines lined the walls from floor to ceiling—and hams, herbs, even hats hung from the ceiling. Glass cases full of jewelry and fancy soaps ran along each side of the room. Barrels of pickles or crackers and boxes of apples and cheese crowded between tables on which sat lamps, plows, and bolts of cloth.

Two old men played checkers near the door beside Audra, and a suspendered farmer stood in the back, hefting a hoe as if weighing it. She did not see Mr. Hamilton or Mr. Harwood.

Audra breathed in the perfume of newness that filled every corner of the mercantile as surely as did the merchandise. She'd always enjoyed stores. Perhaps that explained why she did not feel quite so distressed as she had feared when Mr. Harwood emerged from the curtained doorway to a back room.

"Why, just the gal I was hoping to see," he greeted, his grin welcoming. Between living with Aunt Heddy and maintaining a suitably sober classroom, Audra felt half-starved for smiles.

"Have I received a letter?" she asked, crossing to the glass counter he stood behind.

"It arrived this afternoon." When Audra stepped closer he handed her the folded envelope as if he had kept it aside just for her. "But that's not why I hoped to see you."

That distracted her from the address: Candon, Tarrant County, Texas. "Then why . . . ?"

Mr. Harwood's smile widened. "Because, Miss Garrison, I am fond of pretty things. I hear folks up Euless way are holding a dance tomorrow night. I'd be honored to escort you."

She took refuge in simple courtesy. "Thank you, no, Mr. Harwood. It is against the rules for a schoolteacher to attend such functions."

He must not have wanted her company too badly; his smile did not fade at her rejection. Instead he leaned closer over the counter. "And do you always follow the rules, Miss Garrison?"

She remembered Peter Connors, the rules they'd broken.

"I . . . try to, Mr. Harwood," she managed despite the burning in her throat, then turned and escaped the store, escaped her own boldness, escaped his inappropriate—and futile—interest.

For the first time since her scandal, she longed to go dancing.

Jack leaned even farther over the counter to examine the doorway, as if it might explain Miss Audra's abrupt departure. He hadn't been *that* forward, had he?

"What did you say to that l'il gal, boy?" demanded Charlie Randall from his game at the cracker barrel. Both he and his opponent, old Ned Cooper, were close to deaf, so Jack shouted his answer loudly enough to startle the nester pricing hoes in the corner. "I asked her to a dance!"

Charlie wheezed a laugh. "No wonder she lit out. I wouldn't dance with you neither."

At that, Ned and even the farmer laughed. Jack would have joined them, if only because of how funny Ned sounded, like he had the hiccups. But Audra's expression, before she'd "lit out," had held a touch too much distress for him to find amusement in it, even if she *had* overreacted.

It also made him even more certain that this gal needed to take life a little less seriously.

He dearly wanted to be there when she did.

I am a teacher, Audra told herself firmly, after three whole days of agonizing over her rudeness to Mr. Harwood. *I am a teacher, and shall conduct myself as one.*

She certainly had enough concerns about teaching—from her awkwardness in the classroom to the shortage of adequate books and slates—to remind her of that when she returned to the mercantile. But despite the presence of Ferris Hamilton in the back room, Mrs. Collins pricing calico, and two old men playing checkers, Mr. Harwood brushed her hand with his as he accepted her return letter, then asked her to join him in a picnic.

Audra snatched her hand away from him. "No! Thank you . . ."

she added grudgingly, realizing she'd been rude yet again. "There are rules, sir."

He leaned his elbows on the counter and widened his eyes, dark hair falling over his forehead. "I fear my wishful thinking keeps making me forget that fact, ma'am."

When she noticed how his gaze settled, rather unfocused, on her mouth, she flushed as guiltily as if *she* had done something wrong. Perhaps she had. It had happened before. . . .

Before she could turn away, escape again, he quickly added, "I imagine gentleman teachers don't have such strict rules to follow as the ladies. Now how is that fair?"

He looked innocent enough, but . . . "They have their own rules, Mr. Harwood."

"Such as?" He had rolled up his shirtsleeves for work, revealing tanned, solid forearms against the display case. She should leave now. But . . . she was behaving herself. And they had several chaperones, of sorts, throughout the store. She must not be impolite.

"They mustn't get shaved in a barbershop," she offered.

Jack—Mr. Harwood—drew his head back. "Why not?"

"I do not know," she admitted. "I've never been to one."

Jack's laugh sent tingles through her, immodestly deep. "What else?"

"I've heard gentleman teachers may not frequent pool or public halls."

"But lady teachers can? Now there's a stumper. Do you play pool often, Audra?"

"Mr. Harwood!" She'd obviously stayed too long. Eyes still dancing, he turned his head at an awkward angle, offering her his cheek to slap. When Audra spun to leave, she nearly ran into the minister's wife. "Oh! Mrs. Collins! I am sorry—"

"No need, honey," the older lady assured with her Texas twang, and slid her gaze toward Jack Harwood. "Seems to me our assistant storekeeper here can use a little exposure to decent folks. Perhaps you'll help me convince him to attend church while he's in town."

"I doubt it, ma'am," insisted Jack, so vehemently that Audra forgot about leaving and searched his face instead. He so obviously liked people; how could he dislike church?

"Sunday services are good for the soul," assured the older woman, as if dangling bait.

"I'll take the odds without it, ladies," said Mr. Harwood. As if life were a card game!

"If I have no mail . . ." demurred Audra, finding refuge in propriety once again.

Mr. Harwood protested, "Now, Miss Audra . . ." That was not quite so forward as just "Audra," and if she stopped to scold him, he would only lure her into more conversation. She escaped the store before that could happen.

What was it about Mr. Harwood that drew her away from her own better judgment?

"I'm not the ladies' man you are," drawled Ferris Hamilton once Mrs. Collins had left as well. "But I doubt you'll win anyone by flaunting your godless ways."

Godless ways. Jack hated that kind of talk. He glanced toward the door, to make sure Ned and Charlie wouldn't overhear him, then said, "Go to hell."

"You'd get farther with her if you attended church."

"I don't see *you* reading your Bible regular."

"I'm not trying to seduce a schoolmarm," Ham countered.

Jack frowned at that word. Seduce her? He wanted a stroll, a private conversation, a kiss . . . anything to catch another glimpse of the spirit he feared was strangling beneath those rules of hers. Especially the kiss. He imagined holding her in his arms, weaving his hands into her sorrel hair until its pins gave way and it fell over her shoulders as God had meant it . . .

God? He cleared the distaste out of his throat. God had nothing to do with it. But he might tone down his pursuit of her, just a dram, skittish as she'd proven.

He didn't want to *seduce* her. But he surely wanted that kiss . . .

To Audra's relief, Jack Harwood began to behave himself after that. Oh, he still looked at her in such a way that made her feel dizzy—deliciously so—but was that really *his* doing, or hers?

Against the suffocation of "the teacherage" and her frustration at still not reaching her pupils, her visits to the mercantile became the bright spot of her week. Mr. Harwood intrigued her. When he drawled a word like *ain't* or *weren't* she suspected he did so more for his own amusement than because he did not know better; he obviously had intelligence. His skill with figures, and playful ease in handling money, greatly impressed her.

"I wish I knew how your teachers encouraged you to learn so well," she admitted, buying a length of dark blue ribbon when she would rather have bought green.

His eyes twinkled, as if he saw something far more likable in her than did her pupils, her aunt . . . even, sometimes, herself. "My teachers had less to do with it than plain life," he admitted. "I just enjoy it. Have you never found something you liked so well, it just came . . . natural?"

The way his voice fell husky, on that last question, felt downright improper—but what he'd said had merit. *Plain life* . . .

Perhaps he should be the teacher!

"I'm starting a game in the back room Friday night," Hamilton told Jack in a low voice. He leaned on his new crutch as, one-handed, he took inventory. "You're invited as long as you don't cheat."

Jack resisted the urge to whoop with joy. Behaving himself with Miss Garrison, though a fair plan at first, was wearing on him. She smiled at him more often, and seemed less likely to bolt in his presence. But discussions about books and arithmetic weren't exactly his goal. He longed for some good, old-fashioned sin.

He said, "I hardly ever cheat."

Ferris stared at him for a long, unimpressed moment, then went back to his inventory. "I plan to win back some of that credit before you give half my store away."

Then the door to the mercantile flew open and five young folks, including that poor excuse for a poker player Early Rogers, rushed in. The last was the pretty schoolmarm herself.

At noon?

"Mr. Harwood!" she exclaimed, delighted. "Just the person we hoped to see. Good afternoon, Mr. Hamilton."

Ferris, going back to his inventory, muttered, "Mr. who?" under his breath.

Jack, in the meantime, wondered if maybe he'd made more progress with her than he'd thought. Basking in the glow of her excitement, the way her dovelike eyes shone at him, he could believe just about anything.

She quickly introduced the four "student representatives" before explaining their business. "We have decided upon a project, thanks to the advice you gave me last week—that is, when I came to buy a hair ribbon . . ."

Her eyes widened in dismay, as if she'd caught herself lying.

"Now that you mention it, I do believe we spoke," Jack interceded. "Don't know as I recall taking it upon myself to give advice, though. You weren't there but a minute."

From near the patent medicines, Ferris Hamilton snorted.

Audra nearly glowed before reminding him, "You mentioned that you learned arithmetic more quickly when the numbers stood for something real."

"Did I?" Jack asked, intrigued.

That was all the encouragement she needed. "The next day, I asked my aunt about our shortage of school supplies, and she said the town could not afford more. That's when I had the idea. My pupils and I shall make a project of it, raise money as a community effort. They can use it as a lesson in arithmetic, and we all get the satisfaction of accomplishment."

Gazing down into Audra's pleasure-flushed face—and past it to her primly buttoned bosom—Jack had an inappropriate thought about under what other circumstances he'd like to see her so passionate. "Don't see as how I can take the credit for that," he protested.

After all, he'd been thinking of learning arithmetic with poker and faro, not good works.

Her smile said he was too modest.

"We're here to price slates," announced Melissa.

Jack felt a twinge of something suspiciously like guilt for entertaining such fantasies in front of her pupils . . . although at least two of them, Jerome Newton and the pinch-faced Claudine Reynolds, exchanged secret glances with enough heat to argue the innocence of schoolchildren.

Hamilton said, "They're ten cents each."

"So if we buy ten slates . . . ?" prompted Audra hopefully.

"A dollar," answered Jerome, ignoring Claudine long enough to seek Audra's approval.

With a smile, she gave it. Then she looked to Jack and her smile got downright radiant.

Warmed on a surprisingly deep level by her approval, Jack heard himself ask, "What if Hamilton and I give you a discount, maybe take off three cents per slate?"

Audra and Melissa caught their breath at his seeming generosity. Early, still ticking off fingers from the previous question, frowned at having to start over.

Ham said, "We what?"

"Seventy cents," announced Jerome to Jack. But he said it more like a challenge.

"That saves thirty cents!" Melissa added, looking at him as if he were some kind of saint.

Jack started to feel downright unsettled. He ought not involve himself in this scheme of theirs. It would take them time to raise their money, more time for ordering and delivery. Worse, the whole thing felt suspiciously like a church project. But Audra, too, gazed up at him as if he were worthy of esteem, even by her strict criteria.

Tension began to ease from his shoulders as he gave in to what felt suspiciously like fate. Hell's Half-Acre would be there at the end of the month as surely as now.

"Matter of fact," Jack added, coming out from behind the

counter and heading for the window where the slates sat. "I'll sweeten the pot some. That is," he quickly translated, when the girls looked confused. "I'll add some encouragement to your efforts. You'd best be able to divide by two, because the mercantile will match any of the money you raise. We'll pay for half of whatever you order."

That last he said with a grin at Ferris himself.

Ferris glared murder back at him.

But Audra! Joy and admiration warred for supremacy across her face, and she put an approving hand on his forearm. "Oh! You are a *wonderful* man! Thank you so much!"

Once, in a lightning storm, he'd seen a tree struck barely ten feet from him. The crackle of the air was nothing compared to the electricity that surged through him at her soft touch.

He touched her hand with his own, relished how she glowed up at him. At that moment he thought he could kiss her. It would earn him a hell of a slap, but every male instinct in him, every ounce of gambler's timing, insisted that his chances were ripe.

Not in front of the children.

He moved his hand, let her belatedly remove hers, and fed a little more friendliness and a little less desire into his grin. "If we're to be business partners," he suggested, "maybe it would be forgivable for you to call me Jack?"

The pupils continued to chatter, so involved in each other that they'd missed the near scandal. Not that Jack had ever before avoided scandal. Scandal was fun. So why . . . ?

"I believe that you are right," Audra agreed softly. "For business matters. Jack."

Her lips had never looked more tempting than when forming his name. He ached to taste her—and after a lifetime of making sure he never wanted *anything* very badly.

Well . . . tarnation. He could raise his investment by another few weeks, couldn't he?

Could be that the stakes of this game were a mite higher than he'd first anticipated.

Chapter Six

A teacher must keep her pupils from unseemly conduct.
—Rules for Teachers

Over the next two weeks, Audra increasingly heard a most gratifying opinion: "What a nice man that Mr. Harwood is!" She enjoyed hearing Jack praised so, her faith in her friend validated—even if, strangely, Jack did not. In the weeks Audra had known him, she would not have thought him one for false modesty. But he repeatedly rejected any praise.

"You're the one who figured up this effort," he pointed out when she stopped by the store to check on her mail, or to drop off a return letter, or to price suitably modest calico for a dress. "I'm no more generous than the next fellow."

Mr. Hamilton snorted his agreement at that.

"But, Mr. Harwood, you *are*." Audra insisted one afternoon. The men's laundress had arrived at the store, her small sister and brother with her, and Jack gave each child a candy stick with instructions to enjoy the treats by the stove, where they would be warmer.

Why would he do that except from generosity?

Mr. Harwood just stared at her, bemused, until she dropped her gaze out of modesty.

"Jack," he prompted, almost a whisper. She shivered inexplicably at his low voice.

"Jack," she repeated softly—then hurried to safer conversation topics. "Do you realize that no colored children attend the Candon school?"

"Are you surprised?" asked Jack, blinking.

"Back home . . ." But to continually compare Texas to Wyoming showed poor manners.

Trust Jack to let her say what she truly wanted. "Back home what . . . Audra?"

Despite their growing friendship—platonic, of course!—she knew she should chide his familiarity. She did not. It made her feel less alone, and seemed so small a sin. "We had several colored pupils, and some Mexicans, too. All children should get an education, do you not think?"

"Mmm-hmm," he agreed easily, still watching her face so closely that, when the laundress descended the stairs from Mr. Hamilton's apartments, where she'd gone to deliver the men's clean clothes, Audra seized upon further distraction. "Excuse me—miss?"

Only when the laundress stopped, stiff, did Audra see her tension. "Is this a bad time?"

The colored woman cocked her head at Audra, somehow both curious and resentful at the same time. "No such thing as a bad time, miss. What is it you want?"

"I teach school here, and I wondered why none of—why your little brother and sister don't attend school." She offered her hand, but the laundress only looked at it, then took a step back.

"They attend school," she announced firmly. "They attend school in Mosier Valley."

Audra had heard that name before, mainly when her pupils invoked it to frighten each other. But she'd not realized it lay close enough for a woman to do business between the two towns. She'd thought Grapevine or Euless or Bedford to be closer. "That's where you live?"

"Yes, ma'am." The taller woman turned to the stove. "Lee! Martha! Time to head home."

With a clumping noise, Mr. Hamilton hobbled down the stairs to see them leave.

"Good day, miss," the colored woman said, still sounding somehow angry. "Mr. Harwood. Mr. Hamilton. *Sir.*"

"Lucy." The storekeeper scowled at her from the stairs.

The strange tension in the store didn't recede until the trio left. Audra repeated the name: "Mosier Valley. Is it close?"

Mr. Hamilton said, "Maybe two, three miles. Why?"

"Why do people talk so differently about it?"

The storekeeper stared, as if surprised by her ignorance, but Jack smiled. His smile made her feel warm, safe, special. She did not know how to react except to look away, which she did.

"I hear tell," Jack explained, "the folks in Mosier Valley were once slaves."

"All of them?" She blushed at the foolishness of that question; the country had abolished slavery decades ago! "That is to say—it's a whole town of colored people?"

Jack smiled wider, somehow amused. "Yup. A whole town of them."

Mr. Hamilton said, "Things are different here from up north, Miss Garrison. You'd be wise to keep your distance from the Mosier Valley folk."

She'd thought more highly of him than that. "Surely they pose no special danger!"

Mr. Hamilton said, "They don't. But if you mix with them, the rest of those rules you're following won't be worth a damn."

Audra's mouth fell open at such foul language, but she did not have to rebuke Mr. Hamilton. Jack took care of it for her. "Watch your tongue around the lady, Ferris."

Mr. Hamilton stared at Jack Harwood, and then he laughed. And not at the idea of Audra being a lady—he did manage to gasp, "My apologies, miss." No, he was laughing at Jack.

Jack scowled back, and Mr. Hamilton laughed harder. It made no sense to Audra.

Jack Harwood was, after all, such a nice man!

By the time the slates arrived, Jack had sickened of being nice. He found himself countering a surfeit of daytime courtesy with nighttime wildness. By mid-November, he knew every backroom poker game and every source of bootleg liquor from Grapevine to Hurst. He smoked. He chewed. He cursed. He won and lost ungodly amounts of money.

And he always wandered back to the mercantile before dawn, washed off the smell of cigarettes and whiskey, and fell into bed. The next morning would find him behind that damned counter, wearing clean clothes or even a shopkeeper's apron, ready to mind his *P*s and *Q*s yet again. It seemed wrong; dishonest, even.

But every time he considered leaving, Audra Garrison would come by, and the draw of Fort Worth's red-light district faded. She would raise her dove gray eyes to his with a sweep of long lashes, or blush at something he said, or smile shyly, or solemnly bite that luscious lower lip of hers. And Jack would think: *There's still a chance. Don't give up yet.*

But he began to fear that, in those hopes, he proved even more naive than Audra herself.

And danged if the gal wasn't naive as they came. Even when Jack took a chance on educating her a bit, she fought it. "That Claudine," he warned one day, "is up to no good."

But Audra said, "I'm sure that she has good intentions. She's simply confused."

When he said, "Don't trust that Jerome Newton," she used the term *high-spirited,* as if he were a horse instead of a youth of almost twenty. Jack had seen more damage done by such young men than he cared to relate—especially since the bulk of his anecdotes would contradict the sham of respectability he'd cultivated for his little schoolmarm.

Even when he asked her to step out with him, she would simply say, "Be serious, Jack." And he felt such pleasure to hear her speak his name that he let her go right on believing the invitations were playacting on his part. But sooner or later, her naivete would get her hurt. At her age, Jack could've taken an out-and-out beating and suffered less than Audra seemed to suffer from an unkind word—even from Lucy the laundress's rebuff of her offer of used slates and books for the Mosier Valley school.

"Thank you kindly, miss, but we don't need charity," said Lucy. "We have a fine schoolhouse—it's our church. It's new. And our teacher is college educated. We get by."

Audra's face fell so visibly that Lucy added, again, "But thank you." Then she glanced, concerned, toward Ferris. Did she think Hamilton would fire her over something like that?

Jack didn't particularly care, and ignored both of them to draw Audra aside to suggest she go riding with him and take a look at that fine Mosier Valley schoolhouse themselves.

"Be serious, Jack," she murmured, a weak smile easing the worst of the pain from her eyes, and Jack felt the breathless sense of another close call. Sometime soon, Audra Garrison would run into something that would hurt her too badly to be fixed with mere words.

He couldn't decide if he wanted to be there when it happened or not.

"Where is Claudine?" demanded Aunt Heddy, while Audra and Melissa started supper.

Melissa said, "I think she's outside." But something about the way she spoke, head down, concerned Audra. "Shall I go fetch her?"

"Audra can do it," declared the older woman. "No need to lose two of you."

So Audra put on her cloak and stepped into the slanting, late-afternoon light. She remembered being fourteen, how important it had felt to be alone with her thoughts . . . although she would keep her hands busy with chores at the same time. Could Aunt Heddy remember the uncertainty of becoming a woman? Poor Claudine could not even turn to her own mother, because Claudine's mother had died.

So clearly could Audra imagine the poor girl's loneliness that she did not hear the strange noise until she'd almost come upon it. Startled, she stopped.

Was there an animal behind the barn?

If so, it wasn't an animal she'd heard before—Aunt Heddy had chickens, two old horses, and a few barn cats. This sounded nothing like those. It sounded vaguely like something in pain.

Audra knew better than to approach a hurt animal unarmed, so she found the pitchfork, then investigated. Something about that moaning sound unsettled her deeply, as if she'd heard it before but erased the memory from her mind. Still, she would not let any creature suffer simply for her own comfort! She quietly circled the barn, to the shelter of the woodpile . . .

And she stared in shock.

She'd come upon not one creature, but two—both of them her pupils. And what had them moaning stunned Audra into mortified paralysis.

Jerome Newton—somehow she recognized Jerome, even from behind and staring at his bared bottom—had his pants down. Claudine, the sleeves of her gingham dress dangling to her knees, had wrapped her bare arms around his neck, and was making that moaning sound while Jerome tried to scoop armfuls of petticoats and skirt up off her stockinged legs.

They were—Audra had of course never seen it before, but obviously they were about to—

It looked so ugly!

"Claudine!" screamed Audra, horrified.

Claudine saw Audra and screamed, too. Jerome began to turn, wide-eyed, but Audra covered her eyes before she could see any more of this debauchery—or any more of Jerome.

"Miss Garrison!" Jerome protested, over a rustling of denim. "This isn't what it looks like. I mean, we couldn't help ourselves—"

"Don't tell Mrs. Cribb!" protested Claudine. "Don't you dare, Audra, or I'll tell that you—"

At the blast of a shotgun, Audra screamed again. Whirling, she peeked enough to see her aunt shoulder the double-barreled shotgun she kept to chase varmints away from the henhouse. She still had one shot left and aimed it at Jerome Newton, who let loose an ill-chosen word.

But at least he'd pulled up his pants. No way could he have skedaddled off past the corner of the barn, toward the shelter of the woods, if they'd still hung off his hips the way they had.

Audra shut her eyes again, even though she faced only Claudine's bared bosom now. That seemed awful enough. She didn't cover her eyes, though, because she needed her hands to take off her own cloak and stumble blindly toward Claudine with it until the younger girl took it from her hands and—Audra peeked—wrapped it around herself.

For a moment, the world had seemed a chaos of nudity, gunfire, screaming birds, and scrambling cats. Suddenly nothing remained but a blushing Claudine, a furious Aunt Heddy, silence, and the tang of gunsmoke hanging in the air.

"Did he get your drawers down?" demanded Aunt Heddy, as if that question overrode any of the others—*Are you all right? What were you thinking?*—that Audra might have chosen.

Claudine said, "No. Audra interrupted us first."

"Have you done it before? Don't lie to me, girl!"

Claudine shook her head.

Audra realized that Melissa now stood beside her, staring with shared awe at the drama before them. She welcomed the taller girl's hand on her arm. She felt ill. Another few minutes, and Claudine apparently would have been wholly ruined . . . and in so ugly a manner . . .

She feared she would never stop picturing Jerome Newton's bared bottom, the grimace on Claudine's face, the way they'd fumbled at each other.

Why would anybody want to do something so . . . so ugly?

Was *this* what the gossips of Sheridan suspected her of doing with Peter Connors?

"You will go to your room," instructed Aunt Heddy, grasping Claudine ungently by the cloaked arm and dragging her toward the house. "And you stay there until week's end, when I shall take you home for your father to deal with. Melissa, stay out here. If anyone comes by to ask about the gunfire, say we had a coyote sniffing around. Audra, come with me."

Grateful for her aunt's clear thinking, if not her terseness, Audra obeyed, shaken. Did her married sisters do that? Did her—*No.* She refused to think of her parents!

"Put down the pitchfork," instructed Heddy as they reached the house. Audra belatedly leaned the tool against the wall, then followed her aunt and pupil inside.

Aunt Heddy said, "Do you have something to confess, Audra?"

Audra blinked, startled. "Me?"

Her aunt turned to Claudine, who stood wrapped in Audra's cloak, her sleeves still hanging outside her skirt. "You told Audra not to tattle, or you would tell me *what?*"

Claudine *had* said that. But what could she possibly tattle about Audra?

Claudine's face took on a pinched, angry look. "Or I'd tell you her friend Jack Harwood is nothing more than a professional gambler."

Audra's mouth fell open. "How dare you lie about him!"

"Jerome told me so. He's a gambler, and he met Mr. Hamilton at a poker game, and he's only staying in town because Mr. Hamilton paid his gambling losses in store credit. You think you're so proper and pure, and you've been friends with a gambler!"

Audra swallowed back dizziness. *Jack?*

Perhaps Jack pushed the boundaries of polite behavior, grinned a little too broadly, smiled a little too intimately. But . . . a gambler? Someone who, instead of doing an honest job, made a living cheating foolish people out of their earnings?

Aunt Heddy said, "Write a note explaining why you will not be by the store again."

"But she could be lying!" Audra did not care how childish her protest sounded. She trusted Jack more than Claudine. Jack had warned her about Jerome and Claudine both!

"Audra—"

"No," insisted Audra, even more disoriented by this accusation than by the scene she'd interrupted behind the barn. "I will not be rude to him on mere gossip. I shall ask him myself."

"You will do no such thing," commanded Heddy. She dragged Claudine into the bedroom to pack and to speak in private.

Audra took her aunt's cloak to hurry to the mercantile before it closed. Disobedience or not, she would ask Jack herself, give him a chance to explain . . .

But as soon as she reached the store, as soon as she saw him look up from the counter in surprise—playing cards in his hand—she knew the truth.

Jack Harwood was so obviously a gambler, she'd been blind not to see it from the start.

Chapter Seven

Teachers will not associate with people of questionable character.

—Rules for Teachers

"How *could* you?"

Audra Garrison stood before Jack—an Audra he'd seen only in his dreams. Slips of sorrel hair escaped her bonnet to brush her flushed cheeks and neck, but her fingers did not dart out to tuck them back into order. Her bodice expanded and receded with deep, desperate breaths, and her eyes—

Passion flamed in those large gray eyes. Here stood no malleable, fragile china doll. Here stood a lady with grit. And she was gunning for him.

"How could you make such fools of us?" she demanded, clutching at the glass counter. "How could you let us believe you were honorable when in fact you are a . . . a no-account . . ."

He waited, wary and fascinated at the same time. Ferris Hamilton hobbled closer from across the store. "Is anything—"

"A *cardsharp!*" accused Audra.

Ham spun and began to limp wisely away.

Obviously Audra knew. More than anything, Jack felt relief. The masquerade had ended. Stiff with anger, Audra raked her accusing gaze across him, but for once it was *him* she saw.

"I'll venture that you disapprove," he guessed, folding his arms.

"Do you deny it?"

"I've never once denied it." He spoke carefully, as to a skittish animal, but she jerked back.

"You did *so!*" Then her gaze fell away from his, haunted, as she apparently reviewed their brief history. "You said . . ." she began. "You called yourself . . ."

He waited for her to work it through—and Lordy, but he wanted to hold her. His hands itched to grip her shoulders, if only to decide if he felt heat off her or a chill, or both. Tension charged her so subtly that tendrils of her hair quivered. Standing across the counter from her prickled at his skin. *This* was why he had stayed in Candon—this strong young lady.

Yet even as he admired her outrage, it began to crumple. *She* began to crumple, eyes brightening, lips pressing tight, and he couldn't stop his own attempt at comfort. "Now, Audra . . ."

Her head snapped up and her glare struck him. "How *dare* you be familiar with me? I don't even know you. Did Mr. Hamilton realize that he was taking in a . . . nothing but a . . ."

She turned her back to him, looking at Ferris, who quickly occupied himself with some inventory. From Audra's sharp huff, it seemed she disapproved of the unspoken admission. It was not surprising; she disapproved of quite a bit today.

"A no-account cardsharp," Jack finished for her, using her previous words.

She nodded a single, jerky nod.

No-account. Now *that* bothered him. He'd always considered himself a particularly admirable example of a cardsharp. He leaned his elbows on the counter, bending closer to her. "And have you known many cardsharps in the past, Miss Garrison?"

She spun back to face him, chin high, cheeks flushed. "Of course not!"

"So how would you know we're such a bad lot?"

Her mouth opened in outright astonishment. As if she were so worldly-wise, herself.

"If I'm the only gambler you've ever had truck with, and I struck you as a decent enough fellow until now, what makes you assume any different about the lot of us?"

"I assume different because I've been told so. By my father, my brother—by people I *trust,*" she added. "And you *aren't* decent. You let the whole town believe you were a respectable, law-abiding gentleman. You let us . . . *me* . . ."

She swallowed hard.

He spoke carefully again. "I let you believe what you wanted to believe."

"And you did nothing to disabuse us of it!" She might have been accusing him of high treason, from the way her mouth pursed primly around the words. Tarnation; if he did grasp those shoulders of hers, would he rather kiss her or shake her? Lucky for her, he was too much of a gentleman to do either. That thought annoyed him.

"Could be folks ought not be told what to think," he fired back. "Could be someone as intelligent as you might not wait for scoundrels to declare themselves before she recognizes 'em. Could be, Miss Garrison, that as long as you insist on holding yourself so all-fired distant from fellows like me, you dupe yourself, no assistance required. Maybe instead of marching down here to scold me like I'm one of your pupils, which I am *not,* you ought to be thanking me for not taking worse advantage of that cursed innocence you've been yoked with."

"Yoked?"

"Downright shackled." Jack stalked around the counter to get closer to her. Much closer. Her eyes widened as she looked up at him, but she stood her ground. "Not everyone in this world waits for permission, and not everything that's the least bit fun is a sin."

Her eyes narrowed at him, as though he were crazy. Maybe he was, expecting her to understand.

"But you've got those Sunday-morning blinders on," he pushed on. "You've been harnessed up for respectability as surely as if your folks or your minister or your aunt put the traces on you themselves, and you just stand there and let 'em do it."

He could smell her, some kind of fancy soap covering her own, richer scent. The fit of her dress molded the swell of her breasts, the nip of her waist. He realized that he wanted something a lot earthier from her than a kiss. The idea seemed blasphemous . . . and liberating.

He watched her throat clutch when she swallowed, followed the tip of her tongue when, gazing up at him with wary fascination, she licked her lips. They seemed so close now.

"You're trying to confuse me," she accused, her voice barely a whisper.

"I'm trying to free you." His voice softened. "Take a gamble, Audra Garrison. What's a sterling reputation going to do for you except hold you in that suffocating job and find you a boring husband who'll just loop on more chains? Loosen those corset stays . . ."

And of its own accord, his hand brushed lightly down her ribs to the flare of her hip. Lady or no lady, she *was* hot—hot and starched and real. And she did not wear a corset.

She shuddered, caught her breath, but continued to stare up at him, dazed.

He leaned nearer, brought his lips close enough to hers that he could taste her breath. "What," he whispered as he closed the last few inches between them, "do you have to lose?"

But with a cry, she twisted away from him—away from the hand that softly cupped her hip, away from the kiss he could see she wanted, away from the truth of his arguments. "No!"

And, low-down cardsharp or not, aching for her or not, Jack let her pull away.

"You are an unfeeling cad!" she accused, backing away. Apparently she put distance between them over giving him the slap he knew he deserved.

"I came here to tell you, in person, to stay away from us," she announced, running shaking hands down the sides of her gown, backing away. She bumped into a table but refused to turn her back on him. "Stay away from my pupils. Stay away from my aunt. Stay away from *me*."

"I may know you better than you think," he insisted. "I know that suffocating yourself for fear of making a mistake is a lot worse than actually making one."

She stopped at the door, eyes brimming with pain and thus paining him, too. "No," she whispered. "It isn't. And you don't know me at all."

Then she spun away from him, escaped to her proper, regimented little world—a world he'd vowed never to return to.

Tarnation.

"You think he meant to kiss you?" asked Melissa, dipping water out of the rain barrel and into the bucket Audra held.

Jack Harwood's face floated before Audra's unfocused gaze, his blue eyes almost black with an emotion that looked unnervingly like hunger. Even more disturbing, instead of frightening her, his gaze had sparked an answering hunger within herself. His hand at her side felt oddly protective, oddly gentle . . . for a masher's. His coat had smelled of the mercantile, a delicious mixture of new merchandise, clean wood, apples, and a faint, familiar whiff of tobacco. Perhaps the tobacco, which she associated with her father, explained why she had not pulled away immediately.

Or perhaps respectability proved a greater challenge than Audra had feared.

"I *know* he meant to kiss me," she corrected, bracing the first of their two pails against her knee as its weight increased. "Right in the store—in front of Mr. Hamilton!"

"I can't believe Mr. Hamilton would stand for it!"

"Perhaps he would not have." But suspicion whispered that perhaps she should not hurry to see people in so favorable a light. Jack Harwood had taught her that.

She put down the first bucket, lifted the second with the protection of her leather work gloves, and listened to the metallic ring of water tipped into it from Melissa's dipper. She'd rather not think of Jack as having anything valid to teach. The things he had dared say to her . . .

"Well, good riddance to bad rubbish," decided Melissa. She

sloshed water in her hurry to finish the task and get them out of the chill wind. "Sorry."

Audra smiled acceptance, too grateful for the friendship to mind a little damp. For almost a week she had lived with the sharp memory of her encounter at the store, which overrode even her disappointment in Jack and her regret at her own gullibility.

How could she have allowed such an unwise friendship as one with a—

"Have you ever been kissed?" asked Melissa, and Audra lost her grip on the second pail.

It fell to the ground, drenching both their skirts. "Melissa!"

"The widow Cribb can't overhear," insisted Melissa with a laugh, rescuing the bucket and handing it to Audra. Then, leaning deeply over the rain barrel's edge, she collected the last of their water, one foot off the ground and her voice echoing. "I just wondered, is all."

Aunt Heddy and Claudine had left Candon for the weekend to see Claudine's father about her recent misbehavior. Neither Audra nor Melissa knew if the girl would return or not.

"At least wait until we go inside!" Audra again propped the bucket on her damp-skirted knee and noticed that she would now have to polish her shoes.

"There's nobody to hear us but the animals."

But Audra took comfort in repeating one of her father's sayings: "Better safe than sorry."

She and Melissa were using their weekend of autonomy to pamper themselves in a way that, while not immoral, would likely annoy Aunt Heddy. They were treating their skin with buttermilk and taking the time not only to wash their long hair but to treat the ends with a special family recipe, to soften it before a final rinse in herb-scented rainwater. Now they added to the morning's dissolution by laying their damp dresses and petticoats out to dry and continuing their toilette in their wrappers. For the first time since she'd left Wyoming, Audra got to talk girl-talk.

"Yes," she finally admitted, pouring warm water over Melissa's hair. "I've been kissed."

When Melissa tried to sit up with a squeal, Audra pushed the girl's head back over the washtub. "It was all very proper," she insisted, to set a good example, and continued to carefully ladle lavender-scented water onto her friend's blond hair. "His name was Peter Connors and he was my beau. He kissed me on the cheek at my fifteenth birthday party."

Odd, how tame that now seemed. It once had been the most romantic thing ever to happen to her.

"You have a beau!"

"*Had* a beau," Audra corrected, squeezing the excess water from Melissa's hair. She steeled herself against the familiar sense of panic at the thought of the scandal, but time and distance seemed to be leaching its power. "I am a teacher now! Teachers mustn't have beaus."

"Teachers mustn't court—that does not mean they can't have beaus back home." Melissa accepted a muslin towel to further dry her hair.

Audra poured more rainwater into the big pot on the stove to warm, then bent to use the water left in the tub to dampen her own hair and start the process Melissa had just finished.

Melissa snatched the tub out from under her. *"No!"* Then, at Audra's surprise, she added, "The widow Cribb isn't here today—you deserve to have fresh."

Touched that Melissa had noticed her aunt's stinginess with the bathwater, Audra still protested. "We have fresh water for the rinse; no reason to create more work before . . ."

But Melissa had already carried the tub outside to empty. With a sigh, Audra picked up her silver-backed brush and began to draw it through her reddish-blond hair until the water on the stove warmed. Not that anybody would notice her hair anytime soon . . .

Melissa returned with the empty washtub, her face flushed from the chill.

"Sit by the stove," insisted Audra. "You ought not have gone outside with wet hair."

Melissa rolled her eyes, but did as told. "I *long* to have a beau," she shared. "To step out together on Sundays. To dance all night in his arms."

Checking the water, Audra thought about stepping out with Peter, dancing late into the night. She'd felt proud to be on his arm, flattered that he had chosen her. But she could not remember feeling anything powerful enough to merit the dreaminess in Melissa's tone.

Not about Peter.

"Have you ever done *more* than kiss?" asked her friend now.

"Melissa!"

But they were not teacher and pupil today—merely two girls boarding together—and Melissa laughed at Audra's shock. "Claudine has done more, and you're older than she."

"Melissa!"

"We know she has! We all but saw them!"

Too much this week, Audra had thought about . . . well . . . what her sisters, when they spoke of it at all, simply called "that." Did all married couples really do *that?* What about unmarried girls like Claudine? What about women who took money for it? Was it as horrid as it looked?

She also remembered the hunger in Jack Harwood's eyes, the press of his hand on her hip, and her face heated. "I think," she said carefully, dipping out enough water to wet her hair, "that should stay between Aunt Heddy, Claudine, and Mr. Reynolds."

She used her mother's special hair soap, sent all the way from Wyoming.

"I don't blame Claudine," Melissa admitted, unwrapping her own hair and beginning to comb it. "If I were to kiss anybody, I'd kiss Jerome Newton. He surely is a good-looking boy."

"They both behaved disgracefully! Ladies should not give favors so freely."

"But surely we have to trust *someone* with our . . . favors. If we're ever to marry, that is."

Audra carefully washed away the soap, then applied the conditioning lotion to the length of her hair before wrapping it in a towel Melissa had discarded. Then she broke pieces of rosemary into the now-hot rainwater on the stove.

She was in no position to give advice about whom to trust with one's affections.

"Don't you want to marry?" insisted Melissa, standing to help her. "Someday?"

Audra pictured her parents in quiet conversation, her oldest sisters' shining eyes as they looked at their husbands—and the way she'd felt when Jack Harwood grinned at her.

She snapped herself out of that foolish reverie. "Of course I do!"

"Then why are you in Texas if you had a beau in Wyoming?"

Audra had been reaching for a bottle of vinegar; now she clutched it so tightly her knuckles went white. Here it came again—the scandal. Would it haunt her forever? Or might she possibly disarm it with the assistance of a friend who could help her follow the rules?

She put down the vinegar. "I would like to tell you something. But you must promise not to ever tell anyone else. Especially not Aunt Heddy."

Melissa's eyes rounded at the seriousness in Audra's tone. "I swear!"

Still, Audra hesitated. She'd hurt herself so badly in the past, especially the recent past, trusting too readily. On the other hand, she and Melissa had lived in the same house for a month now. Though teacher and pupil, they'd found an ease between them, as if they could move from being friends to something closer to surrogate sisters. And, oh, how Audra missed her sisters.

"Would you like me to spitswear?" asked Melissa, eyes gleaming as she raised her palm toward her mouth. It seemed so like something Audra's sister Laurel would have done, Audra could not help laughing as she grabbed the younger girl's wrist.

"No! I trust you. Truly."

"Then tell me!"

So, adding the tangy vinegar to the spiced rinse water and

leaving it to simmer, Audra made herself remember the end of the respectable life she had once known.

Peter Connors had courted her for some time. He had offered to walk her home from school from the time she turned twelve, but she'd explained that she could not have beaus until she turned fifteen—and so he'd waited. Occasionally he had tempted her with a surprise gift, or "accidentally" met her in town, but each time she'd reminded him of the rules and, graciously, he'd obeyed. Still, by the time she turned fifteen and Peter's courtship officially began, complete with a kiss on her cheek, no one else came courting. Everyone knew that Peter had set his cap for her.

Luckily, she thought Peter Connors one of the nicest, most polite boys in town.

For almost a year they'd attended parties and dances together, went on Sunday-afternoon drives, and sat together in her family's parlor, where her parents or sisters could chaperone. Audra's mother fretted that she would marry too young. Her plainspoken father sometimes had low words with Peter, which had always ended in Peter's wholehearted agreement to whatever instructions he had received. Audra's five sisters, older and younger alike, asked questions like Melissa's—had Audra and Peter kissed? Had they more-than-kissed?

But of course they had done nothing of the sort. Audra's three older sisters seemed to have attracted the most, well, unsuitable of men. She saw how that upset their father and determined never to bring such distress to her family. Peter sometimes held her hand, though he let go before anyone noticed. Anything more, they could reserve for their engagement, then their marriage.

But then, somehow, something went wrong.

"He'd gone away to college," she told Melissa now as they began to mix honey, lard, and wax to soak their fingernails. "To become a banker, like his father. And when he came back for the Christmas holidays, he seemed different."

"Different how?"

Audra struggled for a gentle way to frame Peter's change. "Less . . . polite."

And Melissa's eyes widened with understanding. "Oh."

Sitting with her in the parlor, left alone for a moment, Peter had tried to kiss her again—on the mouth! When she pushed him away with a surprised protest, he'd scowled at her as if *she* had misbehaved. Walking her home from church, later in the week, Peter boldly put his arm around her waist, with the same result. Only later did he offer a begrudging apology.

She should have told her parents; she knew that now. But . . . this was Peter! And she was one of Jacob Garrison's daughters. Everyone in town knew that to accost one of the Garrison girls was to take one's life into one's own hands.

Surely she was overreacting.

Still, when Peter borrowed his father's buggy for a Sunday-afternoon ride, Audra had felt misgivings. Her sister Kitty had even asked if something was wrong. But Peter's family, taking Sunday dinner with hers, had stood right there. How could she decline his invitation without making a scene? Besides, she *had* gone riding with him in the past. And as late in the afternoon as it was, they would not go far. Peter agreed to her father's usual instructions that they stay on the main road, where folks could watch out for them. What could it harm?

But despite his promise, Peter had barely left the town limits before he tried to take a side road off toward the river and its concealing trees. When Audra protested, he argued that it would be fun. Only when she threatened to jump from the moving buggy did he reluctantly pull the horse to a stop and set the brake, still blessedly in the open.

She remembered feeling relieved that she need not embarrass them both. "He said it would be more romantic to do it in private," she told Melissa now, keeping her voice steady. "And then he asked me to marry him."

At least Melissa's face showed doubt as to an appropriate reaction. Some of Audra's schoolfriends hadn't understood why she would hesitate, much less feel somehow let down by the long-awaited, now anticlimactic proposal. They seemed to feel that the rest of the afternoon had somehow been Audra's fault. That Melissa understood better reaffirmed Audra's decision to share the story.

"So what did you say?" asked her friend now.

"I said we should wait until he finished college before making so big a decision." She'd hoped that once he moved home, Peter might again become the safe, quiet boy she'd known most of her life. That strange desperation he'd brought home for the holiday frightened her.

"What did he say?"

More than anything except the scandal itself, that had most upset Audra. She'd answered as properly as she knew how. She'd made her alternate suggestion in her gentlest voice. She had not robbed him of all hope. But Peter had refused to accept her answer.

He'd argued with her, as if she did not know her own mind. He'd pleaded with her, as if mere sympathy would sway her—and about so important a decision! He'd shown her the ring he'd bought, as though she would change her mind for a piece of jewelry. When Mr. Scott, riding out toward his ranch, called to them to make sure they hadn't had trouble—parked there off the main road as they were—Peter had barely contained his rage at the interruption.

Once we're engaged, we can be *together,* Peter had insisted. When Audra, confused, pointed out that they *were* together, he'd laughed a surprisingly ugly laugh.

Melissa waited, fascinated.

"He took it badly," Audra summarized. "So I asked him to take me home."

Melissa nodded her support at the decision.

"But . . ." Here came the hard part. "He was angry, and he whipped his gelding into a canter. I tried to jump out of the buggy, but fell back into the seat, and it started running . . ."

Oh, but she'd been frightened! The wind had roared past her ears, torn off her bonnet, stolen her hairpins. The buggy had bounced and tipped horribly as it hit a rut here, a rock there—at one point the gelding had raced right over a small coulee, and

Audra had shut her eyes, sure they would die, but instead they had flown over it—flown!—and landed with a lurch that should have broken the axle. Peter had laughed, tried to hold her protectively, but she'd beaten him off of her with her fists, like a scene on the cover of a dime novel. She'd grabbed the reins from him, tried to pull in the horse, but it felt like trying to pull back a train.

Only then did Peter realize they were out of control.

He took the reins back and tried to stop the gelding himself, then yelled curses at it when he hadn't the strength. Finally Audra had managed to pry the right rein out of his hand, and shouted over the noise for them each to take one. Together, with their joint strength, they somehow slowed the horse, then stopped him.

In the middle of the rolling Wyoming foothills.

At least Peter had had enough sense stay as far on his side of the seat as possible. Only knowing that the buggy would be easier for the menfolk to track than she would be, walking alone, and that December in Wyoming was no time to go afoot, had kept her from stalking away from him.

Now in Texas, unbelievably far from that horrible afternoon, Audra wiped her hands clean, then stood to set the rinse water off to cool, to strain the herbs out of it. "By the time my brother found us, the sun had already set," she told Melissa calmly, as if she had not thrown herself, weeping, into Thaddeas's arms.

"No!" Like any well-bred girl, Melissa understood what that meant.

Audra nodded. "My family knew that we hadn't . . . that I . . ." No, she could not even say what she'd escaped, only to be accused of anyway. "But my reputation . . ."

"Just for staying out after dark?"

"Several hours had passed before anyone found us." She decided not to mention that when Peter had returned home from college four months later, he'd had a wife with him. The new Mrs. Connors dressed and spoke crudely, raising serious doubts about her background, and she was quite obviously "in the family way." Obviously Peter had flouted the dictates of society, and if he would make a baby with this new bride of his, before their marriage, then he might have behaved so with Audra.

Or so the worst of the gossips surmised.

"It was terrible," she admitted. "I felt as if people were looking at me all the time, in the store, at church. Some girls in town weren't allowed to spend time with me after that! Then the superintendent of schools came to visit and told me that it would be better if I did not take the teaching position they had offered.

"So when Aunt Heddy mentioned that Candon had approved a second teaching position, it seemed the best thing for everybody," she finished. "And here I am."

"Does your aunt know all this?"

"I don't think she knows all of it, but Papa did talk to her. You see why I must do a good job now. You see why I can make no more mistakes."

Melissa nodded firmly. "And why Mr. Harwood did such a terrible thing, befriending you when in truth he was a—"

"A man of compromised character," supplied Audra quickly, not wanting to face the harsh reality again so soon. Just like Peter, Jack's deception had stolen from her the comforting illusion of the person she'd thought him to be. She missed that illusory friend.

Melissa stood, tested the water, and nodded—it was not only soft and wonderfully aromatic with the herbs they'd added, but had cooled just enough to rinse out Audra's hair.

"Well, your secret is safe with me," Melissa declared, while Audra moved her chair to the washtub and unwrapped her hair. "I'll do anything I can to help keep your reputa—Oh, my God!"

Audra should have reprimanded her for the blasphemy. But her entire being seized up as she stared in horror at the thick length of hair she had just freed from the towel. Melissa's exclamation echoed over and over in her head: *Oh, my God. Oh, my God. Oh, my God.*

Bright yellow streaks striped her red-blond hair, like the pelt of a colorful skunk.

Chapter Eight

Teachers may under no circumstances dye their hair.
—Rules for Teachers

Recovering from the initial shock, Audra began to rub at the strange color on her hair. Hard. It made no difference, and her thumb wiped off no stains. "What is it?"

Melissa made a whimpering sound.

Perhaps it would wash out. She reached for the mason jar of her mother's precious hair soap, then eyed it with suspicion and went to the drain board for Aunt Heddy's lye soap instead. Splashing plain pump water onto the bottom length of her hair, she began to scrub.

The yellow streaks stayed. Panic tightened her throat. "*What is it?*"

"You used the wrong towel," whispered Melissa.

Audra spun to face her. "What?"

"Oh, Audra, I am so sorry!"

Pulse pounding, Audra stared at her friend. "Why? What are you sorry for? What is this?"

And Melissa said in a very small voice, "It's hair dye."

Audra stared, her legs gone weak. She tried to sit with quiet, ladylike grace but missed the chair and sat hard on the wooden floor instead. Puddles of water that she'd splashed moments before soaked, cold, through her wrapper and into her drawers. "Dye?"

"Bleach, actually. To lighten it. I—" Recognizing the uselessness of words, she stopped.

"It's against the rules for teachers to dye their hair," said Audra dumbly.

"It was an accident," insisted Melissa. "You used the towel I'd wrapped around my hair while the dye set, and so where your hair touched the towel . . . It was an accident."

"Under no circumstances may a teacher dye her hair. Nice women do not dye their hair. *Floozies* dye their hair!"

Melissa's face paled, and Audra regretted the last comment. Then she looked at her garish hair and did not regret her words so much after all. She could not teach school with dyed hair. Without a position, she would be sent home in disgrace.

Panic began to sting her eyes.

"We'll dye it back," suggested Melissa, kneeling beside Audra, touching her shoulder.

"Two wrongs do not make . . ." But she was in disgrace anyway. What choice did she have? "Do you know how to do that?"

Melissa swallowed. "Ma only taught me to lighten my hair, not darken it back again."

Hope plummeted and panic surged again. "Then what should I do? We can't go from door to door, asking people if they know how to darken hair! What sort of woman *would* know . . . your mother being an exception, I mean," she added awkwardly.

"My father's people came from Bavaria," Melissa defended, taking her hand back. "He liked girls with light hair, so Ma lightened hers. Then she had to make sure I looked like her. . . ."

Uncaring, Audra stared at her long, damp, skunky hair. *Dyed!* Not only would she be sent home in disgrace, but everyone in Sheridan would see their doubts about her confirmed.

And after she had tried so hard . . .

Only when she felt a wail of despair building in her chest did Audra recognize how uselessly she was behaving. She tried to breathe more deeply, to calm herself. She'd never been the kind of woman who sat on the floor crying about her fate—not for long, anyhow—and did not intend to start now. She came from stronger stock than that.

She was a rancher's daughter. If her father could face rustlers and stampedes, surely she could somehow face this.

"Beet juice," she said, her voice lower now and barely breaking. "Beet juice stains anything; perhaps it will help."

"I'll find you some beets," assured Melissa, scrambling to her feet. "We'll fix this, Audra. I promise—we'll fix this!"

Audra closed her eyes and wished she felt so confident.

Jack should probably have left town already, but he wasn't sure Ferris could run the mercantile alone just yet. It wasn't the fellow's ability to limp around that concerned him, either, but the amount of laudanum Ham was downing.

"You might ought to go easy on that stuff," Jack suggested more than once, only to be told to mind his own damned business.

At the rate Hamilton was going, Candon's mercantile *would* be Jack's business—literally. And he didn't want it. He enjoyed the companionship, but he was no storekeeper; he was a gambler. Half the town knew it. Why not move on to Fort Worth and let Handy Jack return?

Still, he hated to leave Ferris alone like this. And Jack couldn't figure out who to ask to watch out for him except maybe the minister. His skin crawled at the very thought of talking to the reverend, much less inviting the fellow to butt in on Hamilton's self-chosen path to misery.

In the meantime, he served more customers than Ferris himself did, played poker at night, and, what with the schoolmarm not showing up once, hardly noticed that a week had passed.

Then, Saturday, Audra's pal Melissa showed up and bought nothing but a tin of beets.

"Everything all right?" asked Jack, counting out her change and pretending not to notice her damp hair or poorly belted dress. Most ladies wouldn't sweep their porch without first belting their dresses, much less hike into town that way.

"Me?" Her voice sounded higher than normal. "I'm fine. Why would you think—" She stopped herself. "I shouldn't talk to you," she reminded him, and left.

"You're bad for business," noted Ferris from the corner.

Business is doing just dandy," Jack shot back, "I'm not the one alienating folks with my sour disposition." Ferris had even had some kind of words with their laundress, serious enough that her cousin delivered the clothes all week.

Hamilton took a swig of laudanum and said nothing.

Not an hour later, Melissa was back and needing walnuts.

"I believe we have some," said Jack, leading her to the proper bin and scooping shells into a small sack. "Beets and walnuts? Sounds like an odd recipe you ladies are cooking up."

Even odder that they planned it so poorly as to make two trips to the mercantile in one afternoon. Plenty of folks came by the store every few days, to check mail or trade news, but most didn't shop but once every week or two.

"It's not a— Never you mind," insisted Melissa, and made her purchase. She was short a penny, and Jack fronted it to her. As soon as she left, she broke into a run toward the teacherage.

"Now that is mysterious," Jack mused aloud. "Aren't those gals alone this weekend?"

"You leave those girls be," warned Ferris.

Jack folded his arms and scowled at the man. "And here I thought I'd head right down there and invite myself to tea. Thank you kindly for helpin' me see the error of my ways."

"They're none of your concern."

"I believe I was here when Miss Garrison informed me of just that." Although, for someone who ought not concern him, she surely had stayed on his mind a good deal of late. Especially that last afternoon when she'd lit into him. He remembered with almost painful clarity the warmth of her dress under his hand, the fire in her eyes, the way her lips had parted in silent, instinctive invitation, when he had leaned closer to . . .

She'd wanted that kiss. The more he remembered it, the more certain he felt. But hell, if the gal wanted to rob herself of the joys in life, it wasn't his damned business.

Still, when young Melissa returned for a third visit, he'd been waiting for her. This time she came straight to him and, in a low voice, said, "I have to talk to you."

"I thought you weren't talking to me."

"In private."

Jack took a step back from her. As soon as he found someone to nursemaid Hamilton, he meant to leave this burg. Compromising a local schoolgirl would in no way help him do that, unless it led to him being tarred, feathered, and ridden out on a rail. "You being a lady and all, how 'bout you say what you need to where Ferris can keep watch."

It amused him to think how Audra would have approved of his suggestion.

Melissa, however, leaned nearer him, murder in her eyes. "Charlie and Ned are on the porch. There's nobody to see us go but Mr. Ferris, and you can keep him from telling. Threaten him or pay him or something. But I've got to see you in *private*."

And, bold as that, she marched into the back room.

Hamilton arched his eyebrows at Jack.

Jack narrowed his own eyes at Ham, then followed Audra's pupil into the back room—at least, into the doorway. He didn't step all the way in until Melissa said, "Audra needs your help."

Then he not only pulled the curtain, he took the girl's arm and swept her into a far corner. "What was that?"

"Audra is in trouble and she needs your help." Melissa took a deep breath, obviously distressed. Jack noticed that she wore gloves, unnecessary for a nicely crisp day like today and unusual except on Sunday. One of her wrists looked purple over the edge of the white material.

Had someone bruised her? Had someone hurt Audra?

His voice came out sounding dangerous. "What's wrong?"

"We need to find a . . ." The girl hesitated, looked at her hands, and self-consciously pulled the glove a little higher.

"Spit it out."

She took a deep breath. "We need a sporting woman."

Jack blinked at her, unable to reconcile her request with his fears.

She stared stubbornly back up at him.

He shook his head, then ran a splayed hand through his hair. "I don't think you realize what you just said. Now what is it, exactly, that you gals need?" The only thing that kept him from laughing was how upset she looked, so upset that, if it weren't nearly impossible, he'd have thought she knew what she was truly saying.

Then she said it again. "A sporting woman. A . . . a soiled dove."

He stared.

"A daughter of sin," she tried, increasingly desperate, and he held up a hand.

"I've figured that part out," he assured her. But it made no sense. He could think of one reason anyone needed a whore, and that applied only to men. Mostly. Although actually, he had heard tell of some woman who were surprisingly drawn . . .

The idea made *him* blush, and Jack Harwood did not blush easily. Those stories were plumb crazy. And even if they weren't, this was Audra they were talking about!

Melissa shifted her weight impatiently. "You're the only person I could think of who might know any," she explained. "Being a scoundrel and all."

"What would either you or Miss Garrison need with a—a sporting woman?" he demanded, defaulting to her euphemism of choice. Some of his annoyance at being lumped in with prostitutes and outlaws and such came out in his tone.

Melissa set her jaw stubbornly. "I can't tell you."

Well, he knew how to trump *that*. "Then I can't help you."

"But you've got to! Audra's very reputation is at stake! She—" The girl looked away, obviously working out how much she would have to tell him. "Something has happened to her, and she has to fix it before her aunt gets home and finds out or she'll be ruined. The only person we can think of who might know how to . . . to fix this . . . is a woman of loose morals. Since you have loose morals, I thought you'd know someone you could send over."

Somewhere in the middle of her speech, Jack figured it out—and he wished he had not. Audra was such an innocent, virginal little thing. But it was the only way any of this made sense.

She was in trouble, her reputation on the line.

She had to fix it before her aunt came home and found out.

Only a whore would know how to deal with it.

She'd seemed pure as a nun since she got to town, as far as he knew—but then, she'd been in town for only a week or so longer than he. The very fact that she'd left her home to come live with her aunt, where nobody knew her, just added more fat to the fire. And what had she said when he had tried to tell her that fear of making mistakes was worse than mistakes themselves?

She'd said no, it was not. As if she *knew.*

"My God . . ." he said softly, a hollow place in his chest where he'd thought his heart was.

Audra Garrison was with child. She'd caught herself a baby . . . and she was looking to get rid of it before anybody found out.

"My God," he repeated.

Melissa stomped her foot. "Can you help us or not?"

"I . . ." He knew of no whores in the immediate area—with no saloons, prostitutes had to keep an even lower profile than gamblers. But he'd never seen a frontier community without *someone* servicing the needs of its men, maybe a widow, or someone from the poor side of town.

He cleared his throat. "I'll see what I can do."

"Good." She walked to the curtain, then paused. "Be discreet," she warned, aiming a finger at him. "We don't need Widow Cribb hearing about us inviting shady characters over while she was gone."

Again Jack felt a jolt of annoyance. Odd, since she was right. Although if Audra was truly in the family way, she'd hardly be one to . . .

But no, he'd seen enough of life to know that the woman was not always at fault in that. "I will be the soul of discretion."

"Good. And hurry." She peeked past the curtain, making sure nobody watched, then vanished through it, only to almost immediately pull the curtain back again. "One more thing."

Jack stared at her, still in shock.

"I'd like to buy some brown shoe polish, but I need to put it on credit."

"It's on the house," he assured her faintly.

She stared at him.

He translated. "Free." That, she understood, and she vanished into the mercantile proper.

Jack watched the curtain swing back into place and felt ill. No wonder the poor gal had been so desperate to follow the rules; she knew she'd broken a big one and feared nature's consequences. And there he'd stood, preaching at her—*preaching*—to try making some mistakes. He'd forgotten that women paid a higher price for their mistakes than menfolk did. And now . . .

In a saloon outside Abilene, he'd seen a prostitute die from attempting an abortion herself. No way in hell would Jack let that happen to Audra Garrison. If he had to, he'd find a local "sporting woman." But he hadn't worked here for weeks without learning the mercantile's stock, even items ladies like Audra or Melissa wouldn't know to request.

Especially since Ferris kept them discreetly here in the storeroom, where nobody would come upon them by accident.

Jack went to the shelf that held patent medicines, specifically those cures not discussed in polite society, some of which could even be confiscated as "items for immoral purpose." The only boxes he knew well had an incongruous but respectable picture of Queen Victoria on the side—crepe rubber condoms. Ever since Abilene, Jack had no desire to sow his wild oats in fertile fields. Beside those sat bottles of Cupidene Vitalizer: Manhood Restored, and even—*yes.* A bottle labeled Dr. Wade's Cure for Interrupted Menstruation.

Jack felt somehow unclean just picking the thing up. But if Audra needed help, this was safer than anything a whore could do to her . . . wasn't it? *Includes cathartic powders!* the label read. It didn't say anything about beets, walnuts, or . . . shoe polish.

Taking a deep breath to steady himself, Jack slipped the bottle into his coat pocket and stepped out into the mercantile proper. Ferris Hamilton, standing by the counter, scowled at him. Apparently they'd had a customer, and the poor fellow'd had to take care of things on his own.

"Glad to see you're up and about," said Jack. "I'm going out."

"Where?"

"Wherever I want." Then he paused, checking the store for customers. He leaned closer to Hamilton. "Where would a fellow go to find a woman amenable for sport?"

Ham seemed unamused.

"I'm thinking . . . Grapevine?" The railroad went through Grapevine, after all, though it would be a long ride to get there. "Mosier Valley?" A poor community like that might—

Hamilton said, "Get the hell out of here, Harwood."

"I'm just asking—"

"Well, go ask somewhere else. And stay the hell away from Mosier Valley."

If Jack had not been in such a hurry, he would have pursued that further. But he had weightier issues on his mind. He had to find a discreet route to the teacherage.

Audra was in trouble. He'd do what he could to help her.

The panic felt like a ringing in her head, made her hands awkward in their repeated attempts to fix this.

But some mistakes could not be fixed. She of all people knew that.

Audra did not expect the shoe polish to work, but she tried it anyway. As long as she had something to do—one foot in front of the other, one attempted cure after another—she could rein her panic back to mere dizziness, mere clumsiness. But that last hope ended in streaky, mud-dull hair and brown splotches on the blue calico of her wrapper. She had no more ideas, no more directions.

She hadn't meant to. She'd tried so hard not to. But she'd broken the rules. Again.

The school board would dismiss her. Aunt Heddy would send her home. She would have brought disgrace on her family not once, but twice. Just imagining her father's disappointment, she covered her face with her hands, elbows on the table. Nothing would ever—

Melissa leaped to her feet even as, with a gasp, Audra heard a soft knock on the back door. No, not company! Not *now!*

Even if discovery was unavoidable, she foolishly wanted to postpone it a little longer.

"I sent for help," insisted Melissa, which was of little comfort. "Wait here."

Audra stood, awkwardly pushing her wet, heavy hair behind her shoulders to disguise the worst of it—the part closest to her head had escaped damage—and backed away from the intruder. Apparently it wasn't who Melissa expected; the girl's greeting was a surprised, "You're alone?"

"I might be of use without bringing someone else in," drawled a too-familiar voice. How easily and immediately she recognized it should have surprised Audra, but she could react to nothing more than the shock of it.

Jack Harwood. Here. Now.

Could her day get any worse?

As soon as Jack ducked through the doorway, his blue eyes sought her out. To his credit, he looked at her kindly enough, hat already in hand. He seemed concerned, even sympathetic.

Only when Audra felt the sting of tears did she recognize how sympathy endangered her precarious sense of control. She had been away from home for a month now, and she longed for someone's concern with an almost physical ache. But she could not trust his, of all people's.

"You sent for *him?*" she asked Melissa, confusion warring with embarrassment.

"He was supposed to bring someone with him!"

Jack said, "Seems to me, the fewer folks know about this, the better." His hushed tone seemed to show that he understood the magnitude of Audra's dilemma. That felt as dangerous as the concern.

"But what . . . ?" Belatedly Audra realized her rudeness in

not greeting him properly. Then again, he should not even be here—propriety demanded she order him out. Why did the man always seem to arrive with dilemmas for her at his heels?

Too emotionally battered to sort out her warring obligations, she went with her instinct. "Good afternoon, Mr. Harwood."

"It's all right, Au— Miss Garrison," Jack reassured her gently, stepping to her and taking her hand in one of his. His palm felt dry, soft, protective. "You don't need to act brave. Your friend here gave me a fair picture of what's happened. I'm here to . . ."

For a moment, her multicolored hands distracted him. The walnuts had stained even worse than the beets. But he recovered quickly and cleared his throat. "I'm here to help, if I can."

The surprise of his appearance began to fade, allowing the afternoon's crisis to rush over her again. Audra sank onto one of Aunt Heddy's chairs before her knees gave out. At least this time she did not overshoot it. "That is kind of you, but I doubt anyone can help me."

Not releasing her hand, Jack sat on the chair closest to hers without being asked. "As you know, I am not unfamiliar with the seedier side of . . . that is . . . the mistakes folks can make. I . . . I am assuming this was a mistake."

She'd never seen him speak so hesitantly. "I wouldn't do something like this on purpose!"

"No, ma'am." He said that firmly enough, at least.

"Now everyone will think I'm . . ." How could she say it? But at least Jack Harwood himself lived outside the rules. His eyes held no censure. "Loose," she finished, agonized.

"Not if nobody finds out," he assured her earnestly.

Did he mean . . . ? Audra looked from the handsome man across from her, to Melissa, to Jack again. Was this why Melissa had fetched him? He knew about this kind of thing?

Hope mingled with a darker, less defined emotion as it occurred to her *how* Jack Harwood must know about this sort of thing. He obviously did not dye his own hair—it was too natural a shade of dark brown for that—so he must know women who did. But of course. He was a gambler, and gamblers associated with who knew what measure of lowlifes?

She withdrew her hand from his, unsure why that angered her so. She'd known the truth about him for a week now, after all! And he *was* here to help.

"You can make sure nobody finds out?" she asked, more coolly than before—but too desperate for his help to throw him out.

"I've got something we can try, anyway."

She nodded. She would try pretty much anything. But when she nodded, some of her hair caught on her shoulder and, in doing so, caught Jack's attention as well.

He pulled his gaze from her shoulder back to her face . . . but then it crept back, as if of its own accord. He stood for a better look before sitting again, eyeing her with puzzlement.

She resisted the urge to close her eyes in shame—even if he did not mean to shame her.

"Miss Garrison," he said hesitantly. "I do not wish to be insensitive at a time like this, but . . . what in tarnation has happened to your hair?"

The contrast of his observation against what had already been said alarmed her somewhat. Something was not quite right—something other than the tragedy she already faced. "I thought Melissa explained it."

"So did I." Mesmerized by the horror that her hair had become, he reached out, caught a shank of it in his hand, then drew more of it over her shoulder. Shoe polish came off on his fingers. He studied them for a moment, then raised his confused gaze again to her. "You dyed your hair?"

Something about the warmth of his hand brushing by, so close to her cheek, stole Audra's grasp of words even to answer him. So Melissa did.

"Well, that's why you're here, isn't it?" the pupil demanded. "To help us fix it before anyone finds out."

Jack looked at her. Then he looked at Audra, his eyes bright, searching.

Then he said a rude word and began to laugh. He had an infectious laugh, melodic and full, but Audra had no idea what was so funny about her ruin.

He laughed until he fell out of his chair. And even that did not stop him right away.

Chapter Nine

Teachers who engage in unseemly conduct will be dismissed.

—Rules For Teachers

Audra did not understand. Her life lay in ruins and this man, this *gambler,* was laughing?

"Stop it!" commanded Melissa. "How dare you laugh at her!"

Then Audra felt even worse. She'd become a laughingstock.

Somehow Jack Harwood caught his breath, but even then he lay on his back on Aunt Heddy's kitchen floor, knees up, grinning to himself. That he was there, much less prone, felt wrong. Everything was wrong.

"I thought you came to help," Audra reminded him coldly.

He sat up, seemed to be fighting another bout of laughter. "Yes, ma'am, that I did. I just . . ." Looking away, he chuckled.

Audra turned away. "You are the only one here who finds this amusing! I'll lose my job, go home in disgrace . . ."

Jack scrambled around her chair to half kneel beside her, bracing an elbow on an upturned knee, ducking to see her face. "Hold your horses there. It can't be all that bad, can it?"

His eyes still danced, amused, but at least some of the concern had returned. This felt amazingly inappropriate, him beside her, his chest by her thigh . . . but he wasn't touching her.

She'd never been told not to let a man *kneel* by her . . . perhaps because the topic had never arisen.

"Hair dye is against the rules," she explained quietly. "And if teachers break the rules, they lose their position."

"But this was an accident," Jack insisted, as if to convince her. "You said so yourself."

If only it were so simple! "Rules are rules, no matter one's motives. Without consequences, they might as well not exist at all."

"And that would be a bad thing because . . . ?"

How could he ask that? Rules helped society function, kept ladies like herself safe, enabled one to differentiate between the people one could trust and those who . . . well . . .

If rules did not matter, then her struggle to stay within their confines would be meaningless and leaving home unnecessary. She could not bear to imagine that! Jack was a gambler, perhaps a drinker as well. He broke rules on a regular basis.

"I thought," she said again, "that you were here to help."

He gazed up at her for a solemn moment, his thoughts seemingly deep. Then he shrugged, smiled, and the impression vanished. "That I am. Let's get this . . . shoe polish? . . . out of your hair and eyeball the real damage first, shall we?"

That he touched her hair again when he said it did nothing for her frail composure. There *should* be a rule against men kneeling so close to women.

Nobody had thought of it before, was all.

By the time they'd washed Audra's hair twice more, Jack could see the hopelessness—for her hair, anyhow. What the gals hadn't ruined right off, they'd surely abused with their attempted cures. The end result reminded him of the multicolored mottling on a tortoiseshell cat.

Still, it was easier to fix than an illegitimate child. Every time he thought of the medicine bottle in his pocket, he wanted to laugh again. The urge lingered long after the humor of the situation should have waned. He reckoned relief kept him so tickled.

The pure lady he'd thought Audra to be remained just that—pure—which for some reason kept him cheerful as a jaybird.

Although the pain in her gray eyes, surveying the results of the second wash as she combed her hair by the stove, sobered him some. Aroused him, too—when had he ever watched a young lady, much less one as lovely as Audra, do something so innocently intimate? He'd never seen her hair down before this afternoon. But they soon realized as it dried that her "accident" could not be hidden. And he could see that the realization nearly shattered her.

"You mean to tell me," he asked, still resisting the concept, "that you'll be dismissed for an accident?"

"Yes." Audra sighed, studying her hair instead of him. "That is what I mean to tell you."

"Those sons of—"

"Watch your language, please." But she could not even muster up a glare for him.

Her misery pained him, no matter its cause. "My apologies."

"You were supposed to help," noted Melissa, hovering at the edge of the room. "Or bring someone who could."

"Someone . . . ?" Obviously Audra hadn't helped with that scheme—more proof of her continued purity. Sitting with her tortoiseshell hair almost to the floor, her face wan in the light of the setting sun, her large eyes overcast with pain, she was the prettiest thing he'd ever seen.

"It was suggested that I find a sporting woman who could help you out," Jack explained.

Audra's eyes widened and her mouth fell open.

"And you didn't," accused Melissa.

"I don't know any," he defended himself.

Audra closed her mouth, looking at him with unsettling intensity and . . . hope? "You don't?"

He wanted to claim that he wasn't even sure what the term meant, but while Jack Harwood might bluff now and then, he was no liar. "Not locally, no."

"Oh." She lowered her gaze, long lashes hiding her disappointment, and continued combing her hair.

"Then what good are you?" demanded Melissa. He was beginning to wonder if he'd misjudged Claudine.

"Well, I know that even if we *could* find us a sporting gal, she could no more put Audra's hair to rights as restore her own—" *Oops.* Best not mention virginity around ladies. Especially virgins. "—reputation," he finished lamely.

Audra's pupil wasn't satisfied. "How do you know?"

"Because I've seen enough women with dyed hair to know it never looks natural."

"That depends," Melissa said stiffly, "on how one does it."

Jack said, "Don't put on airs. I knew you bleached your hair soon as I saw you." That nobody had yet said *how* Audra contrived to dye hers added credence to his observation.

Melissa's face fell—not that he had much sympathy for her. Likely she stood at fault in this whole mess. "You did?"

"I did."

When Audra said, "I didn't," he could hardly make her out. She'd bowed her head under the weight of more than just a yard of damp hair.

It spoke of her distress, he thought, that when he took her hand again she didn't pull away. She had such a dainty hand, despite its residual stains. She didn't deserve this, minor though it might seem to him. "That," he told her, "is because you don't know the kind of folks I do."

"But if I'd been smarter from the start, I could have been more careful. Now . . ."

Oh, Lordy. Was she starting to cry?

"Don't you give up just yet!" For the second time that afternoon he found himself on his knee beside her chair, to better see her pinched face no matter how she tried to turn away from him. "No need to pack your bags just yet. We just can't dye your hair back, that's all."

When he touched his fingertips to her jaw and drew her face toward him, he saw that she was indeed crying. They were quiet, exhausted tears, but they got his thumb just as wet. Her voice came out too high. "Then what can I *do?*"

He should know? Not that it took much thought to hit on the

obvious choice. "You know those rules of yours fairly well."

She nodded.

Jack took a deep breath. "Is there any prohibition against teachers *cutting* their hair?"

Both girls looked at him with wide eyes. Cut Audra's hair? He might as well have suggested she strip naked as do something so unladylike as cut her hair short.

"It's drastic," he agreed quickly. "I'm not saying it isn't. But is it against those rules?"

Audra raised her chin, swallowed hard, and gave it some real thought. "No," she admitted finally. "But I'm sure that's only because nobody imagined a teacher ever *would* cut her—"

"Rules are rules." He used her own words. "Didn't I hear tell that motives aren't at issue?"

It amused him to watch the play of emotions over her pretty, china-doll face—disbelief, then shock, then curiosity. She was considering it.

Jack began to grin. Maybe those blinders of hers weren't on so tight, after all.

After curiosity came hope and then, even better, rebellion. And he'd thought she was beautiful *before* she set that chin of hers! "You are right," she decided, her voice gaining strength. "There are no specific rules against a teacher cutting her hair."

He longed to kiss her, tortoiseshell hair and all. "The top part looks decent."

Her return smile came more tentatively, hope alternating with dismay. Good girls wore their long hair down and good women wore their long hair up. The only decent ladies he'd ever seen with short hair were recovering from serious illness. But really, with the hand she'd been dealt, did Audra have any chance but to bluff?

Hope won out. "Will you do it?" she asked him, and dropped her gaze. "Jack?"

At that moment, he would do anything in the world for her.

"I would be honored."

* * *

Audra could not believe she was letting him do this to her. Actually, she could hardly believe he was even there, much less alone with her and Melissa—unchaperoned!—in Aunt Heddy's house. That, she knew, was just plain wrong.

So why, instead of her initial shame, was she almost beginning to enjoy it?

The haircut was exquisite torture. Unwilling to let herself think ahead to the trouble her new coiffure would cause, she focused on the moment . . . and to her amazement, took subversive pleasure in it. Jack stood behind her chair, his body a wall of warmth against her back. Despite his efforts at cheer, she heard the unsteadiness of his inhale before he actually made the first cut.

More than anything else, that hint of empathy from him reaffirmed her decision.

Her hair made a faint, gritty noise as the sewing shears sliced it away. A long, streaked shank fell to the floor beside her.

Melissa, watching from across the room, put a fist to her mouth to muffle whatever protest might escape. Audra looked at the amputated length of hair and swallowed back nausea.

Jack, behind her, took another overly deep breath and Audra followed his example. Too late to turn back now. "In for a penny," she said, only a little tremulous, "in for a pound."

"That's my girl," said Jack—not that she *was* his girl! But the part of her that craved concern hungered equally for praise. She did not rebuke him.

His fingers brushed the back of her neck as he lifted another lock of hair, then another, holding it carefully away from her skin before slicing it away. Such sure hands he had. Soft, gentle—and yet the sensations that sizzled through her at their touch were not gentle at all. Sometimes, when he made a cut that demanded he rest his knuckles against her shoulder or throat, her eyes drifted shut of their own accord. It should frighten her, the intimacy she felt with this man, this *gambler* behind her. Perhaps it did frighten her—but it excited her, too. Every bit of her felt alive, even bits that he was not touching.

Especially bits he was not touching. The sensations warmed secret parts deep inside her.

And shockingly, instead of fighting it, she savored it as she would sugar candy. Nobody had to know . . . did they?

"Well, looky here," murmured Jack, fingering ends of her shorn hair. His soft drawl only spread that seductive warmth. If he were to move his hand a bare inch, caress her cheek, or touch her lips, she wasn't sure she could object.

Not that he would want to do any such thing, of course. She had made it clear how poorly she thought of him just last week. And now, with her hair gone, how could he possibly find her attractive? Perhaps this was her punishment for her and Melissa's vanity this morning, for caring so much about their hair as to use rainwater and herbs and special soap. . . .

"What is it?" asked Melissa, and Audra tried very hard not to envy the girl's long, clean, brightly blond hair.

Jack leaned nearer Audra's cheek. "You've got curls," he said, his breath caressing her cheek even if his fingers did not.

"C-curls?"

"What with all that weight gone, you've got the prettiest sorrel curls I've ever seen."

Oh, my. He thought her pretty, even now? Her eyes drifted shut again as she held that tremulous, liquid feeling tight inside her, tried to make a memory of it. Heaven only knew when she would ever again be so intimate with a man.

The idea of behaving as she should—avoiding this feeling in the future—saddened her.

When Jack finished and steered her to a mirror, she shut her eyes again. He stood there behind her, holding her shoulders, waiting patiently for her to face what they had done. If she leaned back a little, he would support her entire weight. She knew he would. Then she could not open her eyes because she knew she'd blushed at her own daring thoughts.

"In for a penny," he reminded her, humor thick in his voice. So she opened her eyes.

The horror she'd expected was indeed there, clear in the lamplight. Her hair! All that hair, kept so carefully and brushed so faithfully since childhood, gone! No more chignons, or long braids wrapped around her head like a crown; she did not have enough left to tie up in a ribbon. She might as well be standing here in her undergarments as without her long hair.

Which, with Jack right behind her, watching her face in the mirror, was indeed a shocking idea. She and Melissa ought not even have a proper man visiting, much less after sunset, much less *him!* And yet . . .

In his gaze she saw none of her own dismay reflected back at her. From over her shoulder Jack Harwood seemed satisfied, even admiring of what he beheld. When she tried to look at her new coiffure from his vantage, she saw that it *did* swoop into curls. He'd cut it carefully, so that it framed her face in a neat cap of red-gold instead of sticking out like straw, the way some girls' hair did when they had to chop it off because of lice or high fever.

It seemed almost artistic, what he had done. Her head felt wonderfully, amazingly light.

She met his eyes in the mirror and, even if he ought not be here, her gratitude felt too great to smother, even for something as important as propriety. Especially after the things she had accused him of! "Thank you," she said softly.

"My pleasure, darlin'," he assured her, equally quietly.

"I think it's wonderful!" added Melissa, startling both of them. Audra spun to face her, and Jack took a quick step back. "You could start a new fashion trend," she added.

Audra laughed weakly. "I doubt it. I may yet lose my job."

"You didn't break any rules," Jack reminded her with his more usual cocky grin.

Now that they'd done the deed, she could not believe anybody would accept that argument. But least she had attempted *something.* "That may not matter."

"Depends on how you play it."

She sighed. "Unfortunately, Mr. Harwood, this is not a game." But she attempted a wan smile. He had not judged her this evening, not once. She could do no less.

"Jack," he corrected, eyes dancing again.

"Jack," she repeated, surprised at how it became easier to smile around him.

"You might enjoy life more if you treated it as a game."

He'd said something similar at the store, hadn't he? *Take a gamble,* he'd said. . . .

And after she had said such horrible things to him!

"Melissa," she said, "please go feed the animals. I wish to speak to Mr.—Jack—in private."

Melissa hesitated, looking from Audra to Jack and back.

"I have short hair!" Audra insisted, and Melissa nodded agreement. Compared to the hair, what did she have left to lose?

As long as Jack behaved himself, anyway. And he'd proved trustworthy so far this evening. He could have taken advantage of her more than once this past month, but he had not.

He'd said something about that at the store, as well, but she'd refused to hear.

Melissa lit a lantern and left—and Audra and Jack were suddenly alone. Together.

He cocked his head, obviously intrigued.

Crow was best eaten warm. "I owe you an apology."

He shifted his weight to a hip-shot stance, folding his arms. "Why would that be?"

"For the things I said last week. In the store."

"As I recall," he noted, "you called me a cardsharp."

She nodded, and he smiled. It was a slow, somehow naughty smile. "Audra, darlin', I *am* a cardsharp."

That flustered her—both the smile and the *darling.* "But you are a *nice* cardsharp."

"Such an animal has been known to exist now and again." He was still smiling.

Audra tried to find order in tucking a strand of stray hair back into place—but her fingertips told her it was all stray hair now. That flustered her almost as much as his smile.

"I did not believe you when you said so before," she stammered, looking down to avoid the fascination in his eyes as he gazed at her. "That is why I must apologize. You helped me a great deal this evening. Even after I behaved so rudely, you came here and helped me. And before—when I asked you not to mention meeting me at the schoolhouse—you did that, too. No matter what happens with the school board, I owe you a great deal. If there is ever anything I can do for you . . ."

But, oh, that sounded all wrong! Despite fighting it, she looked quickly back up—and was caught. "That is, if you ever need a favor . . ."

That sounded better. Then he said, "I might could use a favor, at that," and his voice came out so husky, his gaze focused so intently on her mouth, that she knew she was in trouble. And yet, as with the haircut, she found a new, subversive pleasure in the alarm that shivered through her at that realization. She did trust him . . . but he was no gentleman.

Unfolding his arms and leaning closer, Jack proved it.

The press of his lips to hers frightened and fascinated her; his mouth somehow drew her into that wanton moment so that she was no longer Audra; she was simply . . . pleasure. She felt the scratch of his evening whiskers, breathed peppermint edged with fresh tobacco, and over it all savored his warmth, enveloping her. His arms encircled her, his lips took hers again—or still—and through the lowering veil of her lashes she watched his eyes drift closed in sleepy contentment.

Then her own eyes shut, and still he kissed her, and it felt delicious. His fingers wove into her shorn hair, cradled her head, held her still as something—his tongue!—teased her lower lip. *Oh, heavens!*

She felt more alive than during the haircut. Every bit of her. *Especially* the deep-inside parts!

When Jack straightened from her, and her eyes opened, it felt like awakening from luxurious sleep. It felt dreamlike, even yet. His blue eyes danced in the lamplight, and she found something else to feel grateful for—his encircling arms holding her up. She felt so light-headed she could swoon, foolish or not. Peter Connor's kiss had felt nothing, *nothing* like that!

On some level she knew she should fight this. She knew this

was wrong. But she barely had the strength to duck her head, to brace it against the brocade vest he wore. Another level reminded her that she wasn't the woman she'd been this morning.

She had short hair. . . .

Even now Jack rested his cheek against her curls. "Oh, Lordy," he said with a gasp . . . and the tickle of his breath sent the most incredibly languorous feeling down her spine, sweet as molasses.

She had to rein in those shivery feelings. She *had* to! Even if she would not slap him—had she not practically invited this?—she must stand alone. "Please," she whispered against his chest.

"Please what?" She could hear the smile in his voice as it sent more shivers through her. His hand had slid down from her scalp to cradle the back of her neck, so tender . . .

"Please let me go."

There. She had said it, though not without extreme effort. And, to Jack Harwood's everlasting credit, he did just that. She was not sure she could have pushed away.

Especially not after he whispered, "Yes, ma'am," against her temple.

Somehow she kept from falling in the sudden, cold void that followed his release. She forced herself to face him, afraid of seeing . . . what? Anger, she supposed. Peter had been so angry when she had rejected his advances.

But Jack watched her as he had in the mirror, if a little sleepier. Admiring. Fascinated.

Her hands itched to reach out to him. Her mouth tingled, hungry. What was happening to her? Somehow she managed words. "I should not have let you do that."

"Why is that?"

When she looked away from the temptation of his warm eyes, his surprisingly soft lips, he ducked his head to hold her gaze. She had to answer. She owed him that much.

But it was so hard to remember the *right* answer! "Because I am a teacher," she managed finally. "If they let me, I have to . . . it is my *responsibility* to set a good example."

Yes, that was it. With each reason, her back felt stronger, her stance minutely more sure.

But when Jack brushed a curl behind her ear, she did not have the power to push his hand away. "Who is going to know?"

Oh, she wanted to lean her cheek into his palm; longed to sink against his firm chest; ached to kiss him again. Never had she so doubted her ability to behave herself. But she must not kiss him again! Ever! She prayed for Melissa's return. "*We* will know. *Do* know!"

"We also know how good it felt," he reminded her, and leaned closer. "How good it could be if we do it again . . ."

She shut her eyes. "Please . . ."

His body sheltered hers; his breath brushed her cheek. "Didn't you like it?"

"That's not . . . not the point. Please, Jack. Please go."

And the kiss never came. Worse, she felt bereft that it didn't. She *was* a hoyden!

"Your call," said Jack. When she opened her eyes, he was collecting the coat he had removed before cutting her hair. "Good luck with the school board."

She opened her mouth, but did not know what to say. Before tonight she would have known. She would have known whether to slap him or simply rebuke him. She would know whether to wish him good night or to tell him not to call upon her again. There were rules for it, for all of it!

But he ought not have come in the first place, and she was as responsible as he for their behavior this evening. Rules did not apply with Jack, and their absence left her at a loss.

At least, until he opened the back door to leave. Then she spoke from something desperate, deep inside her, instead of from any learned etiquette. "Jack!"

He stopped, looking over his shoulder at her.

"Thank you," she told him, and could have wept with relief when he smiled. It was not his best smile, but he was so very handsome, even a weak upturn of the lips was a joy to see.

"You're welcome," he said—then continued out.

She followed to the stoop, in the puddle of lamplight spilling out of the house. "Jack?"

He turned to face her again, though he did not stop walking. He merely walked more slowly, backward. "Yes, Audra?"

"I . . . I did like it."

His grin flashed, white, from the shadows. "Matter of fact, I got that impression."

They were hardly being discreet. Perhaps she should ask him to keep this a secret, as she had before. Somehow, though, she could not. It seemed insulting to consider it. If word got out, it would be true and by no means undeserved.

"Audra," he called softly. He'd stopped walking.

"Yes?"

"You keep your head up when you face down that school board. You didn't break any rules. Remember that."

To her shock, she laughed. It sounded panicky, likely the result of this overwhelming day, and she pressed a hand to her mouth to try to capture it. Heavens! She'd broken too many rules to count! She only hoped she could have a second chance. Or a third chance . . .

"Audra?" Now she could not even see Jack's teeth or white shirt. Just shadows, hiding the source of his soft drawl.

Even the sound of her name felt scandalously intimate . . . and she savored it. "Yes?"

"Just so you know," he said. "That wasn't the favor."

And then he was gone.

Chapter Ten

Neither may teachers cut their hair immodestly short.
—Rules for Teachers (modified)

Perhaps he'd been in too great a hurry to leave town. After that kiss, Jack doubted dynamite could blast him out of Candon.

He thought about that kiss whenever possible—while he mis-stocked a shipment of ready-made shirts, when he stretched out on his pallet in Ham's back room, and while he shaved. He'd enjoyed kisses before, of course. But kissing Audra—that was a whole different game! She hadn't reeked of cheap perfume or tasted of rouge or sweat, but of clean things—fresh air, clear water, sunshine. And the way she'd responded! Women in the past had kissed him with more . . . assertiveness. But compared to Audra's slow unfolding, the shuddering catch to her breath, the kitten sound she'd made as she sank willingly against him . . .

There was no comparison. Everything Jack had known of sport before now seemed gaudy and cheap, somehow a form of trade even when no money exchanged hands. Audra gave her kiss from someplace so pure, he barely recognized it.

But he recognized enough to figure to stay awhile longer. Besides, such interesting things were going on! Over the next week at the store, Jack got to hear every bit of it.

Someone had been seen riding out the west road after dark the other night. Since the dreaded Mosier Valley lay to the west, folks were advised to keep their doors locked.

Mrs. Estry's widowed daughter Nora broke with her current beau, Fred Bowen, after church. That hope for marriage over, bachelors from Dallas to Fort Worth got spooky. Nora Parks had already been in the mercantile twice to buy gewgaws and exchange how-dos with Ferris Hamilton. Not surprisingly, Jack noticed, Ham was *not* cutting back on the laudanum.

But the biggest news, on more tongues even than what Nora Parks had shouted at Fred Bowen in front of God and everyone, was how the new schoolmarm had cropped her hair.

"Is that so?" Jack would murmur, measuring rice, wrapping lengths of fabric, or climbing a ladder to reach a particularly unusual item high on the shelf. Or, "You don't say."

But they did say, and often. Apparently the gal had not even offered a good reason—trust her to protect Melissa even now. Did she have lice? Headaches? Had she sold her hair for money?

"Isn't that the gal's own concern?" Jack would ask, handing a candy stick to a child or retrieving a tray of jewelry from the glass case. But she was teaching children, after all, and children were everyone's concern.

Audra had certainly called that one right.

The most foolish fear of all was that Audra was one of those mannish women from back east, the kind who meddled in politics, smoked cigars, rejected marriage, and might well bring about the end of civilization as they knew it. Rumor had it her mother was a suffragette, after all.

There, Jack would just plain stop working and fold his arms. "Has she done a mannish thing since she's been here?"

"She cropped her hair!" noted Nora Parks. Jack felt thankful that, as a known dissolute, he'd escaped being branded prime husband material. Nora Parks was a shrill, skinny woman and he entertained suspicions about how her first husband had died.

He said, "And I hear your father hasn't had truck with tobacco since his fever, three or four years back."

She narrowed her eyes at the implication. Her mother still bought cigars on a regular basis—but she smoked those in private. That was what truly turned Jack's stomach about so-called respectability. Most of it was just plain lies.

Then the door opened, and in walked perhaps the only truly respectable person in town: Audra Garrison herself. She'd dressed sedately in a broadcloth coat with bone buttons, puffed sleeves, and a high neckline, but her bonnet couldn't keep her sorrel hair from curling softly about her china-doll face. Her cheeks were flushed, either from the cold snap that had blown in or, more likely, from the stares she received upon her entrance.

Jack swallowed, remembering her silken hair against his fingers.

She scanned the room, a hunted-doe look to her eyes as folks averted their faces. Yep, this was some respectable town, all right. Finally her pained gaze sought out his.

He smiled what he hoped she would take as encouragement. "Good day, Miss Garrison," he greeted, clearly enough that everyone in the store could hear. "You are looking particularly lovely today. Did you do something different with your hair?"

Audra's eyes widened—but her spine stiffened, too. Vulnerability hardened to disbelief.

"Or am I just being a lowlife cad again to say so?" he challenged, and held her gaze.

She caught on quick. "Yes, Mr. Harwood, you are," she scolded. "A gentleman would be more respectful."

He snapped his fingers. "That would be the problem, right there."

She looked down almost quickly enough to hide her blush. Did she think about last Saturday as well? When she looked up, she'd schooled her expression into one so prim, he longed to kiss it off her. Hell, he longed to kiss her until she couldn't remember what the word *prim* meant. "I came here for my mail, Mr. Harwood," she said. "Not for abuse."

"As soon as I finish here, I will be right with you, ma'am. With the mail, that is."

Then he looked back at the widow Parks and lowered his voice to say, conspiratorially, "There you have it. The woman is obviously out of control. Will this be all for today?"

"Yes," said Nora stiffly as he wrapped the ribbons in a piece of brown paper. "It *will*. And in the future, I would prefer to be serviced by the store owner himself."

"I imagine you would." Jack smiled meaningfully. Being a widow, she took his meaning.

On her way out, the widow Parks took Audra's hand and said, "You mustn't let men like that fluster you, dear. Just limit your dealings with them to what is absolutely necessary."

Audra watched her go with the cutest expression of confusion on her china-doll face.

"What in h—in all that's holy are you trying to do to me?" demanded Hamilton, limping from the opposite counter with his crutch. "Are you trying to put me out of business?"

"Not without assistance." Let Ferris run his own damn store. Starting tomorrow.

In the meantime, Jack finally had a moment with the prettiest schoolmistress this side of the Mississippi. "Miss . . . Garrison, isn't it?" She turned back to him, still confused, until he added, "I apologize if I was too . . . bold earlier."

But remembering that boldness—Saturday night's, more than this afternoon's—he was careful not to say he was sorry.

Audra stepped closer to the counter, gray eyes eagerly searching his. "I may have made the same mistake recently."

"Now, I didn't call it a mistake." He grinned, and she blushed. How refreshing to see an honest blush.

Ferris startled them by announcing, "I'll help Miss Garrison. Go put some of those ribbons back in order, Harwood."

Damned if the storekeeper hadn't limped all the way over without either of them noticing. *Now* Ham decided to take charge?

On the bright side, Audra looked as dismayed by the interruption to their double entendres as Jack felt.

"No need," he insisted, feeling his grin harden into a grimace. "I'm doing just fine here."

Ham narrowed his dark eyes. "I don't want the lady to think she can't shop here without being insulted."

"I don't," Audra assured him quickly.

"See?" said Jack. "The lady doesn't think that."

"And she won't, either, if I have anything to do with it."

Jack's eyes narrowed. Did Ferris's concerns for Audra run

elsewhere? Now that he, Jack, had finally started to loosen her up, Ham thought he was going to limp in and impress her with this protective, I-own-the-store humbug?

"It's all right," insisted Audra, looking from one man to the other. Jack wondered which one of them she was reassuring.

"Mr. Hamilton?" Fate intervened in the form of their old laundress. Her cousin had come by for the past two weeks. Now the original woman was back, hovering uncertainly just inside the doorway, dark hands fidgeting with the red shawl she wore over a yellow gingham dress.

New gingham, Jack noticed, with the increased awareness of having kept shop for a month now. But in the same room as Audra, the laundress might as well be wearing rags.

"Lucy," said Ham, almost losing his balance when he turned. Even after he'd caught himself, half with the counter and half with his crutch, he closed his eyes for a frustrated moment. Maybe he'd put too much weight on his leg. "You came back."

"Yes, sir, I'm considering it. Depends on the conditions. Of employment, I mean."

Jack hadn't survived by his wits for this long to miss such an opportunity. "Why don't you see to our clean clothes, Ham, and I promise to behave myself around the schoolteacher."

He expected Ham to resist him—especially if the man was setting his cap for Audra—and why wouldn't he be?—but Ham just said, "Yes. We'll discuss your employment," and limped toward the back stairs to show Lucy the laundress their dirty clothes.

Finally—with the exception of Ned and Charlie, and their ever-present checker game by the cracker barrel—Jack and Audra were practically alone. And Ned and Charlie were about deaf.

"Now, where were we?" Jack asked, propping his elbows on the counter to better gaze at the loveliness that was Audra.

"I believe," she said quietly to her gloves, "that the subject of mistakes came up."

Oh. That. "And when they aren't mistakes at all," he reminded her, smiling again at her dismay. "In fact, I believe congratulations are in order. You kept your job after all."

"Barely," she admitted. "They put me on probation."

"And that would mean . . . ?"

"If I do anything questionable, I'll lose my position."

"Ahhh." Since she didn't put *her* hands on the counter, within his reach, he straightened and occupied his hands checking the new mail. "How's that any different? Except that your hair's prettier and you can get away with more than you thought."

"It's *very* different! I'm under suspicion now. Everyone . . ." She glanced over her shoulder, just in case, and lowered her voice to a near whisper. "Everyone stares at me."

Well, if she meant to whisper, he'd just lean closer, to better hear her and whisper back. "Even if everyone were, and they aren't, what's wrong with being stared at?"

"I hate it! It's like before, like . . ." But whatever she meant by that, she stopped.

"Maybe everyone stares at you because you are so intensely beautiful, you erase every other thought in their heads?"

She stared, going vulnerable again. Lordy, he needed to kiss her! Now that he knew how soft and warm and pliant she felt, it took all his willpower to keep his hands to himself.

"Or could be that's just me," he teased.

Her focus retreated to her gloves again. "You ought not talk like that, Mr. Harwood."

Mr. Harwood? "Jack," he reminded her.

"And we ought not call each other by our first names."

Uh-oh. And after all the headway he'd made Saturday. Unsure how to turn her, he glanced with frustration at the letters he'd been shuffling. "Well, looky here! One from Wyoming."

When she reached to take it, he held on for a moment, so that they were practically holding hands—joined at the letter.

"Jack!" she hissed in warning, so he let go.

"Why, Miss Garrison," he murmured. "How scandalously informal of you!"

With a huffing sound, she stuffed the letter into her coat pocket. Normally she spent longer gazing at the handwriting, and she patted her pocket to reassure herself of the letter's presence. "You truly are incorrigible, aren't you?"

"Among other things." Since he was leaning over the counter anyway, he propped his chin on his hands. "As long as I'm being incorrigible, Miss Garrison—when can I see you again?"

She met his question with so blank a look that, for a moment, he wasn't sure she understood. Then she said, "I'll be back before the end of the week to mail my reply."

He laughed. "I was hoping for someplace we can talk. Without you staring at the shelves behind me or me going through seven letters ten times before I find what I'm looking for."

Actually, he was hoping for someplace they might do *more* than talk. But he knew better than to mention that part.

"You went through them ten times?"

"I want to see you again." *Touch you again. Kiss you again.* Just watching her mouth form words was sweet agony. He felt like Ferris must, of late, with his laudanum—addicted.

"Outside of the store?"

She was not increasing his confidence in her ability to teach school. "Yes, Audra," he agreed. "Outside of the store."

"That's not possible!"

Well, of *course* it was possible; they'd proven that. What she meant was, she didn't want to do it—or to *risk* it. "I see," he said, disappointment curdling into annoyance.

"I'm on probation now," she pointed out, silently pleading with him to understand. And maybe he would have accepted it, if she'd just been disappointing him. But here she stood, using her rules to hide from something *she* wanted just as much as he did.

That, he truly hated to see.

So he played his trump card. "I believe you still owe me a favor, darlin'."

Disbelief darkened her face. Jack schooled his expression into complete nonchalance, watching her work through her shock, then her hurt, then—beautiful as ever—her outrage.

"Perhaps I *do* owe you a favor, *Mr.* Harwood," she said in a hiss. "But I am not about to let you manipulate me into something against my conscience! How dare you consider it? I obviously misjudged you, sir, and I . . . I hope that you will at least do me the honor of not mentioning what has transpired between us again. Good *day!*"

He was so busy admiring the kind of backbone she grew when cornered that he didn't interrupt until she turned away. Then he said, "Hold it," and she spun back.

"Hold it? I am not a horse, Mr. Harwood!"

"Jack." He smiled. "And that's not the favor either."

She scowled at him, suspicious, from beneath that cute little hat, those soft sorrel curls. "*What* is not the favor?"

"Meeting with me."

She opened her mouth. Then closed it. Then she did both again. "Oh," she finally said.

"But I'd best meet with you to tell you what the favor is."

Suspicion became wariness. "Why can you not tell me here?"

"Because it has to do with— Ferris!" he greeted more loudly, hearing the awkward clumping on the staircase before Ham appeared. "You haven't been with that laundress this whole time, have you? This store has a reputation to uphold."

He realized he was pushing his luck even to imply that Ferris would have anything to do with a colored woman, but even so, he did not expect the murderous glower that hit him.

"Lucy left the back way," the storekeeper said. "I was resting." And likely dosing himself with more laudanum. Jack had mentioned the favor to stall Audra, but even as he did, he knew just what he could ask from her.

"I'm glad you did," he told Ferris now. "High time you healed up and let me go my dissolute way."

"Nothing's stopping you."

Nothing except for a decent chunk of credit, maybe his conscience, and the pretty girl standing beside him. Audra slanted her eyes toward Ferris and mouthed the word, *Him?*

Jack sent her the barest of nods, then continued his second conversation. "No need to get rude about it. As you can see, I didn't even chase away the schoolteacher in your absence."

Audra widened her eyes at him, as if Ferris would not have noticed she was still here.

"Do whatever you want," groused Ham, clumping off to his chair by the opposite counter. "Just don't use me as an excuse."

"You're the owner of this fine establishment," assured Jack agreeably, then dropped his voice. "I'd like you to talk to someone for me. About him."

She hesitated. "Someone respectable?"

He folded his arms in challenge. She wasn't the only one who could do "holier than thou"; he'd learned from experts.

She had the grace to drop her gaze. "I'm sorry."

Then he felt guilty. "Considering my own reputation, I'd prefer someone respectable speak for me."

"About what? To whom?"

Not so fast. "Where can I meet with you?"

She considered it—and he held his breath. This was what would really test whether her upbringing was truly irreversible and would stifle the poor gal forevermore.

Relief warmed him when she finally nodded. Then she said, "I am practicing piano at church on Sunday afternoons, for Christmas services."

Church? "Not church."

"Why not church?"

For his own reasons. "Who walks you home?"

She looked wary again. "Nobody."

"Then I will."

"That's against—" She stopped; he'd narrowed his eyes at the mere hint of rules.

"Someone was seen skulking toward Mosier Valley a few nights back," he said. "Could be dangerous, you walking alone."

"You don't believe that." He liked that she hadn't adopted the townsfolk's fear of their colored neighbors.

"No, but anyone who catches me walking with you might." She hesitated, glanced back to where Ferris sat ignoring them, then bit her lip and looked at Jack again.

He put on his most innocent face, the one he used when holding aces or better. When she leaned closer, he restrained himself from pressing his cheek to hers.

"Just this once," she warned, almost silently.

"Of course," Jack bluffed, euphoric.

She eyed him with suspicion—perhaps she was not so easy a mark as she'd first appeared? But she was too well behaved to put whatever misgivings she felt into words.

All the better for him.

"Is anything wrong, Miss Garrison?" called Ham from behind the other counter. Maybe he'd noticed more than they'd thought. He surely would, if Audra did not better hide the flush that pinkened her cheeks.

"She's trying to get me to go to church," Jack called back with complete honesty.

Ferris Hamilton laughed at the very concept.

With a sigh, Audra turned to leave the store, pausing in the doorway to slide her troubled gaze toward Jack one last time. She surely took things seriously, didn't she? He winked at her, and she left almost as quickly as Nora Parks had. But unlike Nora Parks, Audra was blushing.

That had to be a good sign.

Was it possible to acclimate oneself to sheer terror?

Audra hardly knew how she survived the week after her haircut. First, she had to face being a hoyden—she'd kissed a gambler in her aunt's kitchen, and enjoyed it! Then came the terror of church the next morning, and her aunt's return with a suitably chastised Claudine. The school board met and, though formally disapproving of her coiffure, they offered her one last chance.

One. How could she risk that by meeting Jack in private?

But she knew how. She risked it because she owed him, not just for helping with her hair but for looking at her with admiration instead of censure, for reminding her to keep her head up, for holding her as if she were something precious.

She owed him.

She could think of little else, after that. She struggled with her pupils, but she thought about Jack. Saturday felt interminable. Sunday's services lasted forever and ended too soon. After dinner she considered claiming illness to stay in, but how could she respect herself if she added lies and cowardice to her growing list of sins? So she put on her coat, walked to the church, and dutifully practiced the Christmas carols she would play at the end of the month, letting the familiar music distract her as little else could.

But still she felt terror. Or something very like it.

She was meeting with a man. She had become a woman who would meet with a man, a gambler, in secret. Were they discovered, she would have no excuse. At least with Peter she'd been a victim. Her family hadn't blamed her. This time . . .

They simply must not be discovered.

Too soon, the slant of pale November sunlight through the church windows told her to go home. Audra played a few more chords on the piano—music made her feel close to her mother. Then she closed the lid, put on her coat, and left the church.

Nobody stood outside waiting for her.

Her shoulders sank—with relief or disappointment? She hurried for the wooded path that would take her back to Aunt Heddy's. Live oaks, she'd heard, would not shed their green-black leaves until spring. Cedar and loblolly pine were evergreen. Used to the snows of Wyoming, which by now would have worked their way down the mountains and across the plains, she could hardly believe it was December, Christmas music aside. Occasional clumps of prickly-pear cactus increased her displacement. Cold wind stung her eyes, and she felt desperately alone.

And then she heard a whistle: *We Three Kings*.

She stopped, looked around, her aching heart starting to beat again.

It sounded from above her.

There! Stretched casually across a low tree branch, grinning down at her like the Cheshire cat in Mr. Carroll's *Alice in Wonderland*, was Jack Harwood.

Maybe it *was* possible to acclimate oneself to terror. To do anything but turn and run was to disobey her employers, shame her family, betray promises she'd made even to herself. And yet, unable to resist his dancing blue eyes, the silliness of his position, Audra smiled happily back.

Chapter Eleven

Teachers may not use liquor in any form.

—Rules for Teachers

At Audra's approach, Jack pocketed the playing cards he'd been using to busy his hands in the chill air. Then he regretted it. Was he trying to hide who he really was?

Yep. Probably.

She wore the same coat as before, sleek and somber, and another understated bonnet. This Sunday-school Audra would likely risk a great deal if she thought he—or his soul—truly needed her. But if she knew he mainly needed another kiss, she would avoid him like . . . sin. So despite the welcoming smile on her clean, upturned face, Jack would play this one according to Hoyle. Until he eased her into a better appreciation of sin, anyhow.

Thus the cards stayed in his pocket as he hopped down from the tree, landing lithely beside the little schoolmarm. He even tipped his hat to her. "Good afternoon, Miss Garrison."

She averted her face from his nearness. "Mr. Harwood."

Well, hadn't that been fun? He'd rather be kissing her. *Don't kiss her.* No, he'd do whatever gentlemen did when meeting with ladies. In secret. Whatever the hell that was.

He saw by the slant of her lashes that she watched him, sidelong. Her seeming interest made his ears ring pleasantly . . . or maybe that was the echo of her fine piano music. Her hands might look small, but her music proved them intriguingly deft.

Be a gentleman, Jack. He cleared his throat. "Thank you for meeting with me."

A shy smile touched her pretty mouth, then vanished. "You're welcome."

He offered his arm. Her gloved fingers stretched toward it—then curled into a fist, and she withdrew them to beneath her chin and shook her head. "I'd best not," she explained, gray eyes apologetic. "Then I really would be walking *with* you."

"As opposed to our walking in the same direction, at the same time, in the same place?"

She nodded solemnly.

Poor, deluded Audra! If men had the God-given right to ruin their life in whatever manner they saw fit, Jack supposed that should go for women, too. But he surely did hate to see someone do it with her pretty eyes closed. Especially when he would so enjoy enlightening her on the subject of what she was rejecting.

As they walked, a mockingbird called two separate snatches of birdsong down at them from the trees in rapid succession, one melodic, the next sharp. Acorns crunched beneath their feet. It occurred to him to wonder if Audra *should* trust him, considering his obsession with kisses, but she'd enjoyed their kiss, too. He was sure of it, would bet everything he owned, down to his fifty-dollar gold piece and Jürgensen watch. She might call it a mistake, but that wasn't the real Audra talking, not the one with fire in her eyes and a lilt in her laugh, not the one who had melted against him as he held her. The gal calling it a mistake was the inhibited Audra, the hurt Audra, the Audra who didn't see her right to throw off the weight of all those rules and make of her life what *she* wanted it to be.

Even now she sneaked little looks at him while her sense of propriety had her trying to hide it.

"Nobody's watching," Jack pointed out. "If you've a mind to stare, you just stare away."

Pink flooded her cheeks and she tried to hide that, too, pressing her gloved hands to them.

"Nothing wrong with interest in another human being," Jack assured her. "Even a cardsharp. I reckon I'm the first one you've met; that must make me quite the novelty."

She slid her hands up to cover her eyes, too.

"And I'm surely looking at you. Is that so low of me?"

Silence, and the back of her bonnet.

"You're the one raised to know this kind of etiquette," he reminded her. "So you will have to clue me in." Finally he eased a few muffled words out of her.

"It's not polite to stare."

"How else am I going to memorize what a pretty schoolteacher looks like on a gray December afternoon?"

Her hands might have fallen from her face, but they twisted at each other, and she chewed with agitation on her lower lip.

"See how ignorant I am in these matters? I'd have figured the polite response to a compliment was at least a thank-you."

She was walking faster than she had before. "That would mean I accepted it."

"No harm there. I offer it freely. No strings attached."

"Tell me about the favor," she pleaded. "The one you couldn't mention at the store."

Luckily he actually had a favor to request. Not that he felt quite right turning poor Ferris over to the godly. It seemed . . . intrusive. He soothed his conscience by remembering that Ham could tell any well-meaning busybodies, including him, to go to hell and how to get there—assuming he didn't need or want the help. What came off a tongue loosened by laudanum might not be polite, but it could be surprisingly honest.

"I'd like you to speak to someone," he admitted. "About Hamilton."

"What about Mr. Hamilton?"

The words tasted bitter. "I believe him to be a mite too dependent on painkiller."

Audra cocked her head, confused. Lordy, what if she couldn't grasp the idea of an addiction? Nice girls were kept ignorant about so many of the world's evils.

"Ah," he stalled. "Um . . . you know how most respectable folks hold against spirits?"

She nodded, then surprised him. "Do *you* imbibe?" She looked down, flushed again. "I apologize. That is none of my concern."

Normally he found folks minding their own concerns refreshing. So why did her question please him so? "I have partaken now and again," he admitted, despite the urge to lie.

"Doesn't it burn your throat?"

Jack narrowed his eyes at her. "And how would a lady like yourself know that?"

She would not meet his gaze, so he stopped and caught her coatsleeve, too intrigued to worry about repercussions. She peeked up at him through a fringe of red-gold hair. "You must not tell a soul," she whispered.

Jack felt hollow. His voice came out flat. "You drink?"

"Just once!" By the guilt shadowing her eyes, one would think she'd just admitted to bank robbery. "Four years ago. I had a toothache, and Mama gave me medicine so that it would not hurt so badly when the dentist pulled it. But later my sister Laurel told me the medicine was whiskey. She made terrible fun of me—she called me a booze hound—until Papa stopped her."

Jack fought a laugh at her obvious trauma. "I see you are a more worldly woman than I had imagined."

She rolled her eyes at him, perhaps less gullible than he sometimes thought.

Well, of course she was. Here she stood, a dissolute herself! "So what did you think of the devil's brew?"

"It was terrible! It tasted awful, and it burned my throat and my nose, and I coughed. I can't think why it's so popular."

"I will admit, it is an acquired taste. But did you by chance get a sort of warm, easy feeling around your heart? After you stopped coughing?"

Audra thought about it, then looked quickly away again, flushed, and nodded. Damned if he wasn't feeling a sort of warm, easy feeling around his heart just watching her.

"That's why it's so popular," he assured her, smiling. Who would have thought he'd be giving the teacher lessons on the joys of drinking! Maybe she *should* stay away from him, at that.

"Oh." She thought about it, then frowned at him. "What has any of that to do with Mr. Hamilton and his pain medication?"

"His pain medication has a great deal of liquor in it," Jack explained.

He did a double-take when she said, "I thought it was opium."

"You know what's in laudanum?"

She nodded. "That is why I am not allowed to take any. The opium."

He would have preferred it immensely if she simply admitted to not taking the drug, without the word *allowed* coming into it. "Then you know how folks can start needing it, by itself."

She nodded. "Like drunkards in the grip of evil liquor."

"So why'd you look lost when I told you Ferris may have gotten himself . . . caught in its grip?" He refused to say the word *evil.*

"Because that's not my business." Disapproval darkened her frown. "I had not realized you were one to gossip."

Gossip? "Well, I'm not telling you just for your enjoyment, Audra. Ham may need help, and I'd hate to leave town until I know he has it."

Pain shadowed her gray eyes again. "Leave town?"

If he wasn't careful, he'd promise to be buried here. "Darlin', you knew I was only helping until Ferris got back onto his feet . . . didn't you?"

She nodded, took a deep breath, and like that, the ache vanished. Efficient, responsible Audra. "Of course I did. It is kind of you to have stayed as long as you have."

He tilted his head, intrigued. "I've greatly enjoyed it."

Her eyes widened; then she looked down again. Getting her trust would take longer than he'd thought. Or—and this idea caught his fancy—was it that she didn't trust *herself?*

"Who do you think could help him?" she asked only a little unevenly, pulling her cloak more tightly around her.

He didn't even want to say it. "Who's the obvious choice?"

"If it were me, I would go to Reverend Collins. He would know what to do."

Jack felt his shoulders relax at her grasping the situation so quickly. "Well, there you go."

She smiled. Then she frowned again. "But why can't *you* ask him? Why involve me in an obviously personal matter?"

Uh-oh. "I don't have dealings with ministers."

"Why not?"

"Because I don't." He could see her dissatisfaction. "You don't fraternize with gamblers; I don't fraternize with ministers." But hers wasn't choice so much as a social obligation.

"But I'm fraternizing with a gambler right now."

Not without a great deal of effort on the part of the gambler, he wanted to say. That might prove counterproductive. Instead he said, "But you're a degenerate booze hound, aren't you?"

Her mouth fell open in shock; then the fire returned to her eyes, her flushed face, and she hit him in the shoulder with her open hand. "I am *not!*"

Laughing, he caught her wrist. At least he'd gotten her to touch him! But then, his fingers encircling her little gloved wrist, he felt himself sober—fast. "No," he agreed, his voice raspier than he'd expected. Her upturned face seemed so close. "I can see that."

Sober? No. Her effect on him surely did mimic that of fine liquor. She stared up at him, eyes bright and lips artlessly parted, and did not try to free herself from the loose manacle of his hand. Weakness washed over him—or was it strength? As with the first warm rush after a shot of whiskey, he couldn't differentiate. He felt as if he were falling, unsure where or if he'd land, and damned if he wasn't going to kiss her despite his good intentions . . .

He'd all but claimed her lips—breathing her breath, feeling her warmth on his face—when Audra spun away from him and wrenched her hand free. "No!"

"Audra!" He reached for her, but she backed quickly away. "I have to go home," she said, looking at anything but him. "I ought not have . . . this is not right. I led you on; I'm sorry."

Led him on? "Don't be sorry, darlin'. You didn't—"

"I'll talk to the reverend," she promised. "Good day, Mr. Harwood."

"Audra!" She was leaving, and he couldn't bear it. He'd

made such progress . . . and not even necessarily toward kissing her. He'd made progress toward talking with her, relaxing her, learning a sweet secret about her, seeing her laugh. Now he'd ruined it. The only thing that kept him from stalking after her was the sure knowledge that she'd simply run faster. "Audra!"

"Good-bye!" she called.

So he said the only thing he could think of to stop her: "My father was a minister!"

And it did, indeed, stop her, if only from sheer shock.

Jack stared at her back and felt guilt—gut-sinking guilt the depth of which he'd not felt in years. He didn't talk about his parents. He'd rejected most of their fervent convictions long ago. Yet here he stood, under live oak and cedar, using his pa to coerce a woman into trusting him.

And yet, even past the nauseating guilt, he felt relief.

Audra turned toward him.

Audra did not know what to believe. Had Jack truly wanted her help, or had he merely lured her here? Was he her friend or a charming libertine? Now he told her his father was a minister. *His* father? He did not even *like* ministers.

He stared at her, blue eyes uncharacteristically raw. But that, too, could be part of a confidence game.

"Are you lying?" she asked, then felt foolish. If he were lying he would hardly admit to it.

But the way his shoulders sloped as he denied it convinced her. Perhaps not that he spoke the truth; she hardly trusted her ability to discern that. But it convinced her to risk the miscalculation of believing him.

As long as she did not touch him again.

"Then how could you be a gambler?" she asked, bewildered.

He drew his head back, incredulous. "Ministers can't have gamblers as sons?"

"But surely you were taught right and wrong as a child."

He shifted his weight, his expression narrowing to something more contemplative. "I reckon you could say I was."

"I don't understand.

"You wouldn't." Perhaps recognizing her frustration, he sighed and turned, frowning in profile. Before she could protest his cryptic answer, he glanced over his shoulder and added, "I learned that right and wrong are nowhere near as simple as folks say. I learned I'd rather be an honest gambler than a hypocritical pillar of the community. So, yes, my pa *did* teach me right and wrong. But his actions taught me a hell of a lot more than his sanctimonious sermons ever did."

Oh, dear. Audra regretted having said anything, felt ashamed to know such a personal, obviously painful thing about Jack—and yet, secretly, she also wondered what it was his father had done. "I ought not be hearing this," she demurred.

He turned to her, cocked his head. "Could be you should."

If she had not already been standing a good length away, she would have put distance between them then. A frightening intensity darkened his face. "It's none of my concern."

"And here I thought you put a great deal of store in doing the right thing."

Was he angry at her? "I do," she insisted.

"Well, darlin', what if by doing what folks tell you is the right thing, you're really doing wrong? That ever occur to you?"

She shook her head, confused.

"How about when you let me stay at the schoolhouse? Was that the right thing to do?"

She remembered the dilemma clearly. "You needed shelter."

"And did you tell anyone about me?"

Of course she hadn't. In retrospect, she felt even more ashamed of involving him in her secrecy than of keeping secrets in the first place. "No. And that was wrong."

"Why? Would it be right for folks to come out in the storm just to make sure I didn't steal your McGuffy readers, maybe to throw me to the weather when they figured out what I was? Would it be right for them to suspect your honor—yours!—just because you did me a kindness?"

Audra wished he were not so convinced of her honor. "You are imagining the worst."

"Am I? And the hair dye, Audra? How wrong were you then?"

"That was a mistake."

"You could have lost your job over it anyway. How could that kind of decision be right?"

"But I *didn't* lose my job."

Jack folded his arms. "What if I told you that someone on the school board, who put you on probation for cropping your own hair, is dallying with the mother of one of your pupils?"

Her mouth fell open. When she wondered whom he could mean, her face heated all the worse. She did not want to know! "That is gossip and slander, Mr. Harwood!"

"I've worked at the mercantile of late, ma'am. I hear things. What does that tidbit do for your take on right and wrong?"

"You're trying to confuse me!"

He strode closer to her and put a steadying hand on her shoulder. Stunned by his argument, his shocking announcement, she did not think to pull away. "I'm trying to open your eyes!"

"What's wrong with my eyes the way they are?"

"Nothing, if you care about appearances over the truth. Truth isn't always what folks tell you, Audra. They aren't giving you these rules to save your soul, you know. They *want* something from you—a docile, compliant schoolmarm to keep their children just as docile and compliant—so they tell you thou shalt not commit adultery when they are, and they tell you thou shalt not covet your neighbor's goods when they do."

She shrugged off his hands and his blasphemy. "You lie!"

"I'm not even bluffing," he assured her. "Where do you think I find the folks to wager with? It's men coveting *my* goods. You hear bad things about gamblers, but has anyone mentioned we couldn't make much of a living if it weren't for so-called decent folks willing to bet on the likelihood that they can take our money before we take theirs?"

He made a horrible sort of sense, and that frightened her. "Even . . . even if all that is true, even if people do try to make me do what they want, you're doing the same thing," she insisted, gulping uneven breaths. "You want to kiss me again!"

The accusation echoed through her head, louder each time, and silence fell between them. A nearby mockingbird tried out a bobwhite's song, then a robin's, then a starling's. As Jack stared at her from beneath the shadow of his flat-brimmed black hat, Audra felt increasingly mortified. What if he *didn't* want to kiss her again? He could probably have women whenever he wanted, loose women who would let him kiss them all he liked.

Then Jack took a deep breath and nodded. "You are right there. I do want that."

She could not tell if her shivery reaction was relief, concern, or both. They were alone on the path, after all.

"But I'm not trying to *make* you do anything," he insisted, holding up his hands as if to show her he was unarmed. "I got the impression you weren't averse to kissing me back."

Had she been that obvious? She covered her cheeks with her fisted hands again, her arms making a shield between them.

"I don't want to do your thinking for you." Jack's expression softened. "I'm not even aiming to upset you. I just . . . it would please me to know that you can judge the world for what it is, to think you can see I'm a man of at least middling character, gambler or not. It would . . ."

One of his raised hands dipped toward her cheek, but apparently he changed his mind. He dropped his hand to rest against his thigh. "I would feel better about you, safer, if I thought you could spot a real villain even if he attends church and follows every single one of those damnable rules that you've piled up between you and the joys of life. That's what I want."

She could not even form her lips into a protest.

"And yes," insisted Jack, low. Though he had not bent nearer, his face seemed dangerously close to hers. "I want to kiss you, Audra. I want to hold you tight and kiss you until we're both dizzy, until we can't remember if it's sunrise or sunset and we don't care, until you figure out that kissing is one of the *right* things in life and that denying what you truly want, for the sake of someone else's rules, is wrong. I may be a gambler and even a scoundrel, but I'm honest with you, which is more than I can say for half the folks you're worried about catching us.

"What I'm wondering now, Audra, is how honest you are with yourself."

He backed away from her far more gracefully, more purposefully, than she'd retreated from him moments before. He held her gaze for the longest time, not smiling at her, not visually caressing her . . . just watching. Expectant, as if he expected the best from her—whatever that was.

Then he jerked his chin toward the west. "Sunset," he said—and turned and strode away.

Sunset? Audra stood on the path, alone with the squirrels and the birds and her jumbled thoughts. When she finally placed the importance of sunset—her aunt expected her home; those were the rules—she didn't know whether to laugh or cry.

Turning herself in that direction, as would any respectable, well-behaved young lady, did nothing to answer that question.

Chapter Twelve

By act, word, and deed, teachers will uphold strict educational standards.

—Rules for Teachers

"You may go now." Audra watched her pupils scramble from their desks to the door, nodding to those who called "Good-bye, Miss Audra."

"Would you like me to wash the blackboards for you?" asked Jerome Newton, lingering as usual. As usual she shook her head, trying not to avert her eyes. He *was* behaving himself. But she avoided his company even so, and relaxed when he left.

Worse than her pupils' relief at the end of the day was her own. She sensed she was failing them—and herself. What was she, if not a teacher? She used to sit on the front steps in the morning, watching her sisters leave for school. Her mother would make her a lunch to carry around the house, like those her sisters took, so that she felt more like a big girl. Once Audra was old enough to attend classes, school proved just as magical as she'd hoped. She'd measured her life by the levels she'd advanced, the textbooks she'd used, the awards she'd won. She could imagine nothing better than spreading that joy to others.

But here she stood, months into the term, failing miserably in school for the first time in her life. Even the pupils who behaved seemed bored, frustrated, confused. She did not know how to explain ideas that had come so easily to her.

Frustrated herself, Audra sat at her desk to read the fourth-level compositions while she still had light. The first composition was terrible; the pupil made two spelling errors in his first sentence. She braced her elbows on the desk, etiquette or not, and hid her face in her hands.

The squeak of the schoolroom door surprised her. She looked up, startled. "Charlotte?"

"Miss Audra?" Charlotte Calloway sidled into the room, lunch pail dangling from her skinny, twelve-year-old arm. The buck-toothed girl with brown pigtails rarely spoke in class. Today Audra had caught her hiding a dime novel in her reader. "May I speak with you, please?"

"Of course you may!" Audra stood and moved to one of the seats in front, which had no desks in front of them. "You are always welcome to talk to me, Charlotte. Please, sit down."

Charlotte hesitated, then sat. Then she said nothing, the toe of one high-buttoned shoe drawing circles on the floor. Her eyes were puffy, her nose red.

Audra tried to look as encouraging as possible. Finally, gently, she prompted, "Is this about class today, Charlotte?"

The girl nodded, then, remembering her manners, murmured, "Yes, ma'am."

"Do you understand why it is wrong not to use your class time for the assigned lessons?" Heaven knew, the girl's marks reflected her distraction.

"Yes, ma'am."

"Then we can move on with a clean slate, you and I."

Charlotte nodded, but did not appear consoled.

"Did you want to tell me anything else?" suggested Audra.

"I'm sorry?"

Audra had heard more convincing apologies. Still, better to err on the side of gullibility than harshness. She took one of Charlotte's hands in her own. "I believe that you are, Charlotte."

Charlotte surprised her then by looking up and asking, "Could I take a whipping?"

For a moment, Audra forgot to breathe. "What?"

"I know I done wrong."

"Did wrong." The correction barely squeezed out of her.

"Did wrong. I know I ought to be punished. But . . . I just got to know what happens, Miss Audra! It was wrong to read it in class, but Mountain Kate was just attacked by the bear, and I just got to know if she gets away and marries Cecil."

"Just have to know." Audra had confiscated the book. Now she stared at the little girl, at the child's bright hazel eyes and thought, *She wants to know how it ends. She's willing to take a* whipping *to find out how it ends.*

What have I done?

"I just have to know," whispered Charlotte obediently.

Audra went to her desk, opening the drawer. There lay the book, its paper cover sporting a line drawing of a woman aiming a revolver at a bear as it leaped at her. In the background, drawn in less detail, a man waved a rifle. Obviously Mountain Kate's survival was in her own hands and not Cecil's. When Audra took the dime novel from her drawer, the edge of a playing card caught her attention. She knew that if she turned the card over, she would see hearts.

Oh, hush up, Jack, she thought, and tucked the card deeper into the drawer. Then she brought the book to Charlotte. "Here."

Charlotte hesitated only briefly, then snatched the book with both hands, clutching it to her like a mother recovering her child. "Oh, thank you, Miss Audra! Thank you so much!"

"You are welcome. No reading it during lessons though, agreed?"

"Oh, yes, ma'am!" Charlotte's sigh relaxed her whole skinny body. Then, slowly, the joy faded from her face. Her expression sobered. "I'll take that whipping now, ma'am."

Oh, heavens. "I am not going to whip you, Charlotte."

"But I done wrong. I got to get punished . . . don't I?" Those were the rules, after all.

Audra shut her eyes against an unwelcome chaos of warring thoughts.

"Did wrong," Charlotte corrected slowly, when Audra did not. "I have to be punished."

"Well, yes," agreed Audra. "But was your crime so severe that it merits a whipping?"

Low marks or not, Charlotte wasn't simple. "Um . . . no?"

"So let's talk, you and I, and see if we can think of something more appropriate."

The girl's expression wavered between relief and wariness as she nodded. But she offered little else. She simply clutched the book, as if afraid to lose it again.

Audra thought of stories she'd enjoyed, how she would have felt to lose one before its ending. Not that she ever took one to school! But . . . sometimes, on nights with full moons, she had sat up past bedtime, curled against the window, squinting to make out every word in the silvery light. Even in winter, when she had to wrap herself in blankets and scrape frost off the windows, when opening the indoor shutters might chill her sisters, she sometimes risked it.

Barely a year ago, her father had gotten up in the night and caught her reading *Ben Hur.* Instead of scolding her, he'd simply drawled, "We got lamps, Audra Sue."

The next morning, neither of them spoke of it. She wondered how long he'd suspected her nocturnal disobedience, and tolerated it, but wasn't sure she really wanted to know.

Now the memory gave her an idea for Charlotte.

"Tell me about Mountain Kate," Audra suggested.

* * *

She all but danced from the school to the mercantile an hour later. The wind that had locals complaining of the cold felt delicious. The live oaks and cedars added a Christmasy green to the landscape. She had not read a single composition—but she had reached a pupil.

Finally.

Charlotte Calloway's face had shone as she related the adventures of *Mountain Kate*'s daring heroine. When Audra decided on a book report as fitting punishment, Charlotte stared, then gave her a quick, surprising hug. "Oh, *thank* you, Miss Audra!"

Audra could only imagine what Aunt Heddy and the school board might say if they learned of this. Dime novels really weren't appropriate reading for young ladies! But wasn't it better for Charlotte to read *Mountain Kate* than nothing at all? At least she was reading.

In any case, Audra had not exactly condoned the dime novel; she simply had not condemned it. And—she smiled—that was not against the rules. Yet.

She had to tell someone, so, as soon as Charlotte left, Audra wrote home to her sisters. Then she decided to post the letter right away.

When she entered the mercantile, some of her joy ebbed into confusion. Mr. Hamilton, not Jack Harwood, stood behind the display counter and asked, "May I help you?"

Audra stared, dismayed. She'd spoken to Reverend Collins the day after promising Jack she would. Had that been all he wanted before leaving? Or perhaps he'd been angry at her. He'd *seemed* angry, though she hadn't been sure he meant it for her.

Had he gone?

She almost asked it—*Where's Jack?* Impropriety or not, reputation or not. For a fleeting, panicked moment, she didn't care a fig about her reputation if Jack had left Candon for good.

Then a familiar voice drawled, "Well, Miss Garrison; if you aren't the dew on the daisy."

She turned slowly, half-afraid to trust her ears, but there he sat, across the cracker barrel from Mr. Cooper. One of the Randall boys *had* mentioned their grandfather taking ill.

She pressed her lips together to keep from smiling. In Mr. Randall's absence, Jack was keeping Mr. Cooper company at the checkerboard! He'd never looked more handsome, lounging with relaxed grace in a ladder-backed chair, his coat off and his fine shirtsleeves rolled up. His dark hair fell, mussed, over his forehead. His eyes danced at her, as deep a blue as the star sapphires her mother sometimes wore, and the smile that slowly stretched his mouth reassured her that, though he might feel something toward her, it wasn't anger.

Oh, my! The stove in the center of the room certainly did put out plenty of heat!

Jack looked even more handsome than Audra imagined *Mountain Kate*'s Cecil could. And Jack thought *she* was the dew on the daisy?

"Good afternoon, Mr. Harwood," she said, uncommonly pleased. She barely remembered to add, "Mr. Cooper. Mr. Hamilton. I hope you are feeling well today."

"Fair to middling," assured Mr. Hamilton. "May I help you with something?"

She tried not to look over at Jack as she crossed to the counter. "I wish to post a letter."

But she still relaxed when, behind her, Jack said, "Weren't you just saying that you wanted to sit down, Ham? Why don't you let me help Miss Garrison post her letter."

Chair legs scraped against the floor behind her.

"That's real helpful of you there, Harwood," said Mr. Hamilton. "But there's no need."

"I assure you, I don't mind in the least," Jack said.

Mr. Hamilton narrowed dark eyes over Audra's shoulder. Flattered, she felt the most unladylike urge to giggle.

Then old Mr. Cooper said, "Now, wait a minute there, sonny! You owe me a chance to win back some of that hundred dollars you done took off me."

Audra's urge to giggle vanished. Jack had won money off nice old Mr. Cooper?

A hundred dollars?

As the shock faded, anger replaced it. The Cooper children came to school barefoot at first; now they wore too-large shoes in the hope that their feet would grow into them . . . and Jack was taking from their grandfather more money than the family saw in profit all year?

She began to shake, deep inside. It didn't matter if he'd won it fairly or not. Not *that* much money.

"Where is this going?" asked Mr. Hamilton—he had none of Jack's charm, but at least he attempted politeness—and took the letter from her numb hand before it began to tremble, too. "Wyoming. I should have guessed, hmm? Postage for that will be—"

"Never mind," whispered Audra, and turned away, walking carefully toward the door. She felt that she might fall down at any moment—fall down and never ever want to get up.

"Miss Garrison?" asked the storekeeper.

Jack said, "Audra?" but, despite her encroaching dizziness, she walked faster. The store seemed suddenly overcrowded, lanterns and shoe boxes and spades looming into her field of vision, trying to catch at her coat with every step. But it was a hand that caught her—Jack's hand.

"Audra?" he repeated, his voice low, his tone gentle. He ducked his head around her, concern softening his sapphire eyes, his handsome face. But he was, after all, a confidence man.

When she met his gaze, his expression cooled fast enough. "What—" His gaze darted back to Mr. Cooper. "Oh, *that!* Audra, you've got it all wrong."

"Excuse me," she said, her tone frigid.

"But, darlin'—"

She yanked her arm free of him. "Don't call me darling. Don't even call me Audra! I do not speak to people like you!"

He cocked his head. "By telling me you aren't speaking to me, you are in fact—"

She stomped by him.

"Miss Garrison," called Mr. Hamilton. "You left your letter."

"I'll pay the damned postage," Jack said with a snarl. It

wasn't the first time he'd cursed around her, either, but she'd made foolish excuses for him before. Why, *why* had she trusted him?

"Well, isn't that charitable of you," grumbled the storekeeper. Even as she reached the door—out of the mercantile, the lies, her suffocating disappointment—Audra made herself turn and stalk back in to the counter. She passed Jack, who stood, arms folded, staring at her as if *she* had done something wrong. "Here," she said, digging a nickel out of her reticule and laying it on the glass. "I should not want to owe anybody interest."

Then she turned to leave the store a second time.

"I don't charge interest," defended Jack testily.

Ferris, behind her, said, "Ha!"

"Which is not to say I don't take it when it's offered. Miss Garrison, will you wait a minute and listen to me?"

"No," said Audra, all but lunging for the door.

"You have two pennies in change," called Mr. Hamilton, and Jack said, "Shut the hell up!"

Before the door had completely closed behind her, Audra heard old Mr. Cooper saying, "What did you do—ask the gal to dance with you again?" But before she heard Jack's answer, the door shut and she could hurry away from him and from all the improprieties he'd encouraged in her. She wished she could run, but lady teachers did no such thing.

So she waited until she reached the shelter of Aunt Heddy's barn.

Then she cried.

On Thursday, Melissa went by the store to check their mail. When she returned, she slipped something into Audra's pocket. "For you," she whispered with a secret smile.

When Audra found the privacy to look, she discovered a pink candy heart with crimped edges. She knew Melissa hadn't bought it. How dare he send gifts, as if they were or could ever be on intimate terms! Worse, how dare he corrupt Melissa by using her as a go-between? Perhaps reputation meant little to a confidence man who questioned right and wrong, but hers meant a great deal. She had no intention of letting any man destroy it for a second time!

She stalked into the chicken yard, threw the candy heart onto the ground, and stomped on it. Then she left the bits for the chickens. It occurred to her, watching the white and brown birds flock and peck at the treat, that she'd never before done anything so purposefully destructive in her life. Perhaps she should feel vindicated, or at least satisfied. Instead she felt empty.

It had been a very pretty candy to be wasted on chickens.

"Do not accept any more gifts," she told Melissa as soon as they had a moment alone.

On Friday, their last school day before the Christmas holidays, she gave her pupils arithmetic assignments using chestnuts and gifts and snowflakes. On Saturday, she helped Melissa and Claudine pack before their fathers arrived to take them home for the week. On Sunday, of course, she attended church. Afterward she practiced her piano for Christmas.

Then, as she started home, someone whistled the first few bars of "Silent Night" at her, down from the trees.

Her heartbeat sped up. She walked faster, and heard leaves and acorns crunch as Jack Harwood dropped to the ground. "Audra."

"Go away. And do not send me anything else."

He started to keep pace with her. "I know what's got you so riled, and you have it all wrong."

She turned to glare at him. "I do not care if you cheated or not. Mr. Cooper cannot afford to lose that kind of money." Then she remembered that she was not talking to him and started walking again. He began pacing her again, and he had longer legs.

"You are fixing to be so embarrassed when I explain things."

And he would be embarrassed when she reported him as the masher he was! Audra doubted she had enough venom in her to ask for his arrest—but she might, if he did not leave her alone! She'd stomped on a nice candy heart, hadn't she? "As if I would ever believe you!"

He stopped and said, "We were playing for pretend money."

She made it three more haughty steps before her intention to never again believe him faltered, along with her steps. *Pretend money?*

He was probably lying. Gamblers did that! But . . . what if he wasn't?

"That's right," assured Jack, taking his own sweet time to catch up with her now. "Pretend money. Five dollars for each piece we took; thirty dollars for winning a game. Now"—finally he reached her, stepped in front of her where she could see him without having to actually turn and look—"doesn't that seem like a passel of money, if it weren't imaginary?"

She could not decide if seeing him was a good thing or not. He'd folded his arms in front of him again, his shoulders tense. His eyes smoldered in the shadow of his hat, and his lips were flat, not even a ghost of a smile playing across his usually friendly, usually inviting mouth.

He really did look angry. At her. As if he truly were in the right, and she in the wrong.

Despite her best efforts to keep her thoughts in check, she considered his words. It *did* seem like a great deal of money.

"Not just for Cooper, either. That's a lot of money for *me.* Checkers isn't even my game."

Relieved at the reminder of what he truly was, what he did for a living, she asked, "And pray tell, what *is* your game?"

"Poker—strictly according to Hoyle. That, and seducing schoolmarms."

How could he speak so callously about that! "Stop it!"

"*You* stop it. You're the one judging me. I thought we had something between us. I thought we had a . . . a friendship. Now you won't even talk to me because you think I swindled Ned Cooper out of two hundred and five dollars in checkers."

"A hundred dollars," she clarified.

"It was two-oh-five by time I finished with the old geezer. Point is, that's what has your dander up around me, isn't it?"

That, and so much else! His foul language. His use of her first name. His kisses.

Except . . . in all fairness, she had not been indignant about the kisses until she thought he'd taken money from Mr. Cooper. Rather, until he *had* taken the money! Rather . . .

"You would say anything," she protested, torn. She wanted so badly to be fair. She wanted him to be telling the truth. She wanted desperately, achingly, to be wrong.

But if she *was* wrong, if Jack truly was the sweet man she'd glimpsed over their autumn together, then . . . how could she further withstand the danger that posed to her reputation?

How could she withstand his threat to her very heart? She might have felt brittle and snappish these last few days, but at least she'd felt safe. If she forgave him . . .

"Well, if you don't trust me, ask Cooper yourself. If you shout, he might even answer you." He considered it. "If you shout really loudly, he might even answer you correctly."

And that, she thought, was not a . . . what did one call it? A bluff. She could easily find Mr. Cooper to ask. He would be at the mercantile every single day and could easily clarify . . .

Unless Jack paid him to lie!

Trying to second-guess him exhausted her. But she had to try once more. "Why would someone like you bother playing anything for pretend money?"

He narrowed angry eyes at her. "Damned if I know. Maybe someone's been a good influence on me lately." And with a bitten-off curse, he turned, stuffed his hands into his pockets, and began to walk back down the path.

Away from her.

A good influence? Did he mean her? Audra needed several shaky breaths before she gathered the strength to turn and watch him leave. Then she barely had any breath left to call his name: "Jack?"

He stopped, his back stiff. She'd barely heard her own voice over the throbbing of her heartbeat, the moaning of the early December wind, and yet somehow, he stopped.

She tried again. "Jack?" This time she heard it, too.

"What?" He did not turn. He meant for her to come to him?

But of course he did . . . could she blame him? Good for

the goose, good for the gander. Somewhere she found the courage to halve the distance between them. Then her steps faltered.

She'd been so accusing, so angry. She'd fed his pretty candy heart to the chickens!

"You are right," she said, her voice wobbling terribly.

"How's that?" He still wasn't facing her.

Admit it. "I am very embarrassed."

She stood in the same place, the trees and sky and rocks all stayed the same, and yet it felt as if the ground had crumbled from beneath her. She had made her choice—she chose to trust him, gambler or not. She chose to be around him, proper or not. It might not be within the rules, but it felt . . . right.

Assuming he wanted her trust or her company after this.

To her relief, Jack slowly pivoted to face her. His mouth and jaw looked somehow softer than a few moments before.

"I told you so," he said. Then he grinned, charming as ever.

That was when Audra burst into tears.

Chapter Thirteen

Women teachers must wear at least two petticoats.
—Rules for Teachers

"You're crying," said Jack blankly.

She averted her face as if to disguise it—not that she could hide the hiccuping noise, or the jerk of her shoulders. Still, he caught her chin to investigate. He released it. She was crying, all right, and not prettily, either. She raised not just her hands but her forearms to hide behind them.

So why did he want to hold her so badly?

"What did I say?" he asked, meaning what did he say *wrong*.

She shook her head, curls bouncing.

"Then how did I make you cry?"

She shook her head and squeezed out the words; "You *didn't*."

Well, that made no sense. When she turned further away from him, he stepped around her, still leaning to better see her. "Sure I did."

She shook her head and turned again. A hairpin fell to the ground and her bonnet slid askew.

He kept turning with her. "Then why are you crying?"

"I . . . don't . . . *know!*"

Well, wasn't this a fine fix? But why would she? She hadn't known that she wanted to be kissed, either. She surely hadn't known she wanted to meet with him in the woods . . . although he had no proof that she'd changed her mind on that one, what with her sobbing piteously.

If she'd played the good girl too long to recognize her too-human desires, would she recognize her sorrows? Glancing around them to ascertain their privacy, Jack took Audra in his arms, drew her off the path behind a sheltering stand of fragrant, dark green cedar—and to him. He closed his eyes when she rested her forehead against his shoulder.

How was it he could he feel both building panic and complete peace at the same time? Especially when, on another hiccupy sob, her bonnet knocked him in the chin?

He longed to tell her everything would be all right, to tell her anything if only she would stop crying. But that would take more than his moderate capacity for dishonesty. Instead he made shushing noises and ran his hand up and down the back of her coat, savoring her warmth. "At least make a guess at what sort of feeling's deviling you. We'll work it out from there."

That made her cry harder, but at least elicited a confession; "I'm so ashamed."

Her? Well, he *had* finagled her into a few situations that she might otherwise have avoided—such as this one. "Ashamed of your behavior of late?" he prompted, and she nodded. Her hat, not made to stay on against a man's shoulder, fell off into the leaves and dirt.

Well, if she was ashamed of meeting with him, holding her probably wouldn't help her feel better, now, would it? He determined to let go . . . any minute now.

Then Audra surprised him further. "I've thought so badly of you, just because you play cards. And—" Her wet sniffle was *not* that of a refined lady. "It's not the f-first time . . ."

Jack stopped stroking her back. Him? She was crying not over how she'd betrayed her upbringing, but how she'd disappointed *him?*

He felt suddenly cold, despite the windbreak of the cedar stand. He drew her even more tightly against him and kissed the top of her head. "I don't imagine you were raised to see my kind in the finest of lights."

"It should not matter how I've been raised." She tipped her damp face up toward him. Despite the way her eyelashes spiked together and the hue of her nose, he could have gazed back down at her forever. He'd never seen anything more beautiful than how she looked at him. "What matters is that you are a good, dear man, and I accused you falsely because I was seeing you with my biases instead of with my eyes and ears and common sense—and that was wrong of me."

Tears flooded her pale eyes again; she hid her face in his shoulder. "I've been *wrong*."

Adorable though he found her confession, he felt even colder. Well, it *was* December. He struggled to reclaim his own calm, his sense of humor, but the best he managed was a fair imitation. "And you've never been wrong before, is that it?"

She shook her head and he laughed shakily. "*Never?*"

Even better, she laughed, too, muffled and wet into his shoulder. Then she risked meeting his gaze again, her own eyes damp but begrudgingly merry. "Well, perhaps once or twice."

"But not enough to get used to it," he figured out loud.

She shook her head in silent agreement.

She had to be cold, her face all wet like that. He wasn't wet and he felt the cold bone-deep. Even the joy of Audra's softness, snuggled up against him just as he'd imagined it, did not help against this strange chill in his soul.

Bluff, Harwood. "I'd offer you a handkerchief, darlin', but I haven't one. Would you like to blow your nose on my sleeve?"

She should not have laughed just then, congested as she was—her hands flew to cover her face, but by then she and he were both laughing at her dishevelment. "No!" she insisted, turning her back to him; he loosened his hold to let her. "Oh, heavens! And I have my own . . ."

As she protested, she pulled an embroidered handkerchief from her own coat pocket, dabbed at her averted face, and blew her nose delicately, but then, apparently frustrated, with more human gusto. Only then did she peek back at him. "Your coat!"

He made a dismissive sound, even as she tried to wipe at the shoulder of his coat. Had a woman fussed over his appearance since his mother's death? "You might look to your hat first."

She made her own dismissive sound. "But you wear such fine clothing."

That was because, traveling from place to place, he had learned to keep his wealth portable, such as in nicely tailored clothing. It also helped get him into high-stakes games, and to intimidate low-stakes players.

Jack chose not to explain any of that. Then he felt guilty for the omission. Years ago he'd given up guilt as a useless habit. What was it about this woman that had him regressing?

"I feel terrible," she said, surveying his coat. As if she could have done much damage!

"Don't fret, darlin'," he insisted. "Ferris and I use a fine laundress."

"I mean about how biased I've been against you!"

Oh. That. "You've had plenty of reason to distrust me."

And maybe one or two excellent reasons even now.

Audra collected her bonnet from the ground, slapped the dust off of it, then raised her chin with determination. "No, I have not. You've proven yourself my friend from the start, Jack Harwood. You kept my secret about the schoolhouse, and you matched our funds for slates, and even after I condemned you for being a cardsharp, you helped when . . . when my hair . . ."

"I remember," he said, again admiring those adorable short curls of hers.

"You haven't taken offense when I've insulted you—more than once—and you've worked to make things right between us. I've had no reason to distrust you except wild rumors about cards and gambling. Please accept my apology for so severely and repeatedly misjudging you."

As her face regained its usual porcelain coloring, she resembled a china doll again—complete with a certain stiffness to her expression. It revealed the toll speaking such words took on her—since she wasn't used to being wrong, and all. Maybe that fortitude had something to do with why, after avoiding real ladies for years, Jack found himself attracted to her, of all women.

"Well, don't you have grit," he marveled, smiling.

She flushed and dropped her gaze. "Oh, no, I don't. My father has grit. I just—"

"Have the courage to stand here, risking your job, apologizing for something that isn't even your fault."

"Of course it's my fault. My mother says . . . well, one would hope that a teacher could learn not just from books but from her own experiences."

Oh, would one? "And your experience with me has you thinking you've misjudged cardsharps?" The idea twisted in his cold gut. He'd known plenty of gamblers he wouldn't trust within a mile of Audra; she ought not lose *all* her wariness around them!

He relaxed some when she said, "I've misjudged *you.*" But gratifying though it felt not to have her angry with him any longer, even that didn't leave him breathing easily.

"You think so," he challenged.

She nodded, eyes alight with confidence. "I know so."

Still unsettled, he said, "Well, what if I do this?" And before she could fully react, he took her shoulders in his hands, leaned down to her, and covered her mouth with his. Then he lost track of whatever he'd been trying to prove in the sheer bliss of kissing Audra.

Her lips tasted as sweet, as full as he remembered them. She made a helpless noise deep in her throat, and then sank—was she pulling away? He hoped not, and he wrapped his arms more securely around her, drew her fully against him, turning his head more sharply to better tease her mouth. When her hand slid up his chest, finding purchase behind his neck, her gloved fingers weaving into his hair to caress his scalp and nudging his hat off-kilter, he made his own, more guttural, helpless noise.

Her sweet, peachy scent mixed with the tang of cedar. She smelled so good, felt so soft and pliant drawn against him, that he could imagine nothing better than to hold her, kiss her, forever. Her bosom pillowed against his ribs, her hips against his thighs. His blood burned for her; he felt his body reacting with ungentlemanly eagerness for more, frustrated by the thickness of their coats. Longing to taste her soft skin, he kissed the corner of her mouth and down her jaw, down the delicate line of her throat until her woolen scarf stopped his exploration. He retreated to her ear, kissed it and nuzzled at her curls. She shivered in his arms.

"Mmmm," she said dreamily, her eyes closed.

He took her mouth again, eased her lips apart with his tongue, then boldly flirted with hers. She squeaked, but instead of pulling away she snuggled more securely against him, blindly seeking more. He wasn't sure how to give it to her, wrapped in winter clothing as they were, but he made a go at it. He deepened the kiss, dropped one of his hands to her backside to ease her more firmly against the hard ache in the front of his pants. *Yes . . .*

Still, she did not fight him, did not protest. She clung to his neck and pressed against him, a beguiling combination of innocence and eagerness, as she awkwardly kissed him back.

A twig snapped nearby. Everything stopped.

Caught!

Jack and Audra froze against each other. He held his breath, as if he could stop time, keep the next minute, hour, day from happening. Slowly he turned his head toward their intruder, vaguely aware of Audra, still in his arms, following suit. He half expected to face a shotgun, and doubted he could defend himself, and not just because, lulled by the simplicity of this little town, he rarely traveled armed anymore. No, he couldn't defend himself because he was guilty.

But damn it, she wasn't. Not as guilty as folks would make her out to be. In the seeming infinity before he'd fully turned, Jack's mind dealt out possibilities for getting Audra out of this. Bribes. Lies. Marriage.

Finally, too soon, his gaze met another's, even more shocked than his. Audra, still in his arms, laughed a frightened, broken laugh. The deer spun and, with a flip of her white tail, leaped away toward the Trinity River.

A deer? They'd been found out by a deer.

Jack stared after it, belatedly remembering to blink—and everything else. *Marriage?*

He'd also considered bribing someone, he reminded himself quickly. And he'd considered claiming to have forced himself on her. That could get a man killed in these parts.

Audra laughed again—nervous relief—and tucked the top of her head against his chest so that he couldn't see her face anymore, couldn't kiss her. It was probably just as well.

He felt ill. *Marriage?*

He had to get out of here, had to figure out what the hell was happening to him. He stepped quickly back, hoping their coats masked his arousal. This was *Audra*, after all!

She didn't look quite so innocent as usual. She looked . . . tousled. Her hair needed combing, especially on the side he'd been nuzzling. At some point she'd crumpled her bonnet in her hand. Her scarf had pulled loose and hung askew. And her face! She chewed her damp lower lip, her eyes averted, but despite her obvious efforts to not stare at him, Audra all but glowed.

If she looked so sated after this amount of lovemaking, how beautiful could she possibly become after sharing someone's bed? No, not someone's. His bed.

Lordy.

"My," said Jack after a gasp of breath. He really had to get out of there.

Audra nodded, blushing—and he could not find it in his heart to bolt the way the deer had. He had to make sure she was all right, had to make sure she got home safely. He had to pretend, for just a little longer, to be the "good, dear" man she somehow figured him to be.

Though how she reconciled his lovemaking with that image, he couldn't imagine.

Then he'd figure things out.

"Seems you have a few reasons yet not to trust gamblers," noted Jack appearing unsteady. Audra felt as if her entire world had tipped sideways, but surely this was no new sensation for him.

For some reason, that thought brought a pout to her lips. "You didn't force yourself on me," she admitted, looking at her ruined bonnet. Perhaps she should have fought him the way she had Peter, but she had not wanted to. She'd wanted the kisses, even more as they became shockingly intimate. She'd wanted his arms around her, touching her. She'd wanted *him.*

When had she become such a wanton?

"About that . . ." When she dared look up, Jack was scowling. Still, he offered his arm, and when she took it he led her to the stony path, in the direction of Aunt Heddy's house. "If we were caught, Audra, you *should* say I forced you. You're the one who has to live with these folks. Let me carry the blame."

"But that would be a lie!"

He inhaled through one side of his mouth, considering. "Let's call it a bluff."

"Let's call it a *lie.*"

"I met you here uninvited, didn't I? You told me to leave you alone, and I forced my company on you anyway. Seems to me you'd have a good case."

He spoke some truth, there. She *had* told him to leave her alone . . . but she'd been mistaken. "You didn't make me kiss you."

He looked angry, and she did not know why. "Maybe I did, and you're so danged innocent you just don't know it."

"No!" She stopped walking, so he had to stop, too. His hat tilted at a funny angle on his head—had she done that?—so she reached up to straighten it. He drew a shaky breath, raised his chin as if expecting a blow, then closed his eyes once she lowered her hand. *Odd.* The discovery that she was a floozy stunned her, but the idea that he would abuse their friendship for a kiss upset her more. She refused to accept it again. "Don't you dare make it something ugly. It was . . ."

Confusing. Joyous. Frightening. New. Electric. Wonderful.

"Enchanting," he suggested, almost grudgingly.

Yes, enchanting. She smiled.

"And against those rules of yours," he reminded her.

Which was the tragedy of it. If she could not control these surprisingly dissolute longings within herself, then her only hope was to stay away from him . . . and the very idea hurt her heart. He *was* a good friend to her. But the rules—rules she had agreed to—forbade her keeping company with any man, much less a gambler. That meant any time they stole together would be just that, stolen and unchaperoned. She could too easily find herself in his arms again, savoring the rasp of his rough, masculine cheek against hers, going completely weak as he did truly shameful, blissful things to her ear.

Being the hoyden that she was.

Goodness, just with her arm resting on his, she found herself noticing his solidity, remembering how easily he'd held her up when her own legs gave way against him.

She cleared her throat. "It is," she agreed unevenly, "against the rules."

"Which is not to say we can't speak to each other in the mercantile, of an afternoon," he pointed out. See how agreeable he was being now, how conscientious of her reputation?

And if she *was* a good influence on him—in other ways than this, of course—she had to at least *see* him. "Oh, yes—we can still do that."

"Or exchange hellos on the street," he added.

She nodded. "Of course." A gust of wind rushed crisply past her ears. They might have cold weather for Christmas. It occurred to her that these trees were full of clumped mistletoe.

"Or," said Jack, "if we were to meet on this here path . . ."

She slanted her gaze sidelong, up toward his strong, shadowed jaw, his dancing blue eyes, his lips. If they happened to meet in private again she feared—hoped—she knew what would happen. Even the momentary terror of discovery could not counter such an attraction.

Jack leaned toward her and she held her breath. *Oh, yes.*

Then he straightened and cleared his throat. "I should probably, uh, go now."

Damn, she thought—and then she had yet more to be ashamed of! He was right, of course. Trust Jack to help her help herself. Still, she would be lonely at Aunt Heddy's this week.

"Perhaps I'll see you in the store tomorrow," she said. It came out like a plea. "To see if I have a letter from home."

"Yes. That would be fine. The mercantile." He was backing away from her in an odd way, as if she frightened him.

"Is something wrong?" Had *she* done something—something else—wrong? Had her lack of restraint upset him even worse than it upset her? Was she horrible to kiss?

He stopped and closed his eyes—and when he opened them, after a deep breath, the glaze of fear had melted; he looked as if he liked her again.

"Everything is marvelous, Audra," he reassured her gently. "Except . . ." He stepped closer again, smoothed down the side of her hair—was it mussed?—and rearranged her scarf around her neck. He stepped back to survey his work, then nodded. His gaze dropped to her hand and he winced. "Except your bonnet," he admitted.

She looked down at the poor, crushed hat. And it was from Denver, too! But . . .

"It's just a bonnet," she told him truthfully.

He stared at her, his eyes going sleepy and dark, as they had before he'd kissed her, and she felt an answering shiver of excitement deep within her. *Oh, yes.*

But then he straightened too quickly, grinned too broadly. "See you at the mercantile then, Miss Garrison!"

And, backing away, he waved.

Was someone watching?

Audra turned slowly, fully expecting to see Aunt Heddy—or at least a deer—glaring at her from the cottonwoods between them and the barn. She saw nothing.

Then, when she turned toward Jack, she saw nothing there either. He'd gone.

Well before he reached the store, which was closed for Sunday, Jack had made up his mind. He'd let things get too serious, trifled with the kind of girl a fellow ought not trifle with. Torn between his desires to have more of her and to see nothing bad happen to her, he was paying the price for it.

Sooner or later, so would she.

He went in the mercantile's back door and climbed the stairs to Ferris's one-room bachelor residence. "I'm leaving."

"Don't you ever knock?" demanded Ham, standing hipshot—to favor his bum leg—and tucking his shirt into his butternut pants. "Get the hell out of here."

"That's what I just said," Jack insisted, swinging himself onto one of the ladder-back chairs at Ham's little table, where they generally ate dinner together each night. "I'm getting the hell out of here. I've spent too much time here as it is."

"Ah." Ham glanced out his window, as if watching something, then reclaimed his crutch and limped over to the table, sitting in his own chair. "This is about the schoolteacher, isn't it?"

Was it that obvious? "Don't you go thinking poorly of her," warned Jack, eyes narrowing.

"I'm not thinking poorly of her; I'm thinking poorly of you. Did you get her in trouble?"

"Go to hell!"

"That'd be a not-yet, I'm guessing. So what's got you so fired up to run?"

"It'd be best for her if I'm not around anymore." Jack frowned when he heard his own argument. Best for *her?* Since when had he looked out for others' welfare?

But he knew the odds and Audra didn't. Satisfying as this game had been, he knew that, sooner or later, the wheel would land on black. Audra might not realize she could *ever* lose—until she lost big.

"I imagine she'll be disappointed," said Ham. "Not that I can fully figure out why."

"She knows I'm leaving." He'd told her he would . . . at some point. "I'll see what I can take from the store. Anything left over in credit, you can have for your foul-tempered hospitality."

"Kind of a Christmas gift?"

"Why not?" Then the full meaning of Ham's question, and his sarcastic tone, pierced Jack's determination. *We Three Kings. Silent Night.* "It's Christmas?"

"Day after tomorrow, you dumb bastard."

"Oh, hell." Jack slumped back in his chair. He didn't even bother to argue the slur to his late mother. If he bolted right before Christmas, he *would* be a bastard. "Oh . . . damn."

"That's what you get for not going to church." As if Hamilton went to church himself.

Then again . . . "I could give her a present," mused Jack. "A combination Christmas and farewell gift. Something nice to remember me, cheer her up—assuming she needs cheering."

He suspected she would. That scared him.

"She won't accept it," warned Ham.

"Sure she will." He'd seen some pretty doodads downstairs that he suspected would please her, but it had to be special.

"Ladies can't accept gifts from gentlemen who are not courting them."

There was that word *can't* again. "She might surprise you," Jack predicted, assessing their inventory in his head. A comb and brush set? A jewelry box? Jewelry itself?

"Anything's possible." But Ham said it in that dry way of his, so Jack couldn't tell if he really meant it or not. And what did it matter what Ferris Hamilton thought? He did not know Audra the way Jack knew Audra. *Thank goodness.*

A present would soothe Jack's conscience considerably.

Audra refused it sight unseen. "You're sweet to think of me," she whispered, sliding the paper-wrapped box back to him as slyly as he'd slid it to her. "But it's . . . it's just not right."

He kept his voice equally low; her aunt stood with her back to them, right across the store. "Sure, it is! It's Christmas . . . and I'd like you to have something from me. Once I go."

Disappointment at the lack of news from home had her so peaked, he couldn't bear to tell her how soon his departure would be.

Somehow, in losing her hope of a letter, she'd also misplaced any scraps of rebellion. "No. Thank you. My aunt would be sure to ask about it unless I hid it, and . . . I've hidden so much already, Jack. You're a dear to think about it, but it's just not proper."

Proper? Even now, with her aunt right there, he couldn't look at her without wanting her. He wanted what he'd had—the taste of her lips, her skin, her ear; her softness pressed against his own aching hardness. And he wanted what he'd not had yet, what he imagined, alone on his pallet at night.

If she knew what he did to her in those fantasies, she'd slap him for sure, no matter *how* she'd responded to his kisses. And her aunt would have him arrested.

As if sensing herself as a topic of conversation, the widow Cribb looked up from the wrapped apples Ham had just handed to her. "Do we or do we not have mail, Audra?"

Audra winced and turned to her aunt. "Nothing, ma'am."

"Harrumph! Then we have no more business here—especially not with *that* man." The widowed schoolmarm stomped out, a forlorn Audra in her wake.

Well, tarnation.

Ham limped across the store to Jack's counter. "I don't blame their apples for going bad," he muttered. "If I lived there, I'd go bad, too. So did the schoolmarm take it?"

Jack scowled at him. It was the perfect gift for her, too—so why was it still in his pocket?

"Told you so," said Ham with an uncharacteristic grin.

Jack made a rude gesture.

"Maybe you'll listen to your Uncle Ferris next time."

"She didn't even get a letter from home." The more he thought about it, the more that soured him. He knew what store Audra put in those letters. Today she'd nearly glowed with anticipation. Then, when he broke the news that she had neither letter nor package, her face had fallen so low, nothing he could say or do had lifted her spirits. "Who would send a slip like that across the country and then forget her at Christmas?"

Ferris snorted. "*You* almost forgot her at Christmas."

Jack made another rude gesture, hidden from the rest of the store by the counter.

Hamilton cocked his head in an annoying, thoughtful way, until Jack demanded, "*What?*"

"You really care about her, don't you?"

"You have a point?"

"I do." Ferris drew his crutch in front of him, rested his hands atop it and his chin on his hands, and gazed solemnly at Jack. "I know how you can get your little schoolmarm to accept your present. If you want to bad enough."

All Jack's instincts flared with suspicion. "What's in it for you?"

"Sheer entertainment," Ham assured him, grinning for the second time in one day.

It felt like a sucker's bet, but, remembering Audra's dejection—and after she'd been practicing her Christmas music, for mercy's sake!—Jack took the bait. "Talk."

And Ferris did.

Chapter Fourteen

Teachers must regularly attend church services.
—Rules for Teachers

Audra knew her family could not have forgotten her; something had happened to their letter, that was all. But to spend her first Christmas away, without even written greetings from home, revived the homesickness she'd thought she'd conquered. By Christmas morning, she resigned herself to a dour, lonely day.

Then, at morning services, Christmas found her.

Wreaths of loblolly pine hung on each of the double doors, tied with red ribbon and hung with cowbells. Inside stood a cedar tree, decorated with garlands of popcorn and holly berries, with lit candles. Festive calico bags tied in ribbon, and apples, and oranges, and the shiny round tops of tin cans all hung off its branches, reflecting the light. The mingling of scents, from the sweetness of fruit to the more romantic smell of fresh cedar, soothed Audra considerably.

Thousands of miles from home, with snow a mere memory, it could still be Christmas!

She sat at the piano, reacquainting herself with the keyboard she'd learned at her mother's side, and began "The Holly and the Ivy" from memory. The church filled with the citizens of Candon, sharing handshakes and smiles and Christmas greetings. Audra knew most of them; she wasn't so terribly alone here, at that. Unsure that people in back could even hear her carols, she continued playing anyway. "Lullay, Lullay." "Deck the Halls." "I Saw Three Ships." And perhaps they could hear. Even up front, *she* heard exclamations and then a falling silence when someone entered during "God Rest Ye Merry Gentlemen."

When she saw why, her fingers tangled up the "tidings of comfort and joy." Nobody paid it any mind, including her. She'd never received a better Christmas present in her life!

Jack Harwood, black sheep of Candon, had come to church.

Well, damn. Rather . . . durn.

Even after an adult life happily strayed from the proverbial flock, Jack felt guilty even to *think* a cuss word in church. His pa would've smacked him for a word like *dad-gum,* or *shoot.* Or *durn.* But his pa wasn't here. It helped some to remember that.

With the gaze of just about everyone in town on him and Hamilton, Jack wondered for a moment what *he* was doing here, too. Then he recognized the piano music, sweeter even than it had sounded from his perch in the oak tree, and he remembered.

He'd come for Audra. What the . . . heck . . . had the woman done to him?

At his shoulder, Ferris murmured, "Having fun?"

Audra hadn't gotten him into this mess; Ham had. The storekeeper had used dares, guilt, and finally pragmatism: Did Jack want to see her get her present, or not? It turned out Ham was supplying candy for the church's Christmas tree—the reverend's increased interest in him had resulted in that, if nothing else—and could slip Audra's present amidst the others. But to see her get it, Jack had to attend services.

So far God hadn't struck him down at the threshold. Not that Jack expected to be called home. Not to God's home, anyhow.

Oh, well. He'd dressed decently for it, anyway.

"Take off your hat, you heathen," he muttered now to Ferris, and nodded a hello to those folks he recognized. Surprisingly, that was the majority of them. Some ladies turned stiffly away, affronted that he would dare darken their doorway. Others, especially the menfolk—many who already looked uncomfortable in their go-to-meeting clothes—returned the silent greeting.

None was the person Jack wanted to see. And standing there, hat in hand, hair slicked back and feeling younger than he had in years, Jack marveled at just how desperately he *did* want to see her. He might recognize these other folks, but he didn't fully trust them and their tight-laced sensibilities. Audra he trusted. Seeing her here would go a long way toward reminding him of what church *might* be, toward crowding out some of the darker memories of what, in the hands of hypocrites, it could become.

He followed the call of the music . . . and there she sat at her piano, coaxing joyful notes from it and staring back at him, an expression of wonder on her candlelit, china-doll face.

Jack nodded to her as well.

With a smile she turned back to the piano. He felt surprise at how easily he recalled the words to the song she played, especially since his pa hadn't held with singing. "To save us all from Satan's power when we were gone astray . . ."

Maybe folks don't need *saving,* challenged a voice—his own, years younger and raw with grief—from too deep in his memory. That unsettled him powerfully. He ought not be here, had been in the right all along in staying away from such places.

But to leave now would be rank cowardice.

He found a stretch of bench with a comfortingly clear view of his pretty, short-haired piano player, and he and Ferris sat. As Reverend Collins stepped up to the pulpit, Jack resisted thoughts of other sermons and the miseries that went with them. Watching Audra, how she cocked her head or nodded while listening to her minister, anchored him when the memories might have swept him into darker places than he'd like.

Only once he relaxed into the rhythm of the minister's words—and the relief that Collins might not be the fire-and-brimstone type his pa had been—did Jack allow himself to compare this service to his ragged religious past. The neat, whitewashed Candon church was finer than nearly anyplace Jack's father had preached. His earliest memories leaned more toward outdoor revivals, sweltering daylong sermons in brush arbors. The congregation would fan themselves or mop their faces with handkerchiefs, usually with some children shouting off in the distance, released from their spiritual imprisonment by parents kinder than his. He'd sit beside his mother, itchy in his charity-barrel suit, Ma squeezing his hand in warning anytime he started to fidget.

Of course, she'd mainly kept his fidgeting in check because he'd get worse from his pa if he didn't behave himself. So Jack would sit, sweltering in the Texas heat, listening to his father rant about the perils of damnation, and he would pray that someone would offer his pa a real preaching position at a real church.

Pa tended to go through churches pretty fast. Jack remembered that, too.

". . . in singing, 'The First Noel,' " announced the reverend, and Jack stood only a beat behind the rest of the congregation. He watched Audra as she played and sang—a shame he couldn't pick out her voice amid the others—and took deep breaths of air perfumed with candle wax, fruit, and cedar.

He surely appreciated the smell of cedar lately, since that afternoon in the woods.

When Audra glanced in his direction, he winked at her. Her eyes widened and she turned hurriedly back to the music, a pretty flush on her cheeks . . . and what looked encouragingly like a smile pulling at her lips.

After "Noel" they sat again. The reverend began to read the Christmas story. Jack could almost quote it with him—not from his pa's sermons, but from his mother's daily readings. He surely would have paid a price for winking in church a couple of decades earlier. Worse than the whipping, though, would be his pa's claims that maybe it was Jack's fault, the next time they were asked to move on. They were always asked to move on. And it was always Jack's fault or his brother's or his sister's—until they'd died of fever—or his mother's. Never Pa's.

The older and smarter Jack got, the more he questioned the hypocrisy. He knew the church ladies' casual cruelty. They preferred to turn a blind eye rather than face ugliness in their own congregations. They'd rant against easy targets—drinkers or

gamblers, most of whom didn't give a hoot anyhow. But let someone dare suspect that a banker beat his wife, or a local farmer had locked up his simpleton daughter to starve her, and those righteous women lost their crusading spirit quick enough. Family matters, they would say if pressed, were none of their business.

As if drinking and gambling were.

But had the ladies actually sent the Harwoods packing just because his ma had midwifed an unwed mother? Or was his pa a no-account lying coward?

By time he reached eleven, Jack was trying to get his mother to leave, but she refused. Then things got better for a while. His Uncle Isham, a riverboat pilot, got them settled at a church in Ma's hometown. Even as a ghost of its former grandeur, Jefferson, Texas, was the finest town Jack had ever seen. He'd never met anybody so wordly, so fascinating as his uncle. Isham seemed everything his own father was not. Ma seemed to finally start coming to terms with the long-ago deaths of Jack's siblings.

Then Pa lost the church in Jefferson. Ma hanged herself. And Jack had run off to live on a riverboat. In all that time, he'd never been back to a church—until now.

". . . stand and sing, 'Oh, Holy Night.' "

Jack stood. Jack sang. And Jack regretted ever letting Ferris goad him into coming here, even for Audra. He looked away from her to the yuletide decorations—something else that his pa had denounced as sinful. And he noticed the way little ones kept sneaking glances at that tree, so stoked up with expectation that he doubted they'd heard the sermon.

Not that he had, either.

Still, it eased him some. He couldn't remember being near so many small children at one time, and they proved to be fascinating critters. One tyke, not much more than an infant, stared at him over its mother's shoulder from the row ahead of him, drooling and smiling and occasionally waving its slobbery hand with irrepressible glee. Another child, a little black-haired girl, kept leaning out into the aisle to better see the tree, with an expression so prim she obviously thought nobody could see her doing it. Some of the children's folks seemed right fond of them, too, touching a little head, patting a little back, even kissing a little cheek . . . as easily as if they did it all the time.

It seemed religious folks need not be so mean-spirited as he remembered. He had more sense of how a gal as deep-down kind as Audra could count herself among them, anyhow.

But even as his nausea faded, Jack felt shaken. He'd put too much effort into leaving past ugliness in its grave. Through moderate drinking, immoderate gambling, occasional women, and all-around fun, he'd avoided feeling anything too deeply. He wasn't about to start now, even if those feelings concerned something as pretty and unspoiled as Audra Garrison herself.

Ferris elbowed him in the ribs, and Jack saw that the minister and his wife were passing out the presents. The church became a riot of squeals, gasps, and thank-yous as eager hands unwrapped clothing, dolls, pocketknives.

So this was what Christmas could be.

But as Jack waited for Audra to receive her gift, he couldn't help but feel his own dark gratitude—gratitude that he'd soon be well away from this little farming community and back to the world he'd happily chosen, where he belonged.

And where she, unfortunately, did not.

Audra had never known a better Christmas service.

She tried not to sneak peeks at Jack throughout the service—Reverend Collins deserved her attention—but occasionally she gave in to temptation. Jack looked so wonderful, fresh-shaven with his hair neatly combed, his tailored frock coat sculpting the clean line of his figure, a gold watch chain glinting from his vest. But better than his outward appearance, of course, was his apparent inward transformation.

He'd come to church!

She wondered if her influence had anything to do with it, and fervently hoped so. Some of her behavior, of late, might not seem quite so wicked if she could excuse it as a form of, well, missionary work.

She enjoyed the service but enjoyed watching the children

get their presents more. She'd given her pupils their gifts on the last day of class—new pencils for each of them—but now regretted not saving them for Christmas morning. *Next year* . . .

But that thought sobered her quickly. Would she not be with her family next year?

Could she still teach school, if she were?

Mrs. Collins thrust a package into Audra's hands with a hurried smile, then moved on to distribute other gifts. For her?

Audra stared at the muslin-wrapped square in awe. She had a present? But who . . . ?

The obvious explanation washed over her like rainwater. This time she managed the self-control not to look toward Jack and instead savored the heft and feel of her surprise for a long, increasingly happy moment. What a wonderfully, sinfully clever man! She could not accept a gift directly from him. But she *could* accept an anonymous present from the church tree!

Catching her lower lip between her teeth, suddenly wild to know what he had gotten her, Audra slid off the string and unfolded the dark green muslin. Her hand shook as she revealed a book. *Duty and Domesticity: Being, a Gentle Guidebook for the American Girl toward the Ultimate Rewards of Modesty and Comportment.*

Bewildered, she reread the title twice, then finally remembered to blink. When she realized she was starting to frown, she quickly smoothed out her expression for fear of being rude. She must not turn her nose up at any gift, but . . . *this*?

Somehow it did not seem the sort of book Jack would give.

When she dared peek toward him, he was watching her with interest . . . and curiosity. The book *wasn't* from him? Then who . . . ?

"If you read it faithfully, there may yet be hope for you," said Aunt Heddy from her pew.

"Thank you!" exclaimed Audra quickly, grasping her aunt's bony hand and then holding out the book so that they could both admire its pretty leather cover. "You know how I love to read. And this looks highly . . . informative!"

All gifts should be accepted graciously—unless given by a

known gambler, or a man not officially paying court . . . or both. Perhaps some rules *did* make less sense than others.

"No need to prattle, child," scolded Heddy, so Audra looked back to her book. Modesty and comportment. For a moment, fear flared. Had her aunt noticed behaviors that Audra would prefer never be discovered? Or was it possible . . .

Her rancher father might easily have said the same thing—*there may yet be hope for you*—and in his terse, Germanic way meant it with affection, even humor. Was there more of Papa in his sister than Audra had recognized?

Reverend Collins himself appeared beside her. "Well, aren't you popular today, Miss Garrison!" he said. Before Audra could ask him what he meant, he had pressed a second package into her hand, this one smaller than the first, and moved on.

This time she had to know. She looked toward the bench where Jack Harwood sat beside Ferris Hamilton, both bachelors somewhat adrift amid the celebration around them.

Sensing her interest, Jack widened his eyes with a complete innocence that confirmed it. This gift was from him.

Audra opened it more slowly, savoring the suspense as she slid away an indulgent length of green ribbon and carefully unfolded snowy white paper. Inside she found a wooden box, longer than it was wide. A necklace? Panic warred with fascination. A necklace would be too much. Even anonymously, she mustn't accept it.

But when she opened the box and peeked at its velvet interior, it revealed not a necklace but a pen. A sleek, silver-and-bone, newfangled fountain pen.

She had never seen anything so pretty in all her life!

After simply staring at the pen for some time, admiring its line and slim barrel, she slowly, reverently lifted it from its purple couch, and it fit her hand perfectly. *A pen*! Perfect for writing home to her beloved family. Perfect for marking compositions. Perfect for being . . . Audra.

When she looked up, sought out Jack again, he looked blurry. Was she *crying* again?

"I do not see what is wrong with a simple dip-pen," noted Aunt Heddy, claiming Audra's attention as quickly as that.

Audra held the prize to her chest, as if afraid someone would snatch it away from her, and blinked to clear her vision. "I think it's . . . *enchanting*!"

"Something like that is far too fine for everyday use." Then Aunt Heddy asked the dreadful question: "Who is it from?"

Thank goodness Audra was looking at her pen, instead of at her aunt. If she admitted her admirer, she would be made to return the present—this best Christmas present ever! But to say she didn't know would be to lie. Had she fallen so low that she would lie to keep a gift?

"There is no card attached," she said slowly, turning the box and then, feeling as dishonest as a pickpocket, looking at both sides of the paper wrapping.

Aunt Heddy made a huffing noise, but said nothing else.

Audra carefully laid the pen back into its case, then held the box tightly. This was hers. If she must accept the book in good graces, she would keep the pen as well. She *would*!

"Will you play another carol before we finish the service?" asked Reverend Collins then, so Audra did—with the pen case laid carefully in her lap. She played "Joy to the World."

He'd done it. Darling Jack had managed to give her a Christmas gift. If only she had something to give him!

She glimpsed him once more that morning, as everyone left the church.

"Miss Garrison," Jack said, as she and Heddy passed nearby. "You make beautiful music."

"Thank you, Mr. Harwood," said Audra—and even though he didn't grin, she felt a deliciously intimate shiver as she met his beautiful sapphire eyes. She hoped he could read her own. *Thank you so very much*! "You are too kind."

"That, ma'am, would be right near impossible."

"Audra," warned Aunt Heddy, her tone as dour as ever.

"Merry Christmas, Mr. Harwood," said Audra, backing away a step but reluctant to turn from him. "Mr. Hamilton," she added toward the storekeeper, who'd been corralled by the minister.

"Merry Christmas, Miss Garrison," said Jack—and then he grinned. "Mrs. Cribb."

Aunt Heddy only sniffed loudly, caught Audra by the hand, and led her off toward home. Audra caught a final glimpse of Jack's white teeth, his dancing eyes, before she turned to keep from falling or dropping her precious gifts.

"It is best," said Aunt Heddy, once they were alone, "to ignore men like that. They take anything more as encouragement."

Audra asked, "Men like that?"

"Trouble, child. Men like that feel they have the right to live outside the boundaries of common decency. That makes them trouble."

Audra thought about it a moment, then smiled secretly at the live oak they passed. The cedar break would be along soon.

Then she said, "Yes, ma'am," because her aunt was right. Jack Harwood *was* trouble.

Wonderful, enchanting trouble.

Chapter Fifteen

Teachers may not dress in bright colors.

—Rules for Teachers

Aunt Heddy prepared Christmas dinner in silence, as usual. Audra hummed Christmas carols as she helped. Whenever she truly wanted to smile, all she need do was think: He came to church! The thought glowed through her, warmed her as surely as, well, whiskey might, but without the coughing. As she pumped water, peeled potatoes, stoked the stove, and ground coffee, Audra's heart began to allow her tiny peeks at her own secret Christmas wishes. If Jack was rehabilitated, truly a changed man, then was there anything wrong with her wanting to spend time with him? Teachers must not keep company with men. But the school year would end by May, and then . . . who knew what could happen?

Of course, if Jack *did* court her respectably, there would be no more such displays of wantonness as in the woods or—she flushed—in this very kitchen. They would be strictly chaperoned. But with chaperones came order and safety. They could visit. She could ask after his family and tell him about hers. And if they were, in fact, suited . . .

She dared not pursue such thoughts further. Her fantasy lacked a few significant ingredients—Jack taking up a trade, or the not-so-minor detail of him actually speaking for her. But such particulars could work themselves out, couldn't they?

What was wrong with letting her heart take a . . . gamble?

So caught up was she in her daydreams that Audra did not hear the carriage first.

"Who could that be?" demanded her aunt, looking up from a batch of biscuit dough. "And on Christmas Day!"

"I'll go see," offered Audra quickly, wiping her hands on her apron and hurrying to the front door. Neither Claudine nor Melissa should be returning for a week yet.

She opened the door—then stared at the unfamiliar buggy, its elderly female passenger, and the man hopping down from the driver's seat. For the briefest moment he looked like a young, clean-shaven version of her papa.

"Child, who is it?" demanded Aunt Heddy again.

But instead of answering, Audra launched herself out the door and into the coated arms of her beloved older brother, come all the way from Wyoming. "*Thaddeas*!"

"Oof!" said Thaddeas, arms closing tight around her. He swung her all the way around with her feet off the ground, as if she were a little girl again. "Merry Christmas, Audie!"

Then he set her down, kissed her cheek, leaned back—and frowned a piercing frown, so much like their father's. "What happened to your *hair?*"

* * *

With more biscuits, their dinner easily stretched to feed four. Thaddeas had brought with him their grandmother Garrison, Heddy's aged mother, from the hill country.

"We were supposed to be here three days ago," he explained between bites of dinner. "But the Union Pacific got snowed in south of Denver. Once I reached Texas and fetched *Grossmutti*, the Kansas-Texas line—the Katy, I mean—flooded out for half a day. I am *not* looking forward to telling Elizabeth that Christmas arrived before we did!"

Elizabeth was their mother—Thad's stepmother, though the family rarely saw the difference. This afternoon sharply reminded Audra of it. Grandmother Garrison, *der Grossmutter* to Audra, was Thad's *Grossmutti*—less formal because they'd been close during his childhood. And when Aunt Heddy, who'd raised him while their father trailed cattle, first laid eyes on him, she actually whispered the endearment, "*Liebling*!" As if he were still a child, not a full-grown man and frontier lawyer. He'd looked startled at that.

Then he'd folded Aunt Heddy into a separate hug, more respectful than Audra's.

Now Audra said, "You don't *have* to tell Mother you were late," and Thad gave her that same startled look.

"Of course I do," he said—and that was that.

After dinner, Christmas came all over again with surprises from home. Some gifts were for Heddy, of course, and some for *Grossmutter,* but most were for Audra, including a myrtle green party dress, complete with a lace-trimmed taffeta petticoat.

"You will send it back, of course," noted Aunt Heddy.

"Send it *back*?"

*Grossmutter tsk*ed at her less-than-ladylike response. Filling her arms with fabric, Audra realized she was being possessive about her gifts today. First Jack's pen, and now this. But the gown was so pretty. And Audra felt so weary of wearing solemn colors.

Somehow she managed the words. "I suppose it *is* too gay for a schoolteacher."

"I'm under strict orders," admitted Thaddeas with feigned regret. "Mother wants me to take you out in Fort Worth on New

Year's Eve. We'll rent hotel rooms, so that you needn't appear less than scholarly until we've left Candon. Then you can just be my baby sister for a night."

Audra barely had the presence of mind to put her gown aside before throwing herself onto her brother for the second time that day. No need to crush the fabric, after all.

And since Thaddeas was the man of the family—at the moment—neither Heddy nor *Grossmutter* protested his plan even once.

Later in the afternoon, while the older women caught up on their family news, Thaddeas and Audra went walking to discuss home—her home. Hand in hand, they strolled to the two-room schoolhouse and then the modest center of town.

Audra adored her big brother; eleven years older than even Mariah, he was a protector and mentor. With his serious gaze, Thad somehow mirrored their father's intensity, though Thad was clean-shaven and had brown eyes. He also smiled more than their father did.

Though nowhere near as often as Jack Harwood.

She asked after the ranch and Thad's law practice, and was relieved to hear that both were doing well. Her parents and younger sisters were happy and healthy—"though they miss you," Thad assured her, squeezing her hand. "We *all* miss you." Even her older sisters, whose shocking choices in men had rocked the family for several years now, were happy in their new lives.

"Poor Papa." She sighed—it was a standard comment whenever the subject of her older sisters' romances came up.

"He'll survive," said Thad dryly, then he slanted an amused glance back to Audra. "But I think he's relieved that, as long as you're teaching, you *can't* marry. Pa's had more than enough unpleasant surprises from you girls."

Unpleasant surprises like her going sweet on a gambler?

She defended her sisters and changed the subject. "Perhaps because *you* haven't married."

"When I do, I will choose someone who's an asset to the Garrison family name."

"Oh?" Well, *this* was interesting! He'd always been not-so-secretly in love with a local woman who had broken his heart by marrying a mining entrepreneur. Since then Thad generally refused to discuss marriage, only son or not.

His look clearly said he refused to do so today, as well.

"This is Main Street," she explained now, letting him evade the subject. "A local family is donating land to the railroad, and there's talk of getting a depot. The Candon Lumberyard is down there, and the church. Here's the livery, and that"—she gestured dramatically—"is the mercantile."

But as she indicated the mercantile, her tour got more interesting by far. Ferris Hamilton had just limped around the corner, accompanied by none other than her charming Jack.

Almost immediately, Jack saw them.

Audra was with another man. Holding hands with another man. Glancing up at that other man as if assessing how he might react once she waved to him and Ferris. With no more information than that, Jack found himself hating the other man with a vengeance.

He hated that the other man looked to be older than him. He hated the self-assured *presence* the other man radiated, as if he could take on whatever the world threw at him without breaking a sweat. He hated the fellow's coat and wide-brimmed-hat, both of understated quality. But most of all, Jack hated that the other man was obviously of a caliber such as could step out with the schoolmarm without inciting local panic.

Jack frowned. The story *he'd* heard was that Audra couldn't keep company with *any* man. Maybe, as with so many other "rules," the pillars of the community looked the other way for someone with wealth and position?

"Well, well, well," muttered Ham as the couple approached. Jack didn't bother answering—it would be a cussword anyhow.

What really gnawed at him was how pert Audra looked. Her face shone as she tugged the man forward for the inevitable introductions. Until this moment, Jack would have bet everything he had—except maybe his watch—on the certainty that he wanted his schoolmarm to be happy. It wasn't as if their own . . . friendship could be permanent. It wasn't as if she could find happiness with *him.*

But now he knew he would have lost that bet.

It wasn't noble of him . . . but he didn't want to see Audra happy with this broad-shouldered, brown-haired, respectable fellow who—*damn* him—even drew Audra closer with a proprietary gesture, as they reached him and Ham. And in all fairness, he didn't even know the man. It turned out Jack didn't want to see her happy with anyone but him, and now was a hell of a time to face that.

Not that anyone expected him to be noble anyway, did they?

Audra's dove gray gaze lingered on Jack's face for a moment, and some of that joy shining from her flickered into confusion. He felt even worse, then—he didn't want to see her *un*happy, did he?—and attempted a smile.

He'd seen that dumb Early Rogers bluff better than his smile felt. But Audra returned it anyway, seemingly relieved by his mere effort.

"Thaddeas," she announced, "this is Mr. Jack—I mean, John—Harwood."

Jack reluctantly accepted the man's hand and hated his firm, unpretentious shake. The fellow's brown eyes narrowed speculatively, intense. Jack held his gaze like a dare.

"And this is Mr. Ferris Hamilton. He owns the mercantile."

The stranger moved his attention to Ferris; they shook.

"A pleasure," said Ferris. "Any friend of our schoolmarm's is a friend of ours." *Weasel.*

Then Audra proudly announced, "This is my brother, Thaddeas," and like that, everything made sense.

"Your brother," repeated Jack, trying to readjust. She could walk with the man in public because they were related. Of course she looked happy—she, unlike him, was *fond* of her family. And weren't most big brothers proprietary?

In fact, he could see that this one didn't trust him any farther than he could spit. And he didn't look to be the spitting type.

Tarnation. Could he have played this any worse?

"I didn't realize you had family visiting . . . Miss Garrison," Jack said now, more carefully. Dangerous enough to trifle with a lady. Add a male relative within the same state, and he'd taken his life into his hands.

Although even now, watching how Audra's pretty gaze swept between him and the brother, he surely couldn't fault himself for the risk. She was something special, all right.

"I didn't know either," she said. "They simply showed up!"

"They?" There were more of them?

Audra nodded happily. "Thad brought our grandmother with him. I haven't seen her for a long time. She's a great deal like Aunt Heddy. But smaller."

"Ah." That was a relief. He hoped he could defend himself against grandmothers—small ones, anyhow. Audra's smile was infectious. "Christmas has been good to you then, has it?"

Delight sparkled in her gray eyes as she caught her lower lip between her teeth, then glanced momentarily away. "It's been the best Christmas ever."

"I'm pleased to hear it," he said. If they'd been alone, he would have reached out and brushed his fingertips to her cheek or hair just to make sure she was real.

"You fellows need to be someplace?" asked her brother then, watching the interchange too closely for Jack's comfort.

"Just the livery," said Ham.

"We're on our way to the Bennett place," Jack explained further—maybe to make up for trying to stare the fellow down . . . or maybe to prove that he had moments of respectability, too. "We got some invites to supper; this one appeared the safest."

Audra cocked her head. "*Safest*?"

Jack waggled his eyebrows meaningfully. "One of the other invitations was from Mrs. Estry and her widowed daughter, Nora."

That, she understood. "Oh."

"We won't keep you," said the brother, and Jack shook hands with less acrimony. If he was leaving town anyway, wasn't it better that Audra be occupied with out-of-town guests?

But Garrison's narrow-eyed assessment of him made him itchy, all the same.

"Enjoy Mrs. Bennett's chocolate cake," advised Audra, glowing like a Christmas angel.

"We will endeavor to do our best," Jack assured her, and held her gaze for a moment too long.

Next thing Jack knew, Garrison said, "If you like desserts, come by for strudel some afternoon this week. You could tell me more about the area."

Among other things? Clever. "I'm not from around here," Jack admitted, as annoyed to have to turn down the invitation as he'd been to see Audra on someone else's arm in public. Not that he'd ever aspired to that kind of respectability. "And last time I noticed, I wasn't welcome at the widow Cribb's."

"Jack used to be a gambler," explained Audra and Jack blinked at her.

Used to be?

Suddenly it all made sense—how much store she'd put into his gift, the way she'd lit up when she saw him in church, her open friendliness this afternoon. It made perfect, damnable sense, and he hated himself for having to clarify.

"Not quite, darlin'," he told her softly. "I *am* a gambler."

Garrison's intense brown eyes sharpened, and he glanced down at Audra before returning his gaze to Jack. "That so."

It was Audra Jack looked at when he answered, wishing he could soothe some of her obvious distress . . . even if that distress implied a proper reaction to his familiarity. "That's so."

"But . . . you came to church," she said. "You said someone was a good influence on you."

He wanted to shut his eyes against her pain, to stop it from drawing an equal ache out of him. But he couldn't be a coward, not to her. He winced, but he took the hurt. "I only went to church this once—and it *was* because of someone's good influence. That doesn't mean I've changed who I am, what I do."

The way she searched his face, trying to understand something he'd thought she knew all along, hurt so bad that he almost wished her brother *would* shoot him. Especially if she hadn't been kissing him at all, just some goody-goody she'd fooled herself into thinking he'd become.

"No," she said too softly, low on breath. "Of course not."

They shouldn't do this, say this, in front of Hamilton or her brother. They should say this where they needn't refer to each other as "someone," where he could hold her, kiss her, whisper apologies and "darlings" and comfort . . . as long as that comfort didn't include his own reform.

"But you think so highly of folks, you couldn't help but make that mistake of me."

Her eyes flashed at him. "It wasn't a mistake."

"I'm still a gambler—Miss Garrison." He added that last formality for her brother's sake. Since she was showing less than her usual restraint, the least he could do was bolster her respectability. "Ham here is still a mean-tempered pinchpenny. That student of yours, Jerome, is still a troublemaker. You're an asset to the community, ma'am, but you can't save us all."

He feared she would cry; her eyes shone suspiciously bright. But they also smoldered with determination, and her pretty mouth set into a stubborn line that unsettled him more than a little, beneath the grief of having hurt her.

I can try, her stubborn gaze seemed to say. She didn't realize she'd run out of time.

"Well," said Ham. "It'll take me half the night just to make the livery stable; we'd better get going. Pleased to meet you, Mr. Garrison. Miss Garrison."

"Hamilton." The brother then eyed Jack again. "Harwood."

"That's some sister you have," said Jack, eyeing him back.

"I know," said Garrison. "I'd best get her home. You never know what kind of folks come out once the sun sets."

"This is true," said Jack—which left them both at a draw. Jack turned away first, but not because he was afraid of the brother. He just couldn't bear Audra's hurt any longer. Maybe he could try to meet with her, try to explain further.

Or maybe that would be the most foolish thing he'd done since arriving in Candon.

* * *

Audra could barely breathe, barely think. Jack was still a gambler. He didn't mean to reform. He didn't *want* to reform.

And he and Thaddeas did not seem to like each other.

Now, when all she wanted was to cry alone, or tell someone—anyone—how foolish she'd been and to hear them defend her, she had to hide her distress. There lay the price for her secret affair, for giving her heart outside the boundaries of decent society. She'd enjoyed his kisses, his embraces, but had they been worth this disillusionment?

Especially when she couldn't even blame him? He'd always been honest with her. She had nobody to blame but herself.

The sun set and the sky turned purple as she and Thaddeas made their way down the lane, back to Aunt Heddy's house. The weather was turning cold finally. She saw that Thad's breath misted faintly in the air when he said, "I think I'd best take you home."

"We're already here," she said, only a little shaky.

Thad said, "No. I mean to Wyoming."

Chapter Sixteen

After finishing one's work, a teacher may spend her remaining time reading from the Bible or other good books.

—Rules for Teachers

Thad's announcement hung between them as Audra thought: *Jack's still a gambler. He doesn't want to reform.* Only belatedly did she hear—*Wyoming?*

Suddenly she *wanted* to go home to Wyoming. She wanted her mother's love. She wanted her sisters to share the joy and weight of her secrets. She wanted her father and brother to watch over her, keep her from foolish, scandalous things . . .

Or would they look at her with solemn disappointment upon learning she'd already done them?

Thad wanted her to go home to Wyoming! Finally she managed clarity, alarm. She did not dare look at him for fear of seeing just that look in his eyes, knowing she deserved it.

For fear of what he'd see in hers.

So she kept her head down, her eyes averted, as she asked, "Why should I go back now?"

Thad encircled her protectively. "Reasons you shouldn't have to worry about, Audie."

Which felt better than him denouncing her for the hoyden she was . . . except for the niggling guilt that accompanied her reprieve and something that felt oddly like—annoyance?

She dared peek at him after all. "Why shouldn't I?"

"Because you are my baby sister, that's why," he said.

That answer would have pleased her considerably, once—would have made her feel cherished, safe. But now . . . "I'm a full-grown woman," she pointed out.

He slanted a dubious expression down toward her as he reached toward the gate, but she caught his arm. She did *not* want Aunt Heddy or *Grossmutter* asking questions. Not until she and Thad had this resolved between themselves, anyway.

Go home to Wyoming?

"More grown than not! I've supported myself for three months now."

"With Aunt Heddy," he reminded her.

What she felt *was* annoyance, after all. "Paying room and board from my wages," she reminded him back, standing a little straighter. "I have a position here, Thaddeas. I have responsibilities. I cannot leave without very good reason."

He considered her seriously, then sighed, nodded. "Let's go see to the livestock," he said.

That meant something serious—something he'd rather work through than confront head-on. Swallowing back uncertainty, Audra nodded, and they went to the barn.

Only once Thaddeas was diligently forking hay into the stalls could he admit, "You should go home because that gambler may have illicit intentions toward you. *That's* why."

Standing by the carriage horses, Audra petted Buck's nose, hiding her face in the side of his neck and breathing in his wonderful, horsey smell.

"He called you 'darling'." Even without looking, she could hear the scowl in Thad's voice.

"Oh. That's just—" *Jack.* "Mr. Harwood."

"It wasn't just that. It . . ." The men in her family had never excelled at expressing themselves in delicate situations. "I don't trust him."

You don't know him. But Jack's intentions *were* a little illicit. "He attended church today," she said from behind Buck.

"Men who go to church can still harbor illicit intentions, Audie. And he said himself it was just this once."

Which means he is honest, yes? She thought better of saying that. If she defended Jack too vehemently, too soon, surely Thaddeas would realize what he meant to her.

And Jack *did* mean something to her. Even without her silly daydreams this afternoon, even knowing he still gambled. She was the one who had disillusioned herself, not he.

"You want to think the best of him," accused Thaddeas.

She leaned her cheek against Buck's. "I *do* want to think the best of him. But I know he's a gambler, he smokes tobacco, he may even drink. He is not always as . . . reserved as perhaps he ought to be. At the store, I mean," she added quickly.

"But?" asked Thad darkly. When he forked hay into Buck's stall, Audra lost her cover.

Luckily, Thad turned his back on her to put the pitchfork where it belonged. She opened the bin of ground corn and used the tin can within to scoop feed for Aunt Heddy's hens.

"But I cannot believe he would hurt me," she said, carrying the feed to the chicken yard just outside the barn.

"That's the way confidence men *work,*" Thad pointed out, following. "They gain your confidence. You might not realize his intentions until he's gone, and you're already . . . hurt."

Without thinking, she looked at him for clarification, but he looked away from her curiosity with equal determination.

She continued tossing feed, watching the chickens peck greedily at their bounty. Were she innocent, she might suggest that her brother didn't trust her. But *could* he trust her? She mustn't pretend righteous indignation if she was not in fact righteous.

Instead she said, "Well, none of this matters, because Mr. Harwood is leaving town."

"When?" demanded Thaddeas.

She frowned. "I did not think to ask into the details. Shall I pay him a call and find out?"

Thad's eyes widened—perhaps because she had never used such a tone with him before. Why she had this time, she could not imagine . . . unless it was that she was upset at Jack's departure.

She'd been clinging to an illusion about that, too.

She turned away to school her features—and to carry the tin can back to its bin. When she heard Thad behind her, she reluctantly said, "I apologize. That was rude of me."

He said nothing but—knowing him—he might well have shrugged. He drew several breaths, each as if to speak, before he saw through on that promise. "I'm sorry I upset you," he said stiffly. "I know you would rather think the best of people."

She bit her lip. *He* thought the best of *her*—thought her as innocent as when she left Wyoming.

"I told you not to worry about my reasons," he said now. "And I meant it. Don't fret about your position just now, Audie. I'll see when that fellow means to leave, get to know the townsfolk, and we'll decide later in the week, agreed?"

She didn't *want* to know when "that fellow" meant to leave. But Audra nodded, because it was expected of her.

Or perhaps her brother wanted actual words. "Audra?"

"Agreed," she said, her voice thick.

"That's a good girl," he said, and turned her around and hugged her, which was when tears threatened. She *wasn't* a good girl. She was a disobedient light-skirt who had trysts with a transient gambling man in the woods. She'd kissed him with abandon, she'd accepted a gift from him—and in church!—and now she hid that truth from a brother who only wanted the best for her. She was a horrible girl. Rather . . . woman.

And worse, she had no intention of doing anything to change.

"Audra?" Thaddeas didn't look panicked when he recognized her tears—very little panicked a Garrison man—but he surely did look uncomfortable.

"I've missed you," she said, ducking for another hug. That was, in fact, true.

But she felt deceitful for saying so, nevertheless.

Jack reckoned the brother would be by sooner or later. That it happened the very next day told him something about just how poor a showing he'd made during their initial introduction.

"Thaddeas Garrison, right?" he greeted, more cheerful this time, from behind the counter.

"John Harwood." So they knew each other's names.

"What can we do for you this fine day?"

Garrison's steady brown gaze noted the others in the store—Ned and Charlie, Ham and the widow Parks—then returned, unreadable, to Jack. "Best talk outside."

Jack's nerves went exquisitely still. Had he just been called out? For *kissing* a girl?

Just how much did big brother know . . . or think he knew?

Garrison didn't look to be wearing a gun, so Jack asked with stoic cheer, "Now why would I want to do that?"

Did the man ever blink? "Privacy."

Not that Jack expected him to say, *So I can beat you into a bloody pulp.* Still, a gamble was a gamble; some just proved more fun than others. If this concerned only him, he might refuse just to be contrary. But it likely involved Audra.

How much did he know?

Audra put great store in her reputation. Jack might not worship at the altar of respectability, even hers, but neither would he discount it. So, since he'd already anted into this round some weeks ago, he said, "Fine. We'll have a smoke."

"I don't smoke," said Audra's brother as Jack came around the counter.

Jack paused. "Not even cigars?"

No answer.

Jack shrugged and headed out. "Do you chew? We've got some chaw that Ned over there would highly recommend." As if by way of advertisement, Ned spat not too discreetly into a small spittoon he carried with him.

Garrison silently followed him out the store's front door. Jack was no fool, after all. Behind the store might offer a tad too much privacy.

The day was beautiful, if a mite nippy for these parts. Jack propped a hip on the hitching rail and proceeded to roll a smoke with steady hands. He wondered just how much danger he'd courted when he set out to woo a schoolmarm—and whether he'd endangered the schoolmarm herself. But he kept quiet. If Thaddeas Garrison wanted to talk, let *him* talk.

He did. "You'll leave my sister be."

Which didn't tell what he knew. In time-honored gambler tradition, Jack stalled for information. "Your sister."

Garrison nodded.

"Miss Garrison, the schoolteacher."

"That would be her."

Jack struck a match on his boot heel and, guarding it from the Texas wind, took a long draw. On his exhale he asked, "You think I'd have truck with a schoolmarm?"

Garrison stared at him, unimpressed.

"She's a fine woman, mind you," added Jack, and honestly. Protesting his innocence right off would hardly convince anyone.

Garrison's eyes narrowed.

"But I was of the impression that lady teachers didn't keep company with men." Jack smiled, shrugged. "Against those rules of their'n."

"You one to mind rules?" asked the brother, such an honest question that Jack felt compelled to answer with equal honesty.

"Not as a habit, no."

There you go, said Garrison's silent stare.

"But I was of the impression that your sister is," Jack added, starting to enjoy this. He allowed himself a devilish moment of eagerness. "Do you mean to tell me I'm mistaken?"

That may have been a step too far. If Garrison *had* worn a gun, he'd likely have plugged Jack right there. "My sister's got a soft heart. I don't plan on seeing anybody abuse it."

Not and survive, was his implication. "You don't think she's got a fine head as well?"

"I think she spoke more familiarly to you than she would have at home. I think she put too much store in you attending church."

"It's a small town," noted Jack, and took another drag on his smoke. "Folks speak to each other. They watch out for their safety, even their souls." Or sometimes they just watched.

"You can watch out for yourself just fine." Jack's soul, apparently, didn't merit concern.

"You don't think she can do the same?"

"I don't intend on finding out."

Jack blew more smoke toward the street. "Wouldn't that be Audra's decision?"

Garrison slapped the cigarette out of Jack's hand—had he meant it to arc into the horse trough, or was that just dumb luck? "Listen to me, you fancy-dan son of a buck," he said in a growl. "I don't know what designs you have or do not have on my sister. Could be you're just playing me for a fool, and that's fine; your good opinion isn't any concern to me. But my sister's young, and she's got as innocent a heart as I've ever seen. That's a durned sight more precious than anything you've ever won or lost in any of your faro hells, and by that I'm including women."

Odd how Jack could despise Garrison's arrogance and agree with nearly everything he said at the same time. "Watch the hands," he warned with practiced nonchalance, fisting and then flexing his fingers, just to anger the man further.

From the way Garrison's jaw twitched, Jack thought he succeeded. "You leaving town?"

"Sometime or sooner," agreed Jack noncommittally. He

could keep his cool now that the brother, losing his, had shown his hand. *I don't know what designs you have or do not have . . .* Garrison had no idea how far Jack had gone—how much he deserved that beating. His sister's image remained unsullied.

Which was as it should be. It wasn't merely an image, no matter who she kissed. Was it?

"Make it sooner," said Garrison.

"Not for you, I won't. You and your family left that little gal down here on her own months ago. As I see it, you gave up the right to deal out her life to your liking. If she wants a fellow like me to keep my distance, I assure you she can hold me off just fine all by herself."

"*If* she wants you to keep your distance?"

Jack grinned and touched his cheek where he'd felt Audra's wrath. "She packs a wallop."

How long ago had that been? Why was he still here? At the moment, he guessed it was because he'd just been told to leave.

"You made advances," accused Garrison, low and deadly.

"I offered her tobacco," clarified Jack. "Or something like that." He hadn't made the advances until much later.

Garrison opened his mouth, then shut it. The thought of that must have struck him as incongruously as it had Jack, originally. Then, recovering himself, he tried again. "Here's my piece; make of it what you will. Assuming I let her stay here—"

"*Let* her stay?" challenged Jack.

"If I ever hear tell you touched her or you scammed her or you hurt her, whether she knows it or not, you will not be safe in this country. Even if our family did not have money or connections, and we're doing fine with both, we've got loyalty you can't even dream of, and we would not stop until we saw you at the end of a rope. *Comprende?*"

Hell, if it was his sister, he'd probably feel the same way . . . except for one thing. "Now see, Thaddeas," Jack said, starting to roll another smoke. "May I call you Thaddeas?"

"No."

"That's the problem with protecting folks like your sister from every little temptation that comes along. Not saying I am one, personally," he added, spreading a hand in defense. "But it seems to me you'd save yourself a passel of grief if you knew the gal could protect herself."

"Well, I don't."

New match, different boot. "You should," muttered Jack into the windbreak of his palm, around the cigarette. "She can."

Garrison folded his arms. "Well then, that ought to satisfy the both of us, shouldn't it?"

"It should." Not that it would. Not either one of them.

"You heard my piece," said Garrison. "It stands." And he turned and strode away, somehow as in control—of himself, if not the conversation—as if he'd gotten Jack to cower.

Bastard. Now Jack had to wait *another* couple of weeks before leaving for Fort Worth.

No way would he give Audra's brother satisfaction by leaving first.

Audra loved spending the week with her brother—but she missed Jack. She wanted to talk more with him about gambling, and what drew him to it, and what she might do to help him stop. She wanted him to argue with her, to grin at her, to make her insides go shivery.

She found it so much easier to be bold around Jack than she did around Thaddeas.

For guidance, she read from *Duty and Domesticity: Being, a Gentle Handbook*, etc. It wasn't taking. Logically she agreed with almost everything the author wrote. She understood how a seemingly innocent first step off the path of right thinking could be as foolhardy as stepping off a mountain pathway onto a steep, stony slope, and that as surely as gravity, the weakness of human nature would fight her return to righteousness. But the story of a girl whose penchant for fun had led to her ugly death in a sanatarium seemed suspiciously melodramatic.

Audra had not stepped so very far off the path yet . . . had she? And, despite her affection for Jack, she did not intend to.

Not so *very* far.

Chapter Seventeen

A teacher may not ride in a carriage with any man unless he is her father or brother.

—Rules for Teachers

Sunday night's game, which Jack found at Ernest Varnes's cotton patch north of Candon, had some ways to go before it managed even a nodding acquaintance with friendly.

"Ain't never played with you." Varnes looked Jack up and down with suspicion. "How do I know you won't report us to the law?"

"Could be so I don't get locked up as an accomplice," said Jack.

"I done played with him before," assured Whitey Gilmer, the Candon blacksmith. When Whitey spoke, his voice as big as his shoulders, folks listened. "He's stand-up."

The only reason Jack had sought out this game in the first place was to distract himself. Ferris had gone out and Jack sorely needed some fun. Maybe fun could help him forget Audra Garrison's disappointment in him, Thaddeas Garrison's high-handed warnings, even the dogged awareness that he'd skipped church this morning.

He'd skipped church for nigh on twenty years, for mercy's sake!

"Sit down and shuffle the cards, Harwood," ordered Whitey. Since no one else protested, Jack shrugged off his reservations and took refuge in the familiarity of handling cards.

He was careful not to look too good at it.

Temperatures had fallen considerably over the weekend, and

the cold edged up from the dirt floor of Varnes's one-room cabin, through the soles of Jack's boots, and up his legs. Old catalog pictures papered the walls—especially advertisements for corsets and stockings, from what Jack could see by soot-stained kerosene lamps—and a small potbellied stove smoked up the place. The empty tin cans piled outside the cabin indicated that Varnes used the stove more for heat than cooking. The place stank of dogs and moonshine, sweat and urine. The table was uneven, carved up in some places and sticky in others.

This, thought Jack, remembering fine halls with mirrors and gas lighting and gay music, was what happened when people outlawed gambling. Even the back rooms, where the Sunday games had moved in big-city red-light districts, were a damn sight better than this. Most, anyhow.

"Five-card draw, jacks are wild," he said now, letting Varnes cut before starting to deal.

Beggars couldn't be choosers. Until he got himself out of this so-called civilization to someplace a little more honest, like Fort Worth or San Antonio or even Abilene, Jack reckoned he'd best make do.

Skinny, long-mustached Harv Jefferson from Euless had brought moonshine in mason jars to sell. The sour-mash liquor scalded Jack's throat and brought tears to his eyes. This was what happened when folks outlawed liquor. If Jack didn't leave the dry townships behind him soon, he'd be finding a reason to hit the laudanum the way Hamilton had.

Although the storekeeper seemed to be cutting down. Not that it was Jack's place to keep watch on him. Jack didn't owe anybody here anything, except maybe Audra herself.

"I'm out," he said, tossing in his cards and awaiting the next hand.

Audra . . . A few more hands of poker, a few more swallows of corn-mash liquor, and Jack could hardly keep his mind on the game—or his less-than-companionable cohorts—for musing on his innocent little schoolmarm. He pictured Audra's pretty sorrel hair curling around his fingers, soft as feathers, when he cradled her head. He remembered the feel of her body drawn against him, her own gloved fingers clutching for support behind his neck, and her hungry lips.

Then he remembered her eyes, showing her feeling of betrayal that he still was and would always be a gambler.

He anted up for the next round—at a nickel a game, it wouldn't break him. Had he ever said he wasn't a gambler? No. But she had to go worrying about his business. She was the kind of woman who, well intentioned or not, chased poker players into dumps like this. She looked for evil in a man's pastimes instead of in his heart. Jack had a perfectly good heart, damn it.

In fact, he had four of them so far . . . one more would make a flush.

He took another swig of moonshine, watched Varnes try unsuccessfully to spit tobacco juice at the old dog sleeping in the corner, and just didn't find it as amusing as the other fellows.

"Did any of you read in the *Register,*" he said, tossing a four of diamonds, "how that Carrie Nation woman got herself locked up in Wichita?"

"Who's Carrie Nation?" asked Varnes, discarding a perfectly good queen.

"That ax lady," said Whitey in a growl. Everything Whitey said came out in a growl.

Jefferson, who'd been rolling a cigarette, lit it and inhaled deeply. "The one what murdered her folks up in New England?"

Whitey said, "The one from Kansas. Thinks liquor's a sin."

"Got herself jailed in Wichita busting up a fine hotel saloon and can't post bond," clarified Jack. He felt some righteous satisfaction at that. If it weren't for folks like the now-famous Mrs. Nation and her Woman's Christian Temperance League, he'd be playing cards in a perfectly good bar instead of watching Varnes spit at the dog. Most bars had spittoons.

But he could too easily imagine Audra following in Mrs. Nation's footsteps, given enough time and incentive.

Varnes's moonshine must have packed more punch than he'd suspected, for Jack to make the mistake of even mentioning it. One oughtn't discuss good women in a drinking establishment—no matter how poor the establishment or how many thousands of dollars' damage the woman had done.

Hell, they hadn't even mentioned Miss Lizzie Borden's name outright, and half the country believed she ax-murdered both her folks, no matter what the jury found!

Jefferson raised his jar in a toast. "Well, here's to the law. Sometimes they get it right."

They toasted that, even Jack. The mash liquor was getting better by the swallow. Somewhere along the line, they'd finished the hand and started another.

"If you read the paper," said Whitey in his raspy voice, "you seen they brought that colored son of a bitch into Dallas."

"The man from Corsicana way?" Jack asked carefully. That fellow stood accused of outraging and killing a white woman a few weeks back, but had yet to stand trial. Since white men who committed similar crimes rarely got any press, Jack questioned the facts here.

"If the law could do something right, they'd lynch the son of a bitch."

"Folks have been trying to lynch him," Jack pointed out. "That's why he's in Dallas."

"They'll string him up soon enough," assured Jefferson.

"Why not let the man stand trial?" Jack thought the suggestion reasonable but, faced with three disbelieving glares, he decided not to pursue it.

"Damn them," muttered Whitey, though on the burly blacksmith, even a mutter carried weight. Jack didn't think he was talking about the law *or* the mobs in Dallas and Corsicana. "Thinkin' they can do whatever they want to our women . . ."

From there, talk moved to colored folks in general, and the menace of the nearby Mosier Valley coloreds in particular, and why the world was bound for hell. Seems it had something to do, Jack would later remember, with race mixing and colored folks running for office.

By then, the card playing could not have been less fun. Before dawn, Jack cashed out and left the other three commiserating about how the South would rise again.

He shouldn't have drunk so much. Luckily, Queen was a steady horse, letting Jack take as many tries as he needed to mount. She even knew her own way back to the Candon stables—a good thing. Central Texas boasted few winter days that could freeze a man dead if he fell off his horse, but this might be one of them. But even when Jack dozed briefly, in the saddle, he would jerk awake and notice that his mare headed slowly but steadily back in the right direction.

He'd been in this place too damn long.

With an eight-mile drive ahead of them just to reach the train depot, Audra and Thaddeas left for Fort Worth very early on Monday morning. As her older brother drove the rented buggy onto Main Street, turning the opposite direction from the mercantile, Audra looked back. She thought that, beyond the pool of their swinging sidelights, she saw a single lamp burning in the store window. She turned forward again and huddled closer to her brother, snug under coats and blankets, and she wondered if the lamp meant Jack was awake.

As much as she looked forward to this outing with Thad, she looked forward to telling Jack about it even more. Yes, he was still a gambler, and unrepentant. She could no longer entertain such foolish fancies as those that had warmed her Christmas morning. But he had also proven himself to be her friend.

"Try to get some sleep," suggested Thaddeas, hearing her sigh.

Audra closed her eyes and did try. But sleep came poorly in even the best of buggies; the livery rental, on a dirt road yet, bounced and jarred her too much. And they hadn't made it a mile from town when their horse whinnied into the dark morning and another horse nickered back from the shadows ahead of them.

Audra opened her eyes, glad for an excuse not to continue trying to sleep.

The rider was bundled against the cold, head down so that his hat brim protected him from the wind. Judging from the horse's size and gait, much less her blaze, the man was riding Jack's

Queen. A rancher's daughter, Audra could see that even if she couldn't yet discern bay from roan.

Jack?

As they drove closer, Audra thought the rider seemed slumped in his saddle. Apparently Thaddeas saw something, too; he pulled up on their horse's reins and called out, "Ho! Ho, there!"

The buggy horse obeyed him. Everyone, it seemed, obeyed Garrison men.

"Hello, there, friend," he called now. "Is everything well with you?"

The rider—was it Jack?—took a deep breath, like somebody waking up. Then he raised his face toward them, squinting away from the glare of their lights.

It *was* Jack! In the lamplight, he looked somehow wan, unfocused.

Thaddeas made a disgusted sound under his breath, and Audra winced inwardly on her friend's behalf. How dare her brother make a noise like that about Jack!

"Harwood," he called, trying again to get Jack's attention, though with less audible patience. "Are you going to make it home on your own?"

That cut through Audra's indignation. Was Jack hurt?

"I made it this far," drawled Jack in slow response, his Southern accent surprisingly thick. Then, even more slowly, his gaze focused on Audra, as if he'd just recognized her.

She tried to smile hello, friend to friend, but could not quite summon up the cheer. Was he sick? If he were sick somebody should make him soup, insist that he drink water and tea.

"Mr. Harwood," she greeted, careful not to call him Jack in front of Thaddeas.

He managed a delighted grin of recognition, but somehow it lacked the caliber of charm she'd grown used to. "Audra Garrison!" he greeted, too loudly. "If it ain't the schoolmarm herself. How are you this fine night . . . mornin' . . . Miss Audra Garrison?"

"Go home, Harwood," said Thaddeas, and twitched their horse's traces. The buggy lurched into motion again. And Audra realized—so come-lately that she felt foolish—what was wrong with Jack. She'd never seen it up close before, was all. Men simply did not drink in the company of ladies. Her father and brother would generally walk between the girls and any cowboy or miner celebrating payday with too much enthusiasm. On the very rare occasion that Audra and her sisters were out alone, they knew to take shelter at the nearest respectable business until such men had staggered well past.

If Jack weren't on horseback, he'd be staggering. Jack Harwood was *inebriated!*

"Wait up there," he called now as the buggy moved out. "Are you leavin'? Today?"

Audra said nothing—and not because of Thad's silent disapproval beside her. She had no idea what to say. This man did not seem like Jack at all. Instinct bade her to pretend he wasn't even there. But . . .

He would be all right. Wouldn't he?

"Farewell, my darlin' Audra," called Jack from behind them. In the distance a dog started to bark. She wanted to pull the carriage blanket up over her head from embarrassment for him—and herself. "Don't go choppin' up any saloons, darlin'! Folks arrest you for that."

Thaddeas made a growling noise deep in his chest.

"Please just drive," she said, sounding meek even to her own ears.

"I am," Thaddeas assured her evenly—and to her wary relief, Jack neither followed the carriage nor called anything else after them.

Audra hunched miserably under her blankets and waited for Thad to say something. Finally, when she could stand it no longer, she had to ask, "He was drunk, wasn't he?"

Because if he wasn't drunk, then something was terribly wrong with him, and they had to go back and make sure he wasn't hurt.

But Thad said, "Yup."

"Are you certain he wasn't ill?"

"Yup."

He'd been drinking on a Sunday night. That demon liquor could change someone so fine as Jack certainly corroborated the stories she'd heard about its evils, didn't it?

"He seemed so . . . pathetic," she whispered. That, perhaps, was the worst of it. She knew Jack broke rules, but thus far he'd always done so with a flair that she found, well . . . dashing. Inebriated, Jack Harwood wasn't dashing at all. She resented the loss of that romantic image.

Thaddeas just said, "Plenty of men do."

"Then why do they do it?" Was even a warm, easy feeling around one's heart worth that debasement? Then again, she'd been willing to kiss Jack in the woods because of how warm and easy he made her feel, despite dire consequences should she be caught.

"I guess some folks'll risk a whole lot of tomorrow for a little fun today," Thad suggested finally, shrugging a shoulder.

If only his words did not apply so aptly to her own recent behavior!

By the time they reached Grapevine and boarded the St. Louis Southwestern, the sun had risen, streaking the cold sky with a fan of pink and yellow and then resolving into a clear, bright blue day. The ride to Fort Worth was relatively brief. From the beautiful new Santa Fe depot, she and Thaddeas had to walk several blocks, to Main Street, to catch a streetcar.

"I first saw Fort Worth when I was ten years old," Thad said, guiding her with one hand and carrying their satchel with the other. "With Uncle Matthew, his wife Minna, and Aunt Heddy. Can you guess why?"

Disoriented by the city around them, Audra shook her head. Buildings as tall as three stories loomed on either side of the road. Wires for telegraph, telephone, electricity, and even the trolleys swooped overhead, from pole to pole. Carriages drove so fearfully near the trolleys that, had the streetcars not been slimmer on the bottom than on top, allowing room for buggy wheels, they surely would have collided. Two people even darted in and out of traffic on bicycles. Main Street went on for as far as Audra could see, its buildings seeming to get even taller in the distance despite what she knew of perspective.

"We first came to Fort Worth," Thad said, "because Pa was leaving for Wyoming. For good."

The distraction of that, Audra could appreciate. "To start the ranch?"

"To start the ranch," Thad agreed. A streetcar slowed, its brakes screeching on its rails, as they reached the intersection, and they ran to catch it. Thad helped Audra in first, then hopped on himself as the car jerked into motion. A gentleman stood to make room on the wooden seat for Audra, which she took with thanks. Thad stood protectively beside her.

"It was 1878 . . . March, I think," Thad said, hanging on through the lurch and sway.

"When he met Mother!" Her parents rarely spoke of how they'd met, courted, and married somewhere along the route of a cattle drive, so her sisters often wondered about it.

"You would have to ask them," said Thad, as cryptic as their parents.

A stout matron seated across from her was listening in on Thad's story, but when Audra noticed, she looked pointedly away—as if she could not hear just as well, even so.

"I wanted so badly to go on the drive with him," Thad continued. "But it was too dangerous. He said he'd send for me the next summer. Since he'd never been gone so long before, Aunt Heddy decided I should see him off." He smiled at the memory. "I think she feared he would be scalped by Indians, like General Custer. It was tremendous, Audra! The cowboys drove the entire herd in from the prairie, across the railroad tracks, and up Rusk Street, right over there—two thousand head! Not white-faces, either; they were all tall Texas longhorns. I'd never seen so many cattle. They just kept coming, bellowing like they do, their horns clacking and their hooves churning dust; I could feel the heat off of them. And when they got to the north side of town they went right down over the bluff, swam the Trinity, and bedded on the other side. And there was Pa, bossing the whole outfit like he was born to it."

Audra took Thad's free hand and squeezed it, grateful for the shared memory. She wasn't simply a transplanted northern girl. She had Texas roots—right here.

Loud laughter off the street snatched her thoughts from the heroic image of her father riding into the wild frontier. A trio of men stood, smoking cigars, on the uneven wooden sidewalk outside a place labeled the Cowboy Saloon. The one who'd laughed sounded somehow loud and unsure—like Jack had this morning. Then he cursed, and his friends laughed again.

"Disgusting," muttered the woman sitting across from her.

Now that Audra took notice, as the streetcar carried them farther from the depot, the neighborhood worsened instead of improved. They passed three more saloons and Holland's Free Show Pavilion—a theater, apparently, but hardly a respectable one. Rooming houses boarded the kind of renters who hung their laundry out the windows to dry—even unmentionables! Audra saw more than one pool hall, and a building marked BAR. A cowboy lay unconscious on the sidewalk in front of that one. At least, Audra hoped he was unconscious.

She'd seen saloons before, but never so closely grouped. In fact, she counted more dens of sin here, in one block, than there were buildings on Candon's Main Street. "Where are we?"

The lady across from her said, "This is the Third Ward, dear. You just cover your ears and we'll be through soon."

Thad leaned closer. "That's what Aunt Heddy said when we rode through here. Try not to notice."

"I don't understand." The sight of a man in a familiarly cut frock coat, exiting a saloon and wincing from the sunlight, would not let her close her eyes or cover her ears. That is not Jack, she told herself. But he dressed very similarly, down to the brocade vest and watch chain.

He stepped over the unconscious cowboy without even seeming to notice.

"I understand that we're in Fort Worth—and Third Ward. But . . . what *is* this place?"

"It's called the Acre, Audra," said Thaddeas, watching her reaction with increasing interest. "Hell's Half-Acre. This is probably where your gambler friend stays when he's in town."

Chapter Eighteen

Teachers will avoid indecent, immoral, or offensive places of entertainment.

—Rules for Teachers

It wasn't patience that kept Audra silent until she and Thaddeas reached the Delaware Hotel, past the ugly district he'd called "the Acre." What silenced her was something she'd rarely felt toward her brother—anger.

The gentle elegance of her second-story room, with its walnut furniture and Brussels carpeting, disoriented her after that place. Was this even the same city?

And would Jack really stay there instead of, for example, here? How would Thad know?

While she stood silently, Thad inspected her room, even the window to make sure her view overlooked nothing improper. "Best freshen up before lunch. I'm right next door. If you need anything, knock." He even knocked on the richly papered wall once, lest she might not otherwise grasp the idea. "I've got your key, so I can be here in a blink. Nobody else can get in."

He'd bent to kiss her cheek before she realized he saw nothing different about her. She'd stewed in silent resentment for over eight blocks, and he had not even noticed!

Only when she asked, "Did you do that on purpose?" did Thaddeas blink in surprise.

"Do what? Can't I kiss my own sister?"

"Did you bring me through that place on purpose?"

He glanced at the door, as if picturing the hallway or the lobby downstairs. "What place?"

Would she have to say it? "The . . . Third Ward."

His gaze sharpened with indignation. "The Acre?"

She nodded, her own anger flickering into uncertainty at his surprise.

"For pity's sake, Audra; why would I do something like that?"

"So that I should think badly about Jack Harwood."

"He doesn't do a good enough job of that on his own?" And, in fact, Jack had hardly endeared himself to her this morning. So why did she feel so defensive of him?

Thad's speculative expression—his "lawyer look," the family called it—made her uneasy.

"I disliked that place," she tried to explain, to shift his focus off of Jack.

"You aren't supposed to like it. Decent folks don't—especially with it sitting smack between the depot and the business district." Thad cocked his head. "In fact, I'd say anyone who did like the goings-on in the Acre must be running lean on decency, himself. Wouldn't you?"

"I wouldn't know," Audra parried. "What kinds of goings-on are we discussing, exactly?"

Thad's eyes flared in a moment of distress—some things a man just did not discuss with his sisters! "Goings-on that a lady of your age ought not know about, that's what."

Jack would have told her, she thought pettily, though that might not recommend him. "Then how could I possibly be familiar with people who *do* know about them?"

"I hope you aren't!"

"Well, I'm not." But she could not lie flat-out to her brother, not even when she looked away from his probing gaze. "Except for Mr. Harwood, of course."

"Oh?" Thad sounded somewhat more dangerous than usual.

"And I don't even know if he's someone who would enjoy a place like that."

"After this morning? Believe me. He is."

She had the grace to flush. "I've never seen him that way before."

"You've never seen him late at night before—" At Thaddeas's abrupt silence, Audra had to face him again, to guess what he was thinking. She wished she hadn't. His bright-eyed horror reflected too much of the disappointment she'd feared for months, though cloaked in uncertainty.

"Have you?" Thad demanded—and his voice cracked.

"Of *course* I haven't! How could you think—why, even if he weren't . . ." Weren't what? A gambler? A scoundrel? That had not stopped her from equally scandalous daytime meetings. Confused, she went to the window so that she could look at something other than Thad's concern—and so that, perhaps, he would not see her own guilt. "That's a terrible thing to think."

But was it, if not true, accurate? Her breath misted on the cold glass. Though she'd measured her words, it felt painfully like lying.

"I know," said Thad, after a long moment.

"I do *not* meet with men late at night." Though it *had* been dark when she'd first kissed Jack, in Aunt Heddy's lamp-lit kitchen. . . .

If only to reassure herself, she repeated, "I don't."

"I know," repeated Thaddeas more gently, crossing to her side and putting a hand on her shoulder. She saw his face reflected in the glass above her own. They wore similar expressions of guarded confusion. "I'm sorry, Audie. That man concerns me, is all. I didn't trust him around you *before* this morning. And after everything you went through back home, with Connors . . ."

Oddly, she had not thought of Peter Connors for weeks.

"It upset me, too," she confessed. "This morning, I mean. And then that ugly place . . ."

Thaddeas squeezed her shoulder. "It's been a long morning, Audra. Rest, and then we'll see what the better half of this city has to offer, agreed?"

She nodded, and when he bent to her she kissed his cheek. She did love him.

But when he locked the door upon leaving—to protect her safety, of course; not to limit her freedom—her eyes widened in a fresh flare of uncharacteristic anger.

As consciousness slowly returned, Jack felt sure of only one thing in the world: waking up was a bad idea. Rank unpleasantness lurked somewhere just beyond the blissfully numbed edges of his mind. Even without naming the memory, he knew to avoid it.

But life didn't work that way. His storekeeper friend looked in on him somewhere around dawn. "You sick or something?"

Jack said, "I will pay you cash money to leave me alone."

"I'll take credit," said the voice. "Ten dollars an hour."

Even if his eyes were open, Jack would not have blinked at the atrocious sum. Waking up threatened to hurt badly enough that he'd promise nearly anything to postpone it. "Deal."

The door shut like a soft dynamite blast. Jack sank gratefully back into the senselessness.

Almost immediately, it seemed, the door reopened. A determined streak of sunlight stabbed through it, across his closed eyes. When Jack rolled away his head tried to fall off.

He propped it against the crook of his elbow. "I thought," he muttered through clenched teeth, "that I ponied-up an X-note to keep you out."

"You owe me *three* X-notes so far, but I had to see if we have any more blue yarn for Miz Fuller." The room where Jack slept, behind the main storeroom, held overstock. Ferris proceeded to ferret through it with loud rustling and dragging noises—including that inescapable thud of his crutch. The noise ricocheted through Jack's head, all but drawing blood with every echo. "I'm surprised, Harwood. I thought you could hold your liquor."

Damn consciousness anyway. Now he'd remembered not only that this was Ferris, but that he was Harwood. The unpleasantness—something even worse than the cadence in his head, and the miserably increasing awareness of the rest of his body—couldn't be far behind. "So did I."

"What happened?"

When in doubt, smile. Jack did try. Somehow just the stretching of his lips made his stomach swoop unsteadily. "I believe I must've fallen in with bad companions."

Hamilton snorted. "Likewise, I'm sure."

Jack didn't have the strength to lift a choice finger in response. After what had to be a thoroughly amusing search on Ham's part, he lame-elephant-stomped from the room again.

Jack dragged his blanket more tightly over him—damn, but it was cold!—and tried to burrow back into the safe nothingness of sleep before he fully remembered.

Too late.

Three gambling companions ranting about the dangerous proximity of Mosier Valley.

The sour taste of mash liquor.

Audra in a buggy, lowering her eyes to avoid looking at him.

He'd dreamed the part with Audra, right? He often dreamed about her, here on his pallet in the back room . . . though usually his dreams offered happier encounters than the one that now spun through his memory. He lay very still, simultaneously hot and cold, boneless and yet stiffening with dismay, as if he could possibly resist what was already done. He caught quick breaths, desperate not to be ill, no matter how his throat stiffened and his stomach clenched.

Oh, Lordy.

Jack opened his eyes—and sleep *was* better. He felt cold, frozen bone-deep, but flushed hot and clammy, too, as if his skin and his innards were wrestling with each other. His throat ached with the effort of keeping control. Worse than bodily discomfort, though, was his growing certainty that he hadn't dreamed the meeting on the dark road.

His quick, shallow breaths fought something disgusting inside him, something that might spill out at any moment. As it had this morning when he'd dared accost Audra, drunk?

Desperation bred strength and speed both; Jack found his feet and lunged unevenly for the back door, making it into the cold, dead grass of the wash yard behind the store just in time to lose his battle against Harv Jefferson's homemade liquor.

After, momentarily eased of the nausea, alternately spitting bile from his mouth and gulping bitter-cold air, he too easily imagined the picture he made: a hungover gambler in stinking long johns, sweating despite a record cold snap, on his hands and knees over a pool of his own vomit.

No wonder Audra was gone.

She hadn't even said good-bye?

Jack sat slowly back on his haunches, lost his balance, and fell on his butt, trembling. He wiped at his blurry, burning eyes with the back of his hand. God, but he was pathetic.

She'd seen him drunk. Her. A lady.

He didn't deserve a good-bye. But somehow, like a child believing in Father Christmas, he would have thought Audra would offer one whether he deserved it or not.

Not that he'd ever believed in Father Christmas. He'd just always wanted to.

Cold seeped up from the ground, into his shins and his hips, into his chest. He should get inside. Somehow, struggling not to think at all, he regained his feet and staggered back inside.

Only once the door closed behind him, and the warm air of the store lapped at his tingling face, did Jack realize just how cold he'd been.

It served him right.

He stood for a long while, propped against the door and trying not to think—or breathe—lest he have to lunge outside again. The stockroom crept in circles around him, despite his standing still, until finally, faintly, he heard Ham saying, "Thank you; come again." Then the storekeeper hobbled through the door from the stockroom and stopped, leaning on his crutch, to look Jack up and down.

"Damn," he said.

This time Jack found the strength for the rude gesture. He needed only one hand to hold on to the door, after all.

"How bad did you lose, anyway?" Ham narrowed his eyes. "That store credit wasn't transferable, so if you passed on my IOU—"

"She's gone," said Jack. The almost inaudible words made it bleakly real.

"What?" Ferris leaned closer, then recoiled from Jack's breath.

"She's gone. I saw her leaving."

"What?" Quickly, Ferris rearranged his features. "Saw who leaving?"

"Who the hell do you think?" His head tried to fall off again, but he hardly cared. Beautiful, innocent, captive Audra. And hadn't he done a dandy job showing why she should spread her wings some and live a little? Hell, he couldn't even stand up straight.

"The schoolmarm?" asked Ham cautiously.

"No, the widow Parks. Of course, the schoolmarm! And . . ." Tarnation, but he felt wobbly. "And there I was, booze-blind, making some show of myself. Thank God her brother was with her."

Ham leaned on his crutch, intrigued. "You wouldn't find things easier unchaperoned?"

Jack had never been a violent drunk, but even cheerful, he could easily have gotten "handier" with Audra than she deserved or would appreciate. He might not like the brother, but damned if the fellow hadn't come in useful. "I'd find things easier with her here."

Hamilton snorted, sympathetic as a stump. "You can't go two days without her?"

"Two days?" echoed Jack stupidly, angrily. Audra was *gone.*

"Two days. Her brother took her to Fort Worth to celebrate the New Year."

Jack opened his mouth, then closed it. He inhaled deeply, recoiled at his own breath, and tried again. "Fort Worth?"

"Big place west of here. County seat. Queen of the cow towns. That Fort Worth."

Jack said, "Two days?" Then he couldn't stand the idiocy of

not adding something of his own, no matter the brutal pain of each word. "What makes you figure that?"

"Been tending store all morning—you remember what that's like, right? One customer mentions hearing a buggy go by before sunup, someone else says they've been talking to the widow Cribb, next thing you know, the storekeeper has the entire story." Damned if Ferris wasn't enjoying this; his normally sullen eyes shone. "You thought she was gone for good, huh?"

Two days? Caught between relief and mortification, Jack said nothing. Besides, the world had started to swoop again.

Ham chuckled. "Who would've thought? A schoolmarm's got you tied to a snorting post!"

Even hungover, Jack dismissed the very idea. Maybe Audra Garrison had cherished some fantastic hope of lady-breaking him; more likely she worried about his immortal soul. Even her kind eyes must see she could hitch up to better for the long haul.

Especially after this morning.

All he'd wanted from her was . . . well, more than a lady like her could or should give. But all he'd ever truly *hoped* for was to see her spread her wings a mite; to have the privilege of helping her do it; and maybe, with charm and a little luck, to leave her with memories of him that might be as fond as his memories of her.

He'd probably blown his chances at most of those hopes. But she would be back. That gave him the opportunity to at least apologize, maybe undo the worst of the damage.

Jack looked down at his sorry self and felt ill again—and not simply because of the hangover. "Where's the closest place I can get a full bath and barber shave, maybe new clothes?"

"Bedford, maybe six miles from here, on the main road. Think you can ride?"

"No." He held on to the door behind him, tightly. "But I will be within two days."

"I've got rye whiskey upstairs, if you need some hair of the dog that bit you."

Jack's head pounded like hooves at a horse race, and he was

rapidly starting to feel like the track. One, maybe two shots would go a long way toward burning off the sickness. But he remembered—blearily—Audra looking away from him, embarrassed.

"Much obliged, but no." He spoke carefully, so as not to further annoy his stomach.

Second chances didn't come around often enough for him to chance this one.

When Thad knocked at her door for lunch, Audra took a deep breath for courage and said, "I would like to carry my own room key, please."

Thad blinked at her, surprised, but gave the key easily enough. "If you want."

After that, in moments when she began to worry about either her behavior in the past or the choices in her future, Audra noted the extra weight in her reticule, and it encouraged her. After a lovely restaurant lunch, she and Thaddeas strolled Main Street toward the fine new Tarrant County courthouse, built on a bluff overlooking the Trinity. She ventured to establish her independence even further. "I have decided to stay in Texas, Thad."

"You have?" he challenged carefully, not wavering in his comfortable pace.

"It's not that I don't want to go home," she assured him. "I miss everyone terribly! But I have a position here. How can I abandon my responsibility to those children?"

"You can abandon them if Pa tells you to," Thad pointed out. She was not twenty-one.

"Have you ever left a job halfway?" she asked. "Has Papa, even when he was going against Indians and bandits? I'm his daughter."

"That's different," Thad noted. "Ladies face different dangers than men."

"You would finish the job," she pointed out. "You would stay."

Thad snorted. "A drunken gambler would hardly pose any risk to me."

Why did it so annoy her to hear Jack referred to in that way?

He *was* a drunken gambler! Still, she frowned. "And Mr. Harwood is your main concern?"

"He is." Thaddeas looked both ways, then steered her steadily but unexpectedly across the bustling, brick-paved street. She peeked past him and saw his reason. They were passing the White Elephant Saloon and Restaurant. Through the window it looked rather elegant, complete with cut-glass chandeliers, and the clientele dressed respectably.

"Audra!" chided Thad, low. She stopped staring, but with effort. Apparently uptown saloons were better than others—perhaps in the same way moderate drinkers were better than habitual drunks. Not a month ago, Jack had freely admitted that he drank only "now and again."

"I am certain," she said now, carefully, "that no matter his faults, Mr. Harwood would not force himself upon unwilling women. I believe him to be a man of . . ." The memory of Jack's self-description quietly amused her, even after this morning. "Of at least middling character."

"Audra, you have not seen enough of the world to understand just how ugly drinkers and gamblers can . . ." Thaddeas paused in front of an establishment called the Theatre Comique, then steered her around the corner. "Let's go this way."

"Why?" This time, when she craned around him, she saw signs for the Bismark and the El Paso saloons on what would have been their side of the street. On the White Elephant side stood an establishment calling itself the Club Room Saloon and Ten Pin Alley. No prone forms marred the neatly swept wooden sidewalks. Several of the buggies hitched in front of them rivaled those of Cheyenne or Denver.

"My goodness," she murmured, following Thad's urging onto a quieter side street. "Uptown Fort Worth certainly provides interesting entertainments, doesn't it?"

"They are *not* entertainments," said Thaddeas in a growl. "They are saloons."

She couldn't resist asking, "Do they have gambling?"

"Open-door gambling is illegal here," Thad reminded her stiffly. "It's illegal in all respectable cities." Which would have settled it, except that something about the way he averted his eyes when he said that caught her suspicions. She did not like suspecting Thaddeas, but . . .

"Is there something you aren't telling me?"

"Nothing you need to know."

But she had the key to her own room. And, she realized with fledgling teacherly instincts, her beloved older brother had not in fact answered her question.

She stopped right there on the afternoon sidewalk, so that Thaddeas had to stop, too, and she phrased the question as she might for Jerome Newton. "Yes or no. Do they have gambling?"

Thad scowled at her, but she did not look away. Amazingly, he broke first. "Yes, Audra. Yes! The White Elephant is infamous for its gambling. As long as they're discreet, the law looks the other way."

"Oh." She felt incredible relief that not only might Jack *not* be a drunkard but, if he must gamble, perhaps he did so in establishments like these. And yet . . .

"You wanted me to think it was all horrid and ugly like the Acre, didn't you?" And that, through association, Jack was ugly, too. "You wanted to frighten me home. How dare you!"

Thaddeas continued to scowl. He turned away and asked the cold afternoon sky, "Why did this have to happen on *my* watch?"

"Why did *what* have to happen?"

"You." He turned on her again, gestured toward the bustling street. "These . . . questions!"

She waited for more, but he appeared to have given up. So she made her own painful commentary. "I never would have believed you, of all people, would lie to me."

He took off his hat, ran a hand through his hair, then planted it back on before speaking with careful calm. "I did not lie, Audra. I simply neglected to tell you the whole truth."

And he was not the only person in this family to do that, of late. If he'd known how Jack Harwood had kissed her, much less how eagerly she had kissed Jack Harwood back . . .

She had the grace to look down.

"I am not trying to frighten you," he added. "But it concerns me that, having met a gambler outside of his normal surroundings, you may get false impressions about him and his world. Vice is horrid and ugly, and it supports a horrid, ugly world. That you would even question that makes me even more certain you should come home."

"I do not mean to defend vice," she said quietly. "I am merely trying to understand how you could insist I leave a job half-finished, merely because of a gentleman—"

Thad rolled his eyes but she did not take it back. Jack *was* gentle and very much a man.

"A *gentleman,*" she repeated with desperate control, "whom you barely know, and who in any case means to leave town. Simply because he gambles."

Thad sighed deeply. "We'd better return to the hotel."

"I would like to resolve this."

He closed his eyes, then opened them, nodding. But he took off his scarf—it matched hers, both knitted by a family friend—and draped it around her neck. "We'll walk slowly."

When he offered his coated arm, she took it.

"First," he said, "I don't trust Harwood to leave Candon anytime soon, and neither should you; he's got a comfortable situation there. Second, even if he wouldn't force himself on an unwilling lady, it's not *force* that worries me from his kind."

She tried not to wonder about willing ladies. "His kind?"

"Con men don't use force; they use deception and illusions. They make their prey want what they offer, whether it's papers for a nonexistent gold claim or a chance to win easy money in a game of three-card monte." He eyed her darkly. "Or something even more dangerous for women. By the time their victims realize it's humbug, they're too late."

She wished he did not sound quite so certain—nor quite so sad. As if, as a lawyer, he'd seen that very thing more often than she could imagine. She also wished it did not sound so much like that steep slope off the path of righteousness her book had spoken of.

She said, "But Mr. Harwood has been honest about what he does." Once she'd found him out, anyway. "If he hid his gambling, like people at the"—for the first time, she spoke the name of a saloon—"at the White Elephant do, he could help at the mercantile without suspicion. Isn't pretend respectability just as bad as open sin?"

Thaddeas countered, "You think its better to flaunt one's bad behavior, to imply that there's truly nothing wrong with it?"

"*Is* it really so wrong? Things like gambling, even drinking? In moderation, I mean!" Couldn't one take just a step down the stony slope and still find her way back to the right path?

The longer Thad stared at her, the more she regretted asking him that, no matter how the question haunted her lately. Thaddeas was not Jack, hadn't Jack's easygoing ways or his objectivity. Finally he said, "You're determined to stay in Texas when I leave."

She nodded, but warily. He wore his serious-news face, and that meant trouble.

"I'll allow you to do that on one condition," he decided.

"*Allow* me?"

He narrowed his eyes and confirmed, "*Allow* you."

Since he could legally force her onto any train he chose, she asked, "What condition?"

"That you let me take you back into Hell's Half-Acre."

"What!" Audra stared at her brother, disbelieving, and heard a popping sound from the south. It could be fireworks, celebrants starting the new year—new century!—early. But it might be gunfire. "Thaddeas Garrison! That's not a proper place for me, and you know it!"

"I thought you were allowing for moderate impropriety," he challenged. "You take a look at the virtues of honest sin. See what happens when people make excuses about moderation. Then at least folks like Harwood won't be able to delude you."

Unable to think of a strong enough argument on her own, she invoked her oldest and best protection. "I don't think Papa would like this idea."

"I *know* he wouldn't, but he's not here."

"Couldn't I see some gambling in one of the nicer saloons?" she almost pleaded.

"With the hypocrites? They wouldn't let you in. At least in the Acre, we can probably find some kind of mission or settlement house, some decent women to talk to." They both knew that such charities were the realm of older matrons, not impressionable young ladies.

He was, she thought, daring her. Bluffing! Surely he wasn't serious when he said, "It's Hell's Half-Acre, Audra, or Wyoming. You choose."

And she must not choose Wyoming. "You won't let anything happen to us?" she hedged.

He winced at her choice, but his resolve did not waver. "I will never let anything happen to you if I can help it. That's why we're doing this."

He was not bluffing. Neither would she. So Audra tucked her arm back under his.

"We're going by the hotel first," Thaddeas told her, starting to walk again.

"Why?"

"To ask about missions and to get my gun."

"I thought Fort Worth had an ordinance against carrying firearms," she noted, nervous.

And Thaddeas said, "It does."

Chapter Nineteen

Make your pens carefully. You may whittle the nibs to the individual tastes of the pupils.

—Rules for Teachers

Jack's hopes to raise his image in Audra's eyes—at least back up from slobbering inebriate to charming-but-dissolute scoundrel—hit a powerful snag. She didn't come back by the store.

Rumor held that she and her brother had returned safely from Fort Worth on Tuesday, but he didn't see her. Of course, her self-appointed guardian was probably keeping close watch. By the end of the week, Thaddeas Garrison and his German grandmother had left town, and Jack figured Audra would find some marketing to do. But she still did not appear.

Melissa Smith, returned to the teacherage for the new school term, came by the mercantile on Saturday.

"What can I get for you this fine afternoon?" asked Jack, hoping the blonde at least brought news. "Walnuts? Beets? Shoe polish?"

But she ignored his teasing, simply requesting tooth powder, and when she left—looking uncommonly guilty—he found the pen. Melissa had secreted it onto the counter while his back was turned. He recognized the wooden box with a sense of foreboding.

Inside its velvet-lined interior, along with the fountain pen he'd so enjoyed giving Audra for Christmas, nestled a note addressed simply to"Mr. Harwood." It began with an even less encouraging "Dear Sir."

Jack didn't have to read more to know what was up. He slammed the pen, box and all, onto the counter. "Well, damn it to hell!"

"Hey!" protested Ham, looking from Jack to the glass counter and back. Luckily for business, no ladies were shopping at that moment, though Mr. Trigg hardly looked amused.

Jack ignored Ham and everything else, took the note into the back room, and dropped onto his pallet to stare at her careful handwriting. *Mr. Harwood.* The name looked downright respectable the way she wrote it, but he knew better.

The delicate leaf of stationery smelled faintly of peaches, like she did.

Finally, he mustered the grit to actually read the damned thing.

Dear Sir, Audra had written. *You were kind to give me this lovely pen. However, I cannot accept it. Please forgive my hav-*

ing done so even temporarily. You must be aware that our respective positions forbid all but the sparest of interaction. In the future, I believe a stricter adherence to such expectations is best. In hopes that you have as good a heart as you always indicated, I thank you for respecting my wishes in this. Sincerely, Miss Audra Susan Garrison.

Jack read it again, but it said the same thing—every ten-cent word of it. *Tarnation.* One would think the author of such a letter not only wore a corset, but laced it so tight it squeezed all her spirit right out of her.

Still, he could not pretend Audra hadn't written it. He recognized her handwriting from the dozens of letters she'd mailed to Wyoming. And he recognized her use of whatever rules she could get her sweet little hands around to shield herself from the truth.

Their respective positions, was it?

Jack crumpled the letter in one hand. To hell with Audra Garrison and all other so-called ladies like her. If she truly wanted to sit in judgment, why stop her? She could just become a sour-faced old battle-ax like her aunt!

Then, ruefully, he smoothed the letter back out and looked at it again. *Was* she sitting in judgment? She called him kind, said he had a good heart, and did not—in writing, at least—blame him for anything from the "improper" gift to the kisses to his inebriation in her presence. Could be the schoolmarm wasn't even taking time to judge. Could be she was just running.

As usual, though, he couldn't figure whether she was running from him or from herself.

The only person who might be able to tell him that would be Audra. In a town as small as Candon, surely she'd return to the store within a week or two. Once the impact of whatever had spooked her eased up, anyhow. He would make his apologies. She, decent gal that she was, would accept them. Surely, despite their "respective positions" and his previous mistakes, she would at the very least start conversing with him again! And then . . .

He reckoned he'd settle things with Audra first, then worry about what came next. In the meantime, he carefully refolded the letter along its original lines and tucked it in his saddlebags.

Of all she'd given him, this was the first thing Jack could carry with him when he left.

Audra turned seventeen the first week in January, but ever since her visit to the charitable settlement houses in Fort Worth's "Acre," she felt far older. Maturity felt not a little like guilt. Now that she'd seen how ugly the world could be, she regretted both the innocence that had kept her blind and, selfishly, the loss of that innocence.

Since her return from Fort Worth, she could hardly look at girls like Claudine, or Melissa, or even a reflection of herself, without remembering the residents at the Women's Industrial Home for single and fallen women. She'd seen a silent fourteen-year-old, heavy with a fatherless child, and learned that the age of consent in Texas had recently been raised to twelve. She'd heard the ravings of a haggard, nineteen-year-old "soiled dove" whom the ladies at the home took in after a suicide attempt and learned that most deaths in the Acre were not from shootings or violence but suicides—usually those of "working women."

At first Audra resisted faulting gambling or drinking for such tragedy. But even she could not miss the blame of poverty, nor how gambling and drinking complicated that. Feeling helpless, she stepped in to help change soiled sheets and cook a warm meal before Thaddeas could make her leave. He had not approved. He'd only meant her to glimpse the consequences of vice, then return to her upright, untainted life. But Audra could never fully return.

She'd held a puny, wailing infant who'd recently been left on the home's front steps, naked and still bloody from its birth. How easily could her scandal with Peter Connors, in less civilized society, have turned tragic for her? She wondered if any of the women bearing fatherless children had *not* trusted their men—would they have taken such risks with their lives if they hadn't? And she had felt derelict for never questioning the charmed life she'd thus far led.

Her insistence on helping kept them at the home past nightfall, and the walk out of Hell's Half-Acre, in full celebration for New Year's Eve, became the most frightening experience of Audra's life. The streets reeked of steaming horse manure, of urine and vomit laced with whiskey. Smoky smells stained the cold air—tobacco, kerosene, coal, and even, once, something sickly sweet from an unpainted business with Oriental men guarding the door. Colored men spilled out of places like the Bucket of Blood and the Black Elephant. Even the white men seemed alien, their noise pouring from the many saloons whose open windows testified to the heat of pressing bodies. Audra had recognized a cacophony of warring sounds as piano music, the clink of glass against glass, drunken laughter, angry shouts, and a strange but steady undercurrent of what turned out to be gambling. She'd heard the whirring noise of a wheel of fortune, the rattle of wooden game pieces, and the occasional cry of "Keno!" And she saw men who wore the same finery as Jack Harwood's, men who smiled charmingly even as they relieved their companions of money.

Hell's Half-Acre was almost three acres wide—but she couldn't deny its similarity to hell.

True to his word, Thaddeas kept her safe, but even the elegance of the Delaware Hotel seemed tainted after that. Her brother recognized his error, apologizing so desperately that Audra went dancing with him, per their original plan, simply to reassure him. But she came home from Fort Worth determined to find a way to make her own amends.

She wrote the Women's Christian Temperance Union asking for suggestions. She spoke to Mrs. Collins about forming a Candon Ladies' Aid. She finished reading *Duty and Domesticity,* then packed it with Thaddeas's baggage for him to carry home to their sister Kitty.

Perhaps if Audra had read it but a few years earlier, she would never have joined Mr. Harwood in wandering off the path of righteousness herself. Now that she saw the true dangers of compromising one's behavior, she knew she must not allow him—or herself!—such liberties again. She felt some guilt about that, too. As the lady, she bore the responsibility for setting the moral tone for their acquaintance, and she had failed miserably. She feared she could too easily fail again, were she to see him on a friendly basis.

Considering her weaknesses where Jack was concerned, that meant not seeing him at all.

She hoped he could understand.

Jack did not understand. By the end of the second week, he was in no mood to deal with Ernest Varnes's continued paranoia about the close proximity of Mosier Valley to "our own innocent daughters." Yes, rumor had it that a six-year-old girl in New Orleans had been attacked by a negro. But New Orleans was in another state.

"And not a one of us in this room even *has* daughters," Jack pointed out on Saturday, disgusted by their continued bigotry, as he showed Ernest yet another revolver from the firearms case. He would have preferred to shed his role of storekeeper right about here—putting Ernest Varnes and a new sidearm together felt lower than dealing marked cards, and nearly as dangerous. But Ferris hated Varnes even more than he did, so Jack waited on Varnes, Ferris waited on folks like the widow Parks when needed, and they all got along. More or less.

It wasn't like any man in Texas didn't already possess a shooting iron or two.

"With the exception of Charlie and Ned, over there," Jack thought to add, raising his voice. Charlie looked up, curious, but Ned just continued to stare at the checkerboard. "And their gals have daughters themselves," he added to Varnes.

He wondered at what point he'd gotten so familiar with the lineage of Candon families.

"Damn foolish, if you ask me," said Varnes darkly, spinning the barrel of this latest revolver, then sighting down it by pointing it across the room.

Jack gently nudged both arm and weapon, unloaded or not,

away from the direction of Hamilton and the glassware and toward the back room.

"I know *I* wouldn't do the disservice of bringin' a little girl into this world, just to fall victim to some colored," their customer added.

Ham set a box onto a shelf a little more forcefully than necessary. Noticing, Jack made an attempt to lighten the tension in the room. "Well, Ernest, I do not know how you manage to fight all them willing women off."

Varnes did not get the joke. "I don't know what they think they're doing, living so close to decent folks like us. If you ask me—"

Hamilton apparently lost his battle for self-control. "But nobody *is* asking you, Varnes, 'cause you're ignorant. Those Mosier Valley folks live near the rest of us because their people were brought here as slaves by the white folks who settled this area, that's why. They worked on the Mosier and the Lee plantations off Hurst way. After the war, they were given some of the land as gifts for their loyalty, and they bought more of it, and they settled in to work it, same as anyone else does. They didn't ask us to build a town this close to them, but we did, and they haven't done a damned thing to us since."

"They ain't been here longer'n us!" protested Varnes. "Just look at some of them graves of your own people, next time you ride by the cemetery."

Something about the way he said that made the hair at the back of Jack's neck prickle.

Ferris didn't seem to notice, though. "And we haven't been here longer than them, either. Why not just leave them be?"

Varnes set the revolver on the counter and muttered, "Now ain't *that* a fine question?"

Jack said, "What?"

Varnes just shook his head. "I reckon I'll be doing my business up Euless way, from here on out." Hallelujah, thought Jack—but Varnes hadn't left yet. "We missed you last Sunday, Harwood. You oughtta come by this week. I'm thinkin' we'll have *real* good fun."

Which only reminded Jack that he hadn't seen Audra Garrison since the *last* time he'd had "fun" at one of Varnes's hellhole games. "I believe I'll give it a miss, Ernest."

Varnes narrowed his eyes and nodded knowingly before heading out.

Charlie said, "That feller there could be plenty ignorant without strugglin' to make such a job out of it." And, being half-deaf, he said it loudly.

Their shared laughter eased Jack's mood some, but only temporarily. The mail express came by, and as he sorted the letters he fell across one from the Woman's Christian Temperance Union, the very folks who championed the likes of ax-crazy Carrie Nation.

It was addressed to none other than Miss Audra Garrison.

Enough, decided Jack, slapping the letters onto the counter in disgust. The least Audra could do was let him explain things to her—even if he could think of only one place where the lady could not avoid him.

Hypocrisy it might well be, but Jack Harwood was going back to church.

His resolution wavered when the time came to actually do it. Pretty much everyone stared and whispered, just as they had at Christmas. He didn't even have Ham beside him to deflect their gaping curiosity. But Audra was there, too, and just seeing her, after two weeks too long, was worth every name he'd called himself on the way here, every rebellious self-image he'd shattered.

Audra's sorrel hair curled delicately around her pale, china-doll face from under what looked to be a new hat. Her gray eyes slowly widened the longer she stared, almost comically revealing the inner battle he'd set off within her. Her soft lips—he knew just how soft—parted in silent protest. But that hesitance was pure Audra, too. Knowing that, could he blame her?

I'm sorry I disappointed you, he thought at her. *Let me explain.* Then, not wanting to frighten her, he smiled—and she immediately spun away to face the front of the church again, leaving him alone.

Well, he'd figured she would take convincing.

Jack looked for a place to sit and spotted Whitey Gilmer, the blacksmith—if not a friendly face, at least more familiar than the others—and made his way to sit by him.

"You comin' to the fun tonight?" asked Whitey in a gravelly whisper. In a church!

Then Jack wondered just why Whitey *shouldn't* invite him in church to a poker game. It wasn't as though he'd come for religious reasons himself, was it? Still, he used a thumbs-down gesture to silently indicate the negative before turning to his pious surroundings. He took slow, deep breaths to brace himself against the worst of the memories. It would last only a few hours, and then Audra would speak to him again and . . .

Jack had not planned much past that. All he knew was that whatever else he did with his life, he'd improve on it tremendously by putting things right with Audra Garrison first.

Look at me, Audra, he thought at her. But her spine might as well have been steel.

The woman at the piano began to play "Rock of Ages," and everyone stood. The long-forgotten words came easily as Jack joined the singing, waiting for the crawling discomfort.

But the memories didn't come.

In fact, there was something almost comforting about the bone-deep familiarity of the song. Despite years of absence, Jack did know this world. He recognized the Bible passages. He knew the next song, too; even enjoyed it. And it didn't hurt to occasionally catch glimpse of the prettiest nape in Candon, about six rows ahead of him.

He'd prefer her delicate profile, if she would only turn. *Look at me, Audra. I came to church for you.* But the back of her neck had its attractions, too.

The amusement of watching the youngsters fidget, the ladies silently compare fashions, the younger couples discreetly link hands, the older couples speak volumes with mere glances, and old Ned Cooper fall asleep sitting up . . . all that entertainment was, Jack figured, gratis.

Before he knew it, the congregation sang their last verse and the folks of Candon started the slow process of exiting the church and catching up on news at the same time . . . except with him, of course. Joining their exodus, Jack was not actually shunned—a surprising number of the menfolk nodded toward him or said, "Harwood" as they passed. But what with the moral stance on gambling, it would take more than two visits to church to put folks at ease concerning his soul.

Not that he meant to come back, he reminded himself. But he found himself less set against the idea than he would have expected. He could at least think on it. If he did stay for another week or two, what harm could it do? Especially if it pleased Audra.

Jack figured that if he approached the schoolteacher in sight of God and everybody, hat in hand and leaving a respectful pace between them, nobody would think the less of her . . . even her. If she put her mind to avoiding him, she still might manage it. But surely if she just looked at him—saw him sober and neat, instead of drunk—she would relent.

And here came his chance to find out.

Unlike him, Audra fended off any number of "how-dos" and "good-mornings." But even surrounded by well-wishers, she searched the church grounds with cautious little darts of her eyes until her gaze met Jack's—at which point she looked immediately away. That was fine. He would happily pretend that they were all but strangers.

As long as she let an all-but-stranger apologize to her.

When she reached the bottom of the steps, he made his move. "Miss Garrison? Ma'am?"

Four sets of female eyes turned to him—Melissa's brown and excited, Claudine's dark and intrigued, and the two schoolteachers' identically gray, except that the widow Cribb's eyes were narrowed in suspicion and Audra's were wide and . . . frightened?

He couldn't remember the finer points of his drunken

encounter with her, but surely he would remember saying or doing anything to scare her! Hell, if he'd done anything to warrant fear, her brother would surely have dealt with it then and there. Of that, Jack felt certain.

Still, it was his move.

"I won't take but a moment of your time," he assured her, sounding to his own ears like a traveling salesman. "I just—"

"Young man," said the widow Cribb, interrupting his apology, "there is nothing you could say that would be of any consequence to my niece. Good day."

"It's all right," Audra said softly, ducking her gaze from Jack's surprised glance. "I may have caused a misunderstanding. Let me hear what Mr. Harwood wants; then we'll go home."

The widow Cribb's eyes stayed narrow. But when Audra did not flinch, only waited for approval, her aunt could do nothing but give it in one terse nod. Jack didn't blame her. He'd never seen the little gal look so respectable.

"Mr. Harwood," said Audra, and surprised him further by walking away from the others.

Jack followed, pleased that their words would be private. At least he wouldn't have to call her "Miss Garrison." Along with the apology, he could ask her to come back by the store. In a visit or two, he might convince her to take the pen back. Maybe he could even manage a final kiss before he left.

Whenever he left.

She stopped a stone's throw from the others, still looking down at her feet.

Jack cleared his throat. "Audra—"

"I wish I could be sure," she said quietly, sounding somehow sad, "that you came here for church and not just to see me."

When in doubt, smile. "Does it matter?"

Her gray eyes swept up to him, then back down, stormier after seeing his smile. From the way she worried her lower lip, it did matter. "I asked you to leave me alone."

"I've hoped for two weeks now to tell you how sorry I am that you saw me lit up the way you did. I assure you, I am not accustomed to drinking that much. Haven't touched a drop since, either." *There!* That should please her well enough.

"Thank you for that," said Audra, but it would have cheered him more if she'd not spoken to her shoes. She took a deep breath. "But I did ask you to let things be, between us."

"But that's not what you really wanted," he countered.

The longer she said nothing, the better he liked it. Audra wouldn't lie. He'd bet on it. Then she said, "But what a person wants and what is best for her are not always the same thing." At least she looked at him for that, silently pleading for . . . what? "You are a confirmed gambler, are you not?"

"We've discussed this before," he reminded her, keeping his tone patient. "If I remember rightly, you concluded that you would start trusting your common sense instead of making assumptions about activities you don't even know about. Remember that? By the cedar break?"

She flushed, eyes widening, then looked away from him or the memory, or both. Pressing her lips together, she took a deep breath, then asked, "Do you know of a place called the Acre?"

The Acre? Jack's thoughts stumbled at the unexpected turn. "What?"

"The Acre. Some people call it the Third Ward." She fidgeted, her left hand straightening the glove on her right, then swapping roles. "In Fort Worth."

She'd said the Acre, all right. To ask a gambler if he knew of Hell's Half-Acre was like asking a meat packer if he'd heard of Chicago. "I am familiar with the place," Jack acknowledged, wishing she would look at him again. "It's barely a day's ride from here. But that's not where I'd been a few weeks back, if that's what you're thinking."

"But you have . . . done business there? With people who sell liquor or gamble?"

"They *are* the Acre's reason for existence," he pointed out. "Among other things better not mentioned."

She took another deep breath, then whispered another question. But he *had* to have misheard her this time.

"Excuse me?" he asked, trying not to laugh at his misinterpretation.

"What about . . . with women there? Have you done business with them?"

While he stared at her, frozen, she finally lifted her gaze to meet his. He wished she hadn't. Her eyes somehow begged and damned him at the same time.

Jack opened his mouth—then closed it. Then he opened it again. "I never figured myself to say something like this to you, Audra, but that just isn't the kind of question a lady ought to go asking. Have I ever inquired into what element of men *you've* known?"

The tragic part was, Jack had meant that as a joke.

Chapter Twenty

> *It is expected that teachers set virtuous examples for the pupils.*
>
> —Rules for Teachers

Resisting Jack's charms by remembering his sordid world was failing miserably, even before he retaliated with the one question she must not answer. "Wh-what?"

Jack blinked, obviously taken aback by her guilty response. A wan smile flickered across his too-handsome face, then guttered out before it could fully form. "What breed of . . . *men*?"

But he was figuring it out quickly enough, she could see. His eyes darkened, narrowed—then fixed on hers in amazement. And why not? He was perhaps in no position to judge her past . . . but neither was she his.

The need to escape rose in her like a panic. "Never mind," she said quickly, though with desperate poise, and spun to leave. The nearness of several people—Aunt Heddy, Reverend Collins, and Mr. Trigg—startled her. Had they heard her asking such improper questions? Worse, had they heard her inability to answer the last?

But as the two men strode by her Audra realized, stupidly, that their target was Jack.

"Don't look like the lady wants to talk, Harwood," warned Mr. Trigg, and Reverend Collins added, "Perhaps it would be best if you left."

They were throwing him out of church?

All the while, Jack watched her, his expression slackened into dismay, his silent questions continuing even as Mr. Trigg took him by the arm to lead him off. Only then did Jack twist free from the physical contact—still staring at Audra. "Hands off, Seth!"

Several more of the men in the congregation were moving in.

"Stop it!" insisted Audra, stepping between them and their quarry. "What are you doing?"

"Did this here gambler offend you, Miz Audra?" demanded Trigg.

When she looked at Jack again, he still stared at her. Oh, she wanted to explain to him—if anyone could understand her mistakes, wouldn't he? She'd done nowhere near as much with Peter Connors as she had with Jack; people simply knew about Peter. That alone had not ruined her life, but it had sorely complicated it! Still, Jack was not Peter.

"Mr. Harwood has a name," she challenged now, unsure where her brave words came from but making no effort to stop them. "He also has every right to speak to me, if I allow it, which I did. He would hardly insult me at a church!"

People were staring at the spectacle they made; several women whispered behind their hands. Somehow the threat to her reputation did not worry her as much as usual.

When Aunt Heddy said, "It is time we went home, Audra," it sounded like an order. Audra ignored it to see what Mr. Trigg or the others would do next. At least the menfolk looked uncertain now, glancing at one another but no longer moving toward Jack.

Mr. Trigg said, "A man like him ought not to have business with a lady like you, is all. Struck me as odd, ma'am."

From behind her, Jack spoke, his voice sharp despite the practiced friendliness of his drawl. "Now that *would* be odd. What with the lady's and my 'respective positions' and all."

Only Audra recognized the quote from the letter she had sent him. She turned back to him, dismayed to have upset him so much, wondering how she could possibly have made her necessary requests more kindly.

His formal bow in her direction, complete with a flourish of his hat, seemed to her as uncomplimentary as his tone. "Miss Garrison." He nodded to the others. "Paragons."

Then he strode away from the church, toward the mercantile. Could the others see the fury in his stiffness, or was it just her? She wanted to run after him, to apologize for the others and herself. But what good would that do either of them? If anybody here guessed at the intimacies they'd shared, Jack could meet with true violence. Some apology that would be.

No, better that she stay silent. Bearing the burden of his poor opinion was no less than she deserved. Perhaps it would even make it easier for him to . . . leave.

"What did he say to upset you, dear?" asked the reverend, putting a hand on her shoulder.

Where once she would see only concern, she now felt the walls of authority closing in. "With all respect, Reverend, that is Mr. Harwood's concern."

Aunt Heddy made a huffing noise of surprise, and Mr. Trigg said, "Oh, really?"

Quickly, Audra reviewed the rules for teachers and remembered nothing justifying outright prejudice. "Thank you very much for coming to my aid, Mr. Trigg. And you, Reverend. It speaks well of the town that a young lady has such protectors. But . . ." She took a deep breath, hating to offend them but unwilling to let the incident pass without comment. "But in the future, perhaps it might be wise to determine if assistance is needed, first."

Trigg folded his burly arms. "And just how are we supposed

to tell the difference, with our schoolteacher lookin' like she's about to swoon?"

A significant question. The simplicity of its answer startled her. "You might ask."

With that, she did her best to smile in something close to gratitude toward the cluster of townspeople around her. Then, despite wanting nothing more than to find someplace quiet and think things through, she turned toward the path to Aunt Heddy's.

She had not, she thought sullenly, been about to swoon.

He was a damned fool, was what he was.

Jack could hardly believe his idiocy, thinking Audra would be impressed by a suit, a haircut, by his not touching any liquor since the New Year. Some things, like how long a fellow's transgressions haunted him, never changed. And some things . . .

He kept hearing his own question echo in his head: *What element of men* you've *known,* you've *known*, you've *known* . . . And each time, he saw her go pure white. Audra Garrison never did have a poker face. Until today, he figured it had something to do with her obvious innocence.

Son of a bitch.

Did Audra have some transgressions under *her* belt, as well? *Audra?*

He wasn't sure who he'd rather hurt: Her, for making him jump through hoops to meet those pure and unspoiled expectations of hers? Or, more likely, whatever bastard had taken advantage of her—were it true, that is. She'd left home to live with a distant aunt. Scandal terrified her. Add to that her fine way with kisses—hesitant at first, but she'd caught on right quick—and he just didn't have the ammunition to deny what her pale face admitted.

Here he'd thought he'd fallen in with a puredee lady, and she was nothing more than . . .

But that thought infuriated him most of all, because anyone who thought Audra Garrison *wasn't* a lady, no matter what mistakes she'd made, was a fool. Most ladies who "fell" were, in fact, yanked down by some fellow. He'd lay odds it was the same with Audra.

But it still disappointed him, and his regret disappointed him, too.

He used the rear entrance to the store and bolted the steps to Ham's room, pounding on the door in warning, then stalking in. "You said you had some coffin varnish up here?"

Ferris looked up from polishing a boot and whistled. "Well, don't you look sweet."

Jack began to look behind boxes and above shelves. "Liquor. Now."

"I offered that back when I thought you were going to puke in my store." Ferris went back to work buffing his boot to a high shine. "Maybe I'm not feeling so generous today."

"I'll pay you."

"How much?"

"Whatever you still owe me. I'm leaving." Even as the words came out of Jack's mouth, he knew their truth. He didn't belong here. He didn't belong at Sunday-morning services, or stalking a scandal-shy lady teacher who figured him for a drunken whoremonger.

"I haven't got that much." Ferris put down his boot to tug a small trunk out from under his bed, then opened it up. "Why don't you leave and *then* get drunk? You were figuring on going to Fort Worth anyhow, weren't you? Word has it they run a saloon or two out thataway."

"Fort Worth," Jack pointed out, "is thirty miles of dry townships away from here, and the moonshiners are shy to do business of a Sunday unless they know you." The only one he knew by name was Harv Jefferson, and nothing would tempt him into trying that product again.

So Ferris tossed him a bottle, which he caught. It was a small bottle, barely half-full, but it would do to mark the official end to his foolish attempts at respectability. He wasn't craving the liquor half so much as the opportunity to do something of which Miss Audra Holier-than-Thou Garrison would not approve. Since he didn't know of any whores in the immediate area, and the only poker game was the hellhole at Ernest Varnes's, booze on the Sabbath it was.

He started to turn back toward the stairs, then paused. Ferris Hamilton was a decent fellow. Jack would probably even miss him. "Thanks."

"Pleasure doing business with you," said Ferris, going back to his boot polishing. "I believe I made a profit on it. You drinking it here?"

"I'd drink en route, but the saddle might start drifting out from under me."

"If I'm out when you go, lock up and leave the key under that rock I showed you."

Instead of just agreeing, Jack asked, "Where you going, anyway?"

Ferris finished with the second boot. "Same place I go most Sundays."

"Which would be . . . ?"

"Out." But the storekeeper softened it with a rare grin. "Try to stay out of jail, Harwood."

"Try to stay out of the widow Parks, Hamilton." And Jack finally headed down the stairs.

"Not a problem!" called Ferris, after him. "On my mother's grave, not a problem!"

Once downstairs, Jack settled onto his pallet, uncorked the bottle, and enjoyed the mere smell of good whiskey. *Mmm.* If sin were truly wrong, how come it was so damned tempting?

He remembered Audra confessing her own experience with demon liquor and fought a grin. She would make a damned cute drunk.

Then he wondered if that was how the faceless son of a bitch, whoever he was, got past those scruples and under those petticoats of hers. But that didn't bear thinking about, so he treated himself to a slow sip of whiskey. It burned exquisitely all the way down, leaving that familiar, comforting warmth he was looking for.

It didn't come close to the glowing warmth that Audra Garrison's short-lived admiration of him had fueled. But at least this warmth was real.

And this warmth he could get.

"That was brave," said Claudine. "Standing up to the reverend and Mr. Trigg that way."

Surprised, Audra looked up from her reading. It really was Claudine speaking with such civility! Aunt Heddy had gone visiting, and Melissa was off fussing with her appearance lest Early Rogers come by to sit with her. For once, it was just her and Claudine.

"I did not feel brave," she admitted carefully. "And to be honest, I did not mean to defy anyone. I know they were trying to do what was best for me."

"But *you* didn't think it was best for you," Claudine pointed out. In Aunt Heddy's absence, she held a brush in her lap and carefully combed hair leavings out of it in the hope of making a "fall." While Audra understood her aunt's disapproval of such vanity, she could not bring herself to criticize it. After all, she had short hair and Melissa's was bleached!

"No," she agreed. "I did not approve either of them mistreating Mr. Harwood or using me as an excuse to do it."

"So sometimes what people think is best for us, isn't." Claudine let the hairpiece-in-progress rest on her lap to watch Audra's reaction closely. "Is it?"

Oh, dear. "I have been pondering that myself," admitted Audra.

"You have?"

She nodded. "I'm grateful that people care enough to interfere. And they *do* often have more knowledge of the world than we do. Sometimes," she added, gentling the seriousness of her words with a smile. "But occasionally they *can* be mistaken, as with Mr. Harwood."

"How can you be sure? He *is* a gambler. I truly didn't lie about that."

"Yes. He *is* a gambler," she agreed again. "Which requires a certain aloofness on our part, unkind though it seems. But Mr.

Harwood has always behaved civilly"—*more or less*—"and does not deserve insult for merely speaking to me."

"He has a lovely smile," said Claudine, and sighed heavily enough to drop her shoulders. "I do love men with dimples."

The pang of jealousy that closed Audra's throat surprised her. "It is not his smile that convinced me, Claudine, nor his good looks. I've used my own common sense about Mr. Harwood. I've seen him be kind to children and to lonely old men. He contributed to our new books and slates. He may not always behave appropriately, but neither have I known him to be cruel. Mr. Hamilton trusts him . . . and he has a sweet mare."

Claudine laughed. "A *mare?*"

"My father says you can tell a lot about a man from his horse."

Claudine said, "Jerome Newton wants a fast horse to race on the track in Dallas."

Then Jerome Newton is a fool. But Audra fought back that first reaction. If Claudine received only censure, Audra could hardly hope the girl would speak like this again.

"Jerome is an . . . enterprising boy," she hedged. "I should hate to see him waste his potential on horse-race gambling."

"But Mr. Harwood gambles." That worried Audra. Had Claudine noticed more about her feelings for Jack than she'd meant to show? Or was she merely justifying Jerome—whom she obviously admired—by comparing him to the older man? If Jack knew how his behavior set an example for impressionable boys, would he consider changing his ways *then?* She suspected not.

Wasted potential, indeed.

"Which is why the men at church today turned on him so quickly," Audra pointed out. "A good reputation, once lost, is almost impossible to regain. Once you step off the path of—"

But after this morning, if she pondered that blasted path of righteousness one more time, she might scream from frustration. It simplified too much, left too many questions unanswered.

"They had no idea what Mr. Harwood and I said to each other," she said instead. "But they automatically saw him in the wrong. Why? Because he has not guarded his reputation as carefully as I have. For all they knew, I could have stolen something from the mercantile!"

She warmed to her example. "Suppose Mr. Harwood, not wanting to dishonor me with a public accusation, meets me after church to say that if I will only return it, he will neither file charges nor sully my name. Upset to be so discovered, I cry out. Do you think Reverend Collins or Mr. Trigg would behave any differently?"

"Without knowing that?"

"Without knowing that."

Claudine shook her head. "You're a schoolteacher, and he's nothing but a gambler."

Audra quickly looked down at the book in her lap. "Well . . . nobody should *ever* be described as nothing, Claudine." Especially someone as fine as Jack Harwood, gambler or not. "Part of it is pure luck. I have a good family, while Mr. Harwood—" *Is a minister's son.* But he'd admitted that with bitterness. "His family may have been troubled," she supposed. "But part is choice. I do try to live respectably. He has chosen to gamble, openly, and so is at risk of poor public opinion. It's even worse for ladies, you know. What seems initially harmless can rob a girl of her family, livelihood, community, even self-respect."

Claudine scowled at the fall of hair on her lap. "You're talking about me and Jerome."

Jerome and me. Audra swallowed back the automatic correction—she'd been given a precious chance to teach far more than grammar here, not just to Claudine, but to her own stubborn heart. "No, Claudine, I am not. You are not the only girl to forget herself with a handsome boy." *Or man.* "But you were lucky to be caught. I've seen what can happen to girls who haven't family or neighbors to guard them, or who haven't been raised with proper guidance. I would not wish that on anybody, certainly not on you."

The scowl on Claudine's face softened, and when she raised her dark eyes to Audra, she looked more vulnerable than Audra had ever expected. "You wouldn't?"

It made Audra smile. "Of course I wouldn't."

Claudine went back to work on her hairpiece, and soon was smiling as well.

Audra went back to staring at her book and thinking about Jack's anger. He'd ignored her request to be left alone. And he'd disappointed her, too, embracing a lifestyle that could never mesh with the fantasies she longed to weave around him even now. But she ached to think she'd been lessened in his eyes by what he'd seen in her own. Even if she deserved to be. But . . . did she?

"Miss Garrison?" asked Claudine. "Is it *always* a mistake?"

"Is what always a mistake?"

"To risk one's reputation with a boy. What if you're truly in love? What if he only means to kiss you, and the rest just . . . happens? What if he promises to marry you? Is it still a mistake?"

Audra knew what she *should* say. She should say that girls who behaved so were light-skirted floozies who deserved their dire consequences. But . . .

She remembered kissing Jack by the cedar break, the unnameable joy his lovemaking had ignited in her. Would she forever think of Jack when she thought of kissing? Probably so. He was so dangerously *good* at it.

In any case, she understood now, as she had not before she met him, how easily such mistakes might occur. And to say they always ended in tragedy would be to lie—toward good ends, perhaps, but it was a falsehood just the same. Babies did not, her mother once explained with distressing candor, always result from what men and women did together. And even if a girl found herself with a baby under the apron, most communities would forgive such indiscretion—after time—as long as she immediately married, whether she married the child's father or not.

"I believe," she said slowly, working it out as she spoke, "that two people who truly love each other would endeavor to protect each other, even from themselves. He might be injured or killed before he could do right by her. Or marriage without solid prospects could force them into poverty. Just because it *could* work out does not mean they did not take a dreadful . . . gamble."

"Oh," said Claudine. Then, unexpectedly, "Thank you."

"You are welcome," said Audra. It didn't make the memory of this morning go away. But she thought she understood her dilemma a little more. Jack gambled—and she did not.

Not even for him.

If she could not find comfort, understanding would have to do.

Jack unpacked and repacked his saddlebags twice, certain that he'd forgotten something. Not likely. He felt calmer than he had in weeks, and not because of Ham's whiskey. After that first sip, he'd found himself oddly uninterested in a second, no matter how smooth the liquor.

Perhaps the warmth of the whiskey only reminded him of the warmth he'd lost?

Somehow, corking the bottle had eased him in a way drinking it might not have. Lying back on his pallet to think things through, he fell asleep, catching up on the rest he'd missed the night before. The nap cost him a lot of daylight, but the weather looked clear; with a full moon he could ride past sunset. More important, the rest restored his good sense.

He saw how badly he'd overstayed his welcome in Candon, for one thing.

But that realization did not help him figure out what he needed so desperately to remember. It wasn't something he could pack. Gamblers traveled light. But he wouldn't get far without trusting his instincts. So when whatever it was kept chewing at him, just beyond recognition, he hesitated to leave before he could ferret it out. Had he not done something? Ferris knew he was leaving, and Audra . . . well, despite his efforts to apologize for his previous inebriation, he now saw that was for him more than her. Better for her if he *did* leave on a sour note. The next man who came courting would thus have to prove himself the opposite of Jack before she would look twice at him. She couldn't do much better than that.

So . . . what? What was it he couldn't figure out? He paced the store, the storage room, the back room where he'd slept. He climbed to Ferris's room, but saw nothing amiss there except that the man hadn't emptied his wash water after cleaning up for tonight, wherever he was going. Jack tossed it out the window for him, noticing from the scent that Ham had used their best soap. Jack put that together with the polished boots, and it seemed obvious Ferris had his own trysts to see to. But it wasn't Jack's business how Ham saw fit to ruin his life.

Jack gave up. Likely he'd remember whatever it was halfway to Fort Worth and make the rest of the trip cursing himself. But if he didn't leave now he might stay the night, maybe even search out a local game.

And at that, pieces fell into place like cards in a perfect hand—for someone else. Jack hadn't been invited specifically to a game tonight. He'd been invited to come have what Whitey called "fun." Varnes had called it "*real* good fun"—after lamenting those dangerous coloreds in Mosier Valley—and looking to buy a new six-shooter.

Ferris had lost his temper and defended the Mosier Valley folks. When he'd asked, "Why not just leave them be?" Varnes had said something about that being a "fine question."

The road to Mosier Valley went past the cemetery. Jack remembered Varnes mentioning it, telling Ferris to look at his family's graves "next time you ride by the cemetery." As if Ferris went by the cemetery all the time. But Ferris *had* gone out this evening. To meet a woman.

And in all the time Jack had worked here, he'd seen Ferris show interest in only one woman, speak about more than just merchandise to only one woman, cheer up or sullen down based on the presence or absence of only one woman. But Jack had been so busy conducting his own romance with Audra that he hadn't seen an even more forbidden romance under his nose.

"Tarnation," he muttered, and bolted for the door, then across the street to the livery, leaving saddlebags, keys, and everything else behind.

Ferris Hamilton was seeing Lucy—their colored laundress.

And Ernest Varnes, Whitey Gilmer, and God only knew how many others likely planned to do something about it tonight.

Chapter Twenty-one

Teachers will begin classes promptly at eight o'clock in the morning.

—Rules for Teachers

Candon itself sat relatively high on a gentle roll of landscape, its dirt roads nestled amid a fair amount of brushy timber. The road toward Mosier Valley—and, en route, the Calloway cemetery—sloped downward into a more open prairie of mesquite and tall grass that Jack had heard described as malarial. He could smell the dampness in the evening chill as he rode Queen toward the stone markers that dotted the acre or more of cleared, moonlit burial ground.

No sign of his friend, though he did note the name Ferris on more than one large tombstone. Neither did he see evidence of Lucy, or of a mob out to intercept the pair.

Breathing in through gritted teeth, Jack turned in his saddle, looking for any hint that his hunch would play out. It was then that he saw the trace that branched southward, beyond the last of the gravestones, toward a distant tree line and the Trinity River. For Jack's money, the privacy of timber and the romance of a moonlit river would beat a cemetery for courting hands down. With a click of tongue to teeth, he urged Queen of Hearts onto the narrower path.

Then he heard the gunshot, dug in his heels, and let her take her chances with shadows.

Five white men—including Jefferson, Gilmer, and Varnes—had come looking for trouble. Two sat on mules; one had a shotgun raised. The other three had dismounted to better confront the "perversion" they'd obviously interrupted. Their mounts clustered along the path, spooky and restless from the recent gunshot. Ham's gelding stood tied to a tree across the clearing.

A crumpled quilt and a crutch lay on the sandy, moonlit ground, but Hamilton and his dark-skinned lady friend had backed off of it. Ham stood shirtless on the riverbank, dangerously close to a steep drop over dark water. Behind him, clutching her dress together, stood Lucy.

Jack couldn't remember her last name. Just Lucy.

Of course, since he hadn't bothered to sneak his way up the path, he now reined Queen to a halt with a fine view not only of the players in this melodrama, but of the business ends of a shotgun and Ernest Varnes's new revolver. Another shotgun was trained on the lovers. Pistol smoke hung heavy in the humid air.

Well, hell. He just *had* to be right, now, didn't he? *When in doubt . . .*

Jack smiled. "And here I feared I might've missed the party!"

They might be rubes, but they weren't idiots. Varnes grinned back and did Jack the courtesy of pointing his revolver toward Ferris again. But one of the fellows on muleback—named Mason, if Jack had it right—kept a shotgun on him, and Ernest was likely aware of that, too.

"Light a spell, Harwood," he said. "You got here just in time for the fun, didn't he, boys?"

Jack glanced toward Ham, who stared back, expressionless. Ferris never had been one for showy emotions. Lucy trembled visibly, and justifiably so. This was no lynch mob. Ferris Hamilton could ride away from the whole ugly encounter with nothing more painful than a little shame and some bad memories.

As long as he abandoned her when he went.

It wasn't respectable to lust after a black woman, of course; for some men it ranked just marginally higher than relieving one's needs on the livestock. But liquor up some fellows with basic enough needs, and even the livestock ought to worry. A pretty girl like Lucy . . .

And she was, Jack realized as he dismounted with a creak of saddle leather, very pretty. Despite his recent obsession with a particularly fine lady schoolmarm, he felt a mite ashamed for never noticing before now.

Then again, facing down firearms tended to bring out the regrets in him.

"Well, y'all know me," he noted now, casually, and looped Queen's reins over a nearby bush. "I'm always up for a little fun."

"How do we know we can trust him?" demanded the fellow named Mason. "Him and Hamilton's been workin' together; could be Harwood's here to help him."

"He don't look to be armed," observed Whitey Gilmer, also on muleback.

Tossing a grin in the blacksmith's direction, Jack even opened his coat to better show that he wore no gun belt. "Now isn't that what we're *all* here for?" he asked, downright amiable. "To help my friend Ferris here see the error of his ways?"

He even got close enough to Ferris to pat his shoulder condescendingly.

Ferris shrugged away from his touch as if Jack were diseased. But his eyes . . .

Damn it, Jack couldn't tell if the storekeeper understood or not. Ham had too good a poker face. Poor Lucy, though, obviously bought his act so thoroughly that it pained him to see her wide-eyed fear. Well, he *was* a gambler, wasn't he? Why wouldn't she think a fellow with that track record could be a rapist? Candon's little mob certainly accepted him as their own.

He wondered if Audra might believe similarly. The likelihood downright sickened him.

In the meantime, the others were nodding and agreeing among themselves. Nothing a fellow with a prickly conscience liked more than a rationale that made him the good guy.

"Like I done told you," said Varnes to Ferris. "We just want to share some of what you got. Seems only fair, what with her kind comin' after *our* women."

"You'll have to go through me," warned Ferris.

Behind him Lucy whimpered. "No, honey. No . . ."

"Now, you know we'll be happy to do just that," Varnes

warned him. "Ain't nobody'd make too big a fuss on your account, neither, you sick son of a bitch." It was one thing to entertain oneself with a colored woman on the sly, another to debase oneself so far as to care for her. As Varnes probably saw it, he was giving Ferris an out: fun . . . or violence.

Ferris stayed in. "So be it."

The tension in Jack's shoulders eased at his friend's decision. Violence it was.

Harv Jefferson, also afoot, said, "Ferris, be reasonable. It's six to—"

But by then Jack had as good a drop on Varnes as he'd get. A snap of his left arm released his sleeve holdout, set his hand a breath from Ernest's face as his derringer sprang into it.

"Your 'rithmetic leaves something to be desired, Harv," he called, his tone as amiable as ever. He'd likely looked down a black-eyed Susan a few times more than these farmers. "The count is five-to-two, not including the lady, of course. Call off your boys, Ernest."

Someone exclaimed, "Lady?" But the others sat still, wrapping their liquor-soaked minds around this startling turn of events.

Varnes didn't blink, but he did look a mite bit cross-eyed at the derringer's muzzle. "I can shoot you as easy as you can shoot me," he pointed out, his voice pitched higher than before. This was why fools oughtn't play with firearms. A serious gunman would've already blasted Jack off of him, derringer and all.

Thank God Ernest Varnes was a fool.

"That would make this what's called a standoff," Jack explained gently. "The gamble here is, can you shoot me *before* I shoot you?" Behind him, he heard Hamilton urging Lucy over the edge of the riverbank—and her protesting. He would decide later if he found that endearing, damned annoying, or both, depending on how this played out.

From muleback, Whitey's voice rasped out, "Go on, Ernest! You got a forty-five; all he's got is some sissy gun."

"Forty-one caliber might do the job," assured Jack.

"But . . . but that thing can't hold but one shot," Varnes stuttered, still cross-eyed. "I got six." He'd already forgotten the warning shot that had brought Jack here in the first place, which made it five. And that was assuming he'd been dumb enough to carry it with a loaded chamber.

Jack shrugged his shoulder. "At three inches it'll take more than one shot?"

"But you got two shotguns pointed at you, too," warned Mason.

Those were indeed bothersome . . . but Jack didn't have to point out how little that would matter to Ernest. He just continued to smile, and Ernest went white as the moonlight.

Lucy stopped protesting; instead Jack heard a scuffling noise. *Good.* That should put her out of the line of fire. If she had brains she would hightail it out of here as well . . . but she sounded like a woman in love, and love weakened the thinking abilities of even the smartest gal.

Which told Jack something fairly depressing about his clear-headed Audra.

Just as well. If ever a woman like Audra *did* love him, he'd be a damned fool to be standing here, five-to-two, chancing his life on another man's cowardice.

Over Varnes's shoulder, Mason started to raise his shotgun.

Jack pressed his derringer to Varnes's eyebrow, and the man yelped. Then Jack slid it downward, giving the farmer a chance to close his eye before the muzzle nestled up against his eyeball. No sense risking a ricochet off his skull. "Call off your boys, Ernest."

From the suddenly sharp, familiar smell of urine, Jack guessed Ernest took his threat seriously. Sadly, Ernest might not be popular enough to stop the others.

"I ain't nobody's *boy,*" protested Harv Jefferson.

Whitey Gilmer rasped out, "Harwood, it won't be safe for you to spit around here."

With a quick catch, Jack relieved Ernest of his slackly held revolver. He passed it back to Ham. "Maybe if you fellows go home and sleep it off, we can forget any of this ever happened."

"Not a chance," Whitey warned. "It's still five-to-two."

Ernest, fully comprehending what a fine human shield he made, closed his other eye.

"But each side's got two weapons," Jack pointed out, not mentioning that he and Ferris held mere handguns, while the other side wielded buckshot. If they didn't notice, he wasn't about to educate them. "And you've got to admit, you're the ones that came after Ferris's woman."

"She ain't a woman. She's a colored," said the fifth fellow, a stocky man whom Jack didn't know. He disliked having the second shotgun in an unknown's hands.

"Even if she was a butter churn, that don't make her yours for the taking. No offense, ma'am," he called toward the river. "You boys get along home, now, and nobody has to get hurt."

And for a tense moment, he cherished hopes that things would commence just that way. Then Mason raised his shotgun to his shoulder. "Ain't no way in—"

And the world erupted.

Jack had a passing acquaintance with death, and he'd noticed that if death came close enough, everything else faded. He did hear Ernest Varnes's scream as Jack shouldered him, now unarmed, out of the immediate line of fire—but he noted it only offhand. Just so with the bark of the revolver. Blue flame spurted not a foot from Jack's cheekbone, and he hardly flinched. Horses milled; Whitey cursed; Lucy screamed. But none of it felt as real as the stillness of death.

The stocky stranger lifted his shotgun with what seemed like exaggerated languor, and Jack launched himself to one side, lifting his derringer with the same odd lack of speed. He somehow squeezed off his one and only shot before hitting the ground, shoulder first—

And then, as Jack's momentum carried him over the edge of the riverbank and out of the line of fire, death looked the other way—again—and the world erupted back into a chaos of shots, cries, screams, even the thuds and grunts of his own tumble down the steep, rutted bank. With a splash into silence, the Trinity closed over his head. He might have heard a couple more river-muffled shots before he could struggle to the surface.

Jack's own gasp as he resurfaced seemed to resound into the night, then stilled as he sank back under, echoing with a spray of water as he resurfaced. He lunged for the bank and, after a few handfuls of sand, caught hold of an exposed tangle of cottonwood roots. Holding on against the current, he caught his breath and listened.

He heard retreating hoofbeats and a man crying—"Oh, God, oh, God a'mighty!—"and someone else's moan.

Heavy and wet, Jack used roots and dry grapevine to drag himself back up the eroded bluff. He half expected more gunshots as he pulled himself over the bank onto his stomach. None came. Catching his breath, he pushed up to see what kind of damage they'd done.

Nobody called to God anymore, but a body sprawled across a clump of prickly-pear cactus where the voice had sounded. Farther over, Lucy kneeled on the ground, weeping, her fallen lover pulled onto her lap.

Well . . . tarnation.

Jack had survived. That meant consequences. Unsteady, he pulled himself to his feet and staggered, dripping, toward Lucy and Ferris.

Now he could be scared.

Audra could tell even before class started that something had happened. Her pupils hadn't been so excited since Jerome Newton got back from the Wild West show in October. But when she rang the bell for the start of class, she could see that this news outdid even Buffalo Bill Cody. Some of the pupils backed reluctantly away from the conversation, but nobody actually turned toward the schoolhouse.

What could they be discussing with such animation?

Aunt Heddy startled Audra by snatching the bell rope from her hand. "Do not stand there gaping," the older woman scolded. "*Make* them come!" She rang the bell until its clang made Audra's teeth ache. "School is now in session!"

The smaller children scuttled over then. With a critical look, Aunt Heddy pressed the rope back into Audra's hand and followed her charges inside. Even now, Audra's pupils—though obeying the summons—were still talking as they walked.

Audra took a deep breath and rang the bell again to make her point. Knowing that Aunt Heddy might mark her progress, she wondered if she had to dole out punishments. Obedience would lead these children to become better citizens, which would protect them from some of the world's darker temptations . . .

But, to be truthful, Audra would rather understand what was going on.

And then Melissa darted to her side and tugged at her arm. "Audra!"

"Miss," corrected Audra automatically; she did not blame Melissa for forgetting, but it did seem important to maintain at least the illusion of authority at school.

For once Melissa did not correct herself. She just tugged Audra away from the doorway, around the outside corner, and then announced, "There was a shooting at the river last night."

Which would certainly explain the children's excitement, but hardly the dire solemnity of Melissa's words. Unless . . . had one of her pupils been injured? A church member? Or—

Fear hit Audra then, unbalanced her; only Melissa and the log side of the school kept her from sinking to the ground. A hole gaped inside her, empty and awful. *No—oh, please, no!* Even if it was the expected end for people who lived outside the law . . .

The single, choked word hurt her throat. "Jack?"

Melissa was saying something, repeating it, but Audra heard only the roar in her head. She stared at Melissa's moving lips and saw Jack's grin, Jack's anger, Jack's affection. *No.*

Her friend shook her hard. Breath rushed back into Audra's lungs, and she could hear again. "Audra! You aren't listening to me!"

What was that moaning sound? Why was Melissa's face blurring like that?

Melissa shook her again, with the most beautiful words ever spoken. "It's not him!"

Audra's world solidified once more, trembling but whole . . .

despite the implications of her extreme reaction. "It's not him?" she echoed, desperate to be right, implications or no.

"Well—it *is* him."

Audra grabbed Melissa's arms. "What?"

Melissa shook her again. "Do you want folks to see you like this? Listen. There was a shooting last night, and two men are dead—Forney Wells and Ernest Varnes. Mr. Hamilton—"

"Miss Garrison?" Audra clapped her hand to her mouth against a scream and spun to face Jerome Newton. "It's class time," he reminded her, cocking his head at her obvious upset.

"She'll be in momentarily, Jerome," said Melissa.

The boy actually appeared concerned. "Is she okay?"

She, she, she. Audra took a deep breath, then thought to uncover her mouth. "I am fine, Jerome," she said, marveling at her calm words. "Thank you. But I must have a word with Melissa. Would you please start the others reviewing their spelling words?"

Jerome began to extend one hand, then paused, uncertain. She schooled her features, then breathed more slowly, focusing on her posture. He nodded. "Yes, ma'am. I'd be glad to."

"Thank you, Jerome."

After he vanished, she and Melissa leaned around the corner to make sure that he went into the classroom and shut the door.

Then Audra spun on her friend again. "What about Mr. Hamilton? And what happened to Jack? Mr. Harwood," she added belatedly, as if that would fool either of them.

"I don't know all the details. Nobody wanted to upset the little ones, and there are things they won't tell the girls either. But apparently Mr. Hamilton has a colored wife—or something like that. Some of the sharecroppers found out and tried to lynch them, or rob them, or something. There may have been liquor involved, and there was definitely a shooting."

Drinking. Shooting. Bigotry. She could not be so wrong! "And Mr. Harwood?"

"He was helping Mr. Hamilton," said Melissa, and Audra's shoulders relaxed. Hell's Half-Acre had made it easy for her to doubt Jack; she loved being proven horribly, foolishly wrong.

"And he's not hurt? You're certain?"

"Someone rode out for the doctor from Bedford. From what Early said, though, that was for Mr. Hamilton and Mr. Wells, but he died this morning. Mr. Wells, I mean. They sent for a marshal, too. Audra—Mr. Harwood might be arrested for murder."

Mere moments ago, she would have been thrilled to hear any news except that Jack was dead. Then, anything but that he was hurt. Then, anything but that he'd been part of the mob. Now she pressed her fists against her mouth with brand-new fears. She'd seen how quickly even the kindly reverend had turned on Jack. How could he possibly hope for a jury to acquit him of the murder of simple farmers? "But it was self-defense. It *had* to be!"

"Early says folks are at the store now, deciding all that."

"I've got to help." Audra brushed at her skirts with numb hands. "I've got to go."

Go do what? Other than to see Jack, to be with Jack, to tell him . . . what?

"You can't! There are lawmen there, Audra! And dead people. You'd be in the way, and people might guess at your intentions, and that couldn't help him, now, could it?"

Which certainly gave her pause. "But . . ."

"What possible good can risking your position do, when nothing's been decided? Can't you be of more help to him as the schoolmarm? For mercy's sake—*think!*"

Reluctantly, Audra did. Of course she mustn't rush to Jack's side. Once a decision was made about the charges he faced, then she would know better whether he needed food, comfort, a character witness . . . even her brother, the lawyer, if need be! Melissa was right. Audra had more power as a schoolmarm than as a girl who'd been dismissed for unseemly conduct.

So why did her heart feel an almost physical tug in the direction of the mercantile?

"Perhaps I could send someone to wait for news," she suggested slowly.

Melissa nodded approval. "Early. I don't think spelling lessons help him—"

"Audra Susan Garrison!"

Melissa and Audra winced together, then turned to face Hedda Cribb's disapproval.

"How dare you stand out here gossiping when school is in session! Bad enough were you a pupil, but as a teacher! You are sorely delinquent in your obligations, young lady, and do not think our relationship will keep me from reporting this to the school board!"

Mere months, even weeks earlier, the accusation or threat might have brought Audra to tears. Today she only wondered how her aunt could think of the school board with men dead, injured, facing murder charges. In one moment of terror, Audra's values had shifted in ways Aunt Heddy might never comprehend. Jack could have died. He could have vanished not just from her life but from life itself, and she'd never apologized, never told him that just because common sense bade her to stay away, her heart didn't . . . wasn't . . .

"You will return to your duties at once," commanded Heddy.

Which only heightened the call of the mercantile. But Heddy—and Melissa—had the right of it in one way, at least. Audra had pupils to see to. She'd taken a job, and she meant to do it.

"Melissa, please return to the schoolroom," she said steadily.

"Yes, Miss Garrison." Giving the older teacher wide berth, her friend gladly escaped.

"Melissa was telling me—" Audra began, once they had privacy.

"No excuses!" snapped her aunt, which suddenly struck Audra as rude.

"—about the shooting," Audra finished. "Our pupils may be anxious to discuss it."

"Not during school time!"

"Do you think their minds will be on anything else? I'll . . . I'll use this to explain our judicial system." She prayed the explanation would not end up accompanying a trial.

"Best not speak of such things," insisted the older teacher—apparently the pupils had filled her in at least a little. "I just thank our lucky stars that most of the school board saw you turning that gambler away after church! I cannot imagine what they would think of you had you been too civil with such a man just as this happens!"

Audra could not imagine that they'd be thinking about her at all, compared to the excitement of a double murder. But she knew what she thought of herself. Jack could have died. Depending on whether he was charged with murder, he might still.

Audra's opinion of herself was far from complimentary, proper behavior or not.

"If you will excuse me," she said evenly, walking past her aunt. "I have lessons to teach."

"I am not through with you, young—"

But Audra walked into her classroom and closed the door behind her, silencing anything else the older woman had to say. She knew she would regret her willful action later.

But for the moment, as disappointed with herself as she was furious at her aunt, it seemed the most polite of Audra's possible responses.

Chapter Twenty-two

Teachers should avoid any behavior that might attract calumny or scandal.

—Rules for Teachers

Between the marshal and his deputies, the doctor, and the undertaker—all from larger towns—along with townsfolk come to gawk and one furious widow, the Candon mercantile was nearly bursting at the seams that first morning. But nobody bought much.

Just as well. Between his wounds and his woman, Hamilton wasn't up to making sales, and Jack found himself doing more talking than trading. The marshal, a flinty-eyed fellow of the old school, obviously hungered to make murder charges stick. But despite his clear distaste for the two defendants—one a citified gambler and the other a gimpy storekeeper who'd "started it" by taking up with a colored—he was an honest enough lawman to admit self-defense when he saw it.

Not that he pressed charges against the three surviving attackers, either, despite the fact that Ernest Varnes had been shot in the back by one of his own comrades. In the time it took Forney Wells to die—and he almost made it to dawn—he'd insisted that he wasn't the one who had turned Varnes into such a mean and oozy corpse.

"But he *could* have done it," the marshal noted afterward. End of investigation.

Wells's lead poisoning was likely the work of Ham and Jack together, which made Jack none too comfortable, especially once his widow showed up. The doctor fished out both a .41- and a .45-caliber slug and couldn't rightly say which wound did the deed. But Wells did admit to holding a shotgun. In a contest between shotgun and derringer, Jack won the claim of either self-defense or lunacy—or both. And though Ferris had the revolver, well . . . he had family in the area, old family at that, on his mother's side. That cleared him of the crime as well.

Nothing like small-town justice.

After Wells breathed his last, the Bedford doctor went home. Ferris's wounds—a chewed-up shoulder from what buckshot didn't take out Varnes and a bruised head where a falling branch had struck him, after Wells shot a tree—should mend without further medical attention. By noon, the threat of jail faded and the law rode out as well. While Lucy hid upstairs, the undertaker stayed until midafternoon, time enough for a photographer to arrive and capture both bodies, laid out side by side in front of the store, for posterity. Then the widow Wells got the menfolk to help her load her "no-account" husband into a buckboard borrowed from the livery, so that she could drive him home for a proper vigil.

By that point, since anyone with the stomach to ogle Varnes had already been by, even the undertaker pulled out, taking the second body with him. Then the mercantile emptied faster than a fool's wallet in a game of three-card monte, the smell of blood and sweat finally fading.

Ham, who'd sat in his old corner chair for the greater part of the day, looked wordlessly across the empty store at Jack, then let his head fall back against the wall and his eyes drift shut with relief. Jack sank back against a cold display stove, suddenly a mite shaky himself.

Damn, but he never wanted to face another twenty-four hours like these again. Or maybe, considering the fiasco outside the church yesterday morning, he should stretch that to thirty-six hours he'd prefer to avoid from here on out.

"Mr. Hamilton?" ventured a low voice from the curtain to the back room, and both men opened their eyes to face pretty, dark-skinned Lucy Wolfe.

Jack knew her name now. He'd also offered to take her home, but she'd dared not go. "They might come after me," she'd explained. "I won't bring that trouble down on my folks. I won't do them that way." Regret stained her words. "They may not want me back, anyhow."

Only then had it occurred to Jack that had she been a *white* girl of any distinction, Ferris would be facing more shotguns one way or the other. But Lucy didn't have the protection of a white girl's reputation, even if hers had, as he suspected, been spotless before Ferris came along.

"You can call me Ferris here, Lucy," Ham said now, abashed—for Ham. "Jack's okay."

"I made some tea," Lucy offered, neither agreeing nor disagreeing with him. "I could bring some down for the two of you."

The place seemed to warm at Lucy's offer, but Jack said, "Why don't the two of you go on up? Ham can rest that ground-up shoulder of his, and you can both start figuring on what comes next. I'll stay down here, keep an eye on business."

Ham laughed humorlessly. "There won't be any business, Harwood. Count on it."

Jack said, "Then I won't have to work awful hard at it, now, will I?"

So Hamilton got the hint and headed upstairs with his lady friend, pausing only once at the doorway. "You didn't have to stay, Harwood. Even if you felt honor-bound to defend us, you could have rode off once the shooting stopped, left me to face all this on my own."

Jack probably would have done just that not so long ago. But something had happened to his priorities in this town, something that made him take noble risks for foolish reasons.

Honor-bound?

More than one such reason likely involved the good opinion of a serious, sorrel-haired schoolmarm. But not all of them. Jack said, "Don't confuse me."

"You really *are* okay," insisted Ham before following his own forbidden lover up the stairs. As an afterthought, he called down, "Don't steal anything."

Jack chuckled—then nearly fell off the cold stove when he turned too quickly toward the opening door. There, hesitating in against cold sunlight, stood the last person he'd expected to see set foot in the mercantile again, even before last night's fun.

His world momentarily stilled to dust motes and silence. He'd always thought her attractive, of course. But after the hell of last night and this whole damned day, she now looked so clean, so downright wholesome, that she nearly glowed with it. His eyes smarted just to look at her, but the rest of him eased considerably.

If it wasn't the lovely Miss Audra Garrison herself.

All of Audra's second thoughts and concerns about why she ought not go by the mercantile vanished as soon as she saw Jack in that shadowy, cluttered store.

He seemed so tired!

Half-leaning, half-seated on a display stove, he looked more disheveled than she'd ever seen him, even when he'd been drunk. Something stiffened and dulled his dark hair, as if he'd gotten it wet—but not clean—and then let it dry without benefit of a comb. A day's growth of whiskers shadowed his chin, jaw, and upper lip. His clothes were clean, but obviously thrown on; not only was he in his shirtsleeves, but he'd neither tucked his shirttail in nor had he buttoned its top two buttons. She saw an uneven sprinkling of dark hair below the hollow of his throat before she could make herself look away, flustered.

He seemed so very . . . male. Her common sense made one last try—she ought not be here.

"Miss Garrison," he said, by way of greeting, and pushed to his feet. Not Audra. Not darling. Just Miss Garrison. She looked back, savored the sight of his face again—whole, alive, even welcoming—and, oh, her common sense was right. She should go. She couldn't guard herself against this man, not with him so raw and real and her so very, very glad to see him.

Then she noted his weary eyes and knew she could not desert him on the selfish excuse of her own weaknesses. She must behave herself long enough to be of some assistance.

"Mr. Harwood," she greeted, running her useless palms over her skirt. "Are you well?"

Immediately she regretted the question. Surely if anybody could take care of himself it was Jack Harwood! Even as she thought that, he smiled his usual charming smile. "Considerably improved from the morning. And you?"

Her? "Why—I'm fine. But I'm not the one . . ." She did not know what to say after that. She did not want to insult him again after the horrible questions she'd asked just the day before.

He sighed, shoving his hands into his pockets, and only then seemed to notice his untucked shirt. He stopped smiling. "No, that you're not. You ought not be here, dar—" He stopped himself, then smiled again, this time ruefully. "Ma'am."

No matter how improper, she missed him calling her darling. "I oughtn't?"

"It won't do much for your reputation."

Oh! She had the grace to look down at the toes of her shoes, peeking out from under her long skirt. "I suppose I deserve that."

In the silence that followed, she realized with a deep, squeezing pain that perhaps she'd gone too far, after church, for even the most casual of friendships to survive.

Then Jack said, "Deserve what?"

When she looked up he seemed confused, not condemning, in the half-light.

"You said . . . my reputation. I was rude to you—again—because of your . . . choices. When in fact I've been the one at fault, blaming you instead of taking responsibility for my own weaknesses." She raised her chin. "I apologize for that, Mr. Harwood."

He blinked, more expressions playing across his face than she could read. "You do?"

She nodded. "When I heard there'd been a shooting, and you were involved . . ." Her heart cramped at the too-fresh memory, at the disarray of the store around them, and she took courage from the strength of her feelings. "I was so very afraid for you."

He took a tentative step closer to her. "You were?"

"And—" She might as well be honest. Though she often fumbled propriety around Jack Harwood, his own lack of judgments always encouraged her to honesty. "And afraid for myself, I'm sorry to say. What if you had been hurt, or killed, believing that I thought less of you? I mean . . . it may not seem important," she added, looking down. "But it is for me. When I knew you were safe, that I could still apologize, I had to come. After school let out, I mean."

He said nothing else, just crossed the few feet between them, so that she now had a view of his mud-scuffed boot toes, his creased pant cuffs. She could feel his intense warmth, even from a respectable foot away; could smell a strange but not unpleasant perfume of river, gunpowder, and coffee, along with the deeper, more familiar scent that was simply Jack.

No whiskey, she noted with the edge of her mind. No tobacco, even.

"You came here to tell me that," he repeated, low and uneven.

She nodded, and the way he exhaled—half laugh, half sob—gave her the courage to peek up at him again.

Oh! Jack Harwood was not angry with her. In fact, he was looking at her with such a heady mixture of wonder and even—adoration?—that her heart sped and she forgot how to breathe, both at the same time. The effect made her pleasantly dizzy.

"Oh, darlin'." He sighed, lifting warm, gentle fingers to her jaw. Her eyes drifted shut at the rightness of his touch.

Until she felt his breath brush her lips. Somehow she pulled back. "No!" She managed to turn her back to him, arms crossed tight over her front, fists under her chin, wishing her heart could be contained as easily as that. "I can't!" she said, not looking at him.

She longed for him to take her shoulders, turn her, convince her otherwise. She feared it just as much.

This time he said, "Oh, Audra," almost in a groan. It wasn't with the same passion with which he'd just called her darling, but neither was it as condemning as she'd feared and likely deserved. She'd let him think he could kiss her again. Worse, she *wanted* his kiss, wanted it so badly that surely he could see it.

But she'd chosen staying away over controlling those immodest wants once before. In the end it had proved more painful even than this frustrating forbearance.

"I mean . . . I mustn't," she explained, hating the pitiable tone of her own voice. "I'm sorry. I ought not have misled you. It's just . . . I'm sorry."

She heard Jack's footsteps leave her, but before her heart crumbled, they stopped a safe distance off. "What is it 'just,' darlin'?" he asked, almost in a sigh, but a patient one nevertheless.

When she looked over her shoulder, he'd stepped behind the counter where they kept the mail, so that she would have the safety of a glass case of merchandise between them. He did not appear particularly happy . . . but neither did he look critical.

He even waited, not nudging her on, until she managed to gather enough of her scattered wits to try to answer him. "I . . . I *would* like us to still be friends. If that's possible."

"That is possible," he assured her, blue eyes crinkling in a way that spelled danger.

"But I would like—I *need*—to . . . to behave myself. I promised to follow the rules when I took this job. I promised my father, too. A person is only as good as her word, you know."

He'd always heard the saying refer to men. "And that's a problem because . . . ?"

Her face heated. "I have difficulty behaving myself around you," she admitted, chagrined.

The grin that slowly creased his cheeks, dancing into his eyes, was more than charming. It was downright delighted. "Do you?"

"I would appreciate your taking this seriously," she chided him. Then, recognizing that she'd just used her schoolteacher voice, she had to smile a little herself. Jack Harwood was more of a handful than even Claudine or Jerome could be, but he was a more pleasant handful. "That's why I thought I should stay away," she explained more reasonably. "Why I asked those terrible questions yesterday. I thought if only I could see the worst in you, I could keep myself away."

"And you figured that was the worst of me," he challenged amiably.

"There's *worse*?"

He laughed at that, but sobered all too soon. "Well, Audra—last night I helped kill a man. Most folks would find that worse."

"Wasn't it—wasn't it self-defense?" The idea that Jack, her friend Jack, could be involved in something so nefarious as ambush or murder seemed inconceivable.

"It was," he assured her, just as she'd hoped. "But a man's still dead and his woman widowed. It was an all-around ugly business. I meant what I said when you came in. Being here won't do much for that valuable reputation of yours."

Even if he were mocking her, she supposed she deserved it. But he did not sound mocking. "It would be, were I here for social reasons," she explained primly. She'd rehearsed the argument thoroughly enough, across the course of the day. "But I'm not."

He raised an eyebrow, making her smile at herself again.

"Well, perhaps *some* social reasons," she admitted, flushing. "But I'm also here to offer my assistance."

"Your . . . assistance?"

"That's what neighbors do, don't they?" She considered it. "And friends."

He looked at her strangely. "It has been known to happen."

Which worried her. "We *can* be friends, can't we? Even if I don't approve of gambling? Even . . . even if I mustn't let you kiss me anymore?"

She had let him use her first name, even call her darling. She must draw the line somewhere!

He hesitated, sucked a pensive breath in through his teeth, and her hopes faltered. "You're leaving town," she remembered, feeling foolish.

"I was leaving town last night," he admitted. That alone made her stomach lurch. "But after the . . . trouble . . . I suspect my friend Ferris could use my assistance for another week or so, anyhow. Until we're sure nobody takes it into their heads to try finishing what they started."

The possibility had not occurred to her. "You think they might?"

He smiled. "We held them off just fine before; I figure we can do the same again. It'd be nothing so difficult as trying to be your friend without stealing a few friendly kisses now and again."

His words made her shiver almost as deliciously as his kisses once had—which rather proved his point.

"I cannot be your friend if you mean to behave like a common masher, Jack Harwood," she warned him. At least, she would have to be his friend from a safe distance.

"That would be a shame," he agreed, his eyes laughing at her.

"Yes, it would!" she agreed sternly.

He braced his hands on the counter, and leaned into them. " 'Course, you ought not be my friend anyhow. Considering that you have a reputation to uphold."

Which should be true, as well. She'd be foolish to forget what she'd seen of vice in Fort Worth. To openly befriend Jack Harwood might imply to the school board and the community that she condoned such sins, which she certainly did not.

But to continually avoid him would imply, to herself, that she'd become a narrow-minded ingrate simply for fear of public opinion. His sins couldn't stain her own morality unless she allowed it. She hoped she'd learned enough, matured enough, to allow no such thing.

"I'll see to my own reputation," she assured him. "You do what you can to keep your hands to yourself."

He did not have even the decency to blush. "I honestly don't know if I can do that."

"Then you risk ending our friendship yet again," she warned him, then gave him a shy smile. "And you must admit, it's rather tiring to keep track."

He laughed again. "That it is. How about we take a chance and just see how the cards play out? I will at least *attempt* to treat you like the lady you are."

It pleased her that he still thought she was a lady, even after the things she'd said and not said, even after the way she'd kissed him, held him. *Oh, dear.*

"I'd best go now," she announced hurriedly.

"But what about that assistance?" he challenged quickly, starting around the counter but then, to her mixed relief and disappointment, apparently thinking better of it and staying his approach. "You wouldn't want to give the appearance this was a social call, now, would you?"

She studied him through narrowing eyes, suspecting that he cared more about keeping her in the store for a few minutes more than he did about appearances. Worse, she did, too.

"Is there anything you or Mr. Hamilton need?" she asked, taking refuge in propriety. "Especially Mr. Hamilton. I believe he was injured."

"Mr. Hamilton will be fine," Jack said dismissively. "Doctor said so."

"Oh. That's a relief." She fidgeted with her gloves. "Well, then."

"Could be I need something," he added, his voice thick, and she studied him for sign of what that might be. She quite liked him disheveled. She wished she could run her finger over his jaw and feel the rasp of his whiskers, even wished she could see a little more of that triangle of male chest revealed by his shirt collar. Oh, but she was in grievous trouble.

And it still seemed better than staying away.

"What?" She had to ask twice; the first time it just came out as a croak.

"I don't dare tell you," he teased, and though he smiled, his blue eyes glowed more with unsettling heat than with amusement. "It would end our friendship for sure."

"I'd best go now." Audra all but bolted for the door.

"Maybe you'd best, darlin'," he agreed, softly, behind her.

Neither of them mustered much enthusiasm in their goodbye—but enthusiasm, Audra decided as she hurried home, could remain low on her list of priorities. First she must honor what she knew in her heart was right, including her friendship with Jack. Then she must honor her family and her word, especially in her contract with Candon. In that order.

You can't cross rivers you ain't reached, her father often warned.

Such trivialities as enthusiasm she would deal with if it became necessary, not before.

Thoughts of Audra kept Jack whistling the rest of the day and gave him savory dreams that night. But the true courage of her visit became increasingly obvious over the next few days. Apparently the townsfolk of Candon had no intention of forgiving Ferris for his transgression, at least not as long as Lucy remained. They were driving to Euless or Estill for their goods. Even the postal delivery moved to the lumber mill, with a new postmaster sworn in, so that even for their mail folks wouldn't have to brave the den of iniquity that was the Candon Mercantile.

Tuesday someone egged the store—the only eggs they'd seen, since their supply of eggs, milk, and butter from the farmers' wives had stopped coming in. Their only visitor was an old colored man asking after Lucy. He handed over a worn flour sack, which, Jack assumed, contained her clothes and possessions. They talked, and he left.

Jack went outside to clean the windows then, preferring even the sulfuric stench of rotten eggs to the sound of a woman's sobs. Ferris wasn't fit company for a porcupine, much less a personable fellow like Jack.

The next day someone whitewashed GET OUT—along with several racial slurs—on the front window. Jack hurried to wash off the worst of it before Lucy could see, not that she often ventured where folks might catch a glimpse of her. If the three of them were prisoners, she was the one in solitary, and went only out back for the outhouse or to do laundry.

Hamilton had protested that. "You aren't our laundress anymore, Lucy!"

But when she'd asked him, "Then what am I?" he hadn't known what to answer.

"You gonna do something about this?" asked Jack as they sat alone, playing a listless game of checkers at the deserted cracker barrel.

Ham snorted, wrathful as a stomped snake. "About what?"

Jack moved a red wooden disk from one square to the next. "You're the one who took up with the girl in the first place."

"And that makes me a criminal?" Ferris challenged. "If you could've sweet-talked that schoolmarm into joining *you* by the river in the moonlight, I guarantee she wouldn't stay respectable for much longer than it would take you to hike her skirts—"

Jack slapped the board off the barrel, scattering checkers across the room. "You watch how you talk about her."

He'd reacted faster than he would have guessed possible and now took longer to calm. Only belatedly did he realize an extra cause to his fury, something he'd conveniently forgotten in the excitement. It could be that Audra *wasn't* so pure. It could be that some bastard had already gotten to her. That, as much as Ham's rudeness, made him angry enough to spit nails.

Not that it made a bit of difference to his point. "Audra Garrison," he continued with marginally more calm, "is a lady."

Ham's eyes narrowed. "And you're saying Lucy isn't?"

"Sounds like you're the one saying it. If all she is to you is a good lay, I have other places I can be. And she could use an escort to somewhere a touch less dangerous than this damned town of yours herself."

They sat silently for a few minutes. Finally Hamilton looked up, solemn, and said, "You watch *your* damned mouth. She's more to me than that."

Good. "Then start acting like it."

"What the heck am I supposed to do, *marry* her?"

"Hell, yes. That's what I'd—" He stopped too late for either of them to miss the surprising admission. He'd thought it before, too. Audra Garrison did that to him. "If the gal meant enough to me," he clarified, "and I'd ruined her place in the community, damned right I'd marry her."

Though he pitied the woman so yoked.

"Well, that's fine for you to say, but in case you forgot, Texas has miscegenation laws. I couldn't marry her if I wanted to."

Jack folded his arms. "Do you want to?"

The question hung between them, thick and choking as sour smoke, until Ferris shrugged his good shoulder, the one not in a sling. "I don't know," he admitted.

Well . . . damn. Not that Jack didn't appreciate his honesty. But it didn't do Lucy Wolfe a lot of good. "Well, if a gal *didn't* mean enough for me to marry her, I hope I'd at least take care of her. Make sure she wasn't in the family way. Give her enough money to settle herself elsewhere, someplace folks didn't know her." God, but he hoped that wasn't what Audra had already done in coming here. "Could be the kinder thing, in fact, 'cause I'd surely make one sorry husband."

Lucy said, "That's what I want," and both men looked up guiltily.

"If you meant to ask me," she said evenly, from the doorway to the back "that's just what I'm wanting. To go somewhere and start new."

"Alone?" Ham's voice cracked, and Jack decided he ought to go see to something—anything—out back. Now. Checkers crunched under his boots as he escaped.

He had enough of his own concerns to chew on—what Audra had revealed of herself at church, what he'd revealed about himself right here—that he didn't need to tangle himself further in Ham and Lucy's. Still, despite his usual penchant for not interfering, he was glad he'd brought it up.

Someone shot at the store that night and took out an upstairs window with buckshot.

It was time they did something. *What* they'd do was a whole separate issue.

Chapter Twenty-three

> *Teachers should set aside a goodly portion of their earnings for their benefit during their declining years, so as not to become a burden on society.*
>
> —Rules for Teachers

"Does she know where she'd like to go?" asked Audra, savoring Jack's company from across the counter even more than the sweet tang of the candy stick he'd given her. She felt bracingly rebellious simply by returning here; accepting the candy came easily in comparison.

She tried not to think about slippery slopes off righteous paths.

Even Jack had questioned her propriety when she arrived, after school on Thursday, to ask after their health and safety. Even if Mr. Hamilton and Miss Wolfe *were* married, as she'd heard rumored, that alone would be a scandal without Jack sharing their residence.

She'd attempted to stay away for the week, not just because of Aunt Heddy's disapproval but to prove to herself that she could. Stay away, that was. That she could be Jack's friend without letting her standards of behavior fall by the wayside, as she had before. But when Jerome Newton announced at school that someone had shot up the mercantile, standards of behavior fell in importance next to ascertaining her friend's continued well-being.

So here she was—with nobody else to hear them talk, not even by the cracker barrel.

Jack, leaning his elbows on the counter and his cheek on one fist, watched her mouth with an inordinate amount of interest when she sucked on the candy stick. "What's that, darlin'?"

She took the stick out of her mouth to answer him, as seemed only polite, and he raised somewhat glazed eyes to her own. "Miss Wolfe. Does she—" Then she realized that she already had the answer to one of the gossips' many speculations, right there. "You did not call her Mrs. Hamilton; you called her Miss Wolfe. Does that mean that they . . ." She flushed, hesitant to speak of such things. But if she could ask this of anybody . . . "Does that mean they have not married?"

He sat up slightly, clearing his throat. "Only in the . . . uh . . . basest sense."

"Oh." Her face burned with embarrassment. "That's too bad."

"Neither one's completely set against it, mind you. Ferris is talking 'bout pulling up stakes, relocating somewhere safer, maybe up north. But that takes money, and he'll be lucky if the store doesn't go under first. Lucy—Miss Wolfe, I mean—just wants to . . ."

For some reason, when she started to suck on the hard candy again while listening to him, Jack's attention seemed to wander. This time, even when she withdrew the candy from her mouth, Jack continued staring at her lips for a long, intriguing moment. He seemed fascinated and uncomfortable at the same time, somehow different from when he meant to kiss her.

Testing her observation, Audra tentatively licked the tip of the candy stick.

Jack squeezed his eyes shut as if pained. When he opened them, he reached across the counter and touched her wrist, guiding her hand—and the candy—gently away from her mouth.

"Maybe"—his voice cracked—"maybe you ought to save that until later, after all."

Oh! He'd been the one to suggest she have the treat there, but she must have behaved rudely anyway. She offered the stick to him. "I'm sorry. Do you want some?"

Jack pressed his lips together, the oddest expression on his face, and shook his head.

When Jack Harwood ran out of words, something was amiss. "What's wrong?"

He had to take a deep breath, deep enough to raise and drop his shoulders, before he attempted answering her. "Tell you what, darlin'. Someday you'll get yourself married. When you do, you ask your husband what could be so fascinating about a lady eating a candy stick the way you do, and he'll"—he cleared his throat—"I imagine he'll clarify things further."

The idea of her marrying—marrying anyone but the wonderful, dissolute man across the counter from her, in any case—disturbed her so much, she didn't bother to pursue his strange explanation. And of course she could not marry Jack, even if he wanted to marry her, which he surely did not. He was leaving;

and even if he weren't leaving, he was a gambler; and even if he weren't a gambler, he drank; and even if he didn't drink . . .

Thoughts of his other sins only embarrassed her further. The point was, she could neither marry him nor imagine marrying elsewhere. Perhaps she'd simply become an old maid—like her Aunt Heddy, but without even the past a widow could claim. The thought saddened her—no husband, no real home, no kissing, no . . . marrying *in the basest sense*.

No children except for pupils.

She occupied herself with wrapping the candy stick in a handkerchief, so that she could pocket it without ruining her dress, and prompted, "You told me that Miss Wolfe meant to leave the area, and I asked where she would go."

"That's a fine question," Jack assured her, sounding steadier than he had since giving her the candy. She loved the ease with which he talked to her, as if she could understand almost anything he had to tell her, as if she might even be of some use in arriving at a solution.

"It's one of several we'd best answer if she's to get safely away from here," he continued. "Poorly as the store's doing, we'll do well to afford train passage and funds for food, much less enough to get her settled once she gets wherever she's going. And we can't figure the money until someone figures out a destination."

"How about Wyoming?" Audra asked.

Jack blinked at her. "Wyoming?"

"Where my family lives. The man who runs the laundry there—Sing Lee—used to work for us as our housekeeper until Mama invested in his business to help him get started."

As usual, Jack's smile made her insides swoop. "He was that bad a housekeeper?"

"No, silly! My mother just does things like that. She helped to get Sing Lee's wife into the country, too, despite the Exclusion Acts. So I'm sure he'd do her a favor if she asked. And he often says he could use more help. If Miss Wolfe wanted to go to Sheridan, one of my family could meet the train so that she wouldn't be alone in a strange place, and—"

Jack raised a hand. "Wait a moment, darlin'. You are brilliant," he assured her, which, coming from a man who had faced off five drunken hoodlums with only a derringer—she'd overheard her pupils telling more of the story—flattered her considerably. "But you'll just have to waste breath repeating yourself," he warned now. "Stay here and don't move, agreed?"

She nodded. He turned toward the back room, then paused, turned back, and kissed her. It was a quick kiss, not like the ones they'd lingered over in the woods, but it still tingled through her, especially when his tongue brushed her lips, as if reluctant to end things, as he drew away.

"My apologies," he said smoothly—and not the least bit apologetic, she thought—and then he headed into the back, smacking his lips as he went. He was tasting the candy off her lips!

She'd still not stopped blushing when Jack returned with Mr. Hamilton and a reticent Miss Wolfe. "Now tell them what you told me, Miss Garrison," he instructed, gratifyingly more formal in their presence—but stopping to stand, tall and warm, beside her.

So Audra did, excitement at her suggestion growing.

Mr. Hamilton tended to interrupt. "Maybe she doesn't want to be a laundress anymore."

Miss Wolfe said nothing.

Audra said, "Well . . . I don't imagine that you would have trouble getting a different job if you like, perhaps as a waitress, or a maid . . ."

"Domestic work," challenged the storekeeper, and Miss Wolfe put a hand on his arm.

"It's what I know," she murmured, as if shy to speak at all.

Mr. Hamilton said, "You shouldn't have to work, much less as a domestic."

Then marry her, thought Audra—which only reminded her that, in some unmentionable ways, they *were* married. Audra fought back a blush by studying a selection of jewelry in the glass case, so as not to further embarrass either the nervous woman or herself.

Both Jack and Miss Wolfe dismissed Mr. Hamilton's lastest protest without even arguing it. Instead, Miss Wolfe ventured a question. "You come from a fine family, Miss Garrison. I can see that. Why would your people have doings with the likes of me?"

"Why not? Papa employs colored cowboys," Audra assured her.

Miss Wolfe twisted her dark hands in her apron. "No ma'am. I mean . . ."

"Oh!" Now Audra did blush. Averting her eyes from the couple, she barely caught a glimpse of Miss Wolfe's nod. To be honest, her father *would* be less than pleased to learn that Audra had befriended a fallen woman, much less volunteered the family's assistance.

If he learned of it, she reminded herself, not as guilty as she should likely feel.

"Well . . . I thought the idea of this was to make a fresh start. Why burden people with needless information?" She slanted a secret look at Jack when she said that, pleased to see in his answering gaze, blue and dancing, that he remembered saying it.

"As long as I'm not breeding," offered the woman, regaining Audra's attention.

Face burning, Audra nodded. "Otherwise nobody need know, my family included."

Mr. Hamilton startled them both. "For Christ's sake, she's not a train robber!"

"Watch your language," warned Jack, putting a protective hand on Audra's arm. He even leaned closer and murmured, "Ham's a mite tense nowadays."

She made a conscious effort not to let her eyes drift shut at the sensation of his breath on her cheek, the tickle when his inhalation drew her hair. It kept her from reminding Mr. Hamilton that Miss Wolfe might as well be a train robber, in the eyes of society, as have a baby in the bushes.

"It will be cold in Wyoming," she noted instead. "So if you do decide to go, we must make sure you have proper clothes and shoes. Goodness—have you ever even seen snow?"

Mr. Hamilton huffed. "Of course she has. We do get snow

around here, you know—every other year, at least, and some years more than once." But they had not, that year.

"Mama wrote that for Christmas they had drifts four feet high," said Audra.

Miss Wolfe's eyes widened. "I've never seen *that* much snow!"

"It's wonderful, truly. Once you get used to it. But you'll want to be dressed warmly before you reach Denver. Do you . . . ?"

When she turned to ask Jack about the mercantile's stock, he stood so close to her, watching her face with such obvious pleasure, that her insides swooped again. They were not doing as well being friends as she had hoped—and she refused to consider how she should react just yet. Instead, she cleared her throat. "Do you think the mercantile can help with that?"

"I don't think we're well-enough stocked," he admitted, fascination drowning out any regret in his tone. "Shoes we can do, but there's not much call for truly heavy coats around here . . . except, I'd imagine, every other year, at least." His eyes twinkled as they shared a smile, and, risks or not, she felt so very glad that she'd made up with him—and that he'd let her—that her heart seemed to swell right up against the confines of her chest.

Then she recalled herself. "I may have a solution to that, too," she said, and looked back at Miss Wolfe. "That is . . . if you don't mind assistance from the Ladies' Aid."

"Ladies' Aid?" asked Mr. Hamilton. "What Ladies' Aid?"

"The one holding our first meeting at the church tonight."

The men exchanged doubtful glances, and Miss Wolfe looked down at her bare feet.

"I'm not very popular around here right now," she hedged.

"But do you mind if I at least try?"

Miss Wolfe shrugged.

Jack said, "Are you sure folks won't think less of you for doin' this, Miss Garrison?"

As usual, his concern demanded honesty. "No," she admitted. "But you did not let that dissuade you from doing what was right when you went to help Mr. Hamilton."

"Now, that was different. I'm a man."

That argument, at least, she'd learned from her mother how to handle. She simply stared at him.

Jack tried again. "And my reputation wasn't in fine shape even before that."

Her fingers itched to pat his arm reassuringly, but she held herself back. "I would hope that mine can withstand at least a little controversy, but there is only one way to be sure, which is to test it. In any case, I'm quite sure I'm doing what is right."

It was a heady feeling, in fact, to feel so certain. She knew she would question Jack's latest kiss later—in the schoolroom or in church or while she did chores. But helping Miss Wolfe start a new life seemed so clearly right, she could not imagine how anybody could argue it.

Jack shook his head. "I surely hope someone else figures that out as well, darlin'."

She widened her eyes at his endearment—then noticed that neither Mr. Hamilton nor Miss Wolfe seemed the least bit surprised, and blushed. Had he called her Miss Garrison only for her sake, and not for theirs? Surely they did not know that he . . . that together, they . . .

It occurred to her to wonder if a few kisses would shock a couple who had . . . who were . . . and she felt her blush deepen. This, she realized, explained why young ladies ought not associate with, well . . . wrongdoers. The comparison dangerously minimized one's own sins. But must she wait until she was respectably married, like her mother or the ladies who ran the Women's Industrial Home or the settlement houses, before she could even provide assistance?

Surely, if she kept tight rein on herself, she could risk it.

"We had best arrange a few more things before I go," she said now, dropping her gaze. "But first . . . Mr. Harwood, perhaps you should stand over there."

"Yes, ma'am," he said, his voice thick with amusement—but he stepped obediently to the other side of the counter. She tried to feel relieved, instead of bereft of his closeness.

She could not justify his closeness nearly so well as her assisting Miss Wolfe.

Once the door closed behind Audra, Jack said, "Five will get you ten she does it."

Ferris said, "You're on."

Lucy continued to look at the several sheets of paper Audra had left—a rough train route, including changes; a message to Mrs. Garrison that Jack would send by telegraph the next day; a list of people Lucy could trust. She looked overwhelmed, and Jack didn't blame her—he loved Audra for many things, but until this afternoon he hadn't realized how incredibly useful—

Jack swayed against the counter as the mercantile—the whole world—disintegrated and reformed into something that looked identical and felt completely different. He loved her.

Hamilton, misinterpreting his slump, said, "Too late, friend; all bets are final."

Jack blinked unseeingly at him. Well, of course he loved her. He must've loved her for some time. He loved her innocence and her curiosity. He loved how solemnly she treated issues of character, which had him looking at that virtue a touch more seriously himself. Of course he loved touching her—her lips against his, her body pressed up against him, even the feathery softness of her hair against his fingers. Watching what her mouth and tongue were doing to that candy stick this afternoon nearly undid him. But now he fully understood why such artless gestures on her part packed more punch than the most experienced of seductions.

His physical reactions were symptoms of a bigger predicament: he loved Audra. Well, how could he *not* love her? How could anybody not love her?

He glared at Ferris, who looked surprised.

Lucy said, "You two ought not be wagering over that nice lady as if she were a racehorse. Especially *you.*" She aimed an accusing finger at Jack.

What? A racehorse? Oh. Jack imagined what Audra might think of their bet and inwardly winced. He'd done plenty of late that, while gratifying, might not exactly be *loving,* hadn't he?

"He *is* giving her the odds," Ferris pointed out in Jack's defense.

But Jack sighed. Damned if Lucy wasn't right.

"How about," he suggested, "five will get you ten the Ladies' Aid comes through." He had less confidence when he put it that way, but it seemed marginally better than betting on Audra herself.

Lucy made a disgusted sound and stalked off to the back room.

"I can't take back a bet once I've made it," he called by way of explanation.

She stomped up the stairs by way of response.

Ferris said, "Then my five goes to the bigoted old biddies holding their ground." He made a face. That sounded even worse. "Or . . . if you want to . . . ?"

"All bets are off," agreed Jack, glad to break the rules this once, and they shook on it.

If he loved Audra, really loved her, he wouldn't do anything to hurt her. Not that he would actively have hurt her before, of course. But now, how could he risk even indirectly hurting her? He couldn't talk her into meeting him in the woods again. He shouldn't have stolen that kiss in the store today—though he had no idea how he could have stopped himself, and it had been delicious. She shouldn't even be in the store. Or, to be honest, with him.

Loving Audra, he thought glumly, would be nowhere near as fun as liking her had been.

But all he had to do was think of her—gray eyes alight with idealism, sorrel curls catching golden glints of sun, china-doll cheeks flushing with what she obviously took to be immodest thoughts—and he knew there was nothing more worthy of protection. Even from himself.

The women of the Ladies' Aid could speak of nothing but Candon's recent scandal.

"Shocking!"

"And such a poor example for the children!"

"How do you explain something like this to a ten-year-old? That's what I'd like to know."

Audra sat back and listened—*Close your mouth and open your ears,* her father would advise. The situation *did* set a poor example for the children, after all. But did nobody else find the attack and the vandalism an even worse example? At least the fornication was not *intended* to victimize others.

"That hussy should go back to her own people!"

"I certainly won't spend another penny at that place."

"I've had my husband drive to Bobo's Store in Bedford!"

Tentatively, Audra asked, "What about the blacksmith?"

Ten pairs of eyes turned blankly to her. Then Mrs. Collins asked, "What's that, dear?"

"Has anybody stopped doing business with Mr. Gilmer? He helped ambush Mr. Hamilton and his . . . lady friend. Surely you don't approve of *his* actions."

"Heavens, dear, what lady has anything to do with a blacksmith?"

"That's my husband's concern." As if driving to Bedford was not.

And perhaps most shocking: "*They* were only protecting us from the shameful goings-on by the river! And two of them were murdered for their efforts!"

Murdered? That, and the several nods that answered it, chilled Audra. If these women were spouting borrowed thoughts on loan from their husbands, Jack and his friends might face more danger than she'd feared. How could she, not even eighteen, make a difference?

"Two men and one woman in the same household!"

"And not a one married to another."

"They should be arrested, is what they should be."

Audra tried again. "But Mr. Hamilton and Miss Wolfe *cannot* marry here. It's illegal."

"And rightly so!" declared Mrs. Tilton. "It's an abomination, is what it is!"

"But . . . if you don't allow them to marry, how can you condemn them for not marrying?"

"We condemn them," announced the widow Parks sternly, "for being together at all."

Audra considered pointing out that Mr. Hamilton and Miss Wolfe had fallen in love, but she knew the answer to that one, too—they could just fall *out* of love. People had repeatedly told her oldest sister Mariah that, when Mariah fell for the wrong man. As if it were that easy!

Were these the moral examples she'd been following for so long? They made a better argument for thinking for oneself than Jack Harwood ever had!

Close your mouth. Open your ears. But what about eyes?

Examining the women more closely, Audra realized that only three of them truly dominated the conversation. Several more nodded, but ventured no real points of their own. And almost half the ladies just glanced up from their knitting or sewing on occasion. Could it be that at least some of them disagreed, too, and simply did not wish to draw criticism by speaking up?

Perhaps that was wise.

But it was not right. And for all Audra knew, the noise might indicate their very uncertainty—only a nervous cow would paw or bellow.

She had promised to try. Best get to it.

"Aid," Audra said—but nobody seemed to hear her.

"Do the miscegenation laws include common-law marriages?" asked the widow Parks. "Perhaps we could have them imprisoned!"

"Or insist that there be a morals law in this town!"

So Audra raised her voice. "Ladies' Aid Society."

Everyone in the room looked at her then, even Melissa and Claudine, who were caring for some of the small children in the far corner.

"No need to shout, dear," chided Aunt Heddy.

Well, there was no need *now!* "When Mrs. Collins and I spoke, I had assumed that we would form a Ladies' *Aid* Society. Should that not encompass some kind of giving of . . . aid?"

The three who'd done most of the pawing and bellowing drew back, affronted. But Mrs. Abbott, mother of one of Audra's pupils, said, "What did you have in mind, Miss Garrison?"

And they actually looked to her for a suggestion! She had not felt so tongue-tied since her first week as a teacher. Wasn't someone else supposed to do this part? She'd meant only to speak up on behalf of Lucy Wolfe—and surely she could not *start* with that!

"Well." She remembered something else Jack said. "Mr. Wells left a widow, yes?" When several women nodded, she said, "Perhaps we could help her with some of her chores? Take up a collection toward her debts for the funeral? We could see whether she has any proper mourning clothes, and if not, perhaps someone could loan her an extra dress."

"When my Frank died," said Marilyn Madison, "I could hardly rouse myself to fix a proper meal. I know most of us brought casseroles and cakes earlier this week, but we might take turns bringing an extra lunch to church for her on Sundays, just in case."

"Or send it with folks who go that way, if she don't attend church," added Mrs. Stevens. "When little Abby died, well . . . I couldn't make myself attend church for some months after."

Several women reached across to touch her, to commiserate. Then Audra got to sit back and watch after all. The ladies decided which four would provide Sunday lunches for the next month. Even Mrs. Tilton agreed to bring food on the first Sunday in February.

After that, ideas flew: socks for orphans; flowers in front of the church. But by the time Mrs. Collins asked, "Does anybody else have a suggestion to make?" Audra still had not kept her promise, so she straightened her spine and raised her hand.

Aunt Heddy said, "This is not school, child." Several ladies laughed—but some others, younger, rolled their eyes sympathetically. Perhaps they'd once been Aunt Heddy's pupils.

"I suggest we collect warm clothes so Miss Lucy Wolfe can travel safely north," she said.

Nobody seemed upset at all. Some women smiled encouragingly, seeming to wait for more information. Others stared at her blankly. Then Mrs. Stevens asked, "Who's Lucy Wolfe?"

They didn't know?

"She's the woman at the mercantile," Audra clarified. "With Mr. Hamilton."

The stunned silence that followed comprised the last bit of peace that the first meeting of the Candon Ladies' Aid society saw.

Chapter Twenty-four

Teachers must be home between 8 P.M. and 6 A.M. unless attending a school function.

—Rules for Teachers

Jack enjoyed the still stretch just before dawn, when the world turned gray enough to see its possibilities, but with enough lingering darkness to shelter its flaws. Time was he'd enjoyed this quiet *before* bed. This morning he met it from the other end of sleep, reluctant to desert his pallet or his dreams. But he'd promised Ham and Lucy both—and Audra. So he dragged himself up, washed in bracingly chill water, palmed some food tins, and left for the livery.

Even *after* bed, the frosty morning welcomed him as gently as ever.

The scent of hay, leather, and horses warmed the livery stables. Jack pumped some water for Queen's trough. While she drank he scooped a light breakfast of grain into a feed bag, then slipped it over her ears. Then he sat back on some hay and cut into a tin of oysters to join her, trying to recall the finer details of his dream. Sadly, only remnants lingered . . . though enough to know that he'd deserve slapping, if Audra ever learned to read a fellow's mind.

Several barnyard cats came begging at the smell of his treat, dancing and yowling for his attention, but they had to make do with the liquid in the bottom of the tin.

By time Jack bridled and saddled Queen and led her out, dawn had crept close enough to pick up silver twinkles in the frost. Both his breath and the mare's left a mist in the air, just cold enough to wake him up right. He tried to imagine four-foot snowdrifts and could not do it.

Then he heard approaching footsteps. He and Queen turned their heads in unison.

Audra?

For a moment he thought he imagined her, a ghostly wish appearing out of the gray. But if this were a continuation of his dream, the slight figure would leap into his embrace, fill his arms, kiss him like . . . well, like he knew Audra *could* kiss him. If only she would.

This Audra slowed and murmured comfortingly to Queen as she neared. She held out a fisted hand for the mare to whiffle and praised her equine intelligence at doing so. Only then, petting Queen's nose, did she slide a happy glance toward Jack. Her eyes were the same exact gray color as the frosty morning—and just as invigorating.

He thought: I love her. It unsettled him a bit, gut-deep, but not at all unpleasantly.

"Good morning, Mr. Harwood!" she greeted.

Savoring her smile, her apparent excitement, Jack tugged at his hat brim. "Ma'am."

"I'm glad I caught you," she admitted. A flush of color, even in the gray light, touched her cheeks at her boldness, but she didn't take it back. "I just had to tell somebody, and you were the first person I thought of. I could barely sleep for wanting it."

As with the sweet torture of that candy stick the day before, she had no earthly idea what kind of risqué interpretation Jack could put on her innocent words. He'd wanted it, too.

He took a deep, steadying breath, reminded himself to put *her* good first, and asked, with forced nonchalance, "What's that, darlin'?"

"I did it."

Only when Queen swung her head back and bumped him in the chest with her nose—likely wondering why he'd saddled her if they weren't leaving—did he realize that Audra must mean the Ladies' Aid.

"Did you now?" he asked, approving.

She nodded. "I did! At first I did not think I could—some of those ladies were not so nice as I'd hoped—but I made myself speak up, and they actually listened. Well, not at first. Some thought that to collect warm-weather clothes for Miss Wolfe might reward her for . . . you know. But I reminded them of our duty to help her escape her current situation."

He also enjoyed watching how she loved his horse, petting Queen's blaze and scratching under her forelock, even kissing the mare's whiskery nose as she talked.

In fact, he felt more than a little envious.

"Did you now?" he said again, admiring the play of excitement on her sweet, china-doll face, the glow in her large, fine eyes. "And they agreed?"

"Well . . ." She looked down, suddenly uncertain. "I also said that if they wanted her out of town, better to help her leave than not." Then she peeked back up. "Was that wrong of me? I truly didn't set about it to dispose of poor Miss Wolfe, but I *so* wanted to convince them, and they were being so frustratingly impractical. And it wasn't a lie," she hurried to reassure him, as if he might condemn her otherwise. "But it's not an argument I'm proud to have made."

"You're asking me about right and wrong?" he challenged, increasingly amused, and a giggle bubbled out of her at his observation. Of the two of them, *he* was the dissolute, right?

At least, he hoped he was.

Ducking her forehead against Queen's, she slanted her pretty eyes up at him and said, "Perhaps I am testing you."

Maybe she was and maybe she wasn't, but she *was* teasing him—and he could not have been more pleased. "Well, now," he said, looping an arm over Queen's neck since he could not in good conscience—or at least in plain sight—loop one around Audra. "I doubt Ham or Lucy believe the good ladies of Candon want either of them lingering, so your stating the facts of it oughtn't hurt their feelings none. And if it wouldn't hurt their feelings, I can't see the wrong in it. Especially since it gets them just what they want." Then he smiled. "Did I pass?"

Audra gazed up at him for a moment, then bit her lower lip and nodded.

He wished he could bite her lower lip for her, though softly, and with his tongue to soothe any imagined damage . . . but they were on Main Street. Even the folks who went out this early generally stayed to their own backyards, seeing to livestock or pumping water or carrying in firewood. But he could not know for sure who might be watching him—her—even now.

And if he loved Audra, he would do nothing to endanger her position . . . right?

Toward that end, he forced himself to ask, "Aren't you taking a chance meeting with me in the open like this, schoolmarm?"

He regretted it right off, and not just because of how his question sobered her.

"Oh. Do you think I oughtn't have?"

There she went, asking the dissolute again. This time he chose honesty over protection. "If we were playing by Jack Harwood's rules, you'd have arrived a few minutes earlier and slipped into the stables, where nobody could see either of us."

Audra cocked her head. "But out here, if anybody *does* see us, they can see that all we're doing is talking. If we talked inside the stables, people might think we were . . ."

Jack smiled dreamily at the image. "*If* anybody found out," he reminded her.

Audra's gray eyes flared wider. "Jack! I told you we couldn't do anything like that again!"

Again. As if his fantasies ended at kissing. *Where they should.* But he ignored that prim voice inside him. In fact, it was sounding increasingly like his father's.

"Well then, Miss Audra," he said apologetically, "You just

hold tight to those morals of yours, because I'm having a humdinger of a time doing anything but thinking about just that."

"Just that?"

"The *that* that we can't do." He enjoyed her blush. "It's a fine enough thought that, if there were a way I could shoulder the risks instead of putting you in jeopardy, I would do it gladly." He smiled. "Faint heart never filled a flush."

" 'Faint heart never won fair maiden,' " she corrected warily, eyes wide at his declaration.

He'd better leave here, and quickly, because his heart felt nowhere near faint this morning.

"Well then, fair maiden, before I do something to further lessen myself in your eyes, why don't I head on out to Grapevine and post that telegram to your folks? You've set so good an example with the Ladies' Aid, I'll have to be downright industrious to equal you."

She nodded, and for a moment it was all he could do not to close the distance between them and kiss her. Wasn't that what men and women did, especially when they cared for each other, just before the man rode off? A good-bye kiss, her straightening his muffler for him, him promising to stay safe . . .

The reality that theirs was not, nor ever could be, that kind of relationship walloped Jack hard enough that he regretted those breakfast oysters.

Then Audra said, "You're not lessened in my eyes, Jack Harwood. Just because I need to honor my promises doesn't mean that I'm not tempted."

Lordy. He ached for her in more ways than he'd figured a man could ache for a woman. In fact, instead of resurrecting quilt-tangled images from his dreams, or from this morning's more immediate fantasies of haylofts, he could suddenly think of nothing more physically satisfying than just pulling her to him and holding her, his cheek pillowed on her sorrel-colored hair.

She blushed and averted her eyes from his hungry stare. "I apologize. That was horribly forward of me. I only meant to . . .

That's why we have to be so careful to follow the rules, you see. Most of them, at least. You do understand, don't you?"

And when she again lifted her gaze to his, her eyes pleaded with him.

"I do understand." He swallowed. Hard. "Miss Garrison, every so often I even agree. But that usually isn't when we're face-to-face. So I'd best be off to Grapevine now."

And before he could indulge in any more fantasies of her seeing him off like a favorite beau, he hooked his foot in Queen's stirrup and swung himself up into the saddle.

She held the mare's bridle as he did, and handed him up his reins, just as a girl might see off a beau, at that. But they weren't. A girl with a beau would have chaperones and planned events to attend. A girl with a beau would make sure their families knew one another. Jack was not her beau; he was a gambler who wanted to sneak her away into a stable or the woods and do what honorable beaus waited for their wedding night to do.

Just because he loved her didn't make her less deserving of such treatment. But maybe he didn't love her, not how it counted, because he couldn't just ride away and leave her be. "See, Miss Garrison, there is little I enjoy more than your being horribly forward with me."

And then, only when he had her blushing—was he low enough to hope, even a touch as frustrated as he felt?—he rode off Grapevine way, cursing his damned candor.

This was a higher-stakes game than he'd expected. The longer he stayed in, the more he stood to lose. And, worse, he saw no way she would be taking the pot either.

When a peddler from Arlington, to the south, stopped by Aunt Heddy's with a telegram that afternoon, Audra had a moment of still, clear panic. It had little to do with her aunt discovering the notorious Miss Wolfe's actual destination, either. It had to do with Jack.

He's not coming back! she thought, numb, as her aunt thanked the man and unfolded the yellow paper. As soon as she rejected that fear, another took its place: *He's been hurt!*

Worse was the realization that she preferred the second possibility to the first . . . as long as he could recover. Shamed to discover herself more selfish than she'd ever suspected, she could only stand miserably while her aunt read the telegram, wait for the certain aftermath, and pray.

I take it back. I'm sorry. He can stay away if he wants. Just let him be safe.

But Aunt Heddy read the telegram without looking at Audra once, then apparently read it a second time, and Audra realized the extent of her own selfishness. It wasn't her telegram at all.

Aunt Heddy said, "Melissa, go down the road to the Parkers' home—*walk,* do not run—and ask Mr. Parker if I may ride with him when he goes into the city tomorrow morning. I shall be traveling to the hill country tomorrow. Audra, that will necessitate my leaving the girls in your charge. I need not impress upon you my reluctance to do so."

Hill country—where her papa had grown up! "Is it *Grossmutter,* Aunt Heddy?"

"It is my brother." Aunt Heddy put the telegram down and went into their bedroom while Melissa put on a cloak and slipped out the door.

Claudine grabbed the telegram before Audra could, but for once Audra rejected etiquette and snatched the paper from the girl's hand. *Papa* was Heddy's brother!

Again she felt her moral imperfections when she sank, relieved, against the edge of the table upon reading the cable. Of course it wasn't her papa. Aunt Heddy would not travel to the hill country if a brother in Wyoming had been ill.

But Audra must never imagine such things. The telegram was grim enough: *Matthew hurt mowing. Come quickly. Mutti.* That *Grossmutter* referred to herself so informally hinted as much at the seriousness of the situation—that it warranted a mother's softness—as did Audra's passing familiarity with mowers. A mower could tip, or the horses could spook, or . . .

Claudine took the cable from Audra's limp hand, read it, then said, "She didn't look upset; she looked mad. She must not care very much about her brother."

Audra said, "She's part German," and followed her aunt into the bedroom.

"You could reach the station tonight if you rode horseback," she suggested.

"I never ride horseback." Her aunt, Audra noticed with a chill, was folding her black dress to pack. "In any case, we have no sidesaddle. Nor is it proper for ladies to travel alone."

Audra's mother sometimes traveled alone. Lucy Wolfe would by necessity.

"I'll do my best not to let your pupils fall behind while you're gone."

Aunt Heddy said, "I have no intention of being gone later than midweek; I doubt you can do too much damage in only a day or two."

She *did* sound cold. "But it's your *brother!*"

Aunt Heddy turned. "I am well aware of that. If it were not serious, I would never leave those two impressionable girls under your supervision. You must know that your behavior of late has hardly increased my confidence in you."

That morning Audra had let Aunt Heddy think she was going to the schoolhouse early, then met Jack by the stables instead. Did Heddy *know?* Did she think they'd done more than talk?

"I had hoped that your father's influence would override your mother's," Aunt Heddy continued, emphasizing her words with sharp movements, folding this item or placing that one into her valise. "But you seem determined to intrude in matters which would never concern a real lady. The school board has not yet voiced a complaint to me, but I doubt it will be very long in coming. Do not expect to be offered a position here next year."

Audra opened her mouth in protest, then could not form a word. Too many words jumbled in her throat for any one of them to escape. Did she *want* to live here next year? How else would she teach? Why would the school board voice complaints to Heddy instead of directly to Audra? And beyond that . . .

She prioritized. "What's *wrong* with my mother?"

Aunt Heddy did not deign to answer.

"Mama is the kindest, strongest, most courageous woman I know! And Papa loves her!"

"She is selfish, undisciplined, overindulgent—and over-indulged—and that you even concern yourself about *her* when your uncle lies injured proves my point about your heritage."

Audra felt a rush of rage—but proved her aunt wrong by walking out of the room and starting the slow work of preparing dinner. Losing herself in chores until she calmed down was something her *father* would do, thank you very much.

But it pleased her more to imagine her mother's likely response to such an attack on their family. *Courageous* put it gently. Papa's courage pitted him against the things a rancher *must* face—stampedes and prairie fires, rustlers and floods. Mama's courage pitted her against opponents nobody would blame her for leaving alone. In fact, whereas Papa was expected to face down wolves and Indians, Mama was expected to behave herself. Part of *her* courage lay in ignoring the very people who accused her of "looking for trouble," when she simply did what she knew to be right. Mama had eyes that saw far beyond the strictures of society.

Audra wondered, as she sliced potatoes, what her mother would think of Jack Harwood.

"I will ask the Reverend Collins to stop by at sunset each night while I am gone," said Aunt Heddy, returning from the bedroom, "to make sure the three of you are properly settled in for the night. I expect you to see to all the chores and to attend church on Sunday. Is that clear?"

As if Audra would skip chores *or* church! *I thought we might do some drinking,* she thought. *And gambling. I know somebody who could teach us.*

Out loud she said, "Do not worry yourself about us, Aunt."

Claudine said, "We aren't children, you know."

But that comforted Audra no more than it seemed to comfort Heddy.

* * *

Before Jack reached Grapevine, the frost vanished and the weather lost its edge, becoming downright comfortable for riding, even once he reached the prairie. When he reached the yellow depot, on the south side of the city, he sent Audra's telegram first thing.

It felt odd to send a communiqué directly to the mother—even in Audra's own words—after the thoughts he'd been entertaining about the daughter. What might an established matron, wife of some kind of cattle baron, think of a gambler running errands for her daughter?

He doubted it would be flattering.

Luckily he had other errands to run for Ham.

Despite the absence of a saloon, Grapevine's Main Street could fit five of Candon's and then some. Most of its buildings were of respectable brick, complete with a continuous wooden sidewalk and colorful canvas awnings to protect it. Telephone poles stood sentry along a wide road that, though still dirt, would likely end up paved soon. There was no missing the prosperity around here; Jack figured that had more than a little to do with the railroad depot. As he walked, he noticed the number of stores that obviously thrived. J. E. Faust and Co., advertising "Groceries, Coffins, and Marble," had nine salt barrels stacked on the sidewalk in front of it. *Nine!* Had Ham's mercantile gone through three salt barrels in the time Jack had worked there? The City Drug Store alone could hold Candon's entire general store. Grapevine boasted a dry-goods store, a second grocery store, a feed and ice service store, a hardware store, a photographer . . . a realty company?

As Jack strolled along Main, a thought began to form in his ever-resourceful head. Folks in Candon had been talking about the railroad slated to run past their own town since his arrival, but Jack figured their odds for a depot were worse than those for an inside straight.

What if he figured out a way to increase those odds?

Ferris had asked him to place an advertisement in the Grapevine *Sun,* seeking a buyer for the mercantile, then to ask at some of the local shops about possible interest. Jack hadn't expected a lot. But could be he'd guessed with too few cards showing.

That afternoon found Jack Harwood well pleased with himself. He'd placed the requested advertisement, then spent much of the day canvassing the businesses along Main, including the realty. Folks seemed plenty willing to talk with him, advise him . . . and agree with him that Candon's getting a depot would raise the store's value. It didn't hurt that Jack hailed from Jefferson, the most famous Texas city ever to be ruined by the railroad passing it by.

Somehow, as he worked his way through the afternoon, the possibility of Candon's getting a depot became a likelihood, and the likelihood eased into something suspiciously near fact. Folks' interest increased in direct proportion—and Jack enjoyed just about the most fun he'd ever had that didn't involve playing cards or liquor.

As the afternoon waned, Jack headed back to the depot that had given him so fine an idea and was somewhat surprised to see that Audra had predicted correctly; her mother had replied.

Pleased to help. Send her up. Proud of you. Counting weeks. Mother.

Lordy. Jack stared at the telegram for so long, the telegrapher asked, "You want me to read it for you, sir?" When Jack looked up, blank, the young fellow in the green visor quickly added, "Not to imply you can't read. My handwriting throws some people, is all."

Jack shook his head and gave the fellow a bigger tip than he'd originally planned. Then he pocketed the cable and waited until he and Queen had ridden clear of the city and could take shelter in some barren, grapevine-choked trees to examine it again.

Proud of you. That was the line he stumbled over, and at first he just couldn't figure it. Selfless and caring, hardworking and conscientious . . . why wouldn't they be proud of Audra?

Maybe because she was keeping company with a gambler.

The truth hit Jack low and hard. That was exactly why Mrs. Garrison's kind words gave him more queasy guilt than warm appreciation. He saw, finally, that Audra would suffer from their little romance even if nobody found out. She would think her folks' pride in her misplaced.

Jack folded the telegram, pocketing it. His folks had never claimed pride in him. Could be they were right. All this time, while he was blaming Audra's parents for putting her in harm's way, he'd taken full advantage of their misstep and played the starring role of harm itself.

Worse, he doubted he could stop. He'd told her that just this morning; he understood why she needed to follow those rules of hers far better when they weren't face-to-face.

Maybe he finally understood, now, why she'd tried to minimize their time face-to-face.

He wished he had the willpower to do the same.

Chapter Twenty-five

A teacher may not travel beyond the city limits without the permission of the school board.

—Rules for Teachers

Farmer Parker left for market well before dawn, when the sky had lightened barely enough for his team to keep to the road. Aunt Heddy perched stiffly beside him on his buckboard, her valise clutched against her. She did not turn and wave to Audra, but Audra found herself increasingly unconcerned about such slights. That had to be a bad sign for her, didn't it?

"I don't think so," said Melissa, who came into Audra and Heddy's room to dress after Claudine begged to sleep in until sunrise. "I always thought you were a little *too* perfect, putting up with her as long as you have."

"But she's my elder," Audra reminded her, stripping the sheets from the bed. Since she and Heddy had jobs, Saturday was washday *and* baking day. "And my father's sister. *And* she raised my older brother for ten years. My family owes a great deal to Aunt Heddy, and I mustn't trivialize that through disrespect." She folded the sheets loosely at the seams. "If I become indifferent, something inappropriate might . . . slip out."

"I hope I'm there if it does." Shrugging into her work dress, Melissa grinned.

Unkind or not, Audra enjoyed breakfast far more with her aunt gone and Claudine asleep. Now she and Melissa cleaned the dishes together, discussing the latest fashions and whether Aunt Heddy would protest Audra's recent subscription to a story paper. As they mixed bread dough, Audra quietly admitted that she expected to receive a telegram as soon as Mr. Harwood contrived to deliver it without arousing suspicion.

It felt so good to mention him to somebody, it couldn't be proper.

"Mr. Harwood?" exclaimed Melissa. "I thought he was 'Jack.' "

Audra hushed her and glanced toward the girls' bedroom as she set covered pans of bread to rise. Claudine had behaved far better of late, but Audra still did not trust her with secrets.

"Last time I checked she was dead to the world," assured Melissa. "So talk."

Audra gave in. "I'll admit that I could be . . . fond of him." Even that felt horribly like a fib, since she *was* fond of him. More than fond! "But I am trying to retain some propriety."

"Is *he* trying?" asked Melissa, fetching the washtub to fill from the cistern.

Audra thought of the kiss he'd stolen at the store just this week, thought of how he'd all but asked her to continue being forward with him yesterday morning, and she blushed.

Melissa laughed.

"This is a serious matter!" Audra chided, still blushing, but Melissa still laughed.

Finally, with the sun well up and the wash water ready, they had no choice but to end their private time by waking Claudine. They needed her nightgown and the sheets from her bed. And washing was too grueling a chore—especially in chill weather—to not take all three of them.

Melissa went into the bedroom, then, moments later, bolted out. "She's gone!"

Audra stared, unwilling to risk understanding at first. "What?"

"Claudine's *gone!* She stuffed laundry under her blanket. I guess she left through the window. Audra"—Melissa extended a note—"she says she's eloping!"

Now Audra lowered her stare to the note. That indeed looked like Claudine's halfhearted attempt at penmanship. "But . . . Aunt Heddy hasn't been gone two hours yet!"

It was a foolish, useless thing to say, but Melissa looked sympathetic.

Disgusted by her own cowardice, Audra took the note.

> *It is so romantic! Jerome asked me to be his bride and we are taking the train to Louisiana. I shall write to you from New Orleans as Mrs. Newton!*
>
> *Your friend, Claudine.*

Friend? Friends did not—

But Audra pushed past her selfish concerns, then stumbled at the thought of Claudine's father, thinking his daughter safe in a responsible schoolteacher's care. *Responsible*! If she'd not spent the morning chatting with Melissa, if she had made Claudine get up earlier, if . . .

She forged past the regrets as well. Regrets would always find time to return.

"I have to think," she muttered, grasping handfuls of her apron to keep her fluttering hands busy. "The train means Grapevine. When does an eastbound train go through?"

"You think someone should stop them?" challenged Melissa.

"Of *course* someone should stop them!" Worse, she knew whose duty it was.

"So she marries Jerome. Some people marry young and do just fine."

Mere months earlier, Audra would have been equally innocent. "Does Jerome have a job? Do you trust him to not leave her? Do you think Claudine could support herself or a family?"

Following Audra into the teachers' bedroom, Melissa said, "Oh."

An even worse thought occurred to Audra. "And what if he *doesn't* marry her!"

Memories she'd thought healed now reopened into ragged, painful things. The terror of realizing how little she knew Peter Connors. Her father's rage. The town's reaction when Audra refused to marry her abductor. They'd known her all her life, *knew* she was a good girl, but after Peter, everyone seemed to wonder. At least, it had seemed like everyone at the time.

Melissa obviously remembered Audra's story, too. "She'll be ruined when the sun sets."

That alone had seemed life-ending to Audra only months ago, but she now appreciated how lucky she had been. What if Jerome did marry Claudine, but only . . . well . . . in the "basest sense" of the word? He'd ruin her in deed as well as reputation. If he convinced her to board a train, she would lose even those last remnants of familiarity and safety!

Assuming Claudine were not so shamed by then that she wouldn't even seek help.

Audra began to strip off her work dress, intending to wear something warm enough for the trip and respectable enough to give her some mien of authority once she reached the depot, if she got there in time. She would not wish such ruin on her worst enemy, much less a headstrong girl who, with a little maturity, might yet amount to something.

"What are you doing?" Melissa finally thought to ask, watching Audra strip and redress.

"I'm going to get her."

"What? By yourself?"

Audra pinned on her bonnet, wishing her hair were longer. "She was left in my charge."

"But you're just a woman!" When Audra stared at her, Melissa added, "Your aunt would send menfolk after her, instead of going alone. You're risking your own reputation by doing that."

"If I ask someone for help, they'll know what happened and *both* our reputations will suffer. A woman's reputation is too fragile a thing to risk lightly. I surely know that!"

"Send for Mr. Harwood; he won't tell. Let *him* go after her," pleaded Melissa while Audra found her purse, checking for money for an emergency.

The thought of Jack *did* soothe her. He would understand, sympathize. But . . .

"If Claudine returned with Jack Harwood, she would be worse off than if she returned with Jerome," Audra admitted, leaving the house. Luckily the old horses were tame enough to come when she called to them; she needn't try roping them first. As she led first one gelding, then the other into the barn, she prayed she remembered her father's instructions for harnessing a team. If she rode horseback, she could move more quickly—but she would lose a great deal of respectability if discovered. Returning on horseback with Claudine, especially without sidesaddles, would raise more questions than they could answer.

"You'll stay here," she instructed, setting about the first steps of harnessing Buck and Boy. Bits, then collars—she could barely lift the heavy collars by herself.

"Why?" demanded Melissa, trying awkwardly to help. The gentle geldings practically put their heads through the collars themselves.

"Because someone needs to hang out the wash, do the baking, look normal. If anybody suspects this, Claudine's reputation is lost." Another memory twisted inside her, even more horrible than her immediate fear of not fastening the belly bands and martingale correctly. "The reverend is coming by after supper to check on us, remember? Tell him Claudine and I have gone for a drive, that you expect us at any time. I doubt we'll return home until after dark." Not with an aged team, mostly grass-fed, pulling an old surrey. "He'll likely wait with you. But if we return together, without any men, we may yet get through this."

Melissa stared. "You want me to lie to the reverend?"

Audra looked up from the heavy tangle of traces, straps, and buckles and said something she once would never have thought herself capable of. "Yes. *I'm* leaving the town limits without permission from the school board, and I want *you*—if you can do so—to lie to the reverend."

So much for idealism.

Slowly Melissa nodded. Even more slowly Audra led each horse to step carefully over the shafts and into place and then, with her friend's help, she hoisted the shafts up and hooked them to the harness and collar hames. Her father could have gleaned through some trick of horsemanship which gelding would best pull near and which one off; she just had to guess—and pray that she had gotten even this much right. The tug chains hooked to the evener—*Make sure their tails are clear. Make sure the wagon doesn't ride too close to their heels.*

Yes, Papa.

Twice more, Melissa suggested fetching Jack. It took all of Audra's self-restraint to keep refusing. She longed to have him there, taking charge, telling her that all would be well.

But sadly, he might not be right this time, and with his reputation, he could hardly do anything to help her beyond the harnessing of the horses.

When Audra drove away toward Grapevine, with the canvas sides of the surrey up, as if she expected rain, she did so alone—and with the full knowledge that this could be the most foolish decision she had ever made in her life.

If so, at least she made it for the right reasons.

Ferris Hamilton showed little appreciation of Jack's sales techniques when Jack returned from Grapevine. "You *lied?*"

Depressed and tired, disappointed that he'd have to wait until the next day to somehow get the telegram to Audra, Jack took more offense than usual. "I did not lie; I exaggerated."

"You told people we were getting a depot. For all we know, the Rock Island line might not even come through here—"

"They've got the land already," Jack reminded him.

"—much less stop for a depot. What does Candon have to offer them? Folks'll just go on confusing us with Camden anyhow."

Did the man have no vision? "We'll just come up with something to get that depot, then."

"*We?* Last time I knew, you weren't going to be around much longer anyway."

He'd stayed past the shoot-out at the river, hadn't he? "I like to leave my options open," Jack assured him sarcastically.

"If you think it's such a good business venture, why don't *you* buy the damned store? I can give you a good deal. Especially considering the money you'll make once we get that depot."

What annoyed Jack the most about the suggestion was that for a moment—the briefest of moments—he considered it. He'd all but run the place since October anyhow! And whereas Audra could not seriously consider a relationship with a gambler, a *storekeeper . . .*

Reality doused any guttering hope of that. First of all, a storekeeper who used to be a gambler was still a gambler, especially in a self-righteous town where folks had long memories. Even if people accepted him long enough to keep the store in business—which he doubted—the first time a more virtuous, churchgoing competitor moved in, he'd be finished. And the first time a horse vanished or a wife strayed, who'd be suspected? That gambler who kept store!

He wouldn't do that to Audra—assuming she were gullible enough even to attempt it—and he should be shot for considering doing it to himself. No more cards? No more drinking? Sundays at church, right alongside Whitey Gilmer? To keep appearances he'd either give up fun or give up his honesty about fun. If he turned into one of those hypocrites, how could he help but start hating himself? Or, worse, hating Audra for tempting him into it? Some hope that was.

Jack made a rude gesture, then stomped off to bed. Dreams eluded him.

* * *

The next day, Jack worked on how to deliver Audra's telegram. She deserved to know that her folks had answered; that her mother was proud of her and counting the weeks. But she didn't deserve Jack showing up on her aunt's doorstep, or even tossing pebbles at her window from the bushes, to get it to her. In any case, he didn't know which window was hers.

His only choice was to find a respectable go-between.

Figuring his odds, Jack went by the livery, saddled Queen, and rode out in the direction he'd heard tell he'd find the Rogers farm. He passed the place—easy to recognize from the board with the name *Rogers* carved into it, by their gate—then led his mare into the woods, left her hitched to a tree, and crept up on the farmhouse the back way. Once he had sight of it, he settled onto his haunches and played solitaire in the leaves, waiting for his chance.

Thank goodness the weather, though chill, hadn't dropped to downright cold today; Jack found himself waiting for some time. He saw other members of the Rogers family go about their chores, from little girls in calico dresses to the pleasantly plump woman he recognized from the store as Mrs. Rogers, all of them as towheaded as Early himself. Just as Jack began to wonder if Early'd gone to market with his pa, the lanky boy made a show, protesting something—"Aw, Ma!"—as he got pushed out the back door. Moving awkwardly, likely unsure yet of his big body, Early strode to the chopping stump, collected the ax, and then dragged over a piece of brushwood from a tangled heap nearby and set himself to turning it into firewood for the family.

If Jack distracted the boy too soon, his ma would hear him stop. So he resigned himself to another game while Early strained his suspenders to bring the ax down clean every time.

Only when the kid took a break—long after Jack probably would have—and strode over to the pump to get himself a drink, did Jack make his move. He whistled, low.

At first Early didn't seem to notice. Well, wasn't that just fine? Jack was looking for assistance from the kid with the thickest skull in Candon. He whistled again, then picked up an acorn and lobbed it Early's way. It hit the boy in the shoulder—not bad, thought Jack—and finally Early turned. Jack whistled again, and this time the boy took notice.

First, Early searched the woods with narrowed eyes. When Jack whistled again, he looked over his shoulder at the house, then went by the chopping stump to get the ax before he approached the tree line.

Jack waited until Early had crept nearer, then whistled again.

Early spun, wide-eyed.

Concerned at how handy the boy had proved himself with that ax, Jack stepped out from behind an oak to show himself before Early got close enough to do too much damage.

Early's eyes widened with recognition; then he grinned. "Mr. Harwood!"

Jack put a finger to his own lips, and Early nodded quickly. "I'm glad it's just you," he whispered, stepping into the woods himself. "I was afeared it might be Indians!"

There hadn't been Indians in this part of Texas since before the boy was born. Jack decided not to point that out. "I want you to do something," he admitted, "and I'll pay you."

"Really? What?" Boys this eager ought to be outlawed for their own safety.

But as long as they were legal . . . "I've got a message for Miss Garrison."

"My teacher?" At least Early had sense enough to frown. "What kind of message?"

"It's not from me; it's from her mother." Jack thought quickly. "I was in Grapevine yesterday when a telegram arrived, and I offered to carry it. But I don't want to hurt the lady's reputation by delivering it myself. Will you do it?"

"To the teacherage? Be *glad* to!"

"Don't go telling anyone," Jack warned. "They might misconstrue it." Early looked at him blankly, so he translated. "They might not understand."

Early nodded. "Yes, sir. I wouldn't want to hurt Miss Garrison or Miss Melissa."

So Jack handed over the telegram. Early pocketed it without

looking. He didn't even accept the two bits Jack offered him for delivery.

"But I gotta wash up afore I go," he said—and danged if the boy didn't blush. "I don't want to visit with ladies all smelly like this."

For a moment, Jack wondered if Early were sweet on Audra, too. He told himself it was no concern to him. Audra could hold her own against good boys like Early Rogers. It was the more cunning types like Jack who slipped past her defenses.

Early seemed to be waiting, so Jack said, "You do that. And, Rogers!" Early, who'd started to turn, spun back at the compliment of being called by his surname. "Much obliged," said Jack.

Early kicked the ground. " 'Tain't nothin'."

"The way folks feel about Hamilton and myself lately, I think it is. You're a good man."

Early's proud flush as they shook hands didn't negate Jack's commendation, neither.

And that, thought Jack, was that. Likely he wouldn't see Audra until she came by the store again—not that she should—to deliver the clothing she'd collected or to give Lucy any letters of reference she meant to pass on. And then . . . would he have any more excuses for seeing her at all?

Was that necessarily a bad thing?

A bad thing for him, he thought, more than her.

With no place else to go, Jack returned to the mercantile. Only after lunch—a meal that had improved considerably since Ferris had brought Lucy home—did Jack head out back toward the outhouse and hear someone whistle at him.

His head came up immediately. Indians? he thought, and grinned.

Then he ducked the acorn that flew in his direction, and crossed the yard the rest of the way to the outhouse, which really was the only place folks could be hiding. He also whistled back.

What surprised him was who stepped out from behind the "necessary." Instead of Early Rogers, it was young Melissa Smith, and she looked nearly as pale as her bleached hair.

Jack quickened his step. "What in tarnation are you doing here? This isn't anyplace for a respectable girl, and you know it."

Only then did he fully see how she looked at him with those big brown eyes. She looked downright fearful—and not of anything immediate, like him. *Audra?*

"What's wrong?" demanded Jack, his entire world going still.

"She's in trouble," said Melissa, and looked toward the outhouse.

That was when Early stepped out from behind it, dragging a struggling Claudine Reynolds by the arm. "She's in real big trouble, Mr. Harwood," he said earnestly.

Damn.

Chapter Twenty-six

In emergencies, teachers should not hesitate to ask for assistance from the school board.

—Rules for Teachers

Jack had never risked more on a horse race than he now bet on his race back to Grapevine.

Audra had been manipulated right into a trap—a trap set by that scheming Claudine Reynolds and, worse, Jerome Newton. According to Early, Jerome had "gone sweet" on their teacher sometime before, but Audra hadn't noticed. Nor had Claudine, or she would never have agreed to Jerome's plan to ruin Audra's reputation by luring her out after dark. What Claudine hadn't figured was that Audra would stay out after dark *with Jerome—*

after which Jerome foolishly hoped that, to save her reputation, Audra would marry him.

Marry him? One of her own pupils?

It would be a shotgun wedding of sorts, but to the benefit of the man, using reputation as a weapon instead of a shotgun. Jack would kill Newton before he'd let it come to that. Under no circumstances would that little bastard be rewarded for his trickery . . . or touch Audra.

Queen maintained a strong lope for several miles, hooves drumming along the dirt road in accompaniment to Jack's racing heart, but he could hear her losing her wind. Reluctantly he reined her back to a trot, then a walk. Not that he wouldn't ruin a horse for Audra's sake, even this one. But Queen might be of more use to the schoolmarm intact.

Jack had no intention of letting anyone subject Audra to another scandal.

Claudine hadn't been the only one of the three youths to look guilty. Early confessed to telling Jerome about a lady he'd heard of, a respectable lady who lost her good reputation after a beau cruelly kept her out past sunset. Then Melissa confessed to having shared with Early the same story—"though I didn't tell him who it was about. Really!"

"Who *was* it about?" asked Early, and Melissa said, "None of your business."

But from the big-eyed way she looked at Jack, he knew.

So *that* was Audra's big secret. He ought to have known it would prove to be less than nothing to him. His instincts had insisted all along that Audra Garrison was pure as the driven snow. That anybody could ever have questioned it, especially him, infuriated him.

Mixed with the fury, though, was fear.

What if Jerome, older and bigger, took advantage? Away from the community that knew her and would protect her, could Audra fight him off? What if, Lord forbid, he got her onto a train?

"Dang her," he muttered to himself, sickened by the possibilities. What had she been thinking, going off on her own like that, against all rules? Didn't she know that some of those rules—

schoolmarms not leaving town without permission, not accepting rides with men who weren't relations, not keeping company with folks of questionable character—were to protect her?

But no. Some damned gambler had to go and talk her into questioning every one of those rules, masking rebellion as thinking for herself—and look at what happened.

Queen having caught her breath, Jack spurred her into a trot and then, after she'd warmed to that, another canter. He had to reach Audra before Jerome did.

If he didn't, and she suffered for it, he would never forgive himself.

Buck and Boy made slow time, and Audra had difficulty not urging them to a faster gait than the old team could manage. At least she seemed to have harnessed them correctly, and she knew the route north to Grapevine, out of the cross-timbers and onto the grapevine prairie. At least she had a chance to somehow put to rights the scandal that had shaken her own world by ensuring it didn't happen to another young girl.

But, oh she felt frightened. What if she did not get there in time? Even if Jerome really did marry her, Claudine faced a life dependent upon a man whom she wanted more for his handsome face and charming words than his true character. Where lay the future in that?

Leather-gloved fingers tight around the reins, Audra winced at the personal overtones to her thoughts, but made herself face them. As pleasant as she'd found her Christmastime dreams about Jack, they'd been just that—dreams. She did admire him. Desperately. She admired his honesty, his humor, his tenderness, and his courage. She admired his brilliance with numbers and his ability to put others at ease. She doubted she would ever meet another man who could make her heart race with just a smile, make her whole body tingle—even in deep-down, secret places—with just a look. She couldn't imagine being held or kissed by anyone else, ever.

But they had no real future together, nonetheless.

Any attempted future would mean either ruin on her part or

uncharacteristic restraint on his. She could not bear to put her family through the shame of the former, not even for Jack. And she doubted she could, in the end, bear to put either Jack or herself through the incremental deterioration of the latter.

If they actually married—hard enough to imagine—she married a man who gambled and drank. If he continued—and why wouldn't he?—she risked becoming one of those women with too many children, not enough money, and a husband always out at the saloon. And yet she had no right to cage Jack toward her own ends. He was a gambler. She even loved that he was a gambler. Were he not, he would never have taken so many risks in his pursuit of her. And she'd benefited from those risks as much as—perhaps more than—he had.

But it made him poor husband material—if better than Claudine's Jerome Newton.

The wind across the prairie felt colder than in the timbers, and she pulled up her hood. Would she never reach Grapevine? She could tell by the slant of the sun that night would arrive before she and Claudine made it home.

The surrey began to pass farms and houses again. Finally, Main Street—with its telephone poles and brick buildings and yellow depot—rose into view. Audra drew the team up beside a hitching rail, far enough from the track to keep them from spooking if a train came by. When she hopped to the ground, her legs felt weak from sitting so long. Still, there was nothing to do but walk it off. As soon as she hitched the team, she strode back toward the depot.

A familiar figure, broad-shouldered and dark-haired, stepped out of the building, almost as if he'd been watching for her. She'd made it in time! Jerome had not yet taken Claudine to Louisiana. Audra still had a chance to talk them out of such foolishness!

Instinct itched at her before logic chanced to grasp anything amiss. Jerome *must* know that she meant to take Claudine home . . . so why his smile? And where was Claudine?

Audra slowed her step, wary now. Something felt very wrong. In fact, the way Jerome continued to stare at her reminded her too clearly of Peter Connors, the day he'd taken her riding.

Unwilling to distrust her instincts ever again, even for the sake of helping Claudine, Audra stopped completely. Jerome closed the distance between them with a long-legged stride. "Miss Garrison!" he greeted. "I knew you'd come. Claudine wasn't sure, but I knew it."

Audra said, "Where *is* Claudine, Jerome? I wish to see her."

"I'm afraid you can't," he admitted, ducking his head in the way she recognized from class as his attempt to appear repentant when, in fact, he was proud of whatever trouble he'd caused. It would seem more charming were he not so tall that she could see his face anyway.

What had happened to Claudine? "Why not?"

Jerome slanted his mischievous eyes toward her and confessed, "She's not here."

Not there? Audra tried to grasp his announcement and, for an embarrassingly long moment, could not. She'd known all morning and into the afternoon that Claudine had gone with him. She'd left a note. Why would Jerome be here, eight miles from home, without Claudine? He would not have sent her ahead, would he? Not a fourteen-year-old girl, alone!

Then, finally, Jerome's smile made sense. Claudine had never been here—just Jerome.

He meant to ruin her.

"Not here," she repeated weakly. From the slanting afternoon sun, he'd likely succeeded.

"No," agreed Jerome cheerfully. "But *we* are. Let me take you to lunch, Audra. We've never talked—as man to woman and not pupil to teacher. Once you get to know me—"

Audra slapped him.

Her open palm made such a loud, cracking noise that people on the street stopped to look. Jerome's head turned sharply. His eyes widened over the red handprint that almost immediately appeared, then darkened, across his cheek.

"How dare you?" she demanded—and she did not bother to lower her voice either.

Jerome glanced, embarrassed, toward the people whose attention she'd caught, then tried to smile at her. His smile looked wan, artificial. "Now, Audra—"

She swung at him again, but he caught her wrist in his bigger, stronger hand. "Now Audra," he repeated, his tone more warning than conciliatory. "Stop that."

"Let go of me!"

He widened his eyes at her and hissed through his teeth, "Folks are watching!"

Good! She'd already traveled too far to save her reputation, but she had no intention of risking her safety, too, just to avoid embarrassing herself, much less him.

"You have no leave to address me by my first name, young man!" she scolded, tugging at her hand. At the *young man,* he closed his fist tighter. It began to hurt. "You certainly had no right to presume upon my good nature to lure me away from home. And you have no right at all to manhandle me. Let go!"

Bystanders approached, both from the depot and from across the wide dirt road. "You all right, ma'am?" called a cowboy. A farmer approached from another direction. "Maybe you ought to let the lady be . . ."

And while they had Jerome distracted, Audra pulled a long pin out of her hat and stabbed him in the arm. The ugly sensation of steel piercing skin, then muscle, made her cry out at the same time he did—but Jerome certainly did let go fast.

"*Dammit!* What the hell do you think you're doing!"

Something she should have done to Peter Connors several meetings before she had ever been so foolish as to ride in a buggy with him. "I should have you arrested!"

Jerome's voice spiraled upward. "What did I do? Damn it, that hurt!"

The cowboy, stepping neatly between them, said, "Looks like you're accosting a lady."

"And there are laws against public swearing in this town!" added a businessman with a waxed mustache and bowler hat.

As the danger waned, Audra's strength followed. She

wouldn't get home in time. A second scandal would follow her first.

A fourth man, wearing a deputy's star, appeared. "Public swearing, is it? Would you like us to press charges, ma'am?"

Somehow she kept her chin up, her dignity about her. "Yes, please."

"Miss Garrison!" As they dragged Jerome away, he twisted about to stare plaintively toward her, clearly disbelieving that she would let so terrible a thing happen. What did he think he was doing—had done—to her? Nobody would hang a boy for cursing; likely they wouldn't hold him for long, and by then she would find a way to get word to his parents.

She heard Jerome protesting, "But she's my teacher!"

Someone else said, "I don't reckon they pay her enough. . . ."

And then she was . . . well, perhaps not alone. Two remaining men hovered nearby, obviously as uncomfortable in this drama as was she. She smiled at them, said, "Thank you," and somehow made her way back to Aunt Heddy's surrey—where she stopped beside a tall wheel.

The wide street of Grapevine, similar in size to her hometown of Sheridan but alien as well, bustled along beside her. She supposed she ought to go home now. But it would not do much good. She'd been fortunate in many ways today. She knew how to appear and behave like the lady she was, so that respectable gentlemen came to her aid, just as she knew her father or brother would do for any other lady in such a situation. She had not allowed Jerome to manhandle or manipulate her. But she was having difficulty counting her blessings.

Two scandals, *two!* And after she'd denied herself and Jack so many opportunities to do something truly worthy of scandal.

She heard another horse approaching at full gallop, but only hoped its wild rider wouldn't run her down; she had neither the strength nor inclination to step out of the way. To her surprise the animal slowed, then stopped beside her. Leather creaked; boots thudded to the ground.

"Audra! Are you all right?"

Jack? She turned slowly, disbelieving the miraculous possibility—but it *was* him. Winded and dusty and handsome and concerned, but it was her Jack, come to her rescue.

He took one look at her face and his own fell. "Oh, darlin—I'm too late, aren't I?"

At which concern the miseries and betrayals and fears of her day broke past the last of her defenses and shuddered through her whole body, seared her eyes, opened her mouth in a silent cry that ended against Jack's shoulder as he gathered her, hard, against him. She could no longer fight the tears that came then, wasn't sure she wanted to. Jack's comfort, Jack's strength, Jack's sympathy felt so right that even the shredding, wet ugliness of her grief soothed her somehow. It tore out of her in great, gasping, wordless sobs—not just Jerome's betrayal, but Aunt Heddy's suspicions, Peter Connor's treachery, her miserable homesickness. Safe with Jack—safe to be vulnerable, homely, real—she let all of it gush onto his shoulder and into his loving embrace.

He held her, ran his hand up and down her spine, patted her shoulder. He rocked her against him, kissed her hair where her bonnet hung askew, made soothing, shushing noises. He did not seem to care that they were surely garnering as much attention as she and Jerome had earlier. He just stayed there for her and let her release every bit of it.

Only then, as her tears became gasps of exhaustion and then weary sniffles, did she hear what he was saying to her. "I'm sorry, darlin'. I'm so sorry. I should've gotten here faster . . ."

Dragging in enough breath to actually speak, she pulled back from his shoulder. "No!"

He blinked down at her, surprised, and she ducked her head so that he wouldn't see her runny nose, her swollen eyes. "You got here just in time," she assured him thickly—and then, even if she *was* homely, she made herself face him. He deserved to know she spoke the truth. "Oh Jack, you came just when I needed you most. Thank you!"

He kissed her then, hard, and she tasted salt on his mouth—

her own tears? Barely had his lips released hers, tingling, than she flushed at her own dishevelment. "Jack! I'm a mess!"

"Well, then," he murmured against her hair, his voice as thick as hers but without tears to excuse it, "either blow your nose on my sleeve or use that handkerchief you carry."

Oh! She ventured to reach into her coat pocket and, sure enough, found her handkerchief. She laughed—with distasteful results, which, she realized thankfully, she mostly hid behind white linen. Jack laughed too—almost as unevenly as she—and he helped hold her up, holding her against him, while she wiped her eyes, blew her nose, repaired herself as best she could on a public street.

A public street.

Mortified by the display she'd helped create, Audra backed a step out of Jack's arms, then said, "Sit with me in the surrey?"

"I would be honored." He hitched Queen to the same post that held Boy and Buck and he gave her a hand up into the wagon, as if she'd not gotten here alone just fine. She liked that, once he climbed up, he sat with a proper distance between them.

When she proffered her hand, needing him even now that the emergency had passed, he took it readily enough. He had such tender hands himself, strong and soft at the same time. She wished she could ask him to never let go.

"You came," she marveled, looking at their joined hands rather than braving his face. "How did you know?"

"Claudine confessed all," he assured her. "And in case you're foolish enough to still worry about that little she-devil's safety, she's just fine. So far."

She *was* foolish enough to worry, and smiled gratefully that he knew her so well. Then she admitted, "I won't get home by nightfall."

"Not with this team you won't," he agreed. "But you'd raise your odds considerably if you took the Queen of Hearts."

"Your horse?" Now she did look up at him. The thought, brilliant and daring both, had not occurred to her once. He was still taking care of her, wasn't he? Her chivalrous gambler.

He grinned at her. "She's the only one I can in good conscience offer, darlin'."

She laughed, longing to kiss him again . . . but they *were* on a public street. And Grapevine's citizens had defended her when needed. She would not repay them by setting a poor example.

Not again, anyway.

As for what she would like to do in private . . . She ducked her head, watching their hands.

"She's a fine example of horseflesh," Jack reassured her, massaging her fingers. "Seems to me that, if you leave now, you might make it before that reverend of yours comes a'calling. I'll drive this team of yours back at a pace more suited to their years. With a waning moon and more than a little luck, folks won't recognize the horses or myself—but if anyone comes checking for your surrey in the morning, it'll be right where it should. Is it a plan?"

"It is a wonderful plan," she assured him, probably beaming like a fool and not even caring. She had a chance to escape this horrible, marvelous, wild day unscathed—and all because of a man the rules insisted she avoid!

"You *can* ride, can't you?" asked Jack, not releasing her hand.

"I'm a rancher's daughter. Of course I can ride."

"Astride?"

"We didn't get sidesaddles until we turned twelve." Sitting here beside him, she longed to tell him more about her family, her home, her sisters. She wanted him to know everything she cherished, to know her better, and she wanted to know all about him.

But she also wanted to get home before sunset, and the sun crept farther west even now.

When she shifted to leave the carriage, Jack gestured for her to wait, then jumped down himself and came around. When he didn't release her hand once she was down, she did not protest.

"What happened to the boy?" he asked, as if savoring these last few minutes himself.

That made her smile, too, with unladylike pride. "I slapped him twice, and then I stabbed him with a hat pin, and then he got arrested for swearing."

Jack's delighted laugh encouraged another of her own. "Would you mind if I posted his bond? He ought to learn a few lessons I doubt you or his folks can teach him so well as I."

She hesitated, both pleased that he would defend her honor and concerned. Jerome *was* younger than Jack. "You won't hurt him too badly, will you?"

"Not as badly as he deserves." The dark way he said it, as if drawing and quartering would not be as bad as Jerome deserved, hardly comforted her, so she waited. "You'll see him at church tomorrow," Jack assured her, correctly reading her concerns. "That'll give you a chance to make sure he's still walking. That, and getting him home to his folks before he worries them into asking questions, is all I promise."

She thought: *I love you, Jack Harwood.* And she did, with every bit of her, every thrum of her pulse. If she told him now, frightened him, it would hardly show her gratitude. And if it did not frighten him, he might want to kiss her again, right here on the street.

She knew where he'd be later tonight, where they'd have more privacy than Main Street. So instead of admitting her love out loud, she said, "You are wonderful. Thank you."

"You're wonderful," he corrected. "And you are more than welcome."

"Be careful," she pleaded, reaching up to straighten his coat collar. She'd spoiled his coat again. Thank heavens this man's fine clothes did not get damaged when they got wet.

He looked at her oddly, as if the gesture held more significance than she'd meant. But she could ask about that later, too. "*You* be careful," he cautioned. "Go the back way into town, behind the Parkers' farm, and you might just get in without folks seeing you."

She nodded—then fell into him again, holding him tightly memorizing the feel of him, right down to the imprint of his buttons against her chest. She did not want to leave.

But Jack pushed her gently back from her. "You'd best scat," he insisted. "I'd hate to think I ran that mare as hard as I did and you didn't get home in time."

I love you, Jack. She could barely hold it in—but she did. She readjusted the stirrups on his saddle to fit her own leg length, then lifted her dainty, button-up shoe into the left stirrup and, even after months away, swung easily onto the mare. She started to adjust her cape to better cover the petticoats and stockinged calves displayed by her unladylike seating—but when she saw how Jack was looking at her leg, she so wanted to let him that she pretended not to notice.

It made her feel wonderfully naughty—yet still deliciously safe.

"Soon," she promised, extending a hand which—once he noticed it past her leg—he took.

"Soon, darling," he agreed, and withdrew his fingers with obvious reluctance.

Audra turned Queen around, then rode south, out of town. She waited until the mare had walked almost a mile before urging her into a trot. Once Queen found her gait, they cantered.

She had a race to run.

Jerome looked so pitiable, locked up in a strange city, that Jack didn't have the heart to beat the boy nearly as badly as he'd planned. Which was not to say that, once they got out of town, he didn't make his point in a way that men had always understood. But it felt more necessary than satisfactory now.

By the time they'd approached Candon, respectable folks had gone to sleep—which was as he'd planned it. He let Jerome walk back to his parents' farm from the main road. Then, before he'd reached the town proper, Jack snuffed the carriage lamps, climbed down, and led the team slowly the rest of the way to Heddy Cribb's barn. He heard no neighbors call out in the night, saw no lights lit. As he pulled the barn doors open, then led the team—surrey and all—into its shadows—he suspected that he'd arrived unobserved.

He was almost right. He'd just bolted the doors when a hushed voice said, "Jack?"

He turned, searching the darkness for a woman he'd recognize anywhere. "Audra?"

"Here—I'll light a lamp." In only a moment, a flame burst into the full brightness of an oil lamp, which she hung on the appropriate hook.

God, but she was beautiful. She looked tousled and vulnerable, her calico dress wrinkled as if she'd just woken up, and all the heady, foolish feelings he'd had for her this afternoon, holding her and kissing her and wishing they could be more to each other, all but swamped him.

"Isn't it late for you, darlin'?" he asked, moving to work out how to extract the poor team from the intricate bondage of a carriage harness.

"Yes," agreed Audra, stepping to their off side and starting to unhitch the horses in such a way that he could repeat her motions on the near side, each one after her. "But not *too* late."

Was it his imagination, or did she say that second part as if she meant something more than the obvious? Jack figured he must just be overtired. This was sweet, innocent Audra.

"Did you make it in time? Let me get that, darlin'." He caught the weight of the surrey staves as she unhooked them from the hames.

"Just in time. Reverend Collins was glad to see that the three of us were safely home."

"I imagine he'll make a fine alibi, if anyone mentions seeing you leaving town earlier today," he noted, helping her with the buckles and the straps, then taking the weight of the collars to hang for himself.

"I imagine he will," she agreed. When he leaned around a gelding to see her, she flushed and looked down. But her eyes were bright. She must be nervous, alone in a stable with him this late at night.

Though he knew it was the best thing for her, he just couldn't bring himself to offer that she go in now. Instead they curried the horses, then put them into their stall, where she'd already forked hay and carried water. Jack watched her pet each gelding in turn, scratching behind one's big ears and finger-combing the other's forelock, whispering, "Thank you," to each.

Then she came to him, and before he could stop himself he'd drawn her to him, bent over her innocent beauty, and kissed her. He wanted her to thank him, too, damn it.

She kissed him back in spades.

He'd half expected her to resist—she *was* a good girl, after all! At least until he coaxed her some more. Instead she opened her mouth to his almost immediately. When he teased his tongue into her sweet mouth, her own shyly met it, and she shuddered in his arms.

He probably shuddered in hers. Lordy, but she felt good. She smelled good, too, like soap and peaches—she and her friends must've had their Saturday-night baths—and a little like horses and hay. But she felt even better, velvety and warm and so pliable under his hands. He savored the cushion of her bosom against his chest, the involuntary tease of one of her thickly petticoated knees bumping against his. When she wrapped her slim arms over the back of his neck and moaned soft, muffled pleasure at their mutual exploration of each other's mouths, his body responded fully and completely.

He hoped that, between her innocence and all those petticoats she wore, she wouldn't know just how his body was changing against hers, especially with her arching against him as she was. But he couldn't have stopped the change if he'd wanted to. Worse, he didn't want to.

He would never desire another woman as he did his innocent schoolmarm.

But she *was* his innocent schoolmarm. After too brief an ecstasy, Jack reluctantly drew back—at least enough to see her face. Her eyelids at half-mast, her lips parted and wet, her short, curling hair aflame in the lamplight, she looked sexier than he had ever imagined Audra could.

If he didn't get out of here soon, he risked doing something they'd both regret.

"Oh, darlin'," he said anyway. "Oh, Audra. I can't think of anything I'd like to do more than kiss you like that until the both of us are drunk with it."

And Audra—innocent Audra—said, "Then do."

Jack stared down at her, not even understanding at first. That was something his dream Audra would say. "What?"

"Kiss me until I'm drunk with it. Don't stop. I don't want you to stop, Jack. I love you."

He continued to stare down at her love-hungry face, and his responding emotions, unparalleled to anything he'd ever felt before, nearly drowned him.

She loved him. She wanted him to go on kissing her . . . not to stop. Did she even know what "don't stop" meant? Probably not. She loved him. Kissing her until they both felt drunk would be good, too, though. She loved him?

"Please," she whispered, and he lost any chance at self-control right then.

"Oh, darlin'," he said softly. Then they were kissing too thoroughly to waste more words.

Chapter Twenty-seven

A teacher's skirts may be no shorter than two inches above the ankle.

—Rules for Teachers

For the longest time—an infinity beyond time—they only kissed. *Only?* For once, they'd escaped not only prying eyes but curfews. Until dawn, the night was theirs, and the impassioned ease with which they explored every joyful facet of kissing took full advantage.

Audra and Jack tried kissing with their heads at different angles, or not angling their heads at all, which made them bump noses, laugh, then kiss some more. Her arms draped behind Jack's shoulders and neck, Jack's bracing her back; they needed nothing but each other. They kissed with lips closed—chaste little kisses. They kissed with their mouths open, tongues teasing, exploring, thrusting . . . but in that, some intensity that her body understood better than she did made Audra dizzy. Lips damp, she turned her face into Jack's sweat-salty neck.

"I can't breathe," she whispered, and felt his Adam's apple bob against her cheek.

"You want to stop?" His words rasped out of his throat, horrified and dutiful at once, and oh, she did love him, and she laughed.

"No. Oh, no!" And she meant it. "I just . . . perhaps we should sit down?"

"Here." Jack set her carefully against a support post, then glanced quickly around the stable, found and claimed the carriage robe, and spread it over some hay in the far corner. He also stripped out of his coat, down to his shirtsleeves, for which she was glad. He always wore such fine shirts. "There, now." And, collecting her with a hand on each shoulder, he eased her onto the impromptu chaise, settling himself on one hip beside her, facing her. They weren't quite sitting, but they weren't quite lying down either. At least she knew that, should the world start swooping around her again, she need not spare any attention from the kissing to worry whether she would fall.

"Will that do?" Jack asked, low and quiet, and she loved hearing his whisper. It made her feel intimate, special. So did the way he slid his hand around her waist and pulled her closer to him, the way he leaned his forehead against hers instead of immediately starting to kiss her again. "For a gal who doesn't wear a corset," he teased, "you surely do your share of swooning."

"I do not swoo—" Then the more shocking part of his statement struck her, and she blushed. "Jack Harwood! How would you know what I do or do not wear under my clothes!"

His smile started in his eyes, lifted his cheeks, slowly widened his mouth—and he slid a slow, bold hand up her spine, obviously feeling her back through the calico of her dress and the linen of her shift. "My darlin'," he drawled, low, as she arched into the sensation of it, "a fellow wouldn't need a gambler's hands to tell you don't wear a corset."

Oh! She wondered if she should explain—her mother didn't approve of corsets—but as soon as Jack kissed her again, she let such thoughts drift away to somewhere, anywhere else.

Kissing in the hay was even better than kissing standing up. It wasn't long before Jack had slung a leg across hers, his thigh hard and heavy, and was slowly levering himself over her like a human blanket, plundering her mouth in ways she could never have imagined she'd not only enjoy but . . . oh, enjoy so much.

Over their shivering, tremulous breaths she heard tiny moans and whimpers that had to be their own. Jack seemed to enjoy her whimpers as much as she liked his moans. He began to move on top of her, gently pushing against her with the hardness she thought she recognized in his pants—she'd glimpsed animals enough to understand the basics of mating, though it surprised and intrigued her that humans might be so similarly . . . endowed. She wasn't sure Jack even knew he was doing it; he never did stop kissing her, chewing gently on her lower lip, changing the slant of his mouth on hers again. But she liked it very much.

She spread her legs to give him a little more room, and his weight atop her there felt—*oh!*—even better. She wished she were not wearing so many petticoats.

Jack paused, panting hot air across her cheek and ear. "Kissing," he muttered, voice rough. "We're kissing."

She nodded happily, and he arched back far enough to grin pure delight down at her.

"I'm pleased you like it," he whispered, and she nodded again, so he ducked back in and began to kiss her ear. *And that . . . oh, my!* Between the heat of his breath and the humidity of his tongue and the graze and press of his lips, much less the gentle scratch of his whiskery cheek against hers . . . She never knew an ear could be anywhere *near* so sensitive! When he kissed down the side of her throat, it felt even more . . . whatever wonderous thing it felt like. She writhed blissfully under the weight and whisper of him, wondering occasionally about the hardness in his pants and inhaling his musky scent and sometimes, when a bit of his chin or neck got close enough to her own mouth, tasting him. She explored his strong, taut back under his lovely linen shirt. She felt his ribs and his spine and the way his muscles softened and dipped where his arms branched off, and it felt wonderful, but she wanted . . . something. She wanted even more.

When Jack's lips traced the collar of her dress, she whimpered in frustration. Why did he have to stop there?

He rested his cheek on her shoulder, only his knee and one elbow keeping his full weight off her, and his exhale shuddered, tremulous, across her clothed collarbone. "Darlin', would it be too . . . forward of me if I were to undo just a button or so . . ."

She nodded, then thought perhaps that meant she *did* think it too forward and so shook her head, then feared he'd think she meant for him *not* to, so then she just said, "Please?"

He kissed her again, deep and intimate, and by the time he'd finished kissing her he'd somehow, one-handedly, unbuttoned her bodice to the waist. Perhaps she should have protested, but it seemed she'd spent all their time together on protests and shoulds. Not tonight. It felt too good, the cool night air against her throat, the way he looked at her camisole as if he'd never seen anything so pretty, to consider stopping.

She *loved* him, after all. She loved all of him. And she loved this.

Then Jack went back to kissing—kissing, and touching. While he explored the edge of her camisole with his mouth, dampening the lace trim and scalding her bare skin with his breath, his free hand crept into her open bodice, slid adoringly over her ribs, then continued to glide upward and forward until, before she knew it, he had a gentle handful of her—of her—

And *oh,* it felt wonderful! He stopped kissing long enough to whisper, "Is that all right, darlin'? You can slap me again if it isn't."

She couldn't seem to form any words past the delirium of his touch, the way that part of her body thrust itself up, hard and eager, to fill his hand. She managed only a sort of negative grunt, and he breathed something that sounded like a prayer and proceeded, first with his fingers and then—*oh, heavens*—his lips, to stoke the fire he'd lit in her. He kissed one breast dampening it through the linen of her camisole, making it so hot and then, when he drew away, so rigidly cold. Meanwhile, his hand made love to the other, occasionally skimming her ribs with his fingertips, and he stroked her leg with the inside of his knee.

Yes.

At first she'd felt languid, boneless beneath his lovemaking, but at some point the urges deep inside her began to build a wanton energy. That energy helped her run her hands farther down his back until finally, boldly, she passed his belt and felt the hard perfection of his flank.

He grunted and pushed his lower body harder against her, which she liked. She explored the dip where his thighs began, equally hard and heavy, then slid her hands back up across his flank to his strong, smooth back.

Jack had stopped making love to her breasts—in fact, he had gone very, very still.

"Would you . . . ?" Audra asked, and blushed. She felt like someone else, lying in the hay with him, letting him touch her in such salacious, wonderful ways—but she liked being that someone else, almost as much as she loved him.

Jack stared, wide-eyed, and waited.

"Would you mind . . . taking your shirt off?" she whispered. "I don't know if I can manage the buttons—"

Just like that he reared up over her, yanked the linen from his waistline, pulled the shirt over his head, and tore it off his arms. Goodness, but men had hairy chests! Attractive, though . . .

A cuff link bounced off Audra's shoulder. Then Jack covered her again and he felt warmer, smelled more sensual than before. She rediscovered the planes and ridges of his back, the catch of her palms on his bare skin as arousing as anything she'd ever felt. Through the dampness of her camisole her breasts could feel the scratch of chest hair, the nub of a hard nipple.

They kissed some more, lost in the natural ecstasy of it, for a long, long time. Then Jack asked, "How about you, darlin? Would you mind . . . your bodice . . . ?"

She would not think, only feel, so she nodded and he helped

her wrestle her arms out of their calico prison. Then she wrapped her arms around him, bare skin against bare skin. It felt so right, completely proper. It was Jack.

Somehow, in the course of their kisses, his hands took an interest in her legs. He slid his palms appreciatively up her calves, under her knee—that tickled—and to the top of her stockings where garters held them to her thighs. Neither garters nor stockings lasted long; the hose soon dangled uselessly from her ankles, held by high-buttoned shoes that neither she nor Jack had the patience to tackle. Her feet hardly mattered, considering the sensations he wrung out of her just from the rub of his fingers up her legs. Her deep-down secret places controlled her now, had her praying that he wouldn't stop exploring at her thighs. He slid a hand over the edge of her frilly drawers, over her hip, and then finally, a million kisses later, between her legs.

Her underwear felt wet there, but he didn't seem to mind, and then his fingers did something that sent a jolt of pleasure streaking through her, and she cried out.

She also, with unsuspected instinct, gripped tight to his flank again and tried to pull him more firmly against her most sensitive parts. Jack groaned—a horrible, deep, anguished groan—and stopped kissing her.

She wriggled under him, increasingly fascinated by that hard, hot length in his pants. When he still didn't kiss her, she decided to see for herself, and laid her hand tentatively against that hardness, but snatched her hand away when he convulsed against her.

"Oh, Audra," he all but sobbed. "This is more than just kissing."

"Mm-hmm." She kissed his chest, adored the dark hair there, traced his nipple with a tongue the way he'd done hers.

"I don't know if I can stop," he said with a gasp.

"*Don't* stop."

"You don't even know what I want to do to you."

Since he insisted on talking, she stopped kissing his chest long enough to look up at him. "Then teach me. Just don't make a baby."

He hid his tortured face in her shoulder. "I can't promise that, honey. Maybe some other time, if I'd come prepared, but not tonight."

Something tugged at her memory, an embarrassing conversation her mother had insisted they have when Audra's first womanly time had come upon her, about when babies were most and least likely. Now Audra wished she'd listened more closely.

"It hurts," she confessed, wriggling under him again to ease the throbbing he'd kindled deep inside her. "Not in a bad way, exactly, but . . . Make it stop hurting, Jack."

He pushed himself up on an elbow so that he could see her fully, and even half-naked, he looked more serious than Jack Harwood ever had. "Marry me," he begged, his voice intense.

Yes yes yes yes yes yes . . . the word thrummed with every heartbeat. He wanted her—wanted to marry her! And . . . she mustn't. Tonight, he could have. She might even risk her tomorrows. But to promise them to him, after everything she knew . . . Even if it did not destroy her, she could not risk destroying him.

She licked her lips. "Only in the basest sense of the word," she invited.

Jack felt so hard and tight—damned right it hurt—that he nearly embarrassed himself right there. Audra lay beneath him, disheveled and downright risqué on a carriage robe in the hay, and asked him to finish the exquisite job he'd started, without even the promise of wedlock?

Yes!

But beyond the screaming approval of his body, his mind—and heart—somehow kept him from falling on her right there. He'd never known either his mind or heart had that kind of power. Audra looked too tempting for mere morality to hold him back. She lay there with her arms bare, her slip of a camisole clinging and transparent since he'd finished with it, her dress crumpled both down and up to her waist, and her legs bare right up to the drawers. She was gorgeous. Her tender, pale skin was gorgeous, and the peach-fuzz hair picking up glints of lamplight off her legs was gorgeous, and her gently rounded breasts were works of art, and even the dark thatch of reddish hair in the shadows of her armpits aroused him. She was, after all, Audra. And he loved her.

That, he understood—and so he rolled off of her then and there. Only his love for her had power enough to hold him back after coming so far . . . but he wouldn't place any high bets on how long that would last.

"You won't marry me," he repeated. Somehow that set up an ache in him even more painful than the throbbing arousal pressing against his pants buttons.

"Not now," she admitted, turning onto her side, running a treacherous hand up his chest. "I was thinking . . . But do we have to talk it out now?" She'd slid a leg over him, too, to match the arm, and before he knew it instinct had her straddling him, her eyes drifting blissfully closed. "I don't want to talk now," she admitted, still studying his chest, her voice husky.

Could she be more perfect?

Only if she married him. Even if she wouldn't, that didn't stop him from reaching up to the fine breasts that hung gently toward him. That didn't keep his thighs from tensing under her, readying to thrust upward at her wet, ready heat. He drew her down, hard, onto him, her linen-covered breasts against his chest, and he kissed her more roughly than before . . . but somehow, against her willing opening to him, it didn't seem rough at all, just passionate.

All he had to do was yank off her lacy drawers, open enough of his straining pants buttons to release himself at last, and they could do this . . . but as powerful as that urge was, another equal force forbade it. *Not Audra. You'll ruin the very thing you adore about her.*

Ferris Hamilton's words echoed in his lust-fogged mind—*She wouldn't stay respectable for much longer than it would take you to hike her skirts*—and he refused to make the man right.

"Oh, darlin'." He moaned, shamed by the frustration that burned his eyes. "I'm not willing to gamble with you. You're the one thing I'm not willing to risk . . ."

She kissed him then, as deeply and intimately as he'd taught her to, and whispered, "I love you," again, right against his ear. Then she whispered, "Isn't there some way to make the hurt stop without . . . without taking my . . . without making a baby?"

And she didn't have to ask twice—which was lucky, as deeply as she'd blushed at her own boldness in asking the first time.

"No more clothes come off," he said in a growl, clinging to his last moments of sanity. "If anything else comes off, darling', neither you nor I will be able to stop me."

She nodded eagerly—his good-time girl, who would ever have guessed?—and he set about making love to her on top of her clothing. He rolled her onto her back, suckled at the cloth on her perfect little breasts while his fingers explored up under her pantalets, up against the wet, hot, furry core of her. It was all he could do not to slip them inside, but he couldn't risk it. She enjoyed it as much as he did, writhing and whimpering beneath him, but soon she was all but sobbing in his arms and he knew it would take more than that. He took the gamble of easing her knees wider and kissing them, kissing up the inside of her velvet thigh, tracing his tongue under the lace on her pretty, virginal drawers. Then he proceeded to kiss up those—Audra's readiness for him drew him, filled his nostrils—and, lapping up to the place where her own juices revealed near-transparent glimpses of more reddish curls, he began to suckle at her there.

He'd never done anything so blissfully erotic in his life. She clutched at his head, her cries getting faster, higher, then erupting into a scream that made one of the horses snort in surprise. Jack drank even more of her delicious sexuality while her body convulsed beneath him. Her knees caught hard at his shoulders, and she rode him through her shuddering release.

Then, even once her hips stopped swiveling against him, she was crying again, so he had to crawl back up to lie beside her, terrified that she regretted it now, that she blamed him for making her do something so completely improper.

She looked at him through tear-glazed eyes and asked, "Is it always that wonderful?"

"Never," he assured her. "Just with you." And he kissed her, and he almost wanted to let it end at that—with her—but his body insisted otherwise. She *had* said she loved him. So, as they kissed, he risked drawing her hand against the front of his trousers again. That felt fine, just fine, but not exactly . . . progressive . . . and so then he drew her palm gently up, then down. She picked up on that quickly enough so that he could leave her to her own devices and turn his hands and mouth back to more tempting targets than himself.

She slid her soft little hand up him, slowly, then all the way down, as if measuring him, and his erection strained so hard against the buttons that separated him and her, it really *did* hurt, but he wasn't about to say a thing. She curled her fingers around the girth of him, then traced the different shape at his tip—*oh, lordy*—and then investigated what lay beneath the whole setup.

Jack gritted his teeth, threw his head back, fought it.

Audra twisted around as if to better see what there was to see—*No more clothes come off!*—and then, quick-learning little minx, bent closer and kissed the taut material. At the heat of her breath, before any moisture could even seep through to delight him further, it was all over. Jack's cry shuddered out of him as hot and unstoppable as his seed, wetting the front of his trousers for the first time since his youth. He couldn't even summon the strength to be embarrassed.

Audra reared back from him, eyes wide, apparently not sure what had happened but sure that *something* had. "Oh!"

Damned right, "Oh." Trembling, almost helpless, he somehow caught her with a hand in her curling, wild sorrel hair and pulled her head back to his own. He made love to her mouth as he would have liked to do with the rest of her—not that this hadn't come blissfully close—and held on to her until, as his body slowly relaxed, his mind seemed to reappear as well.

Oh, my. Who would ever have thought?

Audra.

"I love you, darlin'," he admitted hoarsely. It only now occurred to him that he hadn't told her before, and he felt bad for that.

"Really?"

"Absolutely. And not just due to . . ." He slid his hand down her bare arm, savored the feel of her. "I loved you before this."

"This was nice, though," she assured him, and snuggled in closer, not the least bit afraid. *Nice?* His relief nearly undid him. He wasn't sure what he'd do if, because of his inability to control himself, to leave after a kiss or so, he'd frightened her. "I was afraid it would be vulgar and loud."

He narrowed his eyes, didn't mention that they *had* been loud. "Why would you think that?"

She blushed, but refused to answer. "Can we do it again?" She even slid a hand teasingly over his thigh—but he caught her wrist, lifting it to safety before placing it against his chest instead. This had been too close a call. Blissful though it was, it left him vaguely unsated. If she ever held him like that again, she should be guiding him inside of her, hot and wet and virginal . . .

Still, against all odds, virginal. He rolled away from her, fast, before he could change his mind. "We've got to talk, darlin'."

He found his shirt, pulled it on, and, as he buttoned it, left it untucked to better hide the damp spot on his pants. When he looked over his shoulder at her, she'd put her arms back into her bodice sleeves and was trying to pull up her stockings, eyes sad.

He hated to see her sad . . . but damned if he knew what to do about it.

"I love you," he insisted, rising on his knees in the hay beside her. "And you love me."

She nodded.

"But"—and the pain of this surprised him—"you don't want to marry me?"

She hesitated, obviously reluctant to hurt his feelings. "I *want* to marry you, Jack. I've never wanted anyone else like I want you. I'm just . . . afraid."

He managed to help her button her bodice without ripping it off her again. Some initial hesitance he was used to. He accepted it as part of her. "Afraid of what, sugar?"

"Well . . ." She could not even meet his eyes to ask it. "How would you support us?"

The question wasn't what left a hole in his gut—it was the truth behind it. Gambling, while it had its high points, wasn't known for the kind of stability a wife required. In fact, a fellow's luck tended to drop in direct proportion to how badly he needed the money. "I reckon I could do anything I had to. I took to the mercantile quick enough, now, didn't I?"

She nodded, looking down. "Yes. You *could* do anything. But would you be happy?" He stared at her, and finally she risked peeking up at him again. "I love you, Jack. I want you to be happy, not tied down by a wife, or babies, when you'd rather be off having . . . well . . ."

"Fun," he finished for her, low, and the word had never sounded so profane.

She nodded. "Fun."

The *hell* with fun—he wanted her! But some edge of sanity kept him from saying that, because his clearheaded, responsible Audra had a point. It was easy enough for him to give up so-called fun tonight. He'd just experienced something so momentous that to call it fun would be an insult. But what about when times got hard—and times always got hard. He hadn't come far from the transient life his own family had lived, wandering from town to town, living out of charity barrels and handouts, often cold, always hungry. His father had been a preacher, but the family still didn't get the respect any poor, stable dirt farmer would.

Jack had always figured he'd shoot himself before he'd turn to dirt farming.

He stared at Audra blankly, realizing that even *that* life—stable, but no less poor—would be an affront to her. And Ham's suggestion that he buy the store? He'd seen the futility of that. Audra could live better as a teacher than as a wife, and that, too, would chafe as the years passed.

"I suppose we could just have . . . well . . . nights like this," she suggested softly, looking at the stables around them. "When I can get out. It was wonderful, Jack. It's worth the risk."

Become his mistress? Some women that would be good enough for. Not her. How did she think she would face her pupils—*herself?* How would she face her family?

It probably wouldn't be long before regret about her remarkable behavior tonight set in and Jack became the one she couldn't face. He dreaded that moment.

"Early Rogers was supposed to leave a cable for you today," he said, low.

Audra looked up sharply, confused. "He did. But—"

"They're proud of you," he said, voice thick. She flushed, so very pretty in the lamplight.

"They would be proud of you, too, if they just got to know you," she defended him.

Somehow, with the taste of her sex still in his mouth and the feel of linen-covered curls imprinted on his tongue, he doubted that. Really, he had only one choice. He'd flirted with it since his arrival, but this time, if he didn't follow through, they'd be the ruin of each other. "I've got to leave, Audra. If I don't get out of here now, I don't know if I can. And I've got to."

Her eyes filled with tears; one even escaped to slide down her cheek. But she nodded even as she said, "I don't want you to go!"

Her voice wavered pitiably on the last word, and he caught her to him, held her tight, buried his face in her beautiful, curly hair. "Oh, darlin', I don't want to leave you either. But I can't ruin you. I won't let myself do that. I'd die before I'd do that."

They held each other tight for a long, long time. He made vague noises about coming back for her, finding her in Wyoming if he missed her in Texas, and she pleaded with him to do so . . . but surely they both knew that, unless something drastic changed between them, such a reunion would end as painfully as this.

After one last kiss, Jack somehow made his arms let go of her, made himself saddle Queen, unbolted the doors and forced himself to mount. "I love you, schoolmarm," he told her from the safety of horseback. "You're the best thing to ever happen to me. Don't you forget it."

"I love you too, you . . . you gambler," she told him, weeping openly now. "And you're worth every bit of it."

And at that, Jack had to spur his horse the hell out of there.

One thing a gambler had to know was when to throw in his hand.

Chapter Twenty-eight

Teachers each day will fill lamps, clean chimneys, sweep the floor, and clean the blackboards.

—Rules for Teachers

Somehow Audra survived the next day. She attended church, collected clothes from the Ladies' Aid, and delivered them to the mercantile. Jack really had gone; he'd left their pen for her. After that, the day passed in a dreary procession of chores and responsibilities. She missed him through every minute of it. But each minute did make way for the next, even so.

She survived Monday, too, and then Tuesday and Wednesday. It helped that, in Heddy's absence, Audra kept busy teaching both the big children *and* the little ones. The little ones hugged her so readily, and smiled with their whole faces—how could she regret her decision not to have her own children except by a husband who could provide a good life for them? How could she regret Jack's decision to leave her with a chance at self-respect?

Good sense didn't heal her grief at what she lost when he rode away. But Aunt Heddy returned with good news about Uncle Matthew's slow recovery. The week ended; another began. And good sense *did* soothe Audra's self-worth. She still felt lonely, especially in bed at night when unexpected urges confused and complicated her loss. But better loneliness than regrets. Even if she missed Jack worse than she missed her family, worse than she missed her home . . . worse than she suspected she would miss a lost limb.

Audra distracted herself by experimenting with some of his less scandalous lessons. She resumed shopping at Ferris Hamilton's mercantile—after Lucy's departure. Soon townsfolk began to trickle back, too. "If that nice teacher is doing it," they said, "then it must be all right."

The truest rules were those she imposed upon herself. But a good reputation didn't hurt, either. For hers, Audra had only one person to thank. It became a subtle but constant comfort with the passage of time. She would rather pine for Jack as her hero than resent him as her ruin.

And she hoped that, wherever he was, he found some of that same, subtle solace.

"Where the heck do you get your money, Harry?" Jack asked a particularly affluent gambling companion. "Robbing banks?"

He didn't expect an answer, of course, nor did Harry offer one. The big, handsome man with the seemingly endless income just laughed and said, "Worse ways to earn a living."

Jack stared at his hand—four tens, right off—and wondered if gambling weren't rapidly becoming one of those worse ways. He hadn't given a damn what happened to him since riding into Hell's Half-Acre a few weeks earlier. Not since his incredible night with Audra, in fact. Thus, Jack won more money than he'd ever seen in his life, and he didn't even care. Tonight found him tired, restless. But he had no intention of stopping until either he stopped winning or the other players, particularly well-heeled Harry Longbaugh, ran through their stake. Since Harry and his friend were admittedly "just passing through," Jack didn't figure he'd get another chance.

And one just didn't quit in the middle of a lucky streak.

Harry's partner, slightly older and nowhere near as free with his bets, said, "I reckon there's a passel of *better* ways to earn a living, too. Give me three, Red."

The dealer gave Jim Lowe, an amiable fellow with sandy brown hair, the three cards.

Harry took two.

Jack said, "I'll take one," and Lowe said, "Well, heck," and threw in his hand.

Harry said, "Doesn't mean a thing. I'm in for a ten-spot." And the madness started again.

"The problem with earning a living," mused Jack as they played, "is that a fellow either shackles himself to some dull, respectable employment or else he stays free to enjoy a little adventure and ends up with so much durned freedom it . . ."

. . . Costs him the one thing he most wants?

"The problem with freedom," said Lowe, his tone implying he'd warmed to this topic before, and Harry's groan implying the same thing, "is that you find yourself stuck outside the very walls you fought not to get stuck *inside*. Laura, would you kindly fetch me another sarsaparilla?"

"Make it two," said Jack.

Harry added, "And a rye, straight up," and pretty Laura fetched.

The four players and the woman, who appeared to be a "special friend" of Red's, played cards in a small room that until recently had been a prostitute's crib off the dance floor of the Red Light Saloon. Politicians had recently "closed" games in the Acre again, so they just holed up. Other than cramped quarters and more privacy, little else changed. Jack had always believed that, in a game of vice against reform, vice would outlast reform every time.

But he felt increasingly less certain that he wanted to be there when it did.

The Acre still housed its share of rebels, proud individuals living life on their own terms. Harry and Lowe, for example, seemed decent enough—intelligent and friendly. But Jack had met a few intelligent, friendly folks among the Candon church congregation, too.

The more he looked, the more readily he admitted that the wild set bred just as many sheep as the godly flock . . . and just as many skewed values.

Too many folks seemed to be chasing the money instead of the risk. More players than ever didn't seem to realize there *was* a risk . . . until they lost. Twice now, some greenhorn who'd lost fair and square had gone to the authorities and complained about the "illegal" game he'd been happy to patronize until his luck turned. Both times the game ended faster than the constabulary arrived. But the experience still soured Jack considerably.

Did nobody value the risk itself anymore?

The working women of the Acre, too, had lost most of their allure, and not simply because Jack had come so close to *knowing* true quality . . . in the basest sense of the word. Many of the gals still went into the profession for fair reasons—excitement, profit, the usual. But for too many soiled doves, the glitter of their chosen career had gone brass. Despite having places to turn—like the Women's Industrial Home—gals were killing themselves! For all their miseries, they resisted giving up their "easy" money for the lower wages and longer hours of a factory or domestic position. Too many chose death over a future of low income and hard work.

Could be they didn't believe that, even if they sacrificed everything to reform, the world would let them. Jack could understand that. But it no longer put him in gallant company.

He began to think Harry Longbaugh would never tire of losing when a different woman than Laura slipped into the room. Jack had a hard time lately finding real beauty in any hair color but sorrel and any eye color but gray. But something about the lady's solemn face and the neat way she'd swept her dark hair up and back did catch his attention, even as she went to Harry's side, placed a hand on his shoulder, and whispered something in his ear.

She was no prostitute, thought Jack. Or if she had been, she was no more. The way she made her unheard entreaty to Harry, both serious and sweet, seemed more bridal than bawdy.

Lowe leaned closer to Jack and murmured, "You'd do better to look at your cards than at the lady, son. The kid's been drinking again."

"I—" started Jack, to defend himself; heaven knew he had no interest in another man's woman! But he stopped himself, unsure how to say more without insulting someone.

Luckily the lady's intervention seemed enough to lure Harry from his losing streak. The bigger man threw in his cards, then stretched, grinning. Excusing himself, he was escorted docilely from the room at the lady's quiet hand.

The other three finished that round almost as an afterthought—Jack won—and groaned their relief. Nobody was anxious to continue. The game that would not end had finally ended.

"How about another sarsaparilla for the road?" suggested Lowe, his round-cheeked grin admitting that he'd noted his and Jack's shared avoidance of liquor. Jack hadn't made the decision to stop drinking . . . he just didn't want it anymore.

In any case, Jack accepted and Laura was sent for another round.

"Etta's a lovely woman, isn't she?" asked Lowe, leaning back in his chair.

"Yep," agreed Jack, though with no great fervor. When Lowe raised his eyebrows in surprise, Jack explained. "She reminded me of a schoolteacher I once knew."

Once knew. At the horribly final sound of that, he half wished Laura would bring something stronger. But not quite.

"You've got a good eye," said Lowe, impressed. "She *is* a schoolteacher. Was, anyhow . . . among a few other things. Now she's happy enough to be Harry's girl."

Was she? For Audra, becoming little more than "Jack's girl" would seem like a demotion.

"She doesn't look any the worse for wear for her change of station," he noted, imagining—just briefly—that it *could* have been his own ladylove coming to fetch him away from a game. He would have gladly gone, too.

But would it be quite so idyllic were he the one losing? Especially without whatever extravagant backing Harry obviously had? No, he'd made the right decision.

"Oh, she's not in it for the money," Lowe assured him, misunderstanding. "She might not even be with us except that Harry and I are going respectable ourselves. Anyway, more respectable than . . . what was it?" His eyes laughed at the memory. "Bank robbery."

Jack said, "I imagine bank robbery would be a shade more adventurous, though."

"Son, life itself is about the biggest adventure there is—it just took me too dang many years to figure that out. If a fellow can't see the gamble in ranching, or in taking up with a good woman like Harry has, he just isn't looking hard enough."

While Red covered his green-felt table for the night, Laura returned with their sarsaparilla. After paying her, the teetotalers toasted each other, amused by their own abstinence.

"Raised Mormon," offered Lowe, by way of explanation.

"Baptist preacher's son. But that might just be what drove me to drink in the first place."

They laughed together.

"So you're starting a ranch," pursued Jack, dismissing the idea for himself almost as quickly as he considered it. Audra's father was a rancher; no way would Jack try to fill *his* boots, especially without a deuce of experience.

"Could be," said Lowe amiably. "Better than train robbing."

"Bank robbing," Jack corrected.

Lowe's visible amusement deepened. "Son, you must've played an honest game or my friend Harry would've noticed, drunk or not; he's got a worse temper than you'd think. And you have a good head on your shoulders. I see potential in you."

Jack became immediately wary. "And?"

"I doubt you listened to your preacher father about sin any more than I heard my bishop grandfather. But if you'll allow me to offer some advice from a bit more experience?"

Still wary, Jack nodded.

Lowe leaned his elbows on the table, closer and more confidential. "Son, what the hell do you think you're doing with your life?"

Jack sat back, as offended as the older man seemingly expected. Maybe more so. He'd been thinking the same thought so often lately that hearing it from a stranger felt like nagging.

"All I'm saying," Lowe insisted, without insult, "is that it's worth the trouble to notice the trail you're riding now, maybe consider if it's really where you want to go. It's a sight easier to start over if you don't have to leave the country to do it."

Leave the country? Jack narrowed his eyes and asked the one question men in the Acre oughtn't ask. It suddenly seemed important enough to risk. "Who are you, anyhow?"

"Someone with debts to pay." Lowe grinned, tired. "You got some time, son?"

February became March, March crept by, and Texas welcomed spring far earlier than Wyoming did. Though the pupils played outside for recess on all but the coldest days, their restlessness increased with the yellow-green buds on the trees. Smaller children played hide-and-seek and blindman's bluff. The older children played crack-the-whip and catch, or hunted down snakes or rabbits. Thank heavens for the weekly story paper! Its continuing adventures, full of mistaken identities and dramatic rescues and lost loves, were one of the few things that could settle Audra's pupils from physical to mental enjoyments after a romp in the fresh air.

Aunt Heddy protested the "inferior quality" of such literature, but Audra decided to wait until a parent or school board member complained. None did. In the meantime, Audra often used the historical stories to increase interest in history lessons. She enlivened arithmetic problems by couching them in favorite story themes, pirate gold pieces or missing cattle.

And despite increased contentment with her work and with the Ladies' Aid, she felt increasingly restless. She had Jack Harwood to thank for that.

Sometimes, in private moments, she did.

With spring came flowers, both cultivated and wild. Of the two, Audra found she liked the wildflowers more. Bluebonnets, peach and crimson Indian paintbrush, and a mist of goldenrod might grow amid tangled weeds, but they wore bolder colors than Aunt Heddy's roses. More important, with spring came the end of the school year. Audra taught her last class on a Friday, with only Monday's school entertainment and picnic to prepare for. Then, as soon as her father could arrive from Wyoming to collect her, she would go home. *Home!*

"I do want to go home," she admitted to Melissa that Friday as the two of them walked the path where Jack had once met with her, once kissed her. "In fact, I—I believe that once I get there, I shall stay. I'm ready to defend myself against public opinion now, instead of just accepting it. Even if I don't succeed, there is more than one way to teach. But I'll miss Candon. I'll miss *you*." She squeezed her friend's hand.

When Melissa said, "And . . . ?" Audra could not fib by pretending she did not understand, so she said nothing. "If he's willing to come back here to find you, he'll be willing to go to Wyoming. He had enough chances to read the address off your letters."

"You," said Audra fervently, "are such a wonderful friend!" And they hugged each other.

Then Melissa abruptly ended the embrace by asking, "Even if I dyed your hair?"

They were still chasing each other along the path like children, sometimes dodging behind trees in an attempt not to be caught, when Claudine Reynolds ran toward them from Aunt Heddy's house. "Miss Garrison! Miss Garrison!"

Ever since her false elopement, and the danger Audra had faced for her sake, Claudine had behaved with at least a little more respect—for a spoiled, self-centered girl, in any case.

Audra turned, momentarily concerned—then saw the sparkle in Claudine's eyes.

"You've . . ." Claudine almost doubled over, panting. "You have company. Come see!"

Company. Jack?

Audra walked as far as Claudine and put a hand on her arm in silent thanks for the summons; her world had gone so still, she couldn't shatter that hopeful expectation by speaking. Then she began to walk toward the teacherage. Then she began to run.

Until she rounded a turn in the path and beheld the first two of her visitors—and neither was Jack Harwood.

Was it possible to feel disappointment and joy at the same time? She had not guessed just how fervently she'd hoped Jack would return until she saw that he had not. But that didn't abate the pleasure of beholding her two younger sisters for the first time in over half a year.

"Kitty!" Although she'd stopped in shock, for that half moment it took to recognize the two girls hurrying toward her, Audra broke into a run again. "Elise!"

And in a moment she had an armful of both girls and kneeled on the path, holding them to her tightly. *Oh!* No matter what hopes she might leave behind when she left Texas, she would not regret going home to her family! She loosened her embrace only to draw back and examine them both, half-afraid the months had changed her youngest two sisters beyond endurance.

They had not. Kitty, twelve now, looked solemn as ever, with brown braids and spectacles and half-moon dirt marks on her skirt. Kitty wasn't graceful even before a badly broken leg gave her a slight limp, but her gentle spirit compensated. Blond Elise, already the beauty of the family at eight, knew her powers as the cherished youngest child, chattering to Audra even now about the train ride and her new dress and Audra's short hair.

Audra smiled over Elise's head at Kitty, who shyly smiled back.

Only when Elise's chatter included something about Papa did Audra realize that the girls would not travel to Texas alone. She looked up sharply toward the teacherage, and sure enough, two more people strolled toward her, arm in arm, watching her reunion with her sisters.

Audra launched herself toward her parents. Her pretty mother stepped forward to meet her halfway; then Audra was in the arms that she had longed for through more than one heartbreak this year. Mama still smelled of vanilla and orchids. As small as Audra, and only slightly heavier despite bearing seven children, she held Audra tightly enough to break her.

"My sweet girl," Mama whispered, kissing her cheek. Then,

ever fair, she turned Audra toward her white-haired cowboy father.

Papa took off his dark hat. "Audra Sue," he greeted stiffly, gray eyes sweeping her from head to toe with concern his formal posture belied. When Audra hugged him, she felt a completion of something that had broken when he left her. He circled a strong arm around her and held her to him for a satisfyingly long moment.

Then when he released her, and after he ducked his head in response to the kiss she planted on his white-bearded cheek, he said, "I recall teachers showin' a mite more reserve."

"Way back when you were a schoolboy?" teased Mama, in a way that made her appear younger than any matron approaching fifty should.

Somehow the act of sliding a sarcastic look down at his wife undermined Papa's assumed dignity. It didn't help him that Elise began to bounce up and down and ask, "When was that, Papa? Are you as old as Bible times?"

Then he had to glare at his youngest, too, with as heavy an undertone of amusement as he had bestowed on Mama. "Just New Testament," he told her solemnly, which made even Kitty smile.

By then Melissa and Claudine arrived. As Audra made the introductions, she began to sense her mother watching her with unusual curiosity. She thought little of it until, as they started toward the teacherage, Mama held her back several paces behind the others.

"You *are* all right, aren't you, Audra?" Mama asked, a supportive arm still around her.

All right? Only one thing could make her happier.

"I'm fine," she insisted. "It's so wonderful to see you again!"

Mama did not look satisfied. "There's a different look about you. And I don't mean your hair; actually, that's nicely daring. You seem . . . changed, is all."

"Well, I have grown up a great deal," Audra offered.

"That's what concerns me," murmured Mama. Then Elise ran back to see what kept them and she let the subject go.

* * *

Mama's curiosity returned when Papa, making himself useful by cleaning Heddy's stables that Saturday, found a cuff link under the hay. Audra could see—*feel*—disapproval as soon as he came in from his work, even without his aiming it at her in particular. He sent Kitty and Elise outside, then asked with simple authority, "One of you girls recognize this?"

Since only Audra did, Claudine and Melissa said nothing.

"Where did you find that?" asked Mama for the rest of them, and Papa said, "Barn."

A year ago, Audra might not understand the significance of a cuff link in the hay. Now she not only understood, she remembered vividly. Jack's overhasty discarding of his shirt had provided her first and only view of a man's naked chest . . . and, oh, what a chest it had been! Now, even at the moment of disgrace that she had feared since before she'd even done something disgraceful, Audra couldn't regret her indecent behavior.

But she deeply regretted having to confess it.

"Asked a question," prompted Papa, and Audra drew a miserable breath.

Claudine said, "I do. I recognize it from when Audra caught me with Jerome Newton last fall." She looked at Audra. "Back when I thought he loved me."

Papa's expression froze into a mask of his initial anger—it might be his duty to treat his sister's boarding pupils as strictly as his daughters, but the thought that he'd uncovered proof of an already settled scandal hadn't occurred to him.

Mama swept in to save him then, taking the cuff link from his hand and patting his arm. "Thank you, Jacob. Why don't I take over from here?"

He nodded at her, purposefully not looking at the three young ladies before him, then escaped back to the barn even if he didn't need to. Quickly.

Mama waited until he'd left, then said, "I'm sorry, Claudine, to have resurrected that. So that you needn't revisit painful memories, shall we have Audra give this back to its rightful owner?"

"Perhaps Melissa," suggested Claudine quickly.

Melissa widened her eyes at the younger girl. "Me?" Then: "Oh! Certainly. I can give it to Early and he can give it to Jerome."

Mama said, "But I remember that Audra wrote that Claudine and Jerome were found *behind* the barn, not in it. Would you excuse us? I have something to discuss with Audra."

"Audra?" whispered Claudine in amazement as they scurried toward the door.

"You thought it was *me?*" demanded Melissa.

Then Audra, face aflame, stood alone with her mother. She hardly knew where to start, what to say. She'd think more clearly if the image of Jack's chest were not so immediately vivid.

"I assume you'll want this," said Mama, pressing the cuff link into Audra's hand. She did not let go of her hand when Audra took it, either. "Are you certain you're all right?"

And when Audra looked up, she saw no censure on her mother's face at all. Then tears of relief blurred that face beyond recognition. "I . . ."

"Shhh." Mama led her into an empty bedroom. "I'm not angry," she insisted now, sitting with Audra on the bed, holding her hand. "Just concerned. I needn't know how far it went."

Audra gasped. "Mother!"

Mama's playful smile disproved her previous statement. "Well, thank goodness for that. I assume you loved him, whoever he was?"

"I still do," insisted Audra.

"You *do* plan on coming home with us, don't you? If you don't—"

"Of *course* I do! He's . . . he's gone now. It was the right thing to do, and he did it."

Mama gave her a quick hug. "You always were so concerned about the right thing."

"But I didn't tell *you,*" Audra admitted, and Mama laughed.

"Did you really think you should?"

Amazingly, Audra realized she did not. What she and Jack had done was their business and theirs alone. Especially since they'd been responsible . . . more or less.

"Just know that if you ever do want to talk about it, I'm

here. And once we get home, any one of your older sisters would be glad to . . . um . . . advise you. All right?"

Audra nodded, then—independent or not—felt ill again. "Will you tell Papa?"

Her mother almost choked on the idea. "I love him far too much to do that."

Audra thought her revelations were finished after that. But then, settled in church with her family the next morning, she heard excited whispers from the door. She'd heard that murmur before. Twice.

Somehow, just turning to look became the biggest gamble Audra had ever taken.

Chapter Twenty-nine

> *A teacher who performs her labor faithfully and without fault for five years will be given an increase of fifty cents per week in her pay, providing the school board approves.*
>
> —Rules for Teachers

God didn't strike Jack down this time either. But beyond the threat of lightning bolts and whatnot, it wasn't God's opinion that concerned him.

He stood there in the doorway and let the townsfolk stare at him, whisper to each other, and generally appreciate the drama of his prodigal return. Hat in hand, he reminded himself that their opinion did matter—if only because, if he still mattered to Audra at all, public opinion would too. Besides, most were decent enough folks, respectability aside. So he nodded toward all and sundry, touching the gazes of folks who'd frequented the mercantile, and he tried not to smile too charmingly, not to do anything that would brand him as a scoundrel.

Not that he *wasn't* still a scoundrel. He didn't regret how familiar he'd gotten with Audra that night he left . . . though if *she* regretted it, which wouldn't much surprise him, that would surely tarnish things. For another, he still believed that a person had the God-given right to ruin her life in whatever manner she saw fit, even someone as special as Audra Garrison. He'd never appreciated anyone calling the shots for him. So who was he to call the shots for her?

The least he could do was stay long enough to give her what he'd said she deserved all along—the right to make up her own mind, by her own rules.

A teacher oughtn't keep company with men, so he'd stayed away until her term was about over. He'd even used that time to raise his own odds, at least some.

Now he couldn't wait any longer to call.

At his entrance, folks in back turned first. Then, like water rippling outward, people in the middle turned and, finally, those in front. Not Audra.

Jack caught only the barest glimpse of her beyond Whitey Gilmer's shoulder, past Nora Parks's hat—the curse of loving a short woman. But he knew her too-stiff back when he glimpsed it. Along her bench, Melissa Smith and Claudine Reynolds both turned and recognized him. Even Hedda Cribb turned and narrowed her eyes. Two little girls on either side of Audra looked too. One wore dark braids and spectacles that magnified her eyes; the other one, golden-haired, stared with candor. Even an elegant matron whom he couldn't place and a fierce-looking, white-bearded cowboy—or lawman—looked to see what had caused the disturbance.

Jack prayed, and not to God. *Look at me, Audra. Please.*

And, with seeming reluctance, she turned.

In her fine eyes, even half-hidden by Nora Parks's hat, he saw that same pain he'd seen in her from the start: the pain of a gal imprisoning herself. She had her feelings under tight rein, and nothing he could do would ever spring her without her cooperation.

But even while he watched, his hopes sinking, those fine eyes began to shine, as if at sight of him her icy control melted. He still saw hesitance war with hope; relief battle fear. But at least she was letting herself feel those things. At least he did have a shaky chance.

Jack would get nowhere by making a scene in church. So he nodded to her, wishing that single nod could tell her the things she might yet refuse to hear in words. Then he found a seat toward the back, where one fellow actually stood up and moved rather than sit beside him.

But nobody kicked him out. Jack decided to be grateful. It might still be all he got.

Light from the windows crept across the wooden floor of the church. Birdsong and the smell of growing things from outside added to the sleepy, springtime feel of the morning. Jack didn't relive a single moment of haunting childhood sermons . . . though neither did he listen closely to the pastor's offering today. He was too busy hoping he wouldn't create a whole new breed of haunting, church-related memories.

When services ended, he hurried out, lest his presence keep Audra holed up. The girl had once regretted *kisses!* How could she not be regretting their more extreme abandon?

Several folks eyed him warily as he waited, including the preacher. This *was* a risk.

When Audra emerged from the church, Jack saw his stake doubled as the obvious struck him—the little girls, the handsome woman, and the severe-looking rancher were Audra's family. Sisters. Mother. Her father resembled a judge or lawman too closely for Jack's comfort.

If the man had any inkling of what Jack had done to Audra, let her do to him, Jack might not be long on this earth. Jim Lowe, a.k.a. Robert Parker, a.k.a. Butch Cassidy, sure had the right of it there. Life was risk.

And Audra was worth the gamble. At least, in the presence of her father, Jack had extra incentive to keep his hands to himself

. . . assuming the man didn't separate them from Jack's body. Even now, when the littlest girl visibly tired of their chat with the reverend, their father caught her by the shoulder and held her still instead of letting her run off to play. He didn't look like one who suffered misbehavior lightly.

Then the Garrisons descended the steps to make way for the next emerging family. The little blond girl bolted for a cluster of nearby children. What with the interest Jack felt—Melissa's wide-eyed encouragement, Hedda Cribb's narrow-eyed disapproval, and increasingly nervous glances from Audra—he figured he'd best show his hand before anyone forced it.

But this time he'd do it by Audra's rules.

He strode deliberately up to them, right there in the churchyard. "Miss Garrison," he greeted, careful not to call her darling or fill his arms with her or kiss her until they both felt drunk with it, right there, imminent death or not. It had been so long.

Instead he gave her a polite bow and satisfied himself with just being this close.

She searched his face, anxious. He wished he knew what exactly she feared. Her voice came uneven when she said, "Mr. Harwood. Will you . . . be in town long?"

Do you want me to be?

"That depends," he hedged. Since God and everyone was watching, he doubled his stake by facing her stern, white-bearded sire. "I'm guessing this is your family," he said to Audra, feeling nowhere near as confident as he sounded.

She nodded, awkward. It could be that his presence shamed her. It could be that she didn't know how this would go either. "May I introduce my father, Jacob Garrison."

Jack offered a hand. "Sir." When the rancher clasped it in his own then released it with no damage done, he felt relief. The barn remained his and Audra's secret. He had to concentrate to catch the other introductions—mother; Kathryn, called Kitty; Elise.

"This is John Harwood, who used to work at the mercantile."

Once she said the name Harwood, the temperature from the direction of her sire dropped significantly. Pa must've been talking to Thaddeas.

"I hear tell, Miss Garrison," Jack said now, while he still could, "that your school term ends tomorrow. Some kind of entertainment's scheduled, isn't it?"

Audra nodded, waiting with clear questions.

"You'll no longer be under contract as a local schoolmistress after that, correct?"

She nodded again, her confusion slowly clearing as she began to see his direction. Was it that shocking that he might do something by rules other than those according to Hoyle, for once? He guessed it was.

"Then will you be so kind as to permit me to speak with you afterward, Miss Garrison?" Jack quietly held his breath. This was why he'd waited until now, because Audra was worth more than secret trysts and rolls in the hay. She'd always been worth more. Either he courted her openly, or he didn't deserve her. And once her contract ended, he could court her openly.

If she allowed it. And therein lay his gamble.

Audra's smile warmed him far more deeply than even the smoothest of whiskeys.

"Perhaps at the picnic," he suggested. "I hear mention of a box social. Will you be—"

Hedda Cribb said, "The box social is for unmarried girls, *not* for teachers."

Jack swallowed back a few choice names for the battle-ax. "My mistake."

Then Audra said, "Yes," and he felt like he'd just been dealt a third queen, until she added a less committal, "I will be there."

"Then so will I," he promised. He said, "Ladies," to the women, charitably including the widow Cribb. "Sir," he added toward her father, since respect didn't cost anywhere near what doctor bills could. "Miss Garrison. Tomorrow, then."

Audra's mother, smiling pleasantly enough, held her husband's arm quite firmly, as if she had a leash on a bear. So Jack decided to get while he could, until tomorrow anyhow. He would figure how to handle Audra's father if and when it became necessary.

If and when Audra gave him a second chance. That would

depend on her hearing him out, on the changes he'd made, was willing to make . . . and those things he could not, would not change, not even for her.

Audra felt like singing—and like praying. She wanted to hug herself, and she wished Jack had hugged her instead. She felt the last two months of loneliness even more acutely, now that she'd seen him again, now that she could look forward to speaking at further length.

About what? she wondered, dreams and fears taking her imagination in radically different directions. About . . . them? She'd meant to leave with her family, visit *Grossmutter* and Uncle Matthew, then return to Wyoming. What if he wanted her to stay? Could she risk more than she already had—including the possibility of a second good-bye?

After seeing him again, how could she not? Despite her fears and those around her?

Papa growled the name, "Harwood," the way he might say, "hoof rot."

Claudine said, "Him? Audra, him?" and Melissa nudged the younger girl with an elbow before anybody else figured out the context of her question.

Aunt Heddy said, "How dare he? And how dare you behave so brazenly, young lady!"

Audra wasn't the only person in the group to stare at her aunt, but she was perhaps the only one who did not do so with surprise. "Perhaps I should have slapped him, Aunt. The nerve of the man! Perhaps we should have Papa shoot him."

While Aunt Heddy gaped, Papa warned, "I could." He didn't normally set himself against people on such short notice, except sheep herders and rustlers. Thank you so very much, Thad, Audra thought, then steeled herself. "With all respect, Papa, I agreed to speak with him at a public picnic, not to—" *Oh, dear.* Kiss him? Hold him? Let him touch her and put his mouth—

Mama, thank heavens, quickly dragged Papa's glare to herself by announcing, "I say we leave this between Audra and Mr. Harwood."

Papa said, "You would." But he said no more. Normally Audra admired her parents for not fighting in front of her or her sisters, when they fought at all. Now it annoyed her. This wasn't her mother's battle, after all. It was her own.

Finally she trusted herself to ask what counted. "Don't you trust me, Papa?"

The things she and Jack had done together were in no way proper—but at the very least she'd gone into them with her eyes open. When they'd needed to make a painful decision, they'd both used common sense. So yes, she realized, standing straighter. She *did* trust herself!

Papa held her gaze for a long moment—not angry, she thought, but weary, concerned. He hadn't liked anyone her older sisters fell in love with either. A couple of them he still didn't.

He said, "Don't see as I have a choice." No promise of good behavior on his part, but neither was it a command. He was, at the very least, giving her a loose lead . . . or enough rope to hang herself. Either way, the freedom boosted Audra's morale.

As long as she *didn't* hang herself—or get Jack hanged either.

With the arrival of Claudine's father and Melissa's parents and family, the teacherage overflowed with guests. Fathers and brothers slept in the barn, mothers and Aunt Heddy shared the beds, and the five girls slept on floor pallets. Rather, the Garrison sisters lay on a shared pallet and whispered to each other, still savoring their reunion too much to sleep.

"It won't be so crowded at *Grossmutter*'s, will it?" asked Elise, cuddled at Audra's side.

Audra said, "Don't be rude." Then she thought about it and added, "Probably not."

"I like this," insisted Kitty softly. "It's more like home was, before . . ."

She seemed to change her mind, then, but Audra sat up on an elbow and brushed long brown strands of hair out of the twelve-year-old's pinched face. "Before what, honey?"

"Before you all grew up and went away," Kitty admitted. In the pale moonlight through the kitchen window, her eyes unfocused without the protection of her spectacles, Kitty looked even more fragile than usual. "Don't you remember what it was like, Audra? All six of us in two bedrooms, eating together and dressing together and fighting over the silliest things?"

"Of course I remember!" Audra pulled her sister more closely against her. "But Mariah's barely two hours away, and Laurel's claim is only twice that far. And Victoria lives in town! They didn't go away, honey. Not really."

"It's not the same," Kitty insisted.

And Elise, yawning, said, "You did, Audra. *You* went away."

Both of them spoke the truth. Audra wanted to defend herself against a pang of guilt, and she almost said, *I had to.* But that wasn't wholly true, was it? She'd left to teach, of course. Sheridan had denied her a teaching job, and Aunt Heddy had offered one. But she'd also left to preserve her precious reputation, to start over someplace where people didn't know about her mistakes. She'd told herself she did it for the good of her family—but she'd done it for the good of Audra. Now she remembered how she'd resented Mariah's leaving, back when she still had four sisters left at home. By the time Laurel and then Victoria left—happy though Audra felt for them—home seemed increasingly deserted. She had their parents, of course, and Kitty and Elise. But compared to the homes of their childhood, it *had* been lonely.

And then she'd left, too, traveling not a day's ride but half a country away.

"I'm sorry," she told her sisters now. "I can't help growing up, and I won't always live at home, but I'm sorry I moved so far."

"It's all right," Kitty assured her quickly, contrite for having mentioned it, and wrapped her slim arms around Audra, cuddling against her shoulder. "You're coming home now."

Audra thought about Jack Harwood's request to speak to her tomorrow. She'd held her joy at his return tightly to her all day, taking small sips of pleasure from it instead of letting the joy pour over her . . . and now she knew why. The same impractical fantasies she'd not dared consider head-on still danced through her imagination. But they were still fantasies. They had to be, and for reasons far more important than her reputation.

She held her two younger sisters to her tightly. "Yes," she said. "I'm coming home now."

Once she got home, she probably wouldn't want to cry so badly.

The end-of-term entertainment the next day only increased Jack's admiration for Audra. After her fears about her teaching abilities, he'd worried what kind of showing she would make. Not that it mattered to him if she could teach a chicken to scratch. But he knew it mattered to her, especially with her family looking on.

He ought to have known better. Even the widow Cribb's smaller pupils looked to Audra for encouragement as they made their standard little presentations, sang their songs, proved that they could spell and read and count to the approval and applause of their audience.

But Audra's older pupils took the day. Unlike the widow Cribb's charges, Audra's had apparently been given more of a free rein in choosing their recitation pieces. It showed in their level of enthusiasm. Jerome Newton's rendition of "Give me liberty, or give me death!" had Jack ready to do just that—give him death—but he admitted a bias. Early Rogers's and Melissa Smith's recitation of the balcony scene from *Romeo and Juliet* hinted at a mutual interest Jack hadn't seen before now. Little Charlotte Calloway read a story she'd written, complete with gunfights, Indian attacks, swooning women, and true love; most of the parents agreed she had a future in letters. Even Claudine Reynolds surprised Jack, giving a passionate rendition of "The Highwayman," although Jack noted that she took unnecessary relish in the outlaw's bloody end.

Miss Garrison's pupils had not only learned; they'd enjoyed

it. Their pride went beyond the advancement of a grade level. It did Jack's heart good to see the pride Audra felt on their behalf, especially when she sought him out from her place up front to smile especially at him.

Then, insidiously, the townsfolk's satisfaction with their new teacher began to please Jack less and worry him more. For weeks he'd waited for Audra's contract to end, just so he could ask to call on her properly. But what good would it do to court her if she meant to teach again?

He watched Audra's class present her with a surprise gift—a handmade book with all of their signatures in it—and he listened to the applause, watched Audra's pleasure, and he felt like a heel. If he asked Audra to choose him, Jack asked her to choose against a job she loved. Suddenly the argument that it *was* her choice seemed more selfish than he liked.

"What are you looking so long in the face about?" demanded Ferris Hamilton, limping up to Jack without need of a crutch as the festivities ended and preparations for the box social began. Jack had stayed with Ferris the night before, settling a few things there as well, and had been as glad for their continued friendship as he was for the news that his friend and Lucy Wolfe were writing regularly, still planning to reunite once Ham sold his store.

"I am a low-down, good-for-nothing snake in the grass," said Jack, losing track of his sorrel-haired darling in the crowd. The crowd loved her, after all. They gave him wide berth.

"And?" challenged Ham.

"And I want to ruin a good woman's life."

"Ah," said Ham. "You know, if you're talking about the same good woman I'm thinking you are, she might prove harder to ruin than you'd expect."

"Yep," said Jack. He hoped that were true. He also feared it.

Ham said, "The town council likes your idea to get the depot."

Jack said, "Not if they knew it was my idea." That was why Jack had asked Ham to present it. Things had gone mostly back to normal after Lucy had left.

Ham shrugged. "They may already be voting on it."

Jack hoped it worked out, both for the town and his friend. He would not have made the suggestion otherwise. But at the moment he didn't give a wooden nickel about it.

Some kind of commotion caught their attention from the plank table folks had set up to show the box lunches, and Jack's curiosity got the best of him. While Ham wandered off to check on the council vote, Jack headed toward the display of prettily wrapped boxes, tins, and baskets. By time he reached it, the disturbance—whatever it was—had been resolved. This wasn't Hell's Half-Acre, after all, where people turned to fists or firearms to solve their disputes.

Still, Jack suddenly felt wary. He got that same itchy feeling at the back of his neck that he sometimes did in a red-light district, when he had to walk back to his room flush with cash and short on protection. It was the feeling of too many people paying him too close attention.

He didn't vary his pace or his expression as he sought out the cause of his sudden, dubious popularity. And when he followed the gaze of other folks to one end of the table, when any normal man likely *would* have reacted, he couldn't think far enough to respond in any way other than to stare . . . and then finally, slowly, to smile.

He'd attended box socials in his childhood, so he knew the order of play. The ladies brought homemade luncheons and the gentlemen bid on them. When a lady had a beau, she generally gave him hints to which basket was hers—the one with a yellow bow, or bluebonnets—so that they could share lunch and private conversation. Assuming he could afford her.

The widow Cribb said schoolteachers couldn't participate. But the basket on one end of the table, causing its own minor scandal, said differently.

Someone had decorated it with an indulgent length of green ribbon, the kind a fellow might use to wrap a Christmas gift—and from one end of the ribbon hung a playing card.

The jack of hearts.

Chapter Thirty

Women teachers who marry will be dismissed.
—Rules for Teachers

Audra had expected moderate resistance to her offering, especially with its unorthodox decoration. But she had to let Jack know which lunch was meant for him, so she risked it.

It caused more stir than she'd imagined. Aunt Heddy insisted that box socials were not proper activities for schoolteachers. Mr. Trigg reminded her that even between school terms a teacher must behave herself if she wished to be invited back in the autumn.

At which point Audra heard herself clearly say, "Then I quit."

The school board members stared, silent at last. Finally, Mr. Trigg said, "You what?"

"I appreciate the opportunities Candon has given me, and I *am* pleased to be invited back. But if your invitation hinges upon my slighting a kind, decent man who waited until the end of the term to approach me"—*officially, anyway*—"then I must respectfully resign my post."

Reverend Collins said, "Now, Audra, by acting in haste you might repent at leisure."

She'd best tell the truth here, as well. "I have already decided not to return next year, Reverend. My family is in Wyoming. If I cannot find a school there, I will find some other way to teach. But I have no intention of living so far from them again."

Reverend Collins nodded, and Mr. Trigg said, "I see."

"That still does not resolve the issue of your scandalous lunch basket," insisted Aunt Heddy, then raised her attention over Audra's shoulder. "Talk some sense into the child, Jacob."

Audra's stomach knotted. *Oh, dear.* "Jacob" meant her father, and that he said nothing only confirmed his presence. Even without hearing him, she could *feel* him, like an adobe wall at her back. Her father, who often said, "There's no room at the cookfire for a quitter's blanket," had heard her quit a job. He'd heard her disrespect her elders.

And she would somehow deal with his disappointment *after* she settled the issue of her basket. "I believe the purpose of the box social is to raise funds, is it not?" she asked. "And I believe the person who so concerns you tends to donate generously, does he not?"

Aunt Heddy said, "Propriety is not for sale!"

Audra said, "You are selling the companionship of young girls to the highest bidder, Aunt Heddy. How does the presence of a simple playing card denigrate that?"

"Now, Miss Garrison," chided the reverend.

Audra raised a hand to fend off more protests. She did not want to embarrass herself further in front of her father, and she'd said all she could say. Almost. "It is of course the decision of the school board. But if you remove the card, remove the basket, too. I shall lunch with whom I please, whether or not he pays for the privilege. Good day."

And she turned to face her father's disappointment . . . except that Papa did not look particularly upset. Intrigued, yes. But nowhere near as disapproving as she'd feared.

"Your sisters are lookin' fer you," he told her after a long moment of consideration, and offered an arm. She took it gratefully, somewhat light-headed from her uncommon rebellion. Papa thumbed his hat politely toward the others. "Hedda. Folks."

And they left together. Papa did not say anything at all after that, which made Audra increasingly nervous. How much had he heard? What was he thinking about her?

A strange calm settled over her as she thought that at least he was thinking it about the real Audra, not just the careful mask she'd hidden behind, even from herself, for so very long. Still, it was largely to avoid his disappointment that she'd worn that mask at all. She hadn't wanted to hurt him as her older sisters had. She'd never wanted the blame for familial discord.

"I'm sorry if I shamed you," she said finally.

"Didn't hear nothin' that weren't deserved," drawled her father, so unexpectedly that she dared look up at him. "You've not shamed me yet, Audra Sue."

"Not even by quitting?"

"You finish the job?"

"Yes, sir."

"Then you're no quitter." He sighed. "More like your mother than I'd figured, though."

Which made her smile proudly and lean against his arm. "That's not so bad a thing, is it?"

Papa wisely stayed silent on the matter. He loved his wife to distraction—Audra had never doubted that. But Mama did keep him on his cowboy-booted toes.

"I mean to eat lunch with Mr. Harwood," Audra told him now, in the interest of honesty.

"I gathered," he said noncommittally.

"He's my friend." But Papa chose silence again. "You don't approve of him, do you?"

Papa said, "Nope." And she knew better than to argue that he didn't know Jack. Not just now. "But you're comin' home. Don't reckon one picnic lunch—in plain sight—will ruin you."

But he said it reluctantly—except for the *plain sight* part, which came out as a dire warning. Someone had been coaching him on open-mindedness.

Audra said, "Mama's been talking to you, hasn't she?"

Papa said, "Yup."

Audra turned and stood on her toes to give her father a kiss. "I love you, Papa."

He looked away again when he said, "Much obliged."

And I love Jack Harwood, too. But she *was* going home. So why bring it up now?

They joined Mama, Kitty, and Elise on a quilt for the box social, and Audra's basket remained on the table, complete with its playing card decoration.

Before the auction, Mr. Calloway stood and made some general announcements about pride in their young folk and the future of the town. "And, thanks in part to Mr. Hamilton of the mercantile," he said, "the town council has come upon a way to all but guarantee a depot for the town of Candon, Tarrant County." Several folks laughed when he spoke the town's longer name. "It has been suggested that we rename our city Tarrant."

"Well, that makes sense," said Mama, while Audra savored the pleased clamor. Mr. Hamilton could use the boost to his reputation as much as Candon could use the depot.

"Why, Mama?" asked Elise. "Why does it make sense?"

"It's easier to remember," Mama explained, "And it's a more important-sounding name."

"And it won't be as hard to address letters when we write to Aunt Heddy," added Kitty with a shy smile, which made Audra laugh.

By the time the auction began, however, Audra's nerves had too tight a rein on her to allow laughter. What if Jack didn't notice his card on her basket, didn't know to bid on it? What if he didn't *want* to? What if someone outbid him? What if he'd already left?

Early Rogers bid on Melissa's tin. He won lunch with her for six bits, and didn't even seem to mind that her three brothers intended to dine with them. Claudine's father spent two dollars to outbid old Mr. Putnam, to Claudine's too-obvious relief.

Finally Mr. Parker, the auctioneer, held up Audra's basket. He resented it, she could tell. He did not smell it and announce to the crowd that he detected chicken or peach pie. He did not wonder out loud what pretty girl might go with it—not, she suspected, that anyone had not already heard. He only asked, "And what do I have bid for—"

And the wrong voice announced, "One dollar."

Audra felt ill. *Jerome Newton?* Bad enough that, when most bidding began with a nickel or a dime, he'd started so high. But for him to bid at all . . . !

Kitty whispered, "Isn't he one of your pupils?"

Audra couldn't even nod. Not Jerome. He could have the basket to himself, if he won it.

Then, coming to her rescue, Jack's familiar drawl announced, "Two dollars."

Audra spotted him then, and relaxed. Jack could handle Jerome.

"Two dollars and . . ." Jerome paused. "Two dollars and twenty-five cents."

Their audience watched in fascination.

Jack managed a perfect mixture of amusement and annoyance. "Three dollars."

"Wait a minute," called Jerome, and began to confer with several of his friends.

Jack looked toward Audra, an eyebrow raised. She widened both eyes at him. *Help me.*

Before Jerome could gather more funds, Jack called, "I raise my bid to twenty dollars."

Kitty gasped. Or maybe that was Audra herself. Jerome's shoulders slumped.

Mr. Parker said, "Did you mean to say twenty dollars, Mr. Harwood?"

Jack grinned and said, "I rarely make mistakes about money, Nate."

Several of the menfolk laughed, earning various degrees of disapproval from their wives.

"Sold," announced Mr. Parker, and Jack stepped forward to collect his lunch.

Audra gathered up the spare blanket she'd brought, suddenly very nervous. She and Jack had not spoken in private since . . .

Remembering that last time thrilled her, but did little to calm her nerves.

Papa warned, "Plain view," in a tone that brooked no argument. Audra nodded. Some couples headed farther out than others, but she took shy comfort in not being one of them. There was a certain safety to following some rules, at that. And when Jack arrived beside her, tall and handsome as ever, publicly offering his arm, she knew she needed all the safety she could get.

* * *

So this was what it felt like to court a gal in public.

No wonder Jack had never done it before.

First came the challenge of collecting Audra from her family. Her father, staring at Jack from the shadow of his black hat's brim, reminded him of a cougar—certain that it could take him, merely deciding when. But her mother and sisters somehow worried him even more, especially the skinny sister with brown braids, eyes big behind thick spectacle lenses. Kitty, was it?

If Jack somehow hurt this family, her father, at least, could take care of himself *and* Jack—and not in any way Jack wanted to test. But the thought of somehow hurting little girls raised the stakes to even more uncomfortable heights.

Still, he'd anted up, so he might as well play the game through. He exchanged polite greetings. The way Kitty's already big, blue eyes widened when he smiled at her made Audra appear downright forward in comparison. But the little blond princess, Elise, balanced the trio out when she boldly met his gaze and asked, "Are you going to kiss my sister?"

"Not just now," hedged Jack, grinning at her brass, and the imp grinned back.

Then Jack caught Mr. Garrison's murderous gaze and stopped grinning. Only once he'd drawn Audra far enough away not to be overheard did he feel safe enough to start breathing again.

"Sorry," he said, wishing he'd kept his mouth shut. He hadn't wanted to embarrass her.

"No, I'm sorry," Audra insisted. "Elise is somewhat . . . outspoken."

Jack carried the basket. Audra, arm on his, carried a blanket. The blanket gave him the kind of ideas that could get a man killed, especially with everyone in town watching them.

"I don't suppose . . ." he suggested, looking toward a wooded path.

"I promised to stay in plain sight," admitted Audra, apologetic but not disappointed.

Probably just as well. "A little insurance?" challenged Jack.

"Not against you! Against . . ." When he slid his gaze down to her, her blush had deepened adorably. He could stare at her all day and not tire of it, he thought.

"Well . . . maybe a little bit against you," she murmured, smiling.

He smiled back, and that felt better. An unexpected upside to everyone watching was that, for once, everyone saw her with him. Folks could wonder what Jack had that they didn't, never knowing that the most important answer was—Audra.

At the very least, he had her for the afternoon. For the first time, people knew it.

"Well, if we're to stay in plain view, we've reached the end of the available pasturage," he decided now, looking around them. When the breeze blew, snowlike bits of fine white fluff drifted down from a grove of nearby cottonwoods. "Does this meet with your approval, ma'am?"

Audra seemed startled, as if she hadn't been noticing. "Oh. Certainly."

Unless he'd chosen a fire-ant hill or a dung heap, she'd likely have accepted any of his choices. That made him nervous. Considering what he meant to propose, he didn't want her simply agreeing with him today. It gave him too much responsibility, too much culpability if things went wrong. He wanted her to decide for herself . . . even if her decision was no.

They spread the blanket—*Don't think about blankets!*—near some black-eyed Susans and sank onto it with the basket carefully between them. When Audra set about unpacking their lunch it occurred to Jack that, on top of everything else, he got a homemade meal out of the deal.

"I made fried chicken," Audra announced, her voice high. "Actually Mama made it, but I helped. Instead of plucking chickens, Mama prefers that Papa skin them, so I hope you don't like too much fat on your poultry. We made hard-cooked eggs; my sisters collected them fresh this morning. My father's particularly fond of eggs, so I hoped you would be too."

Jack watched her, admiring the uncertain brightness of her eyes, the modest flush across her china-doll cheeks, the way her sorrel curls caught the tree-dappled afternoon sunlight. "I'm fond of eggs," he assured her. He was. But he would eat dirt if she served it to him.

"There's tomato relish, with basil and wild onion," she continued as she fussed with plates, her voice rising in pitch if dropping in volume. "And pie. Everyone probably made pie."

"I don't care what everyone made," Jack assured her, and she finally faced him directly.

"You paid twenty dollars," she said.

"I was ready to pay two hundred."

"Oh . . ." She looked at the food. "Twenty was scandalous enough," she chided gently.

Which made him smile. "Speaking of scandal, I believe I have something of yours." He extended the jack of hearts he'd once left at the school for her. "Now, what kind of a lady would attach an honest-to-dog playing card to her lunch basket?"

When she took it, their fingers brushed. That brief, innocent touch weakened him. "It did create a scandal," she admitted shyly. "But I wanted you to know which one was yours."

Filling his gaze with her, he *did* know which one was his. But did she?

"Even at the cost of your fine reputation?" he teased instead, awkwardly, but when she bit her lip, he wished he hadn't. "Audra—"

"No, you ought to know something, Jack. I *didn't* have a fine reputation at home, and that's why I came here. I had one originally, but I went out riding with a beau one day—"

"And the horses ran off and he kept you out after dark and you wouldn't marry him," Jack finished. She stared at him, wide-eyed. "Melissa told me," he explained. "Without mentioning your name, mind you, but I figured that part out."

Audra said, "Oh."

"Why wouldn't you marry him, Audra?"

She handed him a plate heaped with food. "I didn't love him. I turned him down even before the horses ran away, and I certainly wouldn't marry him after he all but abducted me."

Which was wonderful to know. "Not even to save your reputation," he insisted.

"A reputation is a good thing," she said. "But some things are more important."

"Audra?"

She busied herself pouring lemonade from a clay jug and handed him a glass. But it was her attention he wanted, so he touched her hand gently. She paused like a rabbit caught in the open.

He didn't want to be the predator anymore, damn it!

"I never meant to scare you," he said, reluctantly moving his hand lest even that threaten her. "I've thought about that night . . . when I left . . . I can hardly forget it. That was . . ." He had her blushing now; he suspected he might just be blushing himself, as unbalanced as he felt when he recalled that night. "I've never known anything so fine," he confessed. "But I reckon I owe you an apology for letting it go so far. I know you're not that kind of a gal."

"But I *am,*" she whispered, not meeting his eyes, and her blush deepened. "I . . . I sometimes think about that, too, Jack. You did not force me to do anything I didn't want to." Which relieved but did not exonerate him. "You need not apologize."

"As the man, and the one with more . . ." He swallowed, hating to remind her. "More experience, I think I do."

"For mercy's sake, you proposed marriage! How much more honorable could you be?"

Then she looked up at him, her eyes big. He could see she hadn't meant to mention marriage. Now that she had, she couldn't take it back—but she could try to divert him.

"Eat your chicken," she said softly, giving them both an escape route. "People will begin to wonder what we're talking about."

He obediently took a bite of fried chicken, never lowering his gaze from hers until, halfway through chewing that first bite, he actually tasted it. Then he looked at the chicken leg in his hand, wide-eyed. "This is *good!*" he exclaimed.

"You thought my mother and I couldn't cook?"

"Not like this. This is . . ." He took another bite, savoring it. Only after he'd swallowed did it occur to him that he'd digressed. But Audra was smiling again, at least.

"I meant it," he said, more seriously.

"Liking the chicken?" she asked, purposefully obtuse.

So he put the chicken down. "Marrying you. I ought not have asked the way I did. As if it were only a way to get into your—that is, to ease your inhibitions about . . ." He picked up the chicken and took another bite after all, keeping his attention on the food until Audra uncovered her face and he felt safe to speak again. This time he meant to do it right.

"Audra Garrison," he said now—then thought to wipe his hands on his napkin. "Darlin', you are the finest woman I have ever had the pleasure to meet. Not just the prettiest, nor the smartest, though you are that, too. You are kinder, more honest, more . . . more understanding than I ever knew a respectable woman could be."

"Jack—" she whispered in pained protest.

He knew then that she still meant to say no. So much for his appetite. But she at least deserved to hear his whole pitch. She oughtn't ever have to wonder.

"Hear me out," he insisted. "The world is a finer place for you being in it, darlin'. *My* world is better for you being part of it. I realize that I'm not the sort of man a girl like you would generally yoke herself to, but being as you have indicated a certain return of"—passion? desire?—"fondness," he hedged, "I would be five kinds of fool if I did not at least ask you again to make me a better man by becoming my wife."

There. He'd said it, and properly this time.

He wasn't sure if the fact that Audra began to cry meant he'd done it well or not.

Would she *never* stop crying in front of this man? Audra hated herself for it, especially when Jack began to glance nervously in the direction of her family. He shifted as if to reach for her, then stopped awkwardly. He swore under his breath, then apologized for the language.

"What in blazes do respectable men do to comfort a crying woman?" he demanded finally, clearly as frustrated as he was panicked. That made her giggle, even through the misery of having to reject him again after that beautiful, beautiful proposal. She did love him so much.

"They hold her hand?" she suggested, sniffing.

He took her hand right away—and with his left, he dug into a pocket and then proffered a store-bought handkerchief. She tried to be surreptitious in wiping her eyes, so as not to attract her father's attention. Jack's concern, after all, was not just paranoia.

"You're carrying handkerchiefs now?" she asked, her voice uneven.

"It's a small step toward respectability, but one whose time has come," he assured her.

"I love you, Jack," she said, and watched his eyes close—he was either savoring her confession, or girding himself against what they both knew, from precedent, must follow. "If I were to marry any man, it would be you."

He opened his eyes, and the lack of anger in them relieved her considerably.

"So you don't plan on marrying at all?" he challenged—and with good cause. Distracted by his question, she even stopped crying. What real future was there for a respectable woman besides marriage and children? Audra's mother advocated her daughters' learning to support themselves, insisted that a career could be just rewarding as a home and family . . . but, coming from a woman so obviously happy in her marriage, the argument did not carry as much weight as it otherwise might. Lady teachers could not marry . . . but, for that very reason, most lady teachers retired after only a few years.

Did Audra truly want to grow up alone? *No.*

And could she bear to marry anyone but Jack Harwood? *No.*

But . . . could she marry Jack?

If she risked only her own happiness, she would accept him

in a heartbeat—even as fast as her heart was, in fact, beating. But how could she gamble with the children they would have? How could she gamble with her family's concerns?

Jack waited, and of all people in the world, he deserved an honest answer about her marital plans. "I don't know," she admitted miserably. "I just don't know."

He sat back, watching her, and his face slowly took on kind of a thoughtful look. Soon she could not read him at all.

"How about," he suggested quietly, "if I were to give up gambling in favor of storekeeping. No more poker, no more faro, no betting on the horses."

"You couldn't be happy!" she protested.

He raised one eyebrow at her but, other than that, she still couldn't tell if he felt hope, anger, frustration . . . or nothing at all.

"Could be I've learned to appreciate games with bigger stakes," he challenged. "Could be I'd find myself more than satisfied laying odds on a good woman's happiness, or wagering on a store's ledgers coming up black instead of red."

Oh, she did want to believe him. And yet she'd no sooner flirted with hope than she must reject it. "Do you mean to buy Mr. Hamilton's store?" She'd promised to go home with her family! She *wanted* to go home with them . . . didn't she?

"Nope," said Jack, still amazingly nonchalant—and she realized what he was doing. This must be what people called a "poker face." He added, "I do have a less-than-respectable past to outlive. Seems a place like Wyoming might offer better opportunities."

"Wyoming . . ." she whispered.

"And that's not just to sweeten the pot," he assured her—which, were so much not at stake, would make her laugh. He claimed to be giving up gambling for her—and yet here he sat, more of a gambler than ever. And she loved him for it. He wasn't putting money on the line so much as he was his future, after all, and how could she see anything sinful in that? In fact, she found it so admirable that she longed to follow his example . . . but could she risk it?

She'd never been a gambler, herself. But maybe . . . maybe she could learn.

She looked down at the playing card he'd given back to her, which she'd happened to set on the quilt facedown. "As . . . as *luck* would have it," she volunteered, in a flimsy attempt at nonchalance, "I'm returning to Wyoming myself."

"That so?"

She nodded, then made her own bet. "But I mean to teach. Even if I marry, I would like to continue teaching somehow. I'll have to marry someone who's open to that possibility."

"As luck would have it," Jack said, "I'm especially partial to teachers myself."

Audra suddenly needed to drink some lemonade. Were they doing what she thought they were doing? She felt as if she'd fallen into a game she could not escape—but she did not want to escape it. She wanted only to play it right.

"Papa told Aunt Heddy that there are some mines opening near Sheridan," she noted, as indifferent as she could sound when discussing something of such import. Her version of indifference did not approach his . . . but that was all right, too. Perhaps, just perhaps, this was a game they could *both* win, just by playing. "If so, the coal companies will build towns around them. They won't be high-class, but they'll still need stores."

"I'll keep that under consideration," he said slowly.

Audra put the lemonade down and coolly added, "They may also be desperate enough for schooling that they'd allow a lady teacher to marry, or even to keep company with her"—*Say it*—"her fiancé. Properly chaperoned, of course."

Jack swallowed hard, but otherwise looked calm as a summer morning. "A teacher needs to preserve her reputation."

She nodded.

"I reckon," he ventured, an edge of excitement beginning to undermine his casual tone, "that any lady with good sense would demand a long engagement. That way, any fellow lucky enough to have laid even that much claim on her could prove himself to her and her family."

She had to press her lips together to fight a delighted smile. Surely even her father would consent to a plan like that . . . wouldn't he? If Jack stayed out of trouble—more or less—for an allotted amount of time, what possible argument could anyone have against her marrying him?

Especially her.

And, oh, she desperately wanted to marry him. "How long an engagement do you think she would suggest?"

He inhaled lightly through his teeth, considered it as he might consider how to price a basket of preserves. "Six months?" But his dancing blue eyes gave him away, and she laughed.

"More like two years, I'd think," she countered, and it did sound like forever . . . perhaps because she'd chosen the other extreme.

He began to smile, his poker face slipping. "Nine months? Scandalous implications aside."

Her heart began to smile with him. "Eighteen months."

"An even year."

She could have suggested a year and a quarter, but she didn't want to. Even a year seemed too long to wait—and yet, compared to forever without him, a year of being courted by Jack could rival heaven. "Well . . . *perhaps* she could accept a year," she supposed. "If he really did behave himself. Some unmarried couples might have difficulty doing that . . . I've heard . . ." Her face felt terribly hot again.

"That," he said, "is what curfews and chaperones and other such rules are for, darlin'."

"Oh," she whispered. They stared at each other across a basket, a playing card, glasses of lemonade, and plates of chicken. A butterfly dipped past them, en route to the wildflowers.

"Did we just do what I'm prayin' we just did?" Jack asked finally.

Please, please, please. But she wasn't as much of a gambler as he. Best to face everything up front. "Are you the sort of man who prays regularly, Mr. Harwood?"

"I'm willing to marry into it," he promised, leaving only one more area in which he—and she—must appease her sense of propriety.

"You have the funds to open a store?" she asked reluctantly.

"I do. I might not start big, but if I play it right, it will grow well enough."

Play it right. She needed to know. "Are those funds from gambling, Mr. Harwood?"

"The funds with which I bought this tasty lunch," he admitted, "and the even tastier company, came from just such ill-gotten gains. However, for the business itself, I'm financed from marginally more respectable sources. Ferris Hamilton has promised me a commission on the sale of his mercantile, due to a few prime buyers I've eased in his direction. And I had the luck of meeting an investor with faith in my prospects. I make no promises as to where he got *his* money," he added, poker-faced again, "but he and his partner are cattle ranching in Argentina."

Ranching? For a moment, she'd expected something far shadier. "That doesn't sound so terrible," Audra admitted.

Jack said, "He'd prefer to remain a silent partner. If that doesn't strike you as too . . . speculative a basis for your future."

"As luck would have it," she said, excitement beginning to warm her as they cleared the last of their obstacles, "I'm partial to speculation myself."

"Are you," Jack challenged, his blue eyes seeming to drink her in.

"Especially gambling," she assured him, beginning to lose her breath.

"That is lucky," Jack admitted, his voice rough, and she nodded. So he said, "Audra Garrison, would you consent to marry me after a proper engagement of one year and live with me even if I'm just a storekeeper who owes his start to questionable investors?"

"Do you consent to marrying me even if I make you wait through a proper engagement and if I insist on teaching after marriage?"

"I never dreamed of winning so fine a prize in all my life," he assured her.

So she nodded. "Yes, Jack. Yes, I would love nothing more in the world than to marry someone as kind and as funny and as . . . as *honorable* as you."

"I may not be as honorable as you think," he warned. "But I will endeavor from here on out to be. For you."

"You *are* honorable enough for me."

He reached into his pocket; then his face fell. "I bought a ring. Just in case. Trouble is . . . I paid for it with gambling money."

She might have accepted a store based on ill-gotten gains, though she felt relieved she never need know. A ring? Their whole relationship pushed the bounds of respectability!

"I already have a cuff link that I got in a less-than-appropriate manner, and I adore it. But if you have the other one, best not wear it in front of my father until after we're married."

Jack said, "I am about to kiss you and I do not want to die with so fine a future before me. Just how deadly *is* your father?"

And, oh, she *did* want him to kiss her! "Put the ring on me first, and maybe he won't resort to gunplay."

So Jack pulled a small velvet box from his pocket, opened it, and let it fall uselessly to the blanket as he claimed the ring inside. Then he slid that onto Audra's finger to claim her as well. It was an incredibly beautiful ring, a diamond-cut diamond framed with a small, fiery ruby on either side, and it fit her as well as her hand fit his, as if it had been made for her.

She decided not to ask if the ring had indeed been made for her. Not just yet. Jack's eyes were of far more interest to her than precious gems anyway.

"Once your pa gets to know me," he said, a little breathless, taking her other hand as well and using them to draw her a little closer to him, "maybe I'll win him over."

"Papa isn't won over, Jack," Audra assured him. "Ever."

Jack kneed a plate of chicken out of the way to kneel closer. "You will find, darlin', that I tend to underestimate odds and overestimate chances. I won you, didn't I?"

"No," she said, thrilled by how near he leaned. "You earned me."

He said, "Thank God," but then she cured him of blasphemy by kissing him, in front of God, the school board, her father, and everybody. She longed to fling her arms around his neck, to rediscover all the territory they'd explored before, but Jack held on to her hands tighter and, with the barest tease of lips and tongues, ended the kiss quickly enough to keep things chaste.

Somehow, the simplicity of the kiss held even more promise for their future. They had a lifetime to explore all enchanting aspects of marriage, from its basest sense to its heights.

But she kissed him again, quickly, for all that.

"Here he comes," Jack warned, glancing away—but not letting go of her hands. "And I reckon he'll blame me, instead of his scandalous little schoolteacher of a daughter."

He sounded so mournful that she giggled. Her father wouldn't really *kill* him. Probably.

"I like being scandalous," she admitted. "It's fun."

Jack laughed out loud. "Darlin'," he said, leaning back to kiss her hands. His lips tickled her fingers as he murmured, "As far as fun goes, this is only the beginning."

"I bet you're right," said Audra happily, before turning to beam her pleasure at her approaching father.

Papa's clear disapproval did not diminish when Jack risked leaning close enough to whisper in Audra's ear, "I'll happily cover that bet, ma'am."

She happily let him.

Epilogue

Before the next summer arrived, Jack Harwood survived the longest, snowiest, most frustratingly *abstinent* winter he'd ever imagined—no thanks to Audra.

Well . . . it could be that he owed her something on the survival side. He appreciated Wyoming's frontier spirit. He liked the social interaction of running a general store for the Black Diamond mine—the matrons who shopped early for dinner; the children who came by after school; the bachelors who stopped in for tobacco or just to talk. He enjoyed gambling on what would or would not sell, bluffing suppliers into the lowest prices so that he and his hardworking customers could both rake in the winnings. But he lived for Audra.

On weekends Audra stayed with her family, either in Sheridan or at the ranch. During the week she rented a room from the mine foreman and his wife and taught school for the children of the Black Diamond site. Jack spent every Wednesday evening with her in the Brannons' parlor; drove her home on Fridays, where he took supper with the family; saw her again for church on Sundays, took dinner with her extended family, and drove her back to the Brannons'. She also came by the store after school, to keep an eye on the older of her pupils who congregated at the soda fountain there and to drive Jack slowly crazy with wanting her.

Lucky for her he was either masochistic enough or philosophical enough to almost enjoy delaying their physical union, because *that* part of the winter, his schoolmarm didn't make easy. Often as not, it was Audra who suggested they take a private detour while out driving, or who snuggled against him so perfectly as they kissed good night that he couldn't stop kissing her until the sound of Mr. Brannon's footsteps or—worse—her father's yanked them apart. At other times it was Jack who initiated such things. But he could no longer count on her to steer their conduct as she once had. To his joyful despair, Audra had developed a taste for fun to rival his own.

Once, when they almost lost control of themselves in a stopped sleigh, she even suggested they secretly elope, then not tell anyone unless they got caught together. But Jack needed to prove himself to *himself* almost as badly as to his future in-laws. For that reason, and with much creative use of snow, Audra remained a virgin until their wedding. Just.

They married that following summer on the lawn of her family's Sheridan home. Their minister still officiated, but the church couldn't hold everyone they'd invited. Most of the workers from the Black Diamond site came, either through a connection to her or to him. Any cowboy from the Circle T who wasn't working that day showed to celebrate as well. Half of Sheridan attended in support of the family, including a harried-looking Peter Connors with his shrill wife and three children. Lucy Wolfe showed, of course, along with the Lees. Ferris Hamilton arrived by train from New York City, where he hoped to take Lucy to legally marry. Folks gave the couple sidelong looks, though Mrs. Garrison's obvious approval forbade further commentary, but Ham and Lucy hardly noticed.

Hedda Cribb came north from Texas with Melissa Smith. Melissa wore an engagement ring, although her intended, Early Rogers, had to run his father's gin and simply sent his congratulations. Jack suspected that the widow Cribb's own interests lay more in Thaddeas than in him and Audra. She'd not been invited to Thad's wedding earlier that year, sudden as it had been, and seemed to take great satisfaction in peering critically at his new bride, who, for better or worse, had far more patience for it than would any of Hedda's blood nieces.

Of course rancher Jacob Garrison's daughters, all six of them, attended. As usual, Jack could barely contain his amusement when he considered what his future father-in-law must have gone through with Audra's three older sisters and their surprising choices in mates. No wonder the rancher had never gotten around to killing him. After Mariah, Laurel, and Victoria—not to mention Thaddeas—Garrison must be plumb worn out. Someday, if Jack ever tired of focusing exclusively on Audra, he meant to ask her for the *whole* story of how her older sisters had paired up with their own husbands.

But as he stood by the preacher on that summer lawn—blue sky above, Bighorn Mountains in the distance, orchestral music wafting on the air—and watched Audra approaching on her father's arm, Jack doubted that day would ever come. Her beauty hurt his eyes, made him forget to breathe. Her sorrel hair had grown to her shoulders over the year, but hadn't yet lost its delightful curl. She wore the wedding necklace he'd bought with the last of his gambling money—a diamond framed with rubies, like her engagement ring, to remind them both of her true fire. But the shine in her fine, large eyes outdid it *and* the Denver wedding gown she wore. Any fool looking at her could see on her perfect, china-doll face that she was in love. Even a fool like him.

He still wasn't sure he deserved her, much less the family, the community, the *belonging* that came with her. But he wasn't one to turn down Lady Luck.

As often happened in her presence, he didn't hear much of the preacher's sermon. It all meant that he and Audra would be together forever, and that was more than enough for him. He did hear her promising to love, honor, and cherish him—it seemed to be family tradition to avoid the word *obey*—and he tried to convey with his every word his delight that she trusted him to do the same. And then, amazingly, they'd become Mr. and Mrs. John Harwood. Man and wife.

He about lost himself in kissing her—his *wife*—until her father began to make a low noise like a growl. Reluctantly, Jack and Audra drew back from each other yet again. But he could tell by her blush that he wasn't the only one thinking this would be the last time they'd have to stop.

After a year that had seemed to crawl, the afternoon rushed by in a gala of gifts, congratulations, fine food, elegant music, and dancing—Lordy, but he loved dancing with Audra. His new brothers-in-law gave him advice on how best to keep on Garrison's good side, most of which involved staying out of the rancher's way . . . except for Thaddeas, who, as expected, threatened to kill him if Jack made Audra unhappy. His new sisters-in-law flattered him with attention and welcome, even more than on Sunday gatherings . . . except for Laurel, the "cowgirl," who also threatened to kill him if he made Audra unhappy. His new father-in-law scowled at him, as usual, and his new mother-in-law held his arm and talked quietly with him, reminding him increasingly of his own mother . . . if Ma had married better.

Then, finally, the merry-go-round of celebration came to a stop with Jack and Audra together, alone, at the refined Sheridan Inn. At last.

For a long, quiet moment, standing at the foot of the bed with his bride's hands warm and right in his own, Jack felt almost shy. Their day had been so perfect. Could anything they did tonight live up to a year of expectations? Especially for her?

"Jack?" she whispered, barely meeting his gaze with her own.

He ached with love. The only thing better was seeing her love for him. "Darlin'?"

She ducked her head, then peered up at him through her lashes. "Will you explain about the candy stick now?"

The candy . . . ? *Oh!*

He began to grin. Drawing her closer against him, he whispered an explanation into her ear, her eyes getting wider, and Jack felt exquisitely more aroused by the moment. "It is not," he reassured her, pillowing his cheek against her curls and reminding himself to behave, "the sort of thing one expects a lady to do."

"But . . . Jack . . . ?"

She smelled so good, so clean and pure and real. "Mmm?"

"Does that mean I can't?" Before he'd caught his breath from that, she shyly added, "One of the things I love about you is that you don't expect me to behave like a lady all the time."

"You *are* a lady," he assured her—beginning to tremble with the need to do more than just hold her. "No matter how improper your behavior."

And he kissed her to prove it. The kiss lasted forever, and reminded him what a clever little tongue she had, which reminded him of candy sticks.

"Does that mean you're a scoundrel all the time, no matter how respectable *your* behavior?" she asked when they paused for breath, so hopeful that he laughed. At moments like these, he doubted she'd even mind learning that his number one investor was the notorious outlaw Butch Cassidy. But he didn't try the theory.

"If you want a scoundrel darlin', I am *more* than happy to oblige," he warned her.

"Yes, please," she whispered.

So he proved it—in every way he knew how, and some they invented together. By dawn he barely had the strength to do more than hold her exquisitely soft, naked form tightly against him and murmur, "I love you," over and over again, just about every time he exhaled.

Audra kissed every "I love you" off his lips as the sun rose.

Dear Reader:

I hope you enjoyed *Behaving Herself*. The Garrison family laid claim on my imagination some time ago and I enjoyed bringing Audra to life, especially with a hero as fun as Jack Harwood. I especially liked setting the book in my own stomping grounds, the "Mid-Cities" area of Texas, between Dallas and Fort Worth. In fact, after I began to research Candon (renamed Tarrant before being absorbed into Euless), I came across Tarrant Main Street by accident and learned that ten years ago I had an apartment overlooking that very area!

Although my characters are fictitious, I did try for historical accuracy whenever possible, especially regarding Fort Worth. The notorious White Elephant saloon really was in the "nice" part of town, although it has since been reestablished in the Stockyards area. Hell's Half Acre really did sprawl between the depot and downtown (before reformers finally bulldozed it to build the Water Gardens and the Tarrant County Convention Center). And Butch Cassidy and the Sundance Kid really did spend at least part of the winter of 1900-01 hiding out there, one reason why the renovated downtown is now called Sundance Square. My thanks in particular to the local historical societies and the Old Bedford Schoolhouse for their assistance in this research.

And by the way—at least 75% of the "rules" quoted in this book were the real thing.

If I've piqued your curiosity about Audra's older sisters, I hope you will look for my next historical romance from Leisure, *Forgetting Herself*. You thought Jacob Garrison had problems with Audra taking up with a gambler? Wait until you see how he reacts when his oldest girl, Mariah, falls in love with a cattleman's sworn enemy: a sheep rancher!

I love reader mail. Write me at P.O. Box 6, Euless, TX 76039 (self-addressed, stamped envelopes are always appreciated) or e-mail me at Yvaughn@aol.com.

When cattleman Cody O'Fannin hears a high-pitched scream ring out across the harsh New Mexico Territory, he rides straight into the heart of danger, expecting to find a cougar or a Comanche. Instead, he finds a scene far more frightening—a woman in the final stages of childbirth. Alone, the beautiful Melissa Wilmeth clearly needs his assistance, and although he'd rather face a band of thieving outlaws, Cody ignores his quaking insides and helps deliver her baby. When the infant's first wail fills the air, Cody gazes into Melissa's bewitching blue eyes and is spellbound. How else can he explain the sparkles he sees shimmering in the air above her honey-colored hair? Then thoughts of marriage creep into his head, and he doesn't need a crystal ball to realize he hasn't lost his mind or his nerve, but his heart.

___52321-3 $5.50 US/$6.50 CAN